SUB
ORBITAL⁷

SUB ORBITAL⁷

JOHN SHIRLEY

ALCON
PUBLISHING

TITAN BOOKS

SUBORBITAL 7
Print edition ISBN: 9781803363820
E-book edition ISBN: 9781803363837

Published by Titan Books
A division of Titan Publishing Group Ltd
144 Southwark St, London SE1 0UP
www.titanbooks.com

First edition: June 2023
2 4 6 8 10 9 7 5 3 1

A CIP catalogue record for this title is available from the British Library.

Printed and bound by CPI Group (UK) Ltd, Croydon, CR0 4YY.

*To all the US Army Rangers; those fallen,
and those still fighting*

PROLOGUE

Professor Frederic Dupon strolled beside the Rhone River on a cool night in May. He was walking home from the neuronics lab, and watching the moon rippling on the water. Thoughts of frontal lobe stimuli scans gave way to wondering if he could get his pretty neighbor Hilda to come out and gaze at the moon with him. Didn't full moons have some sort of romantic effect?

He had never subjected the claim to a scientific test.

Dupon heard a soft motor noise, caught a peripheral glimpse of something slinking up closer, long and specter-white. He turned, frowning, and saw an ivory van pacing him, its windows impenetrably black.

His mouth went dry and he hurried on, walking faster. The electric van kept pace. It was almost silent. The only other sounds were the lapping of the waves against the retaining wall and the distant rumble of a jet.

Dupon stopped, to see if the vehicle would pass him.

It did.

And then it suddenly nosed into the curb, blocking his way.

The professor froze, remembering a smartband call from Hans Quorgasse.

"*Dupon,*" the EuroIntel operative had said, "*your work*

has attracted interest in the East. You will need additional security."

"What do you know of my work?" Dupon asked in irritation. *"It is classified!"*

"I know about the spaceflight applications. We're sending some people to support Kessid security."

Dupon relaxed. *The van must contain the men from EuroIntel.* As much as he loathed such skullduggery, at that moment it seemed reassuring.

The back of the van opened, and a drone emerged, about the width of a bicycle's handlebars. It hovered, running a scanning laser over him.

"Professor Dupon?" a filtered voice said. Before he could respond, however, another voice emanated from the drone.

"It's him you idiot," the second voice said. *"Just do it."*

A screech of tires caused Dupon to jump. A second vehicle pulled up — a long black car. Two men clambered out and drew sidearms. One was Quorgasse, from EuroIntel. The other flashed a badge.

"Professor, get in!" he barked.

Before Dupon could react, quick coughing sounds came from within the van, accompanied by a stuttering of muzzle flashes. The two newcomers sprawled backward as their skulls shattered with a precision that became a bloody mess on the hood of the car. Their lifeless bodies crumpled to the ground.

That did it. Dupon turned to run. He heard the hum of the drones following.

Something hissed, and he felt a stinging on the back of his neck.

Tranquilizer darts... fired by drone...

He kept moving—another three steps, and then his legs turned to rubber. He lurched face-forward to the sidewalk.

When he hit the concrete, he thought, dreamily: *This is what it feels like to shatter my nose...*

ONE

Art Burkett drove the Chevy Hydro all too slowly through the Cactus Flats suburb of Armstrong. He'd have driven much faster if it wasn't a Saturday afternoon. The streets were bubbling with kids.

Boys raced on electric skateboards and scooters. Two girls played drone-ball in the middle of the street, one throwing the ball, the other directing a drone to catch it. For a distracted moment Burkett thought he saw an orbcraft soaring above, but then he spotted a smiling dad showing his son how to operate the flying model of a spaceplane.

Maybe get Nate one of those…

His house was part of this development—anyway, it used to be his house, before Ashley insisted on the separation. Technically he was still the co-owner, but it didn't feel that way. The first lieutenant lived on the Army base now—SubOrbital Base Three, a good eighteen miles away from the housing project they'd lived in for four years. Rangers quarters for officers weren't bad, but they weren't home.

These were big houses, all from the same developer, with some variation to break up the architectural monotony. Burkett thought the minor differences so predictable they were just as monotonous, but the development had been built fourteen years ago, in 2027, and its inhabitants had given it character. People painted the houses distinctively, put up quaint little lawn sculptures, seasonal flags, their own choices in foliage—trees, rose bushes, small palms, and desert plants in Spanish-style pots.

The tract mostly housed military families or locals whose businesses catered to the armed forces. There was USAF Sergeant Carlson, in jeans and T-shirt, working in his driveway on a classic muscle car from the 1970s. Carlson glanced up from beneath the hood of the Trans Am and waved at him, and Burkett waved back. He and Carlson had both served in the Second Venezuelan War, and Carlson had flown the heli for Burkett's team, dropping them over a coca plantation with two other squadrons of the 75th Airborne Rangers.

Burkett tried to steer his mind away from that memory, but he seemed to see again the pink-gray dawn light outlining glider chutes, attracting heavy fire from the cartel-funded nationalists camped at the plantation. "Slim" Mersener and Gabrielle Velasquez, shot to pieces on both sides of him before they even hit the ground. Gore, blossoming in the sky.

Feldman's armor protected him some—he only lost an eye, and a lot of the feeling in the right side of his body...

Don't think about that. There's the house.

My house, and not *my house,* he thought bitterly, pulling up in front. Ashley didn't want him pulling into the driveway. Said it blocked her little Hydro II, but it was more than that, or so Burkett suspected. It was symbolic.

"You don't get a place in my parking space, Art, until you change your mind."

Stepping out of the car, Burkett walked up the driveway. He felt a buzzing in his shirt pocket, and grimaced. This was his day off, he was fresh in his civvies, ready for miniature golf with his son. So naturally...

Stopping at the front porch, he took out the phone—aware

that Ashley was watching him through the front window—and read the text.

PER USSPACECOM, IC2, 1LABURKETT: R-INTEL ORDERS:
RETURN TO OPS 3 WITHOUT DELAY, SADDLE UP FOR QRF
BRIEFING & DEP PER. GEN. CARNEY, USAR

"*Dep.*" Deployment.

They were going up.

"QRF" for Quick Response Force, a loose usage of the term considering their style. Another time Burkett would have welcomed these orders. The team had been kept on tenterhooks for weeks, prodded by hints about a deep-insert covert op in Eastern Europe. He'd been feeling that inner keenness, that welcome tension, since the first briefing, and was more than ready for the mission.

But not today.

"Well, what's the word?" Ashley asked. She stood on the other side of the screen door, arms crossed, gazing calmly at him with her crystal-blue eyes. She was trying to keep her expression neutral, but Burkett thought he saw sadness in the set of her mouth. Or was that anger?

"Deployment." Burkett sighed. "Report immediately."

She snorted. "Really?"

"Yeah, Ashley," Burkett said. "Really."

Crisply attractive, slim, long-legged, and tanned, Ashley was five-nine to his six-two, wearing shorts and a peach-colored blouse. Her silky blond hair was short on the sides now, with a ruffled spikiness on top. He missed the long blond hair that had fallen past her shoulders. That style had said "relaxed." This new one was fashionable and pretty but off-putting—at least to Burkett.

Message received, Ashley.

Now she had a Māori-style tattoo as well, resembling a bracelet around her right wrist. The skin still slightly red and puffy around the ink. He decided not to ask her about the tat. Burkett reached out and opened the screen door. The text wasn't classified so he showed it to her. She glanced at it and gave a quick nod.

"The Army has unerringly shitty timing," she said. "As usual."

"*Dad!*" It was Nate, coming up behind his mom. Eight years old, he had her slimness, her blond hair, and blue eyes, but he had the faint makings of the craggy planes of Burkett's face. Looking around his mother, the boy looked worried, glancing questioningly at Ashley as she continued to block Art's way at the door.

"Hey, Private First-Class Nate Burkett," Art said, forcing a smile. "What's up?"

"Gettin' ready to go."

Burkett gave his son a rueful look. "Afraid something's come up." His heart sank as he said it. He handed Nate the phone. The boy peered at the message.

"Saddle up?" the boy said. "*Now?*"

"Yep," Burkett replied, "and you know how it is with the Army. When they say jump, I gotta jump. It's in my contract."

"A fifteen-year-old recruitment contract," Ashley said dryly. "That has to be renewed next year."

There it was—the thorn in their marriage. He wanted to re-up. She didn't. Ashley thought he was crazy not to take a civilian job, one that had been on offer for months now, at triple his current salary. Security consultancy, no risk. Nobody shooting at him.

"You should've been a captain years ago," she continued. "A silver star, two bronze stars, five purple hearts, more combat leadership than…"

Never shouting, laying it out coolly. An assistant prosecutor for seven years, she had all the arguments down. Ashley taught a law class at Armstrong Community College, and wanted to go for a full professorship somewhere, but didn't feel as if she could do it with Burkett gone so much. Not when there was a damned good possibility he wouldn't come back from one of these deployments.

Nate poked around on Burkett's phone, looking a little sullen. Burkett gently took it back.

"You know how it will be when you get to the base, Arthur," Ashley said. "They're just going to make you wait. Why don't you and Nate—"

"*No*, Ashley," he said. "Last time I pulled that they sent a drone to find me. The S-7 is always fueled and ready."

"What you gonna have to do on this mission, Dad?" Nate asked, squinting up at him with his head tilted, his mouth squiggled like he was trying not to cry. Burkett went down on one knee and hugged him. The boy put his head on Burkett's shoulder.

He felt a twisting feeling of shame at letting his son down. *Get a grip*, he told himself.

"Nate, it's a combat deployment," he said. "That's all I can tell you, except that I'm going to be super, crazy, way-way *careful*, and the people I'm going with are going to watch my back. They're the best, son." He leaned back to look into Nate's eyes. "Listen, the instant I'm back, I'm going to apply for special furlough and we're gonna do a lot together..." Mentally adding, *if your mom allows it*. "But right now, I've got to go. Rangers always stand ready."

Burkett gently drew away from the boy, stood up, and stuck out a fist. Lower lip quivering, Nate dutifully fist-bumped him back. Swallowing the lump in his throat, Burkett turned to Ashley.

"We'll talk when I get back."

"Yes," she said, crossing her arms. "We will."

"What are the odds of a hug, Ash?"

Her eyes glinted at the edge of tears. Suddenly she reached out, hugged Burkett—once, and quickly—her arms taut on his shoulders. She never said it aloud, but he knew what she was feeling.

This time is it. This will be the one.

Oddly enough, he hoped it was the real reason for the separation. That would mean she still loved him. Ashley pretended it was about money and her career, but she had knowingly married a Ranger. He figured she was afraid he'd leave her a widow and Nate fatherless.

But what if he was wrong? What if there was some other reason? Something he didn't know about.

She drew back and took Nate's hand.

"Come on, Nate. Me, you, and Jerry'll go to the PCS picnic. There's some fun stuff set up."

"Jerry?" Burkett said. "You and Jerry have plans?" He kept his voice level.

She rolled her eyes. "Police Community Services picnic, Art. I told you about it a week ago. We're doing the face-painting booth for the kids."

Jerry. Sheriff's Deputy Gerald Baker. A vet and an old friend, but one who often let his eyes linger on Ashley. *Maybe*, Burkett thought, *it really is time to leave the Rangers.*

But not yet.

"Right," he said. "The picnic." Burkett took a deep breath, winked at his son, gave Ashley all the smile he could manage, and walked back to the car, feeling like he'd just slung a hundred-pound rucksack on his back. As he pulled out and drove slowly away from the house, he passed a familiar black SUV.

Jerry didn't look his way.

Growling to himself, Burkett wove through the obstacle course of children and families and out to the desert highway.

Now he pressed down on the accelerator.

SubOrbital 7 was waiting to take him, his captain, and a squad of men into orbit for a black-op insert. In less than three hours he might be in a battlefield on the other side of the Earth.

Burkett pushed the car to eighty-five, driving down the long straight highway that split the desert. To either side, cacti were effulgent with thick yellow blooms, almost glowing in the bright sun, and in the distance red-stone outcroppings rose with a curious wind-carved grace. Sometimes Burkett savored the view, but now he focused on the necessary mental acrobatics. Changed his inner center of gravity, turning to fully face the mission.

Closer to the base, his inward shift was almost complete. Through the gate, past the checkpoint. By the time he had changed into his ACU—Army Combat Uniform, complete with the Rangers tab—he was mission-ready. It was something a Ranger learned. Especially an officer bound for combat.

"You've got to be more ready than the non-coms and the enlisted men," Major Corliss had told him, when he first got his first platoon. *"Because you're going to lead those men right into the Valley of the Shadow of Death."*

TWO

Burkett put on his tan beret—something he wore for briefings, not combat—and reported to what Captain Randall Mayweather liked to call the "ready room," though the term originated with aircraft carrier pilots.

This ready room was a rectangular conference structure occupying a small corner of the enormous hangar for the S-7 and its one-hundred-eighty-meter side wingspan mothership. The SubOrbital 7 was there, a taut metallic presence that always seemed to be watching and waiting to be taken to the sky.

Like the old-school ready rooms, there was a central table cluttered with printout checklists, coffee cups—and something new. It looked like a weapon.

The team was already there, in their digital cammie Army combat uniforms, with tactical trousers bloused into their boots and patrol caps on their heads. Captain Mayweather, dressed in ACU, was standing by the conference table in close colloquy with Lieutenant Colonel Baxter. Mayweather was a burly man with graying brown hair, a lined, weathered face, hawkish brown eyes under heavy brows. As ever, he looked friendly in a detached kind of way.

In addition to officers, there were eight men and two women in the insert team. Some of them leaned against the walls, others sat in rickety metal chairs, talking, laughing. Most of them were nervous, but psyched for action. Burkett knew six of these soldiers well—battlefield well—but a couple of them were first-timers for a SubOrbital mission insert.

Even so, they all had Ranger combat experience, and they'd all been schooled in the S-3—the smaller SubOrbital trainer. In addition to being Airborne, the six were certified astronauts.

Lt. Col. Talley Baxter was standing by the briefing screen. An older, broad-shouldered Black man in an Army Service Uniform and beret, he was the base's Drop-Heavy commanding officer. Baxter clapped the Captain on the shoulder.

"Got a hot one for you, Randall."

"Suits me, sir."

Baxter looked around. "Team S-7," he bellowed in a deep voice, cutting through the chatter, "*shut* up and *listen* up!"

Everyone fell silent.

"As much as I'd prefer to go with you today," Baxter went on, "I'm going to be putting out some fires at the Pentagon. We have some burning finance issues." Funding was always an issue for Drop-Heavy. While the public knew about the craft themselves, they were explained away as "experimental," deployed in tests and used only in scientific studies.

The Army's SubOrbital vessels were unspeakably expensive, their cost hidden from the public in the black budget. Their true purpose was known only to a few. This was a constant worry to the secretive Congressional subcommittee that signed off on the program.

"For this mission, you've got three new team members," Baxter went on. "Lieutenant Burkett worked with Alexi Syrkin on a North African paratrooper drop a few years before he signed on with us. Alexi's an experienced SubOrbital hand, transferred over from S-9."

Leaning against a wall, Syrkin gave them a nod.

"We've also got Second Lieutenant Kenneth Carney." Baxter nodded in the direction of a spindly officer standing with his lips pursed, his hands clasped behind him, looking like a man waiting to have a medal pinned on. Unusually pale for a combat officer, he had a bright new M-20 modular pistol on his hip.

General Roger Carney's kid.

Burkett frowned. He hadn't been forewarned about the transfer. Another lieutenant? Carney was redundant, and he wasn't a Ranger. They'd been known to bring Delta Force or a SEAL along on a Drop-Heavy, if the mission called for a specific skill set, but those guys were special forces. Lieutenant Carney was regular Army.

"Finally, meet Sergeant Destiny Andrews," Baxter said. "I believe he served with Lieutenant Burkett in South America."

Burkett nodded at Andrews and got a salute in return. Standing with arms crossed near the door, Des Andrews was a tall, husky, mixed-ethnicity American. A real Ranger. Definitely more promising than Ken Carney. Burkett had read Andrew's file when they'd worked together on a mission in Venezuela. Classical music scholarship with a minor in military history. Andrews left the scholarship behind after just two years, for the Army. Not a normal path for a Ranger, but Burkett hadn't been headed for the military himself, back in the day.

He'd figured on a career as a mining engineer, like his old man.

A small-arms-fire specialist, Des consistently won intra-service target shooting competitions. After Venezuela he'd served in three black ops missions in southern Turkey. Silver Star, Bronze Star, three Purple Hearts. Applied for the Army branch of Space Command, took to astronautics so quick they fast-tracked him for SubOrbital Drop-Heavy. There'd been a good deal of fast-tracking after SubOrbital 12 had crashed in the Pacific. No survivors.

The incident was a puzzle still unsolved.

"I've given Captain Mayweather your orders," Baxter went on, "and he'll relay them to you. Now I've got to go spin my wheels in DC—trust me, you got the easier assignment." There was chuckling at that. "This mission was upgraded to urgent, just in the last few hours. It'll be combat hot, and it's got to go down *fast*. Stay sharp! Keep your heads down and your eyes up." He straightened and saluted them. Everyone went to attention and snapped the return salute.

Baxter nodded to Mayweather, and strode from the room.

The captain tapped his interface and the wall screen showed a map of Eastern Europe. A single country was highlighted, shaped like a mock of the Italian boot, but smaller and thicker, toe pointed west.

"Moldova," he said, "a republic with more than its fair share of corruption. It's crammed in between Romania and Ukraine. It's landlocked, but not far from the Black Sea. Our target is here." He tapped the hand-screen and a glowing spot pulsed on the map. "The Moldovan Plateau, in a remote corner of the Edinet region—not much there. Our target: St. Basil's Monastery. Built in the seventeenth century, abandoned in the nineteenth. Briefly used as a prison in the twentieth century. It's a big fortress-like stone fortification, easy to defend.

"It's a prison all over again for three men who were kidnapped a little less than a month ago. The hostages are Professor Frederic Dupon, a Swiss national; Dr. Jacques Magonier, French national; and... Hold on..."

"Third one," a voice said from the door, speaking in a soft Texas accent, "is Lucius Dhariwal, PhD and Masters in physics. Born in Burbank, California, parents from Pakistan. MIT scientist."

Everyone turned to look.

Sandy Chance was framed in the doorway, slouching casually, hands in the pockets of a wrinkly charcoal blazer, an unlit cigarette in his mouth. The CIA operative was a middle-aged man with short, graying blond hair under a Houston Astros baseball cap. Small blue eyes behind rimless glasses, dominated by a prominent drink-reddened nose. He toyed with the cigarette he wasn't permitted to smoke here, as he went on.

"There was a fourth hostage, Loren Johansen from the Swedish Academy of Sciences. He died in captivity—a heart attack, if our source is correct."

"Glad you found some time for us," Mayweather said dryly. "Sandy Chance, ladies and gentlemen," he said, for the sake of the few who didn't know. "Our sometimes-friend at the CIA."

"*Always* Drop-Heavy's friend," Chance said. He put the unlit cigarette in his mouth, then plucked it out again. "When I'm allowed to be. You want me to finish the briefing, Captain?"

"You were supposed to do the whole thing," Mayweather said, gesturing for him to take the place in front of the big screen.

"Unavoidable delay." Chance sauntered in, taking a flexible hand-screen from an inside pocket. He unfolded it, tapped it a few times, then said, "SubOrbital wouldn't be involved if these guys were just hostages held for ransom. Sure, money was demanded, some even paid, but that's just a cover. These men were kidnapped because of what they know, not what people will cough up.

"This particular cadre of the Eastern European crime syndicate," he continued, "'Thieves in Law,' if you can believe it, is controlled by Moscow. We call them 'TiL.' They're working for the Russian GRU, though only some are aware of it. Normally they're just thuggish, heavily armed, greed-crazed gangsters infesting Bulgaria and Serbia, with tentacles across Eastern Europe. In this case their puppet master is one Vladimir Krozkov, a top GRU spymaster and a big deal in Moscow. Plays footsy with leading high-dollar oligarchs.

"Krozkov's point man in TiL is Mikhail Ildeva—the Bulgarian mob boss of this cadre. He's a man with many skills and specialties, including sex trafficking, counterfeit money distribution, drug smuggling, and extortion."

Ildeva's a Bulgar, Burkett thought, *and so is Syrkin*. Probably why Syrkin was transferred to S-7 specifically for this mission.

Chance gestured with his futile cigarette. "The cash paid to release the prisoners—a release that'll never happen—is the TiL's fee, along with anything Krozkov wants to kick to them. We think Ildeva's been taking Moscow money for a while now." He paused, stared at his cigarette, shook his head, and went on.

"The prisoners at St. Basil's were working on different classified projects that relate to the orbital military—all of which can be applied by Moscow's Orbital Army. Dupon was working on a neural interface with spacecraft controls—"

Sgt. Linda Strickland, the orbcraft's co-pilot, whistled softly.

"Johansen was with Professor Dhariwal, both of them kidnapped near CERN where they were working on a breakthrough in particle beam technology. A technology that, among other things, might be used for a damned scary orbit-to-surface weapon. Krozkov's interrogator of choice is a former scientist with a gift for slow and careful torture, psychological and otherwise—Ivan Lutzoff."

Burkett growled to himself. Anybody using torture pissed him off big-time. Russian interrogators ignored the studies proving that torture yielded unreliable, even bad information. They didn't seem to care if it worked or not. Engaging in torture had to eat holes through the interrogator's soul.

"He's trying to squeeze every bit of applicable tech out of these three," Chance went on. "The prisoners may be cooperating. They won't know that they'll either be shipped to Russia or shot after Lutzoff is done with them." He paused and swept a pointing finger around the room. "We can't let Russia exploit this data—or these men. We didn't know where the prisoners were till yesterday morning—and now that we do, we have to *act*. They're the key to a top-secret program—if what they know is tortured out of them, the Russians acquire an edge like never before."

"Good enough, Sandy," Mayweather said, cutting in. "Consider us motivated. What've you got on defense personnel and ground conditions?"

"The outer walls of St. Basil's are ten meters high, constructed of granite blocks. Inside, most of the central building is still standing, and solid. It's three stories high, top story partly ruined. There's a courtyard with a crumbling old chapel, and two outbuildings. The TiL soldiers bunk in the main building. We think there's twenty-six of them total, mostly on hand for defense due to the size of the place. There are six men who walk a scaffolding snugged to the inside of the outer walls, and they send a patrol out from time to time.

"They're all combat experienced—some of them ex-military, Russian expatriates kicked out of FSB's border troops for their association with TiL. Some are former Bulgarian Army, and eight others are just TiL street soldiers. Weapons—everything from Bizon-4 submachine guns to Kalashnikov-style assault weapons to grenades."

"Ammo supplies?" Mayweather asked.

"Enough for an extended fight, at least. They do have a couple of Kamov drones armed with 40mm mini-missiles. Our source doesn't *think* the area is mined, but you should use a scanner drone to check. Ground conditions: rocky plateau, some cover from boulders and a stand of trees. The S-7 will insert in a valley that's not much more than a wide crevice at the top of the plateau, about two klicks to the south of the target. You'll get a deeper briefing from your captain before you debark from the orbcraft.

"We can't slam this target with mortars or missiles," he continued, "except maybe precision mini-rockets. Prisoners are down under the main building, and it could collapse on them. It's got to be mostly small-arms assault, with drone support. We don't have time for anything else. You're going to have to breach walls and outer doors, move fast, overwhelm the opposition, and get the prisoners out safely, quick as you can.

"We're hoping you can capture Ildeva, as well. Krozkov won't be on the premises, but Ildeva knows a lot about him— he can provide a wealth of useful info." Chance shrugged. "That's it from me. Your captain has satellite photography of the target area. Any questions—ask him." He put his hand to the Bluetooth in his ear, frowning. "I've got to answer this. Good luck!" He hurried out the door, flicking the cigarette into his mouth.

"Don't light up till you get out of the hangar!" Mayweather called after him.

"Captain?" Burkett pointed at the weapon on the table. "Is that a Pike launcher?"

"You called it. Heckler and Koch. Works more or less like the last one... but better. We've got two of them."

"So we'll be testing them in-country—in a firefight?" Burkett didn't like the sound of that.

Mayweather just shrugged. "If we get a chance," he replied. "There were some field tests, but..." He looked as if he was going to say something more, but cut it off, glancing at 2nd Lt. Carney. "Anyway, I'll try it out first myself. Besides, it's not the only special ordnance we'll be testing..."

Mayweather winked at Corporal Dabiri.

Every few years another "world's biggest plane" was announced, and it was usually a mothership configured roughly like the old *Roc*, Paul Allen's Stratolaunch prototype. The S-7's *Mommy Dearest* was a freakishly wide eight-engine aircraft with a wingspan that was huge even for an orbit launcher. Twin fuselages made the huge vessel look like two planes fused together.

It had to be big to carry its baby, SubOrbital 7. The Drop-Heavy program's delta-wing orbcraft, fueled by the latest methane-oxygen mix, was nearly twice as long as the old space shuttles, with a fuselage twice as broad; sleekly flatter, and far more sophisticated. It was also unmarked, because all S-series missions were covert.

The orbcraft that would transport Burkett and his team was clamped to the underside of *Mommy Dearest*'s center wing between the long narrow twin fuselages. Its outer wings each sported four pulsejet engines. As Burkett walked up, the orbcraft's hull was almost belly-down on the concrete.

Every Drop-Heavy mission felt new. Gazing up at the conjoined aircraft, Burkett always felt a sort of awe. The mothership with the attached orbcraft made him think of an old symbol he'd once seen for the 345th Bomber Squadron— an eagle in flight clutching a large bomb in its talons. The mothership was the eagle—but the death-dealing ordnance it was clutching wasn't a bomb.

Bombs don't come back. The S-7 always had.

There's always a first time, he thought.

Burkett walked under the vast, sheltering wings of the mothership to the ramp where the crew filed up into the S-7. Each of the Rangers carried a backpack slung over a shoulder. First came the pilot. 2nd Lt. Ike Faraday had piloted three S-7 Drop-Heavy missions. A compact man, he'd had to cut off his dreadlocks for the Rangers. Athletic, light-hearted but tough, Ike was always willing to fight.

Walking beside him was Sgt. Linda Strickland, twenty-nine years old, from Georgia. Masters in international relations and a degree in astronautic navigation. An up-and-coming star in women's college basketball, she'd blown it all off for the Rangers. Her friends and family had talked about having her committed. A tall, attractive redhead who stayed coolly professional around men, Linda had been a pilot for the 75th Airborne Rangers regiment.

After her came Sgt. Megan Lang, late twenties, with only one SubOrbital mission under her belt. Half Seminole, she was short, dark, powerfully muscular. Lang was usually quiet, but when she spoke it was with a bold incisiveness. Megan had a black belt in karate and had been a women's boxing competitor in college. Southern Christian background.

Next up the ramp was Specialist Alexi Syrkin. Born in Bulgaria, grew up in Oregon. Gunnery specialist and translator.

Wore an Eastern Orthodox cross around his neck. Narrow eyes and high cheekbones. He spoke several Slavic languages. A martial arts master of Sambo—Alexi had once told Burkett it stood for "Samozaschita Bez Orushiya"—and the deadly Systema.

Syrkin had been a sergeant but had killed a man in a particularly grisly way, with his bare hands—a man he was supposed to take prisoner. Because the guy was an armed insurgent, Syrkin was cleared of war-crime charges, but was busted down to corporal. Syrkin's problematic history could've made him a no-go for these elite missions, but they needed him as a translator. He was the only orbcraft-trained man who could speak Bulgarian and Russian. Standoffish, usually close-mouthed.

Burkett would keep an eye on him.

Next up was Second Lieutenant Carney, the General's son. Boarding the S-7 he gaped like a kid going on a *Star Wars* ride at Disneyland.

Des Andrews followed him up the ramp—smiling, excited to be going on the mission.

Hope he feels that way when we get there, Burkett thought. *This one's going to be a bitch.*

Lance Cpl. Kyu Cha strode eagerly on board. Gifted in electronics, especially high frequency radio communication, he was their comm specialist as well as a good combat soldier. Burkett knew the Asian-American had come from a rough neighborhood in Oakland, California. Two brothers in a gang, dad in jail for fencing stolen goods. Raised for a time in foster care. Rough life, but sometimes guys like that made the best Rangers—they were motivated. Never close to his old man, Cha had wanted to be a cop, but also had a powerful interest in space travel. Only orbital military could combine both.

Three others were already on board: Medical Specialist Rod Rodriguez; PFC Lemuel Dorman, a lethal quiet-kill expert; Cpl. Tafir Dabiri, gunnery badass, suit-armor tech, and translator.

It was a good team, Burkett mused.

If and when they rescued the prisoners in Moldova, that'd make fifteen. They barely had room for sixteen people on the S-7, so if they managed to get Ildeva alive—Burkett doubted it—that would be capacity for the orbcraft.

Carney's berth and Ildeva's should've been occupied by more experienced Rangers. Maybe this would be Carney's chance to prove himself. General Carney—in charge of the SubOrbital Drop-Heavy program—had wedged his son into the assignment. Burkett had to admit to himself that he had a prejudice against the young officer.

"How's it look, Art?" Captain Mayweather asked, joining him at the bottom of the ramp. Neither man had rucks or weapons—orderlies from ground crew had already loaded in the officers' gear.

"Good team, mostly. But Carney? Really?"

Mayweather sighed. "He seems to have gotten through most of his commando training..."

Burkett grimaced. "Most of it?" Even after army commando school, Carney couldn't be half as qualified as the others. He'd never been a Ranger.

Ranger training was famously rigorous. An average of only forty-five percent of trainees made it through. Some died in training—of hypothermia or hyperthermia, of snakebite, of drowning, of heart attack. Ranger training was designed to push soldiers close to death, because combat would take them there later. Having Carney plugged into a squad of Rangers was like a spoiled terrier yipping behind a pack of attack Dobermans.

General Carney wouldn't understand—he'd never been a Ranger either.

"Can't we find a reason to scrub him from the mission?"

"He was added to the list last minute—probably so we couldn't do that," Mayweather replied. "I suspect Hassner was transferred out to S-9 so Lieutenant Carney could be dropped on us." He grimaced. "Maybe Rod could say Carney's got flu symptoms, but the General would know what was up. So—naw."

He rubbed his nose. "And the General wants him in the action, told me that on the phone. 'Don't leave him at the orbcraft.'"

Burkett nodded. "I'll keep an eye on him. Maybe he's better than he looks. You said something else about new ordnance, Captain?"

"Yeah, it's another one of those half-tested jobs," Mayweather said. "Talos III, based on the Talos combat suit."

"Talos *power* armor? They finally get one to work?"

"This one's supposed to."

"They always say that."

"It hasn't been tested in combat, but Corporal Dabiri used to be a tester for Talos prototypes, so he's got familiarity. He's going to test this model on the mission."

"Without having tried it before today."

"Oh, yeah." Mayweather shook his head and gave a sour grin. "It's the General's way."

"Why does he *do* that?" Burkett said. "Has he got some kind of investment in the company that makes 'em?" This was talking trash to a superior officer about an even *more* superior officer, but Burkett and Mayweather were tight—they'd each saved the other's life more than once. Mayweather treated him like a man of equal rank.

"Not legally." The captain shrugged. "But people have ways." Mayweather clomped up the titanium ramp and Burkett followed him into the S-7's fuselage.

Thirty seconds later the ramp whirred up and locked firmly into place. A few minutes more, and the S-7 began atmosphere control as the mothership began rumbling onto the runway.

THREE

MONASTERY OF ST. BASIL
MOLDOVA

Frederic Dupon was certain he wouldn't be able to bear it. He was already in pain with his broken nose, and he was endlessly terrified. Worse was coming. Today, they would begin the torture.

"In the natural course of things," Lutzoff had said carelessly.

As Dupon contemplated impending torture, the non-disclosure oath he had signed with the European Union seemed to wither in his mind. It now seemed absurd. Lying on his bunk—heart pounding, belly rippling with nausea—he remembered what Lutzoff had told him, just two nights before.

"You know, Frederic," the oily, balding Russian said, Adam's apple bobbing on his long neck, *"this monastery was built by monks devoted to St. Basil, who was a true fanatic. They came from Russia to build it, all because Basil had a vision. It took many years to complete it, and much determination. Look at it now! Crumbling at the edges, abandoned but for us! Their precious chapel used to store dried meat and toilet paper.*

"Things are built, and they fall apart, Frederic. The European Union crushes national identity a little more each year. Nothing lasts, nothing matters. Loyalty is for family and friends and oneself. I myself do not waste it on anything else. I am—" He shrugged ruefully, and adjusted his white coat. *"—just a well-*

paid hireling. They employ me because I work carefully. I have a special method. Please understand, however, I do not stop till it is finished, Frederic. However—if you choose to help us, we will move you and your mother and father to a safe place.

"We know where your parents are, of course..."

Lutzoff's sinuous rhetoric made sense when nothing else seemed to. Dupon had been transported to the medieval world; dragged into an underground cell, damp and unheated, smelling of rat droppings and mold and shit. They had to use buckets here.

As well, the company of the other surviving prisoners was increasingly odious. Dupon had grown to dislike them intensely. Johansen—the one he'd respected most and the first to be tortured—had died, much to Lutzoff's surprise, it seemed. A weak heart.

Even if Dupon cooperated wholeheartedly, he couldn't trust these men to let him go. Most were Bulgarian mobsters, but their interrogator was asking questions specifically useful to Russian military intelligence, and Lutzoff was a Russian. They might let him live, but in some remote location, and only until his usefulness came to an end.

Then he would be shot, buried in an unmarked grave.

Of that, Dupon was certain.

The door to the cell clanked open and Keruyn, a towering slab of a man with long blond hair and tattoos swarming his thick neck, was there with a cattle prod in one hand. Just behind him was Lutzoff.

"Come along, Frederic," the Russian said, his voice dripping with faux sympathy. "I have something new to try. It will help you make up your mind." Looking theatrically sad, Lutzoff lifted a heavy-duty shop vise into the light. "You see what you force us to do? We start low on your feet and tighten it and *crack*, and *crack* a little more, and we move upward six or eight inches, and we do it again. Then another six inches. Decisiveness grows and grows, as this simple instrument marches up your body. It doesn't make a bloody mess, either. I like that."

Heart hammering, Dupon stood, wobbling with terror—then tried to rush past Keruyn. The cattle prod flashed and Dupon fell to his knees, twitching spasmodically.

Keruyn grabbed Dupon around the throat and dragged him by the neck into the dimly lit corridor, along the musty flagstones, and through the door that led to Hell.

Everyone was in a flight seat except Captain Mayweather. They were buckled in, and the body-conformable smart-netting, used to deal with extreme gravitational conditions, was clasped around each of them. Oxygen masks waited on the seats next to the headrests.

Mayweather held onto the side of the open hatch that led into the flight deck, facing the team.

"It's ten hours later in Moldova," the Captain told them over the rumbling of the mothership leaving the hangar. "When we get there, in a little over an hour, it'll be dark. No moon. Cloudy, weather moderate. Optimum conditions." He paused, then added, "After *Mommy Dearest* hits the air, we've got about twenty minutes before we reach thirty-five thousand feet. There we detach."

Most of them were familiar with the routine, so Burkett figured he was laying this part out for Ken Carney and Des Andrews.

"Six seconds after dropping from the mothership," Mayweather went on, "we'll burn methane and shoot up into lower Earth orbit. A little over an hour after that we'll be in Drop-Heavy position over Moldova. It'll be about one-thirty in the morning when we touch down. Cloudy night, no moon, good time for an assault. We'll move toward the target with maximum pronto. You should have the infil tactics on your hand-screens by now—let's go over it…"

* * *

Minutes later the mothership was racing down the strip for takeoff. Mayweather was in his seat up front. Burkett was seated behind Tafir and Lem Dorman, Carney in front of them.

Cpl. Tafir Dabiri, from Queens New York, seemed restless, adjusting his seat unnecessarily. He was an experienced SubOrbital hand. Reliable and smart. A Sunni Muslim, speaking Farsi but also fluent in Arabic. A believer without being outwardly religious. An engineer and experienced combat soldier, he was physically ripped, and maybe a little too proud of it. All too lively a sense of humor.

Tafir liked to haze SubOrbital newbies.

By contrast, PFC Dorman was relaxed. Curly black hair, heavy eyebrows, slightly crooked smile. Born in Israel, grew up in Philadelphia. His dad was former Mossad. Lemuel was a specialist in quiet kills, earning numerous commendations and two silver stars. He could've been promoted several times but seemed to dodge it.

"I like it better down here," he told Burkett. "Get more action."

Normally a squad would have more PFCs and Specialists, but the necessary skillset and clearances for SubOrbital meant the team was top-heavy with commissioned and non-com officers. They had learned to be tacitly flexible where rank was concerned, at least up to Burkett, who was the XO.

Waiting for takeoff, Burkett watched as Lem calmly tinkered with a setting on his night-vision goggles. Dorman chuckled to himself at some private joke and Burkett wondered what he was thinking about.

"Hey, Lieutenant Carney," Tafir said in a carefully modulated tone. He leaned forward. "Have you been on a combat-ready orbcraft before?"

"I went up on the trainer," Carney said a little defensively—

and loudly — over the rising noise of the engines. There was everything from deep bass-tone roars to a falsetto shriek, with metallic rattling mixed in as the mothership took off. "And I visited USOS 7. Had my weightlessness training."

"Yes sir," Tafir said. "Course, the trainer's not combat-ready—it's not as big and it hasn't been fired on. Two missions ago we were fired on, caught two RPG rounds as we came to the infil. Armor held, 'cept in a couple of places, but sometimes it's like we never quite got it repaired. Hey Lemuel, you hear that rattling?"

Dorman nodded solemnly. "Now you mention it... Whoa—you hear *that*?"

"What?" Carney said, looking around quickly.

"Probably nothing," Tafir said. "You see, Lieutenant, the problem's gonna be when we hit the hard acceleration. You know, sir, once *Mommy Dearest* lets her baby go and we start to burn fuel, this big ol' orbcraft kicks us up to seven gees. That's intense shit. Blacked out one time. I always think the g-force'll snap something in the ship, breach the hull, and we'll suddenly lose air pressure and I'll feel my eyes pop out of my skull..."

Burkett leaned out a little to check on Carney. The second lieutenant's knuckles were white on the armrests. Burkett had wanted to see how Carney would react, but it was time to nip this in the bud.

"Tafir, Lem—*zip it!*"

"Yes sir!" they said together, barely keeping their faces deadpan.

"Carney—ignore those two scared little girls," Burkett said. "They get worked up at the beginning of every takeoff. Some weird paranoid ritual. There's nothing wrong with this craft."

Carney let out a long breath. "Oh, well, I thought so..." His fingers relaxed on the armrests. "I mean, I wasn't..."

Burkett smiled. Being first lieutenant, he outranked Carney—maybe he should give him hell for being suggestible. But it was the guy's first Drop-Heavy flight.

* * *

They soared to the altitude where the S-7 would separate from the mothership. Less than fifteen minutes passed, then one of the mothership pilots could be heard over the radio.

"*Ready for release... launching S-7... good luck and see you at Wyatt's when you get back*," the pilot said. Then he added, "*We're buying.*"

"Roger that," Mayweather said.

There was a metallic screech, a *ker-chunk-chunk* sound, and the bottom fell out of Burkett's stomach as the S-7 was dropped from the mothership. The orbcraft jarred with teeth-rattling force as full windage hit them. At 35,000 feet—10,668 meters— the S-7 used no engine power for six seconds. It shot forward, carried by momentum, to give the mothership time to ascend and veer away.

Six seconds—and then came the thunder of the orbcraft's big engines as it started its burn of cryogenic liquid methane and liquid oxygen. The stage-combustion engine accelerated to three gees in under a minute, going quickly from Mach 1, Mach 2, Mach 3, and up. Supersonic, hypersonic, high-hypersonic, hyper velocity—

The vibrations running through the S-7 changed, becoming fine-tuned, more of a buzzing as they arced up toward the Kármán Line—the edge of space. It was rough for a while, but Burkett loved it, because he identified with the roaring engines and the embodied power of the rising orbcraft forcing its way from the atmosphere—penetrating space, overpowering gravity itself.

It was always badass.

The g-force increased, to four, then five, pushing relentlessly on Burkett, seeming to try to push his face off his skull. As Tafir once said, "*It's wrapping my cheeks around my damn ears.*" Instead of a fighter pilot's pressure suit they relied on the automatic compression of the smart-netting, tightening around them to keep their blood flowing to the brain. Even with the netting, it was harder to breathe because of the invisible giant's hand pressing on his chest.

Then his training kicked in and he used the Hook maneuver, controlling his glottis while breathing slowly, deeply, and firmly, and compressing his abdomen to press blood up into his brain. Still the g-force mounted, until Burkett's vision blurred. Too much of this and they'd all hit G-LOC and black out, despite the circulatory assistance from the netting.

Ike leveled off the S-7 and the pressure eased dramatically. Heavy gravitation dropped away second by second.

Soon, they'd be in microgravity.

Directional rockets snapped into burn and they tilted twenty degrees upward, so that they hit LEO—low Earth orbit— following the curve of the planet as they rocketed northeast, skating along the Kármán Line. Burkett always imagined this part of the flight as surfing on the upper atmosphere.

Glancing out a port, he saw the curve of the Earth swelling, the luminescent blue of the atmosphere showing an indigo band where the air thinned. There were glimpses of cobalt sea and craggy mountain ranges looking brown and purple. There was a wave of nausea as the last of the detectable gravity fell away, like a steep plunge in a roller coaster.

Burkett hoped Carney hadn't eaten anything in a while.

All gear was supposed to be secured before flight, but there was always something that got loose. Someone's hand-screen went floating up toward the ceiling, and Des Andrews cursed softly. It drifted back through the cabin, turning end over end before Burkett caught it. The motion made him slightly dizzy, though. He felt a bit sleepy, too — the first effects of microgravity. His body would adapt, but it helped to move around.

"Keep your seats!" he called out, unbuckling from his own. The smart netting folded back and he drifted upward. He and Mayweather had the privilege of going up to the flight deck and

Burkett always took advantage of it, partly for the practice in weightless motion.

Still carrying the screen, he placed his free hand on the back of Carney's chair to push himself into the aisle and then forward, drifting like Superman out for a leisurely flight. From time to time, he used his hand on the bulkhead or grabbed an overhead ring to keep him on course.

"Hey, Andrews!" Burkett sent the all-purpose comm device spinning through the air. It moved in slow-mo through the air to Des, who caught it.

"Thanks, Lieutenant!"

"Hold onto your gear next time, Sergeant. Not gonna tell you again!"

"You're not, sir?" Des asked, as if skeptical.

"No, next time you'll get that thing stuck an inch into the back of your head!"

Des grinned. "Roger that, sir."

Burkett drifted past Corporal Rodriguez. The medic was leaning back in his seat staring at the ceiling, probably trying to control a little nausea. A medic who knew as much as any emergency room doctor, Rodriguez had close-clipped black hair, dark eyes, a wide mouth. Thirty-six years old, he'd been recommended for the Medal of Honor for repeatedly risking his life under deadly fire to save the wounded. Endlessly compassionate, but unhesitating when it was necessary to neutralize an enemy combatant.

Burkett reached the big flight deck—the cockpit of the S-7— and found Mayweather already inside, floating upright and hunkered a little behind the pilots. He was peering through the front viewport, where it looked as if they were about to plunge from day into darkness. An eerie twilight zone of dusk swept along with the turn of the planet.

As the S-7 crossed the border into the night side, darkness draped over the flight deck and the lights of civilization appeared below, bright gleaming spots competing with those on the instrument panel. The moon was just visible, a gray orb hanging over the Earth's horizon against the blackness of space.

Their engines were silent now, since the orbcraft only needed them for course correction. It had reached its orbital maintenance speed of 18,000 MPH—29,000 kilometers per hour. At this rate they would circumnavigate the Earth in under an hour and a half.

"How's the Roman candle, Ike?" Burkett asked.

"Flying straight and true, Lieutenant. We're coming up on DH ZP in about forty-two."

Burkett nodded. Twenty klicks to the Zero Point, Drop-Heavy terminology for an orbital position directly overhead of the target. Somewhere in Nevada there were landing pods being tested that could drop directly down from Zero Point—they'd be faster, with only the briefest radar-lidar footprint.

But the S-7 had to risk a period of semi-horizontal trajectory as it came down. Still, it came down steeply and accomplished a fast insert.

In a pinch, the S-7 could land on its tail like something from a 1950s science-fiction flick, and at end of mission it could take off from that position, as well. A vertical landing was complex, though, tough for problematic terrain, and too slow for a Drop-Heavy assault, which was all about quick deployment, getting to far places rapidly and quick ground action upon arrival.

Far below, the sharp points of light became few as the orbcraft traveled over the Atlantic Ocean. Ike and Linda muttered over indicator readings and slight changes of course as they corrected for Moldovan airspace.

"Better get back to our seats, Art," Mayweather said.

Burkett grunted agreement and carefully turned around in the open hatch—sudden movements ended with bruises, at the very least—then stretched a hand to grab a ring in the ceiling and tugged himself aft. Queasy but not in any real distress, he drifted past the squad and then caught another ring to turn and angle his body into his seat. This part required some wriggling, but he was soon in his belt and netting again.

"Less than thirty to Zero Point," Mayweather called, settling into his own seat. "Prep for regravitation."

Once strapped in and netted, all Burkett could do to "prep for regravitation" was relax, hold onto the armrests, and prepare himself psychologically.

The pilots began descent, and the S-7 pitched down as sharply as possible while still within tolerable range for atmospheric friction and craft control. G-force on the way down to the Earth's surface was far less, just a pressure on the chest, and a need to control their breath.

The heat was the thing.

As they plunged into the atmosphere, it would reach a thousand degrees on the hull. The titanium-alloy hull was specially treated to lessen drag, which reduced friction, and an under-layer of carbon nanotubes resisted heat build-up. Even so, a cherry-red plume formed around the swept-back wings as they picked up descent speed.

The orbcraft retained one of the old stratolauncher's features—a tail that could be tilted up and over the fuselage, "feathering" against atmospheric pressure to slow them enough to assist braking and keep the vessel controllable.

Sergeant Strickland activated feathering and the orbcraft jolted as the tail tilted into the wind. Carney made a little soft moaning noise as the vessel slipped slightly off course, briefly shaking from side to side, but Ike quickly guided it back into the mapped trajectory.

As they passed through thermosphere, mesosphere, stratosphere, and troposphere, an array of high-artificial-intelligence computers—layered into the hull—controlled deceleration rockets with precise control, firing them rapidly on and off, spreading inertia along the hull so no one area received too much stress. The tiny rockets hissed close inboard, rippling from nose to tail, slowing the vessel. Coming down at so steep a pitch had called for special engineering.

Just ten klicks northerly, Ike eased out of a planned, gradual spiral and flattened trajectory for landing. He and Linda had studied the satellite images, but if some unseen obstacle cropped up at the last moment—some outcropping hidden by an optical flaw—they had to be able to react in time. And there was always the chance that someone at the dear old NSA had erred with respect to the *length* of the impromptu landing strip. Even if the analysts were right, there was no room for pilot error.

Lights out, coming in low, and fully stealth-clad, the orbcraft was only visible against the dark night if its rocketry was spotted. The engines were designed for as much quiet as possible. Methane burned clean and dark blue, and they were landing more than two miles from St. Basil's.

On the wall of the old monastery, four members of the Thieves in Law were caught up in an argument about a pass to go to the village.

As the dispute went on, Stepan Bohdan thought he heard a strange sound and peered off to the south. Was that the rumble of an engine? Then again, there was a road not far away. Probably just a passing truck supplying the military base over at Kezn.

He had his thick, tattooed fingers on the tripod machine gun—but there was nothing to shoot. It was just a cloudy night, few stars visible, no moon. The stand of pines and spruce south of the old monastery nodded in the wind.

Olek Syrkin, alone of the four men, knew something was coming. He'd personally recommended the landing zone, but he was careful not to look in that direction.

Ildeva wagged a stubby finger at him.

"You don't get a pass to go into the village, Olek, because you don't do the work," Ildeva said in Bulgarian. "Half the time I find you wandering around—aimless!"

Not aimless, Olek thought, but he kept his tongue. Instead, he put on a look that was sad and offended. "Mikhail, I am looking around for security! We have prisoners. Some of the locals, they spy on us. Maybe they work for Moldovan secret police. Sometimes I think I hear them breaking in!"

Ildeva gave out a loud, sneering laugh. "Olek, you worry about those pig-slopping oafs? *Ha!* And as for Moldovan secret police, who do you think gave us this place to use? You're not searching for intruders—you're looking for liquor, that's what you're doing." He was a heavyset man with out-of-proportion thick arms and a beard that looked too small for his round face. When he laughed, the multitude of temhota tattoos on his neck and bare arms seemed to squirm in shared amusement. There was a sharp wind cutting across the plateau, yet Ildeva wore only paramilitary togs, untied boots, and a sleeveless T-shirt.

"So, there is liquor hidden here?" Dmytro, a wiry man with a red beard that whipped in the wind, slapped his submachine gun against a bony hip, which was as close as he ever came to laughing. "In this mess of old rocks?"

"Ah, for a time there was," Bohdan declared. He was a stocky, bald machine-gunner, tattooed on his head and cheeks with gorgeous swirls around Slavic crosses. He was half-Russian. A tattered mustache hung over his harelip. "The monks made pear brandy here. Some old bottles, smashed, still stink of it in the cells!"

"Yet you hope to find some hundred-year-old liquor behind a stone, eh, Olek?" Ildeva jeered. "Let me help you, then. You can search for it down in the cells, when you go help Ilyov guard them!"

Olek grimaced as if this wasn't exactly what he wanted. "The devil loves you, Mikhail."

"Go! Or I will tie you face down on Bohdan's bunk! You know Bohdan, he'll fuck anything, and he has no sheep to love here."

The men laughed at that. Bohdan the loudest.

Shaking his head and grumbling, Olek went to the stairs, fingering his submachine gun as he went. He pretended to be resigned, and even a bit bored, but his gut was quivering with rising dread.

They are coming. He was sure of it, and if he could manage not to get killed in the next few hours, he could leave here with them and to hell with the CIA. Yet the risk of getting his head blown off during the incursion was quite high.

His CIA handlers wanted him to stay with TiL, to encourage the others to abandon the monastery—to go with them if they bolted, and continue to be a source of intelligence—but it was in his mind to surrender to the Rangers the instant he got the chance. To declare himself to the American commandos who were coming, and demand to be exfiltrated.

He'd had enough of being a spy. The constant fear of being exposed, weariness of perpetual dissimulation. Now, Olek Syrkin wanted the reward the Americans had promised him for more than two years.

The orbcraft's only light as it approached its landing was in its flight deck—a glow unseen from outside, thanks to the one-way windshield. The S-7 rushed toward the LZ.

A computer-generated replica of the landing topography unrolled toward the pilots, with arrows and numbers superimposed over high-risk spots. A large boulder appeared but the ship's computers—controlling the now-extended wheels—saw it too, and the aft wheels lifted precisely enough to avoid the obstacle. A split second later they lowered again, just in time to touch down.

Ike did the last of the braking himself.

Theoretically the computer could accomplish it, but it wasn't fine-tuned to the feel of the ship in the way Ike was. Forward braking rockets feathered on and off under his controlling fingertips. The wheels braked, too. The orbcraft rollicked as it rushed over uneven, rocky ground toward a hulking granite boulder...

The S-7 slowed... and stopped unnervingly close to the boulder.

FOUR

"I don't know what you're complaining about," Ilyov said.

"How can you not complain in such a place?" Olek replied.

Olek Syrkin and Nerhiy Ilyov stood in the musty, ill-lit corridor outside the prisoners' cells. Ilyov was a much-scarred, remarkably unbathed older man in heavy green paramilitary jacket and combat trousers. He had a matted thatch of white hair. Olek was passing time talking with Ilyov, but his mind was far from chitchat as he looked through the bars in the cell's little window. The three scientists were sullen, listless but, so far, not in bad shape.

Olek sighed. He was already sick of this hallway. The confinement, the cold, the gloominess, the stench. He tried to think of some excuse to slip away, get some fresh air. Perhaps he might have time to take his satellite phone from concealment. To call for word on the Americans.

"Ilyov—maybe I will go and have a pee."

"You piss like a sieve today. This is three times."

"I think that whore in Chişinău gave me the clap. I should not be here. I should go to a clinic."

"Remember, Olek, when you asked to come on this job? You asked! None of the rest of us *asked* for it. Moldova? Out in the wastelands? A *monastery*? But Mikhail insisted that those with military skills must come. He even brought more men than he needed to… and then came *you*! An amateur! Hardly blooded!"

"Oh please, I have done my share of bloodletting for the brotherhood," Olek growled.

"And you *begged* to come, Olek! Mikhail was suspicious, but he is your uncle so he turns a blind eye! Me—I know you are not enterprising enough to be a traitor."

Oh indeed.

"Mikhail is not an uncle—only second cousin. It was my Uncle Denys who told him to let me come. I wanted to prove myself, Ilyov, I always get stuck in small jobs. I wanted to do something big this time."

"Feh! With Thieves in Law you prove yourself by bringing in women and money and drugs! That's what we like. This ransom business—it's not a job for a real soldier. They will give us a share, but still…" Ilyov shifted his assault rifle from one shoulder to the other and nodded toward the cell door. "Watching these frightened, spoiled teacher-doctors. Bah!"

"I am not so happy now that I'm here," Olek admitted, as he wondered if he would have to kill Ilyov before the night was over. Quite possibly.

"So you said, boy—as if you were surprised! No women here, no vodka, not even wine—what did you expect in such a place? Once a week, if we are good little boys, a trip to the tavern. Must be very careful with locals. 'Don't force yourself on the women.' Bah!" He spat at the stone floor.

"Yes, I agree. I think we should have a tot or two of vodka, or at least nalyvka—every night! And—" He lowered his voice. "—Mikhail has his own vodka! I smell it on his breath. He forbids it to us, but he has his own supply!"

"You should not talk of such things. Your uncle won't keep Mikhail from kicking your ass!" Chuckling, Ilyov turned away and lit one of his precious cigarettes, instinctively keeping his back turned so Olek would be discouraged from asking for one.

But Olek didn't smoke—except, back home, a little hashish.

He looked again through the small window in the door. There was a yellow electric light in a cage hanging from the ceiling, connected to a thick orange cable running to a hole in the wall, and out to the generator. It was always lit so they would know what the prisoners were doing.

Two of the men sat on the floor, talking softly, their backs to the least damp wall, their faces hidden by a shadow cast from the corner of a bunk. He had not dared to tell them what might be happening tonight. Ilyov spoke some English, and French—Ilyov had been in a French prison for six years. The prisoners might say something in his hearing.

The nearer one, huddled in his bunk, Frederic Dupon—he would be a problem. Lutzoff had used the vise to break the man's right foot; then he had cracked Dupon's ankle and the lower part of the shin. Olek had to stand guard in the interrogation cell during one of these sessions, and he had no taste for it.

"*Up your limbs we will go over many days, Dupon!*" Lutzoff had said sweetly. "*And yet you are willing to put up with anything for the swine who allowed you to be brought here! Do you think they did not know your danger? They didn't care! A couple of EuroIntel imbeciles to guard a man like you! Now then... let's use rawhide ball to close your mouth, because the screaming disturbs my concentration...*"

Dupon could not walk. He screamed when they moved him, but the Americans would send their strongest men. They would carry him out quickly.

Olek glanced at Ilyov. Yes. It would be necessary to kill him, and soon. Well, the old fellow had lived a long time—he was past fifty. He'd enjoyed many women in his day, and had spawned many children. Every night Ilyov prayed to the saints and made his peace with God.

So then, send him to God.

* * *

Hearing voices, Burkett walked up to the S-7's nose, trudging over gravel in the dull red glow of the orbcraft's underlighting—switched on only because they were in a valley below the enemy's line of sight. He could feel the heat coming off the metal above him.

Dabiri and Faraday were staring up at the cliff.

"Look at that!" Tafir said, shaking his head and pointing at the beetling granite wall. "Two meters! You stopped two meters from a fucking wall of granite, Ike! You practically kissed it!"

"This may be the shortest landing strip, if you wanna call it that, I ever landed on," Ike said, as he peered at the snout of the S-7. "You got my finesse to thank that you're not splashed on that granite wall."

"What'd you do, stick your foot out the hatch?"

Burkett cleared his throat. "Cast your mind back, Tafir, to the last time you looked at the bars on Ike's collar." There was tolerance around rank protocol in the team, but Tafir always pushed it too far.

"Sorry, sir," Tafir said, nodding. "*Lieutenant* Faraday, you stopped two meters from a big fucking wall of—"

"*Corporal?*" Burkett snapped. "Captain wants you to suit up in that piss pot."

"Yes sir." Tafir hurried off into the darkness.

"Piss pot?" Ike asked.

"One of Carney's little test-'ems. Newest Talos combat suit."

"You're fucking kidding me. Sir."

"Nope." Burkett looked up at the cliff wall. "Ike—you did cut it damned close. Did you inspect the wings?"

"Yes sir."

"You send the damage assessment drones?" Launching the DADs was standard procedure.

"Flew 'em over every inch. We're copacetic." He hefted the MK-21 in his hands. "Am I cannon fodder tonight?"

"No, you watch your baby and be ready to support if we call. Set up a tripod defilade near the ramp."

"Roger that."

"Come on." They walked back the length of the orbcraft together. Partway along they met Lemuel, who was skidding down a goat path worn into one of the rugged, steep ridges enclosing the valley. He had night-vision telescopic goggles dangling around his neck, MK-21 SCAR-H in his hands. The 7.62mm × 51mm weapon was a combination of carbine, assault rifle, and medium sniper rifle. A beautiful, eclectic, relatively light weapon—Burkett carried his own on a strap over a shoulder.

"Clear to the west, sir, so far as I can see," Lemuel said, taking off his patrol cap to wipe his forehead with the back of his hand. "And to the east. Megan—Sergeant Lang—reported all clear from there. North looked good but there's rocky spurs blocking line of sight some places."

"We'll get a better look from the drones. Call Lang, tell her I want you both to check out the exit route, then hustle back for final load-out. And put on a helmet, Dorman."

"Yes sir." Lemuel touched his headset, and as Burkett walked off, he heard Lem talking to Megan. "Sarge? Lieutenant wants us to check south AO together, rapid return."

Burkett and Ike continued through knee-high grass and over crumbling rock to the aft of the S-7. A wind whistled over the little valley and a faint precipitation, little more than mist, came and went.

They found Mayweather personally backing the Bravo 7 blast-resistant light-terrain vehicle down the ramp onto the rocket-scorched ground. The armored, tan-colored LTV was a hybrid, capable of using gas if need be but mostly electric, so it would be quiet. It had separate electric cells in its composite armor, to neutralize armor-piercing rounds, the electrical field dampening them before they could explode. There was a 16mm turret up top of the vehicle, and a small launching deck for the two-meter-square armed drones stacked up there.

The LTV had adaptive camouflage that adjusted to backdrop, and its armor was layered for heat suppression, making it hard to see, especially at night, even with heat-signature goggles. It had 360-degree cameras, screen-view remote-control of the drones, and secure comm frequencies. All in all, it was a mobile Tactical Operations Center, dented and scarred because they had used it in combat three times before. Mayweather had never had the superficial damage spruced up. Said it was a good reminder.

Sometimes Burkett thought the Captain was in love with the damn thing. Mayweather's nickname for it was "the Light-Up." As in, *"Let's light the bastards up."*

"Stand clear till she one-eighties!" Mayweather said from the cab's windows. They gave way and he spun the LTV around, facing south. The cliffs around the little valley were steep; the only way the LTV could get out was a rocky slope to the south. They'd head south and double back to the north for the assault.

Burkett went to stand by the open window, watching as Mayweather pulled the drone control screen out from under the dashboard and tapped in commands. Drone 1 started humming, its blades whirling. Its fastener unhooked and it lifted up, wobbling a little before stabilizing about ten meters over the vehicle and to one side, leaving room for the other two. Drones 2 and 3 lifted up, and the trio shifted into a triangle formation, then elevated above the rock walls of the ravine and flew off to the north.

Mayweather touched his headset. "Syrkin? You on perimeter?" A pause. "Get Andrews to relieve you and report to me." He took his hand-screen from its clip on the dash and scrolled through the briefing text. "Yeah. That's who it is."

"Who, Captain?" Burkett asked.

"The spooks' inside man at the monastery. He's been using a satellite phone to talk to Chance. He's given us most of what we've got. I'm the only one here to get this briefing memo, and Chance left it up to me if—"

Cpl. Alexi Syrkin appeared at the open window next to Mayweather.

"Sir?"

"Corporal Syrkin—you have a brother named Olek? Got some iffy connections in Bulgaria?"

Syrkin hesitated. Then he nodded.

"Yes sir. Last I knew, he was working for my Uncle Denys. Who's… more than iffy."

"See, the reason you're on this one is that Olek's here at the monastery. He's our inside man. CIA asset. He's a hired gun, not agency, but he's given us good intel so far."

"Here, sir? He's *here*—at the target?"

"Yeah. He knows we're coming in. He's supposed to do some spot sabotage for us tonight to make it smoother. I'm sorry you weren't briefed—I wasn't allowed to talk about this until we were on the ground and ready. He's asked for exfil—Chance discouraged the idea, but he thinks Olek is going to try to exfil with us anyway. If Olek comes with us, we'll want you to run herd on him. Keep him under your wing."

Syrkin scowled. "Why should the CIA *not* want him to come with us?"

"Because they figure most of these guys are gonna do a runner. If he goes with them, he can continue to report on them. They're hooked up with Moscow."

"Sir—if he wants to exfil, he should be allowed to. He's running a big risk getting us this far."

"I don't disagree, Alexi."

Syrkin was breathing hard, as if he'd been running. "Sir, he's liable to get killed in the op!"

"He knows to keep his head down tonight. With any luck he'll be okay. Are *you* okay, Corporal? I need you frosty."

Syrkin chewed his lower lip. Burkett could see inner struggle in the man's eyes… and then resignation. The CIA and the Rangers had left him no option but acceptance.

"Yes sir," he said at last.

"Grab the rest of the load-out and take your place in the vehicle."

Without a word, Syrkin turned away and strode up the ramp, anger visible in every step.

"He should've been told," Burkett murmured.

"Chance is a fanatic for need-to-know."

"If anybody ever needed to know, it was Syrkin, Captain."

Mayweather sighed and turned to the window.

"You all have your orders," Mayweather called from the LTV cab window. "Light-Up personnel, get in if you're geared up. If you're not, why the hell aren't you?"

The soldiers scrambled to obey as Mayweather focused on the screen. Burkett climbed into the shotgun seat and leaned to see what the drones saw. Mayweather had three windows open, each showing a drone's-eye view. Two kinds of night vision combined—an upgrade on the old green tones—to provide a dull-red and muted blue image and a sharp green of the topography around the valley to the north.

Mayweather directed the drones out to a hundred meter spread and sent them skimming low, in case the TiL operatives had some form of radar going.

Burkett suspected they did. They had too many men here just to guard three prisoners, and they were in an unnecessarily remote, fort-like location. All of that had to be Moscow's idea. The GRU had orchestrated the taking of three important researchers—every one of them working on something exotic with military applications. Meaning they knew there might be an American or NATO black ops rescue attempt.

Had they picked up the short-term blip of the S-7? Was their radar sensitive enough to spot the squad's relatively small drones?

As Burkett watched, Mayweather slowed the drones to a hover just behind the woods to the south of the monastery, a quarter klick from its steel-reinforced front gates. Then he sent Drone 2 straight up, away from the others. He held it at 200 meters and rotated it, looking through its camera eyes for any movement outside the monastery. Vehicles, patrols, drones—nothing yet. Taking care not to come in too close, he directed Drone 2 to circle the ancient structure.

There were men on the outer wall, walking in twos, with others stationed at machine-gun posts — one to the north, one south, and one to the west. A TiL thug seemed to be tinkering with a transmitter dish on the top of the central building. There were a couple of trucks parked in the courtyard next to a chapel with a partly collapsed roof. No one in the courtyard, no one currently visible outside. Lamps and electric lanterns burned here and there.

"They're ready—but not ready," Burkett noted dryly.

"There, Art, see that door on the west side? You can barely make it out from up here…"

At the bottom of the drone's steep angle of observation, the shadows thickened halfway along the western wall, forming a rough rectangle. "That our entry point?" He'd seen it marked in their orders, but it was good to get a visual fix in his mind.

Mayweather nodded. "This guy Olek thinks it's the best way in. It's heavily barred and he can't open it for us—too out in the open—but we'll blow it in and sprint across the cobbles there to the building. He's supposed to have that inside door unlocked—if he doesn't, we'll take that down, too. One floor underground, just inside that door, we'll find the cells, and hopefully the prisoners are still alive."

"Good stealth on these drones. Seems like no one's spotted them yet. Another drone might, though…"

"Yeah." Mayweather did a ping-scan for enemy drones, came up empty.

"No state of alert, looks like," Burkett remarked.

Mayweather nodded. "Area of operations is virginal. Go to tactical readiness. Chest armor only, except for Tafir—minimize the battle-rattle. Assign Beta Team to draw fire. There's a sweet outcropping of granite thirty meters from the south wall. We'll put Beta there. You take Alpha to hit the door—Tafir's some of your cover."

"Yes sir."

Tafir was sharply aware of the others staring at him as he clomped down the ramp in his Talos combat suit. They were ducking one by one into the Light-Up and glancing back as they went. A helmet completely concealed his head and his entire body was covered with complex and heavy-duty combat suit armor.

He chortled to himself and took a place on exterior footing at the back of the LTV, a glorified running board, holding onto a metal half-ring.

"What the fuck, Lance Corporal?" Lemuel said, taking up a place beside him. They were poised like nineteenth-century firemen on the back of the vehicle. "Tafir, you didn't clue us about this knight-in-ugly-armor shit because you wanted to see our faces?"

"Yep."

"You like to see us going 'what the fuck,' right?"

"Exactly right, Private."

"So how come the Captain didn't brief us?"

"You didn't get briefed on it 'cause you didn't have security clearance, small fry," Tafir said.

Lemuel snorted and they gripped the handholds as the LTV started off. "Those suits never work for dick."

"It'll work. It's got smartness, PFC Dorman. Much... smartness. I tested the model before this one. They got the bugs out since then—so they tell me—and this one's been fitted for me."

At least I hope they got the bugs out, Tafir thought.

"You got the adaptive camo skin on that thing?" Lemuel asked, looking it up and down.

"Yeah, more fine-grained than the Light-Up's."

"Ever occur to anyone that we might need to be trained to be around a combat suit? How we going to work with you, if we can't see you?"

"Um… take that up with the General." The suit didn't provide complete invisibility, though it would wrap the backdrop around it, but he had to admit that at night, it would be hard for the other Rangers to see it.

"*Shut the fuck up back there*," the Captain said, over his headset. "*Loud as a couple of huskies in heat.*"

Another problem with the suit's adaptive camo was its tendency to blow through its power charge. He'd have to be sparing with it; he didn't think he could use the semi-invisibility mode. The exoskeleton that was supposed to support the 290-pound armor, computer interfacing, and smart sheathing, sometimes had labored to keep up with weight stress.

That stuff was supposed to have been ironed out, but right now, Tafir's HUD—the heads-up display—bombarded him with way too much information. He didn't think he'd need "electromagnetic field surveillance" or the "kill triangulation" software. Best to shut those two down.

Night-sight built into the helmet was pretty damned good, Tafir thought, looking around. It was simply part of the visor on the helmet that covered his head and face. Walking to the LTV, he'd found the armor to be well supported by the exoskeleton, and the joints flexible enough. No way he was going to be as nimble in this piss pot as without it.

His auto-shotgun had an add-on that communicated with his suit, projecting precision sighting on the HUD. That might compensate for his slowness.

The LTV headed out, past Ike Faraday who was setting up the 10mm laser-sight machine gun behind a movable wall he'd set in place. Mayweather drove, Burkett beside him.

In a few minutes the Captain swung west, then sharply north. Mayweather gauged the rough terrain through his night-goggles, veering around an outcropping now and then.

* * *

In the back of the Light-Up, his back pressed against the steel wall, Alexi Syrkin looked around at the others. Sgt. Des Andrews was across from him, next to Sgt. Linda Strickland. Rodriquez was following the Light-Up in a smaller LTV, essentially an armored ambulance with room for three wounded.

The other soldiers were serious, quiet, centered in their own thoughts as they looked down at the deck. Their heads and shoulders jiggled as the wheels hit rough grade. Next to Syrkin was Sgt. Megan Lang, Lance Cpl. Kyu Cha, and Second Lieutenant Carney. They hadn't seemed strange before. Not during the briefing on the ground, not on the orbcraft. A crew of professionals. But now...

Syrkin glanced over at 2nd Lt. Carney, who looked sickly in the red light of the overhead. He was breathing hard and trying to hide it—clearly he hadn't been in close combat before. Why was he even here?

To please his father, the General.

And why did they bring me along? Syrkin thought. *Because my brother might be a problem?*

"*All personnel,*" Mayweather said over the intercom, "*you know from the hand-screen briefing we're looking to take Mikhail Ildeva prisoner if we can. You had orders to memorize his picture, so you better have done it.*" He paused, then continued. "*There's another man who may ask for exfiltration. He's a valuable agency asset named Olek Syrkin. CIA has not seen fit to give us a picture of him.*"

At that, everyone in the back of the Light-Up looked at Alexi. They hadn't been told. Not much had been done to protect his brother...

"If he requests exfiltration, we'll grant it. Let that be on the record. Watch your fire. Corporal Syrkin can identify him for us. This man is his brother."

"You have a picture of him with you, Alexi?" Linda asked. Alexi shook his head.

"*Squad, check your hand-screens*," Mayweather ordered as the LTV came to a stop. "*It'll show you the satellite image of the AO. We are that green blip just west of the trees, 200 meters from the wall. Beta Team, head north-northeast, through the trees for that big granite outcropping. Undergrowth isn't much in there. Sergeant Strickland is weapons squad leader for Beta Team, follow her, she has it locked in.*

"*When I say follow her lead, that includes you, Lieutenant Carney—you've got the rank, but she has the experience.*" After a moment he added, "*Put your hand-screens away and be weapons-ready. Beta is SBF—draw fire and take down anyone you can on the walls. Watch sharp to repel counterattack. That's it.*

"*Hit your positions right fucking now!*"

FIVE

Olek Syrkin was taut with uncertainty. He sat on a wooden bench, clenching his hands, staring at the prisoners' cell door, as Ilyov spoke with Zelinsky. The TiL stood at the doorway down the narrow stone corridor, to Olek's left. They were bitching, as usual. No sense of urgency about them.

Fingering his submachine gun, Olek thought about nailing both Zelinsky and Ilyov the instant gunfire started up.

Chance had asked Syrkin to set a fire, to prevent the TiL from getting Kevlar vests and ammo resupply. Did Olek have time to do that? Doubtful—and even if he managed it, could he hope to go unnoticed, and escape this slimy rockpile with his life?

If he weakened TiL, it meant the commandos were likely to succeed, and more likely to take him out of here. First he'd have to kill Ilyov, though, because the bastard would object to Olek leaving his post.

Someone shouted down the stairs. Zelinsky waved to Ilyov and went to see what was going on. Ilyov stayed where he was, lighting a cigarette and staring into space. His back was turned.

This was the moment.

Olek drew his knife, switched it to his left hand.

This has to be done fast and it has to be done silently. One mistake, and Ilyov would kill him. The old bastard was strong, and knew scores of lethal tricks. Best not to try and sneak up on him.

He'd sense that.

Cold sweat on his palms, Olek tightened his grip on the haft of the double-edged Karatel knife and walked casually up to Ilyov, not trying to hide the sound of it.

One motion, he told himself.

Olek suddenly stepped in close, slapped his right hand hard over Ilyov's mouth, then stabbed up under the ribcage, nearly vertical, driving the blade in fully and with all his strength—deeply afraid of what would happen if Ilyov had even a slight chance of survival. For a man like this it could not be the kidney stab and throat-cutting maneuver. It had to be the heart—he absolutely must die instantly.

Olek felt three pops in his knife hand, as the razor-sharp blade popped through Ilyov's coat, his skin, and—with a slight delay—his heart.

But Ilyov surprised him. The old gangster stayed upright, struggling to twist away, gnawing at Olek's right hand, trying to force Olek to remove it so he could shout the place down. Olek felt a wrenching, painful strain in his arms and his back as he fought for control.

Then Ilyov snorted blood onto Olek's right hand, quivered, and went limp. Panting, Olek held on and twisted the knife to make sure, but Ilyov was dead. He could smell it.

Olek backed up, step by step, dragging the dead weight down the hall. He turned, cruelly pulling a muscle in his lower back to do it, and dragged the body into the empty cell next to the one holding the hostages. With a gasp of relief, he dropped it into the shadows, then bent to tug his knife out of the corpse, wiping it on Ilyov's coat.

"I'm sorry, Ilyov," he said hoarsely, sheathing his knife, "but you lived long enough. You had your fun, eh?"

Walking a little unsteadily Olek left the cell, closed the door, and looked around. A splashy trail of blood on the floor led back to the cell, and there was blood on both his hands. Some of it was his own blood, from where Ilyov had bitten him.

And here came Zelinsky, down the stairs. "Hey, Ilyov, they want you to…" He stopped, staring at the blood.

"Lutzoff was sloppy this time," Olek said.

Zelinsky was staring at Olek's bloody hands.

Olek shrugged ruefully. "I was trying to clean it up. I tried a rag, got it everywhere. I'll get a mop—"

"Where… where is Ilyov?"

"Oh, he's checking on the prisoners."

Gunfire, from somewhere above. Olek heard Ildeva shouting. The rattle of a machine gun.

It's begun.

Lots of gunfire. Cover for what he had to do next. Zelinsky turned, started up the stairs, but Olek had the submachine gun up, and he fired a long burst. Zelinsky grunted, tumbling down the stairs to the stone floor below.

No point in dragging this one to a cell. No time. The others would be busy with the Americans, and he had to get to the western door alive.

2nd Lt. Linda Strickland was running through the strange blue, green, and red world of night vision—things that were green to the naked eye were dull blue here. She got her team almost under cover at the big outcropping of granite and was two strides away when they were spotted from the wall. They heard Slavic shouting as a spotlight on the roof of the central building sliced down at the Rangers.

She let loose a long burst of NATO rounds at the silhouettes at the top of the nearest wall—a full forty yards away—with her H&K precision-guided integrated assault rifle. Hurried as

she was and unable to use the precision guiding, she simply
slashed the burst across the top of the wall to suppress Tango
fire as she got under cover.

Strickland laid the weapon in a crotch of granite atop a
boulder about five and a half feet high and kept firing to support
the rest of Beta as they sprinted up behind her.

Bullets whined off the outcropping, spattering chips of
rock. She popped off three short bursts at dimly seen figures
atop the wall—one of them vanished with a suddenness that
said *probably a hit*. There was a machine-gun position on
the wall, but it was far enough to the left that it couldn't
sight on them very well from the firing nock. It looked like
the gunner was fumbling to change the tripod position.
She sent a burst that way, but the angle was an awkward
sighting for her, too.

Sergeant Andrews and Corporal Cha found their own firing
positions to either side of her and opened up on the wall, spraying
bullets fast and hard, to draw fire away from Alpha Team.
Second Lieutenant Carney, she noted, was hunkered behind the
boulder, pretending to examine something on his gun.

Deal with that later, she thought, slapping a new magazine
into her weapon.

Sometimes Strickland was almost surprised at how thoroughly
and quickly she slipped into the psychological combat zone.
Since it left her utterly focused and chill to the point of cold-
blooded, it was a very welcome state. In civilian situations—
like at the Rainbow Bar—she felt slow and backward, but
here, the more chaotic the combat became, the quicker she
made decisions.

She ducked down, resetting to double-tap with digital
targeting, then bobbed up and took aim as a round zinged
just over her head. The light-scavenging video-sighter was
on focus, zooming in on a head-and-shoulders silhouette
atop the wall. Was that an RPG launcher in the Tango's
hands?

Strickland centered the crosshairs in the middle of the target's face, just a head-shaped shadow. The crosshairs went green and she squeezed the trigger. The double tap hit the target twice, one bullet knocking him back, the second catching him in the throat. She saw the pink mist as the figure crumpled from sight.

"Tango down," she said, speaking into her headset.

The machine gun had been relocated, and it opened fire on them, bullets raking the top of the boulder. Strickland coughed from granite dust as she ducked down.

Smoke rose from the rooftop of the central monastery building, where Mayweather's drone-fired mini-rockets had struck the communications antenna group squarely. The array was buckled now, its wiring burning, visibly sparking. He couldn't hit the building again and risk bringing the old monastery down on the prisoners.

An enemy drone locked on Drone 3. Two Sedjil missiles knocked the American drone out of the air.

Hellfire. He would have to find another way to take out the machine-gun positions.

Sitting in the Light-Up parked in the woods, Mayweather heard Burkett's voice crackle on his headset.

"Moving in."

Mayweather shifted to Drone 1's cam, seeing Tafir on the small screen as a faint outline obscured by the adaptive camouflage. He was followed by Burkett leading Alpha Team—all of them squat shapes viewed from overhead.

The Rangers sprinted from the tree line to the blind spot under the southwest cornering wall, leaving the slow but steady Tafir to plod behind in his smart armor. Burkett, Alexi Syrkin, Megan Lang, Lemuel Dorman—and Rod Rodriguez, in case the prisoners needed emergency medical. His medevac LTV was parked just inside the woods.

Mayweather watched as they reached the stone wall's corner and rushed down the west side, staying close to the wall to make awkward targets from above. So far, the support-by-fire team was successfully drawing Tango attention and gunfire to the Beta position.

He remembered being a young Ranger with an SBF team engaging in support fire. Their noisy cover fire had gotten them bombarded by artillery, and he'd wondered who supported the support team.

Burkett led the way to their target—the doorway. Mayweather considered drone-firing mini-missiles at the barrier, but it was said to be heavily reinforced—the missiles couldn't be counted on—so Alpha Team brought shaped charges along.

Turning his attention to Drone 2, Mayweather saw the repositioned machine gun set up on a fallen piece of masonry, angling fire down at Beta Team. The weapon was well supplied and slamming the SBF team hard. Des Andrews popped up just long enough to fire a grenade toward the machine gun but it lobbed too high, went over the target, and exploded in the courtyard.

"Here comes your ol' Cap'n," Mayweather murmured, sliding the objective marker on the screen with the tip of his finger, centering it on the machine-gunner. He tapped the find-and-fire button. The hovering drone tilted and zipped through the air to a hover over Beta Team, a hundred meters up—and fired two mini-missiles at the machine gun. Less than two seconds later the gunner was replaced by a ball of white fire. When it cleared, nothing was left but a black smear and twisted metal.

"Tango MG down, Sergeant Strickland," he said. "Resume fire."

"*Thanks, Captain,*" said the voice in his headset. Almost immediately, fire resumed from the outcropping.

Where was Ken Carney?

There he was, firing with the others — ducking down,

bobbing up, firing in the general direction of the wall. Pretty much at random.

The General can't claim we didn't give his kid a chance.

Mayweather piloted the drone high overhead along the walls, searching for the other machine guns. *There.* The gunner spotted him, tilted back, opening fire. A drone at that altitude was hard to hit with a machine gun, and it reported no impacts. Mayweather locked onto the TiL machine gun and tapped find-and-fire.

The rockets launched, and another white fireball sucked up a TiL. He moved on, decided to take out one of the trucks in the courtyard, mostly to sow panic among their opponents. One rocket, carefully placed, and the truck's gas tank went up. He'd leave the other one—the plan called for forcing the enemy out, not necessarily killing every one of them. They'd need the truck to get away.

The drone jarred once, its camera image jiggling on the screen from an impact, but it reported all systems intact. There— another machine gun on the northernmost wall. Captain Mayweather locked and launched.

A white fireball—

Then the drone image jittered furiously and blurred with smoke and fire. He brought it back toward the woods but it flew erratically, one of the rotors down. He spun it around and, despite its wobbling, spotted the enemy drone. It was coming straight at his screen from about ten meters off, and it fired its own mini-missiles. Sometimes it was easy to forget for a moment that a drone firing at his drone's camera wasn't firing right at him. He almost ducked. But his fingers were working, firing back.

Mayweather switched over to Drone 1's view in time to see both Drone 2 and the enemy drone exploding simultaneously, scattering random pieces on the monastery.

That meant there had to be another drone—the one that had taken out Drone 3—but where was it? He heard a warning buzz from the Light-Up's monitors and saw an approaching blip on the scanner. It had located his LTV and was setting up to fire at him...

Mayweather brought his remaining drone back to the LTV—too late. The LTV took a direct hit. Tilting up with the impact, it sent a bone-jarring vibration through the vehicle, knocking Mayweather onto the floor and making his ears ring with the metallic clang of the blast. Instantly, the LTV's interface shut down.

The monitors went black. Only red emergency lights glowed inside the vehicle. The armor had held up, but the D-comm transmitters had been destroyed.

Almost deaf, feeling as if his head were spinning, Mayweather pulled himself up, slid into his seat. He doubted there was time to get out—the drone would be coming from another angle to hit him again—and he hated the idea of abandoning the Light-Up.

Hitting the start button, he was relieved when the engine began to purr.

Mayweather stomped the accelerator and spun the wheel so the Light-Up turned sharply, and then bumped off over the rough ground.

Another explosion, but this time behind him.

Rocks and shrapnel pinged off the armored rear of the vehicle. Mayweather spun it around again and drove into the copse of trees. Thirty-five meters in, he found a place to turn, the Light-Up crawling over a fallen log to set up between two trees for partial shelter.

Grabbing his ordnance, a retrofitted grenade launcher, Mayweather tossed it through the ceiling hatch and climbed up the narrow ladder into the turret. The turret's machine gun wouldn't be able to hit the drone with any reliability, and it didn't swivel in a 360.

"But I do," he muttered, hands shaking with his hurry, ears still ringing as he grabbed the launcher, loaded it with a Pike from its clip.

Something whirred just below treetop level. He couldn't see the enemy drone from his position, but he could hear it. Flipping his night-seeing goggles down, Mayweather scanned the sky—glimpsed the semicircular drone moving overhead. It slowed, paused between the tops of two pine trees, rotated in place.

Must have spotted the LTV.

The TiL drone fired a rocket. The upper trunk of a pine exploded, the tree's top half tilting over and falling with a dusty crash close beside the vehicle. Mayweather had one eye pressed to the sighter and with his left index finger he pressed the laser guidance button. He tracked the straight line of red onto the drone as it slid away for another firing angle.

"Come on, you bastard, keep the pretty light on the fucking thing," Mayweather hissed at himself, struggling to track the drone. The drone had one rocket left... and he had one in the chamber. He smiled and fired the mini-missile. The rocket-motor missile arced up, sensing the laser, changing course to follow it.

The drone slipped to the side. Mayweather fought to keep the laser centered on his target.

"Dammit!"

Then the 40mm Pike struck home, and the enemy drone vanished—except for the bits and pieces that clattered through branches onto the pine-needle turf below.

"What was that?" Rod Rodriguez asked, turning to look back toward the woods.

"Keep your voice down," Burkett whispered. "Sounded like a Pike. Captain's shot something close by."

Alpha Team pressed to the wall on both sides of the side door in the thick stone of the west wall. The rattling of gunfire from Beta Team was ongoing. There was a *swoosh* and explosion down that way—someone in the monastery had fired what sounded like a rocket-propelled grenade. Burkett didn't want to think about what a direct RPG hit could mean to Linda Strickland—and to Cha, Andrews, and Second Lieutenant Carney.

Tafir was fitting the shaped charge, and Burkett wished he'd assigned someone else. The man was an expert, but the thick gloves of the Talos suit were clumsy to work with. It was taking too long.

Burkett wanted an update from Mayweather. "You just blow something up, Captain?" he said into his headset.

"*Yep*," Mayweather replied, his voice crackling with static. "*Some systems down, some working. Waiting for your prompt.*"

"We're about to bust a move, sir."

"*Then get to it!*"

"Roger that, Captain." He leaned over to whisper at Tafir, "You need some help with that?"

"*No, sir*," Tafir replied, stepping back from the studded metal door, his voice a little distorted by the helmet mic. "*Ready for fire.*"

The door clicked—and swung open. Burkett tensed. This wasn't the door their man on the inside was supposed to open.

"Spread out, stay close to the wall!" he shouted, as the TiL gunmen in the doorway opened fire.

Burkett ducked right, firing through the door as he went. Bullets sliced past his head, and he realized that he'd been saved by Tafir stepping in to catch the bullets on his armor. A dozen armed men swarmed into the courtyard that lay beyond, sent as a sortie to flank Beta Team.

Burkett stepped out to fire through the door. Someone screamed, hit by the burst from the MK-21 SKAR-H. The others kept coming as Alpha Team flattened against the wall. Tafir staggered backward, hammered by gunfire from within the monastery—but he didn't fall. The Talos armor held and he swung out one of his two weapons: a Fostech Origin 18 semi-auto combat shotgun with a big drum of rounds attached to it, looking more like an old Thompson than an auto-shotgun. The TiL sortie kept coming, firing—getting close. Then Tafir let loose with the auto-shotgun, firing twelve rounds in three seconds.

The doorway cleared, for the moment.

Plucking a grenade from his hip pack and leaning to peer through the gun smoke, Burkett saw seven bodies on the ground, torn apart by close-range twelve-gauge shotgun rounds, and a spreading pool of hot blood that showed up clearly on the infrared.

The remaining TiL thugs had cleared to either side of the door. Burkett activated the grenade and tossed it in.

"Fire in the hole!"

Dabiri stepped to one side of the door, Burkett to the other, and the grenade detonated. Someone shouted in pain, but Burkett was certain most of the others would have moved out of range. If he led the team through the doorway, they'd be caught in a crossfire from right and left.

"Regroup at the corner, *go!*" he shouted.

The rest of the team sprinted past the doorway and joined him, Tafir stomping after them.

At the corner, breathing hard, Burkett said, "Tafir, prepare to detonate those shaped charges on my order."

"*Yes sir.*" Tafir's snarkiness always vanished in combat. In a firefight he was all business.

"Hold here."

Burkett trotted out partway between the wall and the trees, and fired through the door, moving, firing again, trying to give the impression that the team had taken to the woods. Then he sprinted back to the corner. Several men showed in the doorway, firing toward the woods.

"Now, Corporal!"

Dabiri tapped the signaler on his wrist and the shaped charges he had fixed to the doorway exploded. The screams of the men caught in the back-blast were almost lost in the roar of the quadruple explosion.

"On me!" Burkett shouted. He started toward the shattered door.

"*Lieutenant, better let me go first!*" Tafir called over the headset.

Reluctantly admitting to himself that Tafir was right—his being point was part of the plan—Burkett made the tactical hand signal for *stop* and the team skidded to a halt. Tafir lumbered past toward the opening.

Bullets skittered past them, thumping into the dirt by the wall, fired from somewhere up on the wall behind them. The shooter, Burkett figured, would have to get in a precarious position, leaning over the wall top, to get any kind of shot at this angle. He turned and saw the shooter trying to do just that. But Megan Lang was already in position to return fire, and as bullets kicked up the dirt around her she calmly fired a double-tap into the man's head.

The body fell from the wall onto the ground outside.

"Nice shot, Sergeant," Burkett said, then he turned to follow Tafir through the doorway. The corporal's shotgun boomed repeatedly.

In the courtyard, a TiL thug was on his hands and knees, the side of his face a tatter of bloody flesh, trying to get up. Without a thought Burkett double-tapped him in the head, and before the man's body had hit the ground he fired at another standing near the doorway to the main building about twenty meters away. The TiL gangster staggered and fell. The rest who'd been here were dead, sprawled in smears of blood and offal.

The Rangers double-timed to the door into the main building. As he went, Burkett assessed the courtyard to their right for points of enemy fire. A truck was burning back there, probably lit up by the Captain. It was gouting black-streaked flame. In its light Burkett saw four men moving toward him, about thirty meters off. He squeezed off a burst and one of them went down.

The survivors dodged into shadow back of another truck, firing sloppily as they went. Lang and Dorman and Alexi Syrkin returned fire. A scattering of response fire, and Burkett felt a round smack his armored vest just under his right arm. He stumbled a little, wincing from the bruising impact.

That's gonna smart.

Tafir said, "*Stand back!*" and tried the door. They were all aware it could be booby-trapped and supposedly… maybe… his Talos suit would protect him from an explosion.

The door opened and nothing exploded.

There were two bodies lying face-down on the floor inside. It looked as if they'd been shot in the back. Burkett saw an antechamber, lit by a single overhead electric lantern. In a wall niche a partly broken icon of St. Basil gazed down with cracked benevolence on the bodies of the two men.

The air coming out of the room was thick with the mingled smells of mildew and blood. Tafir scanned the area beyond.

"*Clear!*" he said, and everyone crowded in after him— everyone except Burkett and PFC Dorman, standing in the door recess.

Two shots cracked by from across the courtyard.

"Permission to intercept Tango, Lieutenant!"

"Not enough cover, Lem. Take a knee and see what you can do. You can watch our backs."

"Sir!" Dorman went down on one knee, within the recess, and leaned just enough to give him the angle he needed. He shot into the flame-flickered courtyard. Someone fell from the shadows at the corner of the building, toppling to writhe in pain. Gut shot. Lem kept firing.

Burkett stepped into the dimly lit antechamber. A voice came from a dark stairway at the back of the room.

"Come in, it is me, it is Olek!" the voice said. "Don't shoot me!"

"Olek!" Alexi shouted. Then he said something more in Bulgarian. He turned to Burkett. "It's my brother's voice! I told him to come out, hands up, where we can see no one behind him is forcing him."

"Good thought," Burkett said. "Come on out, Olek! Hands up!"

"What's this chatter about a mole?" Chance asked. He was talking to Dean Rogers, his opposite number in the Defense Intelligence Agency—and thinking he might regret taking the call.

Sanford "Sandy" Chance sat in his office at Langley, toying with a cigarette in one hand, turning down the volume on his phone headset with the other, more than ready for a smoking break. He wasn't particularly interested in this call from Rogers. The mercurial DIA agent was always too loud and too excited about nothing much. There was perpetual chatter about a Russian mole, *somewhere*—and chatter is all it was: a spy in the White House, in the CIA, in MI6, even in the Mossad.

Then again, it had happened for real in the past. There was Philby in the UK. There was Aldrich Ames in the USA, but almost always, nowadays, the chatter was baloney, bullshit, and hogwash.

"Not a lot of people talking about it," Rogers said. After each phrase, Chance could hear him slurping something. Knowing Dean Rogers, it was probably one of those elaborate coffee drinks from HyperBrew. "Just one guy asking for asylum from Russia, Chance, and yeah, it's a guy with a *lonnnnnng* criminal record, hey what?"

Hey what? Chance sighed. Rogers was totally overcaffeinated.

"Okay, Dean, so with a long criminal record, he's probably lying."

"This guy, Pfensky, used to work with Ildeva. Right? He says there's a mole somewhere in SubOrbital. Says he can give us a name if we give him protection, set him up here."

"A name. What good is a name? Unless it's someone important. Is it?"

"He says no, but he's sure it's a guy *close* to power."

"Like—secretarial?"

"Yeah, ex-*zack*-ully."

Chance rolled his eyes. Caffeine and—he'd heard of steroids in the fancy coffee drinks.

"Does he know who this mole is?"

"Nope."

"Area? Location?"

"Nope, *nyet*, not at all."

"What does he want from DIA?"

"Iron-clad protection contract."

"It's a scam."

"Probably. Just thought you should know."

"I'll keep it in mind, but... I doubt it."

"Me too. *Meeeeeee* too."

"Fine, man." Chance cleared his throat. "Got to go, Dean. Stay in touch."

When you've got something real, anyway...

SIX

Olek stepped into the yellow lantern light. He had a submachine gun on a strap over his left shoulder, but his hands were raised. Olek was a pudgy, double-chinned guy with a tattoo on his left cheek of a cobra wearing a crown. He wore a sweat-stained paramilitary outfit, a scraggly beard, his eyes wide, sweat on his forehead.

"Don't shoot, I have killed these two!" Olek yelled, jerking his head at the dead men. "I need gun!"

"The prisoners," Burkett said. "Are they alive?" The theory was they wouldn't be shot by their captors, despite the threats, because Moscow wanted them alive, but Burkett was always nervous about mere theory.

Olek bobbed his head in a frantic yes. "They don't kill those professors! Good information!"

"Where are they?"

"Right here, down below!" Olek pointed at the floor.

"You stay on him, Alexi," Burkett said. "He doesn't need a gun, at least right now, but he can lower his hands. Sergeant Lang, check the stairs. Don't get your head shot off."

"'No blown-off head,' roger that, sir," Lang said. She slipped past Olek, who was talking excitedly in Bulgarian to Alexi.

Another crack and rattle of gunfire from outside. Burkett went to the door.

"Lem, I'm coming out!" he said. "What's the sitrep?"

"I'm just keeping them back, sir." Dorman kept sighting toward the enemy as he spoke. "They're chipping at the wall, and one of them dented my helmet with a round. No injury."

"What's the range?"

"About twenty-two meters. There was a guy on the wall, too, but I took him out."

"Wish I had that Pike launcher. Hold 'em here, pull back if you need to, watch out for grenades—I got an idea." Hearing gunfire inside, Burkett ducked back into the building. Lang was just coming back from the stairs.

"I can hear them talking from the basement. Random small arms fire coming up the stairwell. Didn't come anywhere near me, but they know we're here."

"How many, Olek?" Burkett asked.

"Ildeva is down there," Olek said, "and three more. Ildeva begin to take them out, to get them to the truck—then you come in."

"Okay, everyone hold right here," Burkett said, nodding toward Lang to indicate she was in charge till he got back. "Watch the stairs but stay back from them—and stay quiet." He slapped a fresh clip in his MK-21, switched on his helmet light, went to the dark zigzagging stone stairway, and climbed, listening for sounds from upstairs. Nothing. Just the rattle-snap of gunfire from outside.

There was little ambient light for his night vision to harness in here and he looked closely at the stairs. He didn't want to run into a booby trap or just a hole in the old ruin's floor. Reaching the next floor, Burkett saw a doorway to the right. It was mostly a rubbled-up hole in the wall.

A light flared to the left, stretching out in a seeking beam along the stone floor. Two bearded TiL appeared, the one with the flashlight wearing a white doctor's coat and paramilitary pants. The other one, mountainously big, wore dull-green camo. Both toted Bizon-4 Russian submachine guns.

They stopped and swore as they saw him, but by the time they were ready to shoot he'd flicked the SCAR to automatic burst and was squeezing the trigger, raking them with a full clip so that they danced clumsily with the impacts, and then slid against the walls to fall, shaking, dying, guns slipping from their hands. The fallen flashlight made a spreading pool of blood gleam.

One of the dying men, the gangly one in the white coat, looked familiar—Burkett had seen his face in a file. Lutzoff, the interrogator.

Very good kill, he thought.

Burkett ejected his clip, slapped in another, his free hand already switching to double-tap. He put two rounds in each man's head and waited a thirty-count to see if anyone else was coming.

Not a sound. No flicker of light.

Turning away, he went to the rubble-filled doorway and looked through. The chamber was empty of everything but shadows. The echoes of gunfire were louder here.

Burkett stepped over fallen masonry and picked his way to the window. It was just a rectangular hole in the wall, with some ancient broken glass on the sill. He leaned out just enough to see muzzle flashes directly below—one man shooting toward Lemuel Dorman. Two others seemed to be arguing. One was pointing at the cab of the intact truck, probably arguing for escape, the other toward Private Dorman.

Humming softly to himself—a kid's song from a video his son liked—Burkett took two grenades from his hip pack, pulled the pins, and dropped them onto the group below. The men yelled hoarsely and tried to run—too late.

The grenades blew, shrapnel ricocheting off the stone of the window frame and striking Burkett's chest armor. He drew back, waited a five count, then looked out the window—could see the dark silhouettes of bodies. Ah—but one was still alive. Badly injured, trying to crawl away.

"Good luck, pal," he muttered, turning from the window.

"Lem," Burkett said, returning to Dorman. "Three Tango down, but keep an eye on everything out here."

"Yes sir. Thanks for damping down the noise around here."

"Hey, it was bothering the neighbors."

Burkett returned to the anteroom. He took two grenades from his pack, one smoke and one flash-bang. The other Rangers looked at him and he gave the tactical sign for silence, then squatted on the floor near the stone stairs that led to the basement.

Taking off his helmet, Burkett stretched out his hand, and thumped the helmet's top on the stairway, trying to make a noise like someone going down the stairs.

Close enough. Burkett saw a muzzle flash as a TiL soldier fired up the stairwell, the bullets cracking on stones above as he scrambled back. He activated the grenades and tossed them— flash-bang and smoke.

Slinging his rifle over his back, he drew his M-19 smart pistol.

"Open up on 'em!" Burkett snarled, putting on his breathing mask as the smoke flooded the stairway. "But don't hit Ildeva or the prisoners! Precision or knives—nothing else."

He started down, pressed against the stairwell wall at left, hearing men below cursing, coughing with the smoke.

Tapping his goggles to infrared, Burkett crouched by the door, swung out to see three men down the corridor, all standing, rubbing their eyes, shouting at one another in Bulgarian. There—the fourth man was Ildeva, farther down the hall, standing by a lantern and unlocking a cell door.

Burkett picked his targets, fired, then Alexi Syrkin was suddenly beside him, firing his rifle, double-tap, with precision. Three men went down.

Ildeva returned fire.

Syrkin yelled incoherently and fell back. Burkett aimed his pistol very carefully, then shot Ildeva in the right shoulder. The TiL gang boss spun, dropping his weapon. Burkett turned to Syrkin, saw he was sitting on the floor, clutching a head wound.

Alexi waved at him. "I'm okay sir, go!" Burkett nodded, then stepped over the dead men and moved to Ildeva. Lang crowded up beside him.

"Secure Ildeva, Sergeant. Wound in upper right shoulder. After that, look to Alexi, I think he's got a gouge on his head."

"Yes sir!"

"Rodriguez, I need you with me." The hostages had to take priority. Burkett stepped over the sprawled, groaning Ildeva and looked through the window into the cell. There were no TiL inside, but two sets of eyes looked back.

"Corporal!" he called. In a moment the medic was pushing past him, opening the cell door.

"Lieutenant," Dabiri said, coming in. "I don't want to tell you what to do, sir, but—"

"But you thought you and your armor were supposed to take the lead. You don't have precision weapons. I wanted to make sure the prisoners got out alive."

"I get it, sir," Dabiri said. He turned to the medic. "Rod—I can carry someone, this suit's got a HULC." The Human Universal Load Carrier.

"Here—this man in the lower bunk," the medic replied, gesturing. "Right leg's swollen. Probable fractures. I'm gonna give him a shot... then pick him up carefully. I'll bring my LTV to the western door." He selected a syringe from his kit. Burkett went to the other men, who were flattened on the floor—trying to stay under the gunfire they'd heard from the corridor.

"If you fellas can stand, you're safe as we can make you. Shooting's over... for now."

The hostages got to their feet. He pushed up his night-vision goggles and looked them over in the lantern light. Their suits were rumpled and grimy, they hadn't shaved in some days, but they looked unhurt.

"My name is Lieutenant Arthur Burkett, United States Army."

"Yes sir!" a tall heavy-jawed man said in a French accent. He wore transparent horn-rimmed glasses, and his blond hair spilled to his collar. Burkett recognized him from the file in his hand-screen.

"Dr. Magonier?"

"Yes, I am Magonier, and my comrade in calamity, he is Professor Dhariwal."

Dhariwal was a dark-skinned, slender man with wire-rimmed glasses, a good deal of curly black hair, and a black mustache that had joined with a new growth of beard. He flashed a smile as he took in the new situation.

"You've come to rescue us?"

"We have."

"God bless you!"

"I thought you were an atheist, Lucius," Magonier said, grinning now. Both men seemed a bit giddy at their liberation.

"Maybe not anymore!" Dhariwal said, laughing. "Lieutenant —the injured man, the one your friend in the spacesuit took away—he is Professor Dupon."

Burkett nodded. "I figured he was. It's not a spacesuit— but then again, maybe it is." He got on his headset. "Captain? Hostages liberated."

"*Good job, S-7. Bring them home.*"

"Roger that, sir." Burkett turned to the scientists. "You men able to walk?"

"Yes!" Magonier said, clapping his hands together. "They hadn't started on us in the physical sense, as yet."

"Then right this way..."

* * *

Sgt. Linda Strickland was scanning the outer wall of the monastery, peering over the top of what was left of the granite outcropping, when Lieutenant Burkett spoke over the squad comm.

"Coming out. Status of your position, Linda?"

"No fire in at least fifteen minutes, Lieutenant. Des did some of his fancy marksmanship and took down three with three headshots in about a blink of an eye—and we haven't seen a head since. Whoa—!"

The front gate of the monastery burst open and a truck barreled through, no lights, and fishtailed to Strickland's right, accelerating across the grass to the dirt road beside the monastery. Second Lieutenant Carney was up, firing after it—it was safe to do that now—and then the truck was gone.

"Whoa *what*, Sergeant Strickland?" Burkett asked.

"Group of Tango, dunno how many, just bugged out of here in a truck, Lieutenant. I didn't fire, wasn't sure if they had the prisoners."

Carney shouldn't have fired, either, she thought.

"Nope, we got the prisoners intact—more or less—and our prime captive. Alexi's got a bad graze on the noggin but Lang thinks he'll be all right. Coming out to you... Captain, you reading?"

"Right here." Mayweather's voice came on the headset. "Meet you at Beta Team. Hold there and I'll give you a lift. Rod'll take the hostages along with Syrkin and Ildeva."

"Sounds like we're going home," Corporal Cha said, wiping sweat from his forehead. He squatted with his back to the rock, looking toward the craters left by two missed RPG rounds, and took off his helmet. "That got pretty hairy."

"I'm surprised they didn't do a sortie and come after us," Des Andrews said, leaning to look through the open front gates into the courtyard. Strickland turned to look. The fire was still burning in there, and she saw two bodies sprawled in the flickering light.

"I heard shooting from the west," Cha said.

Strickland glanced down at herself to see if she was bleeding. Sometimes she got a minor hit when she was in the combat zone, and didn't notice till it bled like hell. She didn't see anything this time, but she felt drained, the usual post-fight let-down.

"Yeah," she replied. "I'm guessing they sortied and Burkett caught them with their pants down."

"Sounds right," Andrews said. "I was in his squad once in Venezuela. Half the time he took care of shit by himself, just to get it done. Not much of a delegator."

"Alpha Team had that man in the armor helping them out, too," Carney pointed out.

What a gift he has for annoying me, Linda thought.

A vehicle came along between the trees and the front wall. Not much bigger than a pickup truck. It was Rodriguez, driving the ambulance LTV. He pulled up near the outcrop.

"Who needs treatment?" he asked, sticking his head out the vehicle's window.

"I think Cha stubbed his toe, Rod," Strickland said. "I recommend amputation."

"I'll live," Cha said.

"Good to hear." Rodriguez turned the LTV south, headed for the S-7.

Strickland got a glimpse of Alexi Syrkin and four other men on stretchers in the back. She went wide on the headset. "Lieutenant Faraday, sir? You awake?"

"*Shaddup!*" he answered. "*I've been standing here at this stupid tripod listening to the shooting and tense as a rat with its dick in a trap.*"

"*Does he know he's talking to a lady?*" Lang asked dryly.

"Apparently not," Strickland said. "Seen any Tango, Ike?"

"*Saw a snake once. I let it go.*"

"Rod's coming in."

"*Roger that. Teams okay?*"

"Alexi's hit but not too bad. Everyone's coming home."

"Here they are now," Cha murmured, standing up, watching Burkett lead his team in a fast walk out of the woods. Megan Lang was close behind him, then Dorman walking slow to let Tafir in his suit keep up with him. Lieutenant Carney stood up and squinted at the monastery, his mouth open.

"We're really the last ones here?"

"Yeah, we gotta turn out the lights," Cha said.

Burkett paused about twenty meters away, turned and looked into the darkness, and shouted something. A warning? Was there a stray TiL?

Then a man came out of the woods, a short stocky man with some kind of snaky tat on his face. He was running toward them with a submachine gun in his hands. Burkett said something inaudible.

"Oh," Strickland said, "maybe that's—"

Then she was jolted by the sound of an assault weapon going off just beside her. Spinning, she saw Carney firing at the man with the tattoo. He went down.

"I got one!" Carney crowed. "I got him! He was coming up behind Burkett and…"

Their cold silence made him break off, and he looked at the others—who were staring at him in shock.

"Dude," Cha said huskily. "I think you just shot Alexi's brother."

SEVEN

There was a medical pod in the aft of the orbcraft. Burkett stood in a doorway too small for him, his head bowed under the curving metal of the little chamber, barely breathing as he watched Rodriguez trying to save Olek Syrkin. Like the other two, Olek was intubated.

The other patients in the compartment were Dupon and Alexi Syrkin. Dupon had a cast on his right leg, from the knee down. He was strapped to a cot, half asleep, muttering. Beside him was Alexi Syrkin, his head bandaged. A bullet had dug a furrow in his skull and passed on. He had a concussion—whether there was brain damage, Rod wasn't sure.

Olek Syrkin had been shot three times in his midsection. One round had pierced a lung; another had torn through an intestine. The third had shattered a kidney.

Rodriguez had opened him, was trying to stop the bleeding. He had some pretty sophisticated nanogear to apply, but a lot of damage had been done. The shock was considerable, and Olek's lungs were filling with fluid. As Burkett watched, Rodriguez gave a small shake of the head. Art had seen that before, always when the medic was accepting the inevitable.

"I could try putting him into a coma," Rodriguez said. "I have the formula, but it could do as much harm as good…"

"*Lieutenant, we have Chance on the line,*" Ike said over the headset. "*He's with General Carney.*"

Burkett winced at that. "Carney? Christ. Can you put them through to my headset?"

"*Yes sir.*"

As Burkett stepped away from the medi-pod there was a crackle, and then General Carney's voice.

"*Burkett? I understand my son is A-OK?*"

"Not a scratch, sir."

"*And you have the hostages. So why haven't you hit the skies yet?*"

"Tangos are dead or bugged out, sir," Burkett replied. "We're secure."

"*So you think you can sit on your hands?*" Chance put in, joining the call. "*By now Moscow knows what happened. You think Krozkov doesn't have any friends in Moldova? Get out of there!*"

"We plan to," Burkett said. "If we go to vertical right now it'll interfere with our medic's work on one of our casualties—one of your assets. Olek Syrkin. There was an accident. Friendly fire. He's hit bad."

"*He's not a priority, I'm afraid,*" Chance said. "*How bad is he?*"

"Not good."

"*Probably won't make it either way. Go to vertical and take off. Bring the prisoners and Ildeva back to SubOrbital 3, ASAP.*"

"Can't do it, Chance," Burkett said. "Not without the Captain's authorization. He's loading the Light-Up."

"*Why the hell isn't Mayweather on this line?*" General Carney demanded.

"I thought I ought to field this myself." Burkett's mouth felt terribly dry and suddenly he was very tired. "Frederic Dupon is badly hurt, too. They crushed his leg. Multiple fractures. He needs to go to the nearest safe hospital. We figure we should drop him off at the NATO facility in Corinth. In fact, none of the prisoners—including Ildeva—have any experience with g-force or weightlessness. Last time we rescued prisoners, they went right to the nearest—"

"*Burkett!*" Chance barked. "*Listen to me. They're not safe in Greece. They're not safe in Turkey. Moscow's got operatives looking for them. They don't want them talking about what they've been through, do you understand? And there is the strong possibility of NDS. Moscow has prototypes...*"

NDS. That made Burkett shudder. Nano-Drone Swarms. A cloud of insect-sized machines that ferreted out their targets and cut them into little pieces... But taking the injured into orbit? Burkett shook his head. It wasn't protocol, and it wasn't smart.

"You're saying we have to take them directly back to base?" he said. "A smashed leg with all that g-force? We can be at the hospital in Greece in forty-five minutes. Might save Olek Syrkin's life."

"*No choice,*" General Carney insisted. "*You have the smart-netting to help them out. Hit the skies and bring 'em back here.*"

"*This is Mayweather.*" The Captain's voice came on the line. "*General?*"

"*It's me—and Chance, and your uncooperative first lieutenant,*" General Carney snapped. "*Captain, if you're through shining up your vehicle—get the S-7 vertical and hit the skies with all possible speed. I am ordering you to bring the hostages and the prisoner back here, hot fast!*"

"*That's not protocol, sir, they should go to—*"

"*Enough! You have your orders.*"

Burkett felt he had to say something, even if he risked demotion.

"General—Olek Syrkin needs emergency medical attention right away. The g-force, the stress of going orbital... it would kill him, sir—"

"*I said—you have your orders!*"

Even over the headset, they could hear General Carney's cold fury.

"*Yes sir*," Mayweather said. Not meekly, but professionally. "*Report when you're in orbit.*" Carney broke the connection.

The air was especially close in the medical compartment. It smelled of blood, sweat, and antiseptics.

"I'm not moving this man, sir," Rodriguez said, his voice calm but definite as he checked Olek Syrkin's pulse. "He can't be moved into a seat. He's got three bullets in him."

"We're going to shift to vertical, Rod," Burkett said gently, putting his hand on the medic's shoulder. "Orders from the General." He was squatting in a corner to talk to Rodriguez because Andrews and Lang were moving the groaning Ildeva to a reclining seat. Dupon, groggily drugged, was already out there.

There was a defect in the design of the S-7's medical compartment—at least Rodriguez had said as much. When the ship went vertical for specialized takeoff, the injured strapped into their clamped-down gurneys would end up vertical, as well. The solution, supposedly, was to move them to passenger seats, each of which could recline almost to horizontal. But moving the wounded could be dangerous for them, and the seats weren't set up for IVs and monitors.

"Rod," Burkett said, his voice low but urgent, "we have to go. Some of them got away. Maybe they're in touch with Moscow. Maybe we'll be tracked. Too damn dangerous. I don't want to end up like S-12, man."

Rod shook his head. "I'll think of something, but if we move him…"

Alexi called out, his voice a little slurred. "Lieutenant—how did my brother get shot?"

Burkett grimaced. "He went to get a hand-screen belonging to Ildeva. Said he would be right back, but he didn't come right back—and we thought he'd decided to leave with TiL."

"You left him. Didn't you, Lieutenant?"

Burkett took a deep breath. "We couldn't wait anymore. Then I heard him call out—he was coming up behind us... and he was running and he had that gun. Lieutenant Carney thought he was a gangster coming to take revenge or something. He..."

"And he shot him."

"Yes. I'm sorry, Alexi, but... yes."

"Olek risked everything for the USA. You left him behind and you shot him. Maybe he was supposed to be shot. Maybe that was the plan. Maybe the CIA wanted him dead... Maybe—"

"No, Alexi—just no. It was a stupid accident." *Caused by a stupid man.* "We're trying to save him. You know? He's..."

"He's gone," Rodriguez said tonelessly, reaching out to close Olek's eyes. "Doesn't matter if he's moved now."

Syrkin said something in Bulgarian. The bitterness in his voice was translation enough.

"Alexi—I'm sorry about your brother. It was..." But it wasn't bad luck. It was stupidity—Carney's. "I'm... I'm sorry you lost him." There was nothing more he could say. "Lieutenant, let's you and me move Alexi into a seat." He didn't want Syrkin to have to lie there contemplating the corpse of his brother. "I think he'll be all right."

"Oh, yeah," Alexi Syrkin said, laughing softly. "I'll be just fine. Just fine..."

The orbcraft's movable supports were flush with the hull on it's underside. As they prepared to depart, two short, powerful struts under the rear hull were thrust out to either side of the front wheels.

The top-section of the aft struts began to push forward, using up an enormous amount of stored power to do it. A technology more than a century old had been drafted for the next stage: two big titanium rack-and-pinion gears rolled up the groove from the aft toward the nose of the craft, the gears meshing with a ridged rack, their forward ends pressing against the resistance of the rocky soil to push the S-7's nose upward.

It was "going vertical"—slowly tilting up, shifting its angle a full ninety degrees with respect to the Earth's surface.

Additional sitting supports, wider on the bottom, extended from the rear to either side of the exhaust ports and held the tail in place on the ground, shifting a little for near-perfect vertical so that the orbcraft—its tail no longer in feathering position— was aiming straight up at the sky.

Burkett now lay on his back, in relation to the ground.

The engines on the wings and the enormous engine in the tail of the S-7 roared to life. The entire vessel shuddered, then began to lift up on the rockets' thrust. The struts closed back into their grooves as, wobbling only slightly, the spaceplane rose steadily, flame lacing through billowing smoke all around it.

And the orbcraft lifted above the little valley.

Then Burkett felt a powerful punch in his back, transmitted from the tail of the orbcraft as full acceleration kicked in. It was as if its engines were kicking him, personally, toward orbit.

Roaring upward, the orbcraft rose on a tail of fire, gaining speed, exerting itself against the pull of the entire Earth. The engines put out seven million pounds of thrust to break free. Faster, ever faster the vessel rose, with accompanying increase in gravitational force.

Frederic Dupon screamed in pain.

The S-7 reached low-Earth orbit, two thousand klicks up—twelve hundred miles—when Burkett saw blood floating in the air.

It was Alexi Syrkin's fault. He'd been scratching at his scalp wound, which was sewed up and bandaged, but he'd loosened a suture and irritably pulled off the bandage. A fluid ounce of blood was floating up into the air. He hadn't said anything about it. Alexi just lay back in his reclined seat, gazing up with a look of sour amusement at the blood droplets wobbling above, some of them merging into larger drops. Each little quivering dark-red sphere reflecting a fish-eye view of the S-7's cabin.

"I can see my face in them," Syrkin whispered as Burkett floated up with a special suction device for liquid spills. After the small vacuum sucked up the crimson blobs, he called out.

"Rod? Your patient's bleeding over here."

Rodriguez was seated forward and hadn't seen the blood. The medical specialist was brooding because he hadn't been allowed time to do a quick g-force training session with the released hostages—and because of the agony Dupon had gone through. Now the medic whipped off his seat belt and netting. He floated up, one hand holding a white and red bag, turned with his knees tucked up against him so he didn't accidentally kick anyone, and used a ceiling ring to tug himself to the aisle and back toward Syrkin.

"Alexi, I hope you didn't do that on purpose," Rod said, drawing himself down into the empty seat next to his patient. "That'd be way against regs. Also, hella unhygienic."

"I don't think it was intentional," Burkett said. "I saw it from back there—he was scratching. The thing was annoying him…"

"I could feel blood coming out in the takeoff," Alexi said, absently, as if he was thinking about something else entirely. "Squeezed out of me like juice from a blood orange. Started to itch."

"G-force got it started," Rodriguez said, catching another ascending drop on a piece of gauze. "Hold very still now…"

Burkett went forward to the freed hostages. Dupon was reclined, and snoring. The medic had given him another shot. He floated down beside Professor Dhariwal.

"You look like a ghost in the cinema when you do that," Magonier said.

"I feel pretty solid," Burkett replied, smiling. "Damned tired, to tell you the truth. You fellas seem to have gotten through the climb, though—how's the microgravity treating you?"

"Queasy," Dhariwal said, "but I manfully keep from throwing up."

"Good job. It can be hard to clean up. Rod'll show you how to use the ol' space toilet, if you need to vomit or pee or whatever. Personally, I hope to get back on solid ground before I have to use one. Hate those things."

Magonier gazed around him in wonder. "They say we still have weight in orbit, but I do feel weightless. Everything is quite strange. I'm so glad to be here and so shocked to be here, all at once. C'est fou."

"You probably don't feel like eating yet?"

"No, just some water, if you please," Magonier said.

Dhariwal nodded. "Me, too."

"I'll see that someone gets it to you."

"And Lieutenant," Dhariwal said, "thank you. I thank all of you. I saw one of your Rangers was shot. Will he be all right?"

"I believe so. It wasn't too serious."

"Tres bien," Magonier said, leaning back and closing his eyes.

Dhariwal took off his glasses and rubbed his eyes. "I'm surprised we didn't go to a hospital somewhere, maybe Turkey?" He set the glasses absentmindedly in his lap and they began floating away. Burkett grabbed the glasses and handed them back.

"I was surprised too, Professor. Some orders are… surprising."

PFC Dorman drifted up to them. "Can I get anything for our guests, sir?" he asked.

"Squeeze-bottle of water, show 'em how to use it up here. Anything they ask for, if we have it. Maybe wet cloths, for a little clean up."

"Roger that."

Burkett noticed Mikhail Ildeva, scowlingly shifting in his seat across the aisle. He was wearing only a sleeveless T-shirt above the waist, so that Rod could get the battlefield dressing on his wounded shoulder. Ildeva noticed Burkett looking at him.

"Captain sir," the Bulgarian called, awkwardly waving a hand cuffed to the armrest. Burkett floated over, tugged on a ring, drew his legs in so his feet didn't clop anyone. "I'm a lieutenant, not a captain."

"Yes, yes," Ildeva said impatiently, his accent thick. His English seemed limited. "It was you, put bullet in me—pain is too much."

"I'll ask the medic to give you a shot. He had to dig around a bit to get the bullet out, so it's going to hurt for a while. You'll be okay."

Ildeva stuck out his lower lip and furrowed his brow, mentally translating.

"What you do with me?"

"You're going to the USA to tell us what you know. You're an internationally known criminal, so maybe after a nice long interrogation you'll be turned over to Interpol."

"You will torture? The water boards?"

"They outlawed all that in 2030. No torture of any kind," he replied. "That's all I can tell you, because it's all I know."

"If I'm hungry?"

"Are you?"

"No. I am sick in this place!"

"When you're hungry, you'll eat. If you need the bathroom, our medical specialist will take you to it." Burkett called to Rodriguez, "Give the prisoner some morphine, Rod, will you?"

"Sure thing, Lieutenant."

Burkett turned, tugged on a ring, let himself drift to the flight deck. He caught the edges of the hatch to keep from bumping into Mayweather, who was once again crouching in the air behind Ike and Linda.

The S-7 was still on the dark side of the Earth, and Burkett could see stars through the windshield, above the arc of the planet. They would soon vanish in the glare as the S-7 orbited to the sun-washed side of the Earth.

They were going home, and he was free to think about his family. About Ashley and Nate. *Was* Ashley still family? It still felt that way to Burkett, but did it feel that way to her?

Worrying too much, he told himself. It was the let-down, the crash from the adrenaline high of battle. Now he really felt the ache, the deep bruise left by the bullet that had hit his Kevlar. If it'd been up a few inches it would've hit him above the armor, smashed its way into his chest. One well-placed bullet from a Dragunov, one well-hidden landmine, one scattering of friendly fire, and Ashley would get the official visit.

And then she'd have to tell Nate.

Friendly fire. Lieutenant Carney. Olek Syrkin. Would there even be an inquest? The op was covert, *big time* covert, and it'd probably be buried. Like Olek Syrkin.

Alexi's brother had been a United States asset. He'd risked his ass to make the mission possible. Sure, the CIA had offered him incentives—a big paycheck at some point, citizenship in the USA, all of it—but he'd risked being caught and shot or, more likely, *tortured* to death to find out who'd recruited him. He'd have died hard.

Instead, Olek "died stupid." Shot by a blundering amateur whose old man had eased his way through West Point, had gotten him on the mission so he could sweeten his record.

Hadn't he seen how Burkett himself had been reacting to Olek, back in the monastery? Talking to him.

I didn't have my gun pointed at him.

But little Kenny Carney hadn't assessed the situation. He'd opened fire—shooting damned close to his own XO. Second Lieutenant Carney could easily have accidentally shot First Lieutenant Burkett, too. His own XO.

Burkett shook his head. He experienced a depth of disgust he hadn't felt in many years.

MOSCOW, RUSSIA

Vladimir Krozkov filled the little china cup with coffee poured from the brass samovar, added a lemon peel, placed it carefully on its saucer and carried it neatly back to the glass table where Feodor waited at the edge of the balcony.

The balcony was enclosed by bulletproof glass; overhead it was darkly tinted, for shade. It was a sunny day in Moscow, and as Krozkov sat down across from Feodor Smyrnoi, he could see much of the Kremlin. Across the square were the colorful domes, the overwrought architecture of the Cathedral of Christ the Savior. The sun made the colors bright, as if the Kremlin were brand new. As always, at this time of year, tourists—mostly from America—were taking pictures of the cathedral.

My little American friends, Krozkov thought, amused.

The glass had other qualities besides being proofed against bullets and small missiles. It looked iridescent from the outside, so no one could see in, but he could see out. He'd always been wary of lipreaders. This penthouse was his home as well as his primary office, and he had given it plenty of thought. He had it swept for listening devices twice a week.

Krozkov regarded his visitor. Feodor was his top aide, but the man was a bit absurd. A pinch-faced fellow with red-brown hair and a beard clipped with near-microscopic precision, he had a tan that looked too dark for him—without it he was pasty as an uncooked roll. He spent far too much time under the sunlamp. Like Krozkov, he wore casual summer clothing: khakis, and a butter-yellow shirt for Krozkov; Feodor in a white one, sleeves rolled neatly up to show his skinny walnut-colored arms.

Feodor looked into his empty coffee cup. "Perhaps I need another," he said, in colloquial Russian. He was indirectly asking for permission.

Krozkov's Russian was a little more formal. "Feodor Ivanovic, you have had two coffees and this my first—and I will have no more. Such strong coffee! It's your health I'm thinking of. Already you're a nervous man, very tense. Endless coffee, and you'll give yourself a heart attack at only fifty years of age. Here." He pushed the plate of tea cakes toward Feodor, beside the hand computer that held the purpose of their meeting. "Enjoy the tea cakes."

Feodor frowned at the cakes and Krozkov chuckled inwardly. Krozkov had chosen tea cakes for the meeting because they were covered in powdered sugar, and he knew Feodor would not want to touch them—it would get powdered sugar all over his sculptured mustache and beard.

Feodor flicked his eyes suspiciously up at him.

He thinks I'm perversely toying with him, thought Krozkov. *And what a peculiar little perversion it must seem!*

In truth, it was one more variation of his means of keeping his close associates off balance. Just little things, so that they were always a hair's width on the defensive. So that they always felt their lower rank, though Krozkov made a point of never overtly bullying anyone. It had to appear that he was in command through sheer charisma. If anyone pushed back hard, he simply disappeared them, without comment.

The others got the message.

He was not short on charisma. It was one of the many gifts the Holy Father had bestowed on him. He went to church once a month and said, *"Thank you for making me who I am."*

Sometimes he thought he detected a curiously attentive silence in response. Such strange feelings one got in the cathedral…

All this passed through his mind in a flash as he nodded toward the hand computer. Feodor put a pleasant, businesslike expression on his face and unfolded the device. It started out the size of a large smartphone, but opened up it became seamlessly smooth, and as wide as the old laptops. He muttered voice commands; it scanned his irises, and he made some haptic passes over it that always looked mystical to Krozkov.

Then he passed it over. "You see," Feodor said, "the satellite imagery is definitive. It's one of their SubOrbital covert operations craft. The reports of the survivors suggest United States Army Rangers. The question is, should we expose them on the world stage? Let everyone know they've engaged in this reckless adventurism, this assault on Moldovan national sovereignty—an act of mass murder, in fact."

Krozkov looked at the memo accompanying the satellite shots.

"The Thieves in Law say the prisoners escaped alive. Hence, my friend, the Americans can perhaps use the testimony of the hostages to justify their operation. If the prisoners are taken to the USA, they will fill the news media with their claims and charges. They will weep on camera about torture. They saw one of their own die in our custody. That will summon the 'How sad, how pitiful!' All the usual. It could lead to onerous sanctions."

"We can insist that we had nothing to do with it. It's all the Thieves in Law's doing," Feodor said, shrugging.

"American intelligence seems to know that this branch of Thieves in Law is our asset. It may be that this Olek Syrkin— who is suspected of being a traitor—is with them, and they have Ildeva. They will talk, and worse, these men—Magonier, Dupon, and Dhariwal—are intrinsic to NATO's orbital military plans, intrinsic to EuroIntel, but most especially they are developing technology that the Americans will use against us.

"They are the key researchers. That is why we took them, and Lutzoff was stupid enough to get himself killed. He sent us little of use. So what has to be done is obvious, and there is no time to consult with our beloved leader."

Feodor blinked. "You do not ask the President?"

"Anatoly will understand. There is no time for procrastination. I will give the orders. It will be done carefully. With deniability. But—it will be done."

Feodor opened his mouth to protest, but Krozkov silenced him with a gesture. Taking his phone from his pocket, he made the call.

EIGHT

"Alexi? How you holding up?" Burkett was crouching in the narrow aisle beside Syrkin, holding onto an armrest to keep from floating away. Syrkin was still staring upward as if the blood was still there.

"How do I *feel*? How do you think, Lieutenant! You people used my brother and then you shot him. And what's going to happen to Lieutenant Carney? Nothing."

"I'm going to file a recommendation that he's court-martialed," Burkett replied quietly. "We all had orders to watch out for Olek. He should have paid attention. But—friendly fire happens, Alexi. I lost a very good friend that way and it hurts like a son of a bitch. It must be way worse when it's your brother—has to be. I'm just lucky Carney didn't shoot me too. Hell, he missed me by a hair, man." Burkett wished he could think of something better to say. "I don't even like my older brother, but if it happened to him, I'd feel it. Hard."

Syrkin chuckled sadly. "I didn't like Olek much either." His voice was slightly slurred. Rodriguez must've given him a Xanax or something, Burkett figured. "I didn't even know him so much," Syrkin went on. "He was my half-brother, raised apart from me. In Bulgaria. He came out to America when he was a teenager, tried life in the blessed US of A with me and my folks. I got to know him some, but he didn't like the... the way women are in America. He thought they were insolent or something.

"He didn't like it when the FBI came and interviewed him," Syrkin continued. "Somebody told them he had connections to Bulgar mafia—the TiL in Los Angeles. I didn't trust him so much. I didn't like the way he talked about America. But a couple of assholes tried to beat me up for my phone one time and he came rolling up on them and *bam*—man, he rubbed their faces in the dirt for it. Really stood up for me. And you know…" He licked his lips. "Bowling is very big in Eastern Europe."

"Is it?" Burkett was a little confused by this seeming non sequitur.

"I didn't know how to bowl. He showed me how, when he lived with us. He was very patient with me, until I was able to make a lot of strikes. It increased my confidence a lot. He said, 'If you can learn that, you can learn most anything.'"

Burkett nodded. "He had some wisdom."

"He didn't have enough wisdom to keep away from gangsters, but you know, we grew up without our father. My dad's brother, he was always a street guy, and he was another father for Olek."

"Understandable he'd go that way," Burkett said. "I'm not sure I'd have done anything else if I was in his position."

Syrkin looked at him, in a sidelong kind of way. A look of cold suspicion.

"You're managing me, Lieutenant, saying stuff like that."

Burkett shook his head. "I mean it. Alexi, I'm deeply sorry we lost track of Olek. This is on me, too. I should've kept him close—shouldn't have let him slip off for the intel. I'm guessing he wanted to get a cash reward from the CIA. We found the intel on his body." Which was now in a body bag, floating in a storage closet. "But… when he didn't come back…"

Burkett had been chewing it over in the back of his mind since Olek Syrkin had been shot. Part of Alpha Team's job was to pick up all the intel they could, but there hadn't been time on this mission.

He ran the events back in his mind. Olek rushing off into the darkness. Then Tango shooting at Lemuel from a rooftop. Burkett getting involved in identifying the point of fire—at which point Olek took off. Long minutes had passed—then the Captain was ordering them to rendezvous. Burkett figured Olek had lost his nerve, was actually blowing off the exfil…

"I told Alpha I'd get them to Beta and the Captain, then I'd go back and make sure of Olek," Burkett said. "We went through the woods toward Beta's position, then Olek came out behind us…"

Syrkin closed his eyes and Burkett wasn't sure he was listening.

"He was a hero," Alexi murmured. "He wanted relocation and money, but it was Olek who saved those prisoners. Gave us what we needed to find them. Moscow would never have let them go. He saved them, Lieutenant, and we shot him for it."

Burkett heard a thruster-burn and felt the orbcraft change course.

"*Lieutenant Burkett?*" Strickland's voice in his headset. "*Captain? We have a blip. We're trying to figure out if it's space debris but… I don't think so. Moves like a bogey.*"

"We'll talk again, Alexi."

Burkett pushed off a little too hard, so that he had to catch himself on the bulkhead up front, sending a stab of pain through his right side. Maybe the bullet that struck his Kevlar had cracked a rib. Ignoring the pain, he made his way onto the flight deck.

"What we got?"

"We're evading… whatever it is," Ike said, "but it's following us!"

"Where's the Captain?" Burkett asked.

"Right here," Mayweather said, drifting up from behind. "How close is it, what velocity?"

"Velocity," Strickland said, breathlessly now, "is… it's accelerating! It's—"

"Hold on for evasion!" Faraday yelled into his headset, hands moving over the controls. Burkett and Mayweather clutched the sides of the hatch as the S-7 fired its main thrusters and underside pitch thrusters, veering up relative to the Earth, heading to a higher orbit. The vessel trembled with the acceleration and the inertia nearly yanked Burkett loose from his hold.

"It's following—still accelerating!" Strickland called over the roar of the thrusters.

"Firing port lateral—" Faraday began.

A reverberating metallic crash rang through the S-7 as it was struck aft, and the orbcraft wrenched sharply to starboard. Someone screamed and Burkett was torn from his handholds and thrown back, tumbling through the air, smacking his head on the back of a seat—then Rodriguez caught him.

The orbcraft whipped into a new angular velocity as Faraday regained control. Inertia snatched Burkett from Rod's grasp and flung him to port, sending him into the bulkhead. Burkett struck curving steel with his left shoulder and grunted with the pain.

Rodriguez unhooked from his seat, pushed toward him, helped Burkett to an upright position—the medic's face was blurred.

Hit my head, too.

"Thanks for that ballpark save, Rod," Burkett said. His eyes cleared and, looking dazedly around, he saw Mayweather disentangling himself from Des Andrews. Burkett grabbed an overhead hold-ring with his right hand. His left arm was numb. Faraday and Strickland frantically called out corrections and readings.

"Lost port-lateral thrusters six through eleven," Faraday said into the headset.

"Lieutenant, how's your head?" Rodriguez asked. "You got a little blood there…"

"Just dinged a little, Rod. I'm okay. Check on those scientists, will you?"

"Yes sir. Best stay put till you're sure you don't have a concussion, Lieutenant."

Rodriguez moved off toward the civilians. Heart banging, Burkett looked around for fire or smoke.

Nothing so far.

Everyone was talking at once and an alarm siren was wailing.

"Air pressure stable," Strickland said.

The orbcraft steadied but a variety of items floated over the seats—pens and hand-screens and a patrol cap and someone's jacket. Some of the Rangers were getting up to see what they could do.

"Switch off the alarm, goddamn it," Mayweather called out. "We're alarmed already!" It shut off. "And keep the talk down to what's necessary!"

"You okay, Lieutenant?" Dorman asked, drifting up to him. "Saw you smack that bulkhead. Feel like anything's broken?"

Some of the feeling was returning to Burkett's left arm and he stretched it.

"Doesn't feel like it. Shoulder hurts, but not like a fracture."

"What the hell happened, Lieutenant? Debris strike?"

"Debris doesn't change direction to hit you. Missile impact." Burkett tugged on the ring, sailed back through the cabin—clumsily, his boots clunking once into a chairback. Head buzzing, shoulder throbbing, he kept going, working his way into the aft compartments passage, where he floated up to the rearmost hatch.

It was inset with a thick glass window that looked out on the storage deck, a large compartment with a curved ceiling. Most of it was taken up by the two LTVs. There were crates locked down to either side, heavy weapons racks, extra oxygen. Two oxygen tanks floated in the air, knocked loose from their moorings. If the chamber had been breached, the tanks would've been sucked to the crack in the hull.

Then he spotted it: the bulkhead on the right was misshapen, dented inward. Faraday had veered just before impact, so the missile hit them glancingly, detonating but not penetrating their armor. Nevertheless, it had done some damage.

"*Burkett?*" Mayweather's voice in the headset. "*We've lost some of our systems. Long distance comms are down, some of our thrusters aren't answering, and Strickland thinks we're leaking fuel. Air pressure's steady. What've you got back there?*"

"Indication of impact in the aft hold, but no breach, sir. I'm reluctant to open the hatch without a pressure suit. It could be a slow leak."

"*Get back up here. But, uh—put Private Dorman on it, to keep watch back there. Leave it sealed for now. Have Andrews, Cha, Dabiri, and Lang go through every other compartment on the craft, inspect for damage, and report. Let 'em know what you think happened.*"

"Yes sir."

Squinting against the pain in his head, Burkett floated forward, issued the orders, saw that the air litter had been cleaned up— Lemuel was chasing down the last bit—and noted Rodriguez checking over Ildeva. He guessed Rod had given Dupon a strong painkiller, because the scientist's head was drooping, his arms limp in the air.

"What has happened, Lieutenant?" Magonier asked as Burkett passed. His first impulse was to put the man off—but then, whatever the S-7 was in for, the civilians were in for it, too.

"We think someone hit us with a missile. We don't know who yet. Good news is we're not losing air pressure. But—we have some systems damage. Going to assess that now. Call Rod over if you need anything." He pushed on before the scientists could press him for more information.

"You okay, Art?" Mayweather asked as Burkett pulled himself into the flight deck.

"Nothing broken, Captain. You?"

"I'm good. Andrews has a bloody nose from my kneecap."

"Any more bogies?"

"Not so far, Lieutenant," Strickland responded. "But we're off course—in a whole different orbit. Evasion and impact threw us into Compass orbit. We're about 2,040 klicks up."

"*Compass*? Jesus…" That was MEO—medium Earth orbit. They were seriously out in space now. "We going to have to evade satellites?"

"There's still a lot of empty out here, but maybe."

"I hear something about a fuel leak?"

"Yeah," Mayweather said, the syllable a sigh. "Tank two. It's going fast."

"Any chance of an explosion?"

Faraday and Strickland looked at each other. Ike cleared his throat. "Um… not impossible. The methane's vaporizing, could accumulate in empty spaces in the tank, and there's oxygen mixed in with it. A spark…"

Burkett's mouth was suddenly paper dry. "Can we use the fuel anytime soon? I mean, if we try to use it—does it increase the risk of a detonation?"

"Actually—yeah, it does."

"We got time to patch it up, somehow?"

"That'd take a lot of plan-and-prep," Faraday said. "Not sure we could carry it out without risking an explosion. That methane's melting."

Burkett nodded. The methane-oxygen mix was kept frozen, and they were on the sunny side of the Earth now. Likely the break in the hull allowed the exposed tank to heat up—the cracked tank released vaporized gas into the space between the hull and the tank. The gas was steadily seeping into space, but on its way out it was danger-hot. He shook his head—and the pain from the motion made him regret it.

"It'll leak out before we can use it. Safest thing would be to jettison the tank." Frowning, he added, "I should know if that's possible, but I don't."

"There is a way to do that," Faraday said. "That section of hull opens from here—if its motor is still functioning—but that's a lot of fuel we'll lose if we dump the tank. We had just enough to start with."

"We'll have to figure something out," Mayweather said. "There's high risk of an explosion. Jettison the damaged tank, Lieutenant Faraday. Make sure it leaves our vicinity tout suite."

"Yes sir," Ike said, opening the cover on a control panel.

"Are the comms down, Sergeant?" Burkett asked.

"Long-distance comms, yeah," Strickland said. She winced. "I should've sent a message to base when we were first being targeted, but—"

"You were busy," Mayweather said. "You didn't have time, and the two of you got us through this intact."

So far, Burkett thought. Why should there be only one attack on them?

"So, who fired this thing at us?" Faraday asked.

"Could be a mistake." Mayweather shrugged. "Maybe accidentally triggered."

That seemed far-fetched to Burkett. "You think it was surface-to-orbit, sir?" he asked.

"Radar, lidar, and heat signature suggested it came from behind us, at the same orbital altitude," Sergeant Strickland said. "And it tracked us for a while—following a parallel course."

"Meaning it wasn't fired from the surface," Mayweather muttered. He rubbed his forehead. "That leaves our own stations, some kind of accidental missile launch, or the Chinese, or... the Russians."

"We just got all up in Moscow's face," Burkett said, nodding.

"Krozkov," Mayweather muttered.

"It's a good possibility. He won't want our guests to make it to debriefing."

Mayweather took a deep breath. "Once we make absolutely sure we're not losing air pressure, our priority is to communicate with control, and then get back to base. Meaning we have to assess our thrust and navigation capabilities, and available fuel."

Getting to the geosynchronous point for re-entry within reach of Base Three might be possible, Burkett guessed, but re-entry meant using large amounts of fuel for braking and course correction. Without that capability, they'd burn up in the atmosphere.

"We could link up with a fuel source," Faraday suggested. "If we could communicate our position."

"Don't they have a fix on us all the time?" Burkett asked.

"We have a transmitter that gives it to them, but it's down," Strickland said dourly. "Its power source is near the impact area. Smashed."

"Then we have to repower it," Mayweather said. "Let's finish damage assessment. I'll assign teams."

"We've lost track of the S-7," General Carney said. He sounded angry, though there was no particular reason to be angry at the other two people in the conference. "They're not responding to comms."

"Hell's fucking bells," said Sandy Chance.

"Maybe it's not as bad as it sounds," Sgt. Susan Prosser offered. "Could be a comm systems failure."

"Failure from what?" Carney snorted. "Got to have a cause."

The three of them were talking by video conferencing. Chance from Langley, Carney and Prosser from SubOrbital One—mission control for every S-series flight. She'd been off duty till the call.

Chance was in his office—he'd gotten in not long before, on a red-eye and couldn't sleep. Now he was nursing a triple espresso at CIA headquarters. The place had high-quality espresso machines.

Glancing out a one-way window, he watched as a helicopter

landed in the blue-tinted morning light. He recognized the silver-and-red heli. That would be his boss. He'd hoped she wouldn't be in the loop on this quite yet. Hard enough to defend the Drop-Heavy program without shit like this. Syl Blackwell, the CIA director, might think that SubOrbital had just lost all deniability.

"Well, Chance?" Carney demanded. "What're you people going to do?"

Chance studied the two of them, each sharing half the screen. Carney was a white-haired, narrow-jawed, clean-shaven man, his eyes a little too close together, the skin around his mouth lined from being perpetually pursed. Susan Prosser was sixty; a plump woman with kindly blue eyes but a no-nonsense air. Her long white hair was in bangs and tied back in a braid. Without time to get into uniform, she had on a light-blue frock.

Chance spread his hands. "I'll talk to our Russia and Bulgaria specialists, and I'll loop in relevant departments in the IC." More precisely the USIC—United States Intelligence Community. Something *from* everyone and something *for* everyone in US intel. "We have any satellites that could look for them, Susan?"

"We're on that," she replied. "Comprehensive sensors all round." Sergeant Prosser, an Army Airborne specialist in satellites, was chief of operational interface on the Drop-Heavy program. She had a proprietorial air about the job. "We'll find 'em, but I can tell you already that they're not on course. They'd have been seen by Orbital Station Three; OS Four too, by now."

"Any chance they've had a major incident, Prosser?" Carney asked. "Or been shot down?"

"We tracked them into orbit and halfway home. So if something serious happened, it was in low Earth orbit."

"It would have made a big damn explosion, if it'd blown up," General Carney said, massaging his long chin with the ball of his thumb. "Someone would've spotted it."

"Someone probably has," Chance said, then hastily added, "if that's what happened."

"It'll be a global PR nightmare if that craft is destroyed," Carney muttered. "We have to ask ourselves if we're going to lie about who was on board, and what the mission was about."

"Either way, we say as little as possible," Chance replied automatically, but he suspected that before this was over, SubOrbital's secrets would go viral.

NINE

I should hate this, Linda Strickland thought as she began the spacewalk. *Because we're all in major danger. This is a huge responsibility, and we have three civilians—important ones—to get home safe.*

Yet every time Sgt. Linda Strickland did a spacewalk, she was thrilled. She'd been tired before suiting up, needing food and sleep, but drifting along the outer hull, she felt energized and wide awake. Her silver-and-black biosuit was about as tight-fitting as a wetsuit, giving her a comfortable range of motion. It was connected to the ship by a long safety tether.

Its helmet, much like a glass-dome bell jar, was actually made of transparent aluminum, though its coating blocked dangerous solar radiation. She had a far better view than the old-style astronauts.

The S-7 was directly over Baffin Bay, between Canada and Greenland. She could see the chartreuse and rose-red shimmer of solar radiation gathered in the aurora over the gleaming white arctic...

Linda breathed slowly and deeply as she drew herself along the outer hull using maintenance handholds, tugging her way to the rear fuselage. Her boots were equipped with magnets for walking on the hull, but she wanted to get to the job more expediently.

Floating on a short tether attached to her left hip was a case of tools, and the metal box of the replacement power conduit. She had the latest SAFER unit on her back—something like a metallic backpack—with small navigational nitrogen-gas jets to use if she needed them. For the moment, she felt in better control using her hands. A small camera strapped to her forehead took in everything she saw.

Out here she was in no danger of losing touch with the S-7— she and the orbcraft were moving along at the same speed. In a way, it didn't feel as if they were moving at all. She'd done eleven space walks: four during her training, and seven after she'd become a trainer on Orbital Station Eight, before being transferred to S-7. Strickland had more experience than anyone else aboard in "the great airless outdoors," as Tafir called it, so she got the assignment.

Linda was reasonably confident she could get the job done, but there were risks...

Her biosuit was the best available, but this new model was so thin—not needing air pressurization, using titanium-coil membranes to pressurize her body—it made her feel exposed.

She passed close beside the orbcraft's reaction control system jets, each one big enough to fry her suit and her with it, if a course-correction pod burned at the wrong moment.

Ike wasn't going to touch the controls for the RCS thrusters while she was out here.

But suppose there was another incoming missile? He'd have to burn whatever was needed to evade it. The Captain would order it—he'd have to prioritize the safety of everyone aboard, wouldn't he?

If she were in his place, that's what she'd do.

The thoughts flickered quickly through her mind and were just as quickly pushed aside. Being scared was something a Ranger handled routinely. It was like learning to handle electricity without being electrocuted. She had to get rid of the fear before it became panic.

A different kind of fear arose in her. It was an aching fear of failure. If she couldn't get the emergency-power unit properly attached to the comm system, they wouldn't have the long-range communication they were going to need to call for help. There was limited oxygen aboard, and little fuel. Everyone was counting on her—not just aboard the S-7. The United States itself was counting on her. Chance had made it clear that this mission had long-term consequences.

Linda Strickland focused on the work in front of her.

"*In the moment and on task.*" That was the mantra at Station Seven.

Up ahead, just above the main engine's exhaust port, she could see black impact marks left by the enemy missile. There was no air out here to feed a fire, but superheated expanding gases from the warhead had cooked the insulating cells on starboard rear fuselage, near the main rocket array's exhaust port. The tail fin was bent just a little out of true, the metal near the fuselage wrinkled.

"You seeing all this, Ike?" Linda asked.

Faraday's voice crackled in her headset. "*Hell yeah, we got a bent stabilizer. That'll be fun when we're trying to land.*"

As she drifted nearer the impact area, she saw a long rectangular gap where a fuel tank had been ejected. A thin plume of blue gas trailed after the S-7—methane from the fuel leak, clinging to the orbcraft's mass.

Handholds became fewer and farther between, so she deployed the joystick for the SAFER jets, swiveling it out from the side of the backpack. She fired a tiny lateral jet to tilt herself in the right direction and cautiously aimed her trajectory toward the hull, pressing the joystick's button very gingerly. It didn't take much.

There was a heads-up display panel just below her helmet glass, and the 3D arrow was pointing down and ahead, guiding her to hull plate 1733, near the enormous cones of the exhaust ports. The gas jet hissed and she angled down to the underside of the rear fuselage. There she spotted it—the battered panel that contained the power node for the comms.

Becoming suddenly aware of the sound of her own rapid breathing in the helmet, Linda caught at the edge of a blackened, bent-up panel, her hands in counter-pressure gloves holding onto the sharp edges. The serrated edge of the damaged panel was under her gloves.

Bracing herself, her left hand holding onto the inside edge of the open panel, she tugged at the broken piece, trying to pull it out of her way. It came loose too suddenly and she lost her grip on it; the panel flew at her, banging hard into her helmet. The transparent metal remained uncracked, but the impact sent her floating backward, away from the S-7 at surprising speed. Angling toward a lower orbit, she had a mental image of her tether snapping...

Of burning up in the atmosphere.

Focus, she thought. *In the moment and on task.*

Linda reached the end of the tether and it jarred her, but it held. She pressed the SAFER's joystick almost convulsively, not aiming properly, and found herself spinning. The Earth blurred by, vanished, spun past again...

She fired a different jet on her backpack, one that hissed counter to her spin, and it stopped her with a jerk.

"Oh *jeezus*."

She was floating in space—and gazing down at the Earth. It was all she could see.

"Linda!" Faraday called. "What's your status?" Drifting behind him, Burkett heard the alarm in Ike's voice.

"What's up?"

"Saw something fly at her, lost the image," the pilot muttered. "Yo, Sergeant Strickland!"

"*Knocked off the orbcraft,*" she said, over the radio. "*Panel was looser than I thought. Hit my maneuvering jet wrong, got myself in a spin. Got myself out of it. On my way back to the orbcraft.*"

"Linda, where exactly are you *now*, goddammit?" Faraday barked.

"Ike," Burkett whispered. "Chill."

"*Maneuvering back to S-7. Uh—ten meters out. Almost there. Going to complete the job…*"

"How about if we send assistance?" Faraday said, breathing hard. Burkett could tell he had some kind of real bond with Linda. Probably not romantic. More like… being two Rangers who worked closely together.

"*Negative on the assist. Almost there. Don't understand how that piece of the hull came off so easily, so fast…*"

"Is the robotic strength enhancement in your gloves turned on?" Burkett asked.

"*The… oh crap. That was it, Lieutenant. I didn't realize it was on. Haven't used the newest biosuit before.*"

"Another one of the General's little surprises," Faraday muttered.

Burkett looked back into the main cabin, saw Mayweather floating near Frederic Dupon, talking to him. Dupon was frowning. He looked scared and angry. Beyond Mayweather, Lem Dorman was leading Magonier and Dhariwal back to their seats, having taught them how to use the space toilet. Magonier looked like he might throw up from the foray into weightless motion, but Dhariwal was smiling, seeming to enjoy swimming through the air.

Sergeant Lang had taken over for Dorman at the storage compartment. Tafir Dabiri had finished his inspection—no further damage—and was floating beside Alexi Syrkin's seat. Syrkin had his hands balled into fists, and was shaking them as he to spoke to Tafir.

Syrkin worried Burkett. Should he place a guard on him?

Sergeant Strickland switched on the electromagnets in her boots, so she could crouch on the hull, and employed her robotics-enhanced gloves carefully to force the instant-metal out of its tube to affix the power unit. The applicator ran an electric current through the liquid, causing a chemical reaction that hardened the metal into a flameless weld.

Done.

"Ike, I've got the battery attached to the hull. Can you confirm that power is shut down in the comms? I'm going to splice the cables."

"*No juice anywhere near you,*" Ike said. "*But use the current tester, just in case.*"

She glanced at the oxygen indicator on her HUD. On the low side. The splicing tool was a bit clumsy through the gloves, but she made it work. She glanced again at her oxy indicator. Less than a quarter of her air remained.

Making herself take very slow, calming breaths to use less oxygen, she continued methodically splicing. It took her a few tries to meld the thick broken cables to the comm unit. She had to do it with exquisite care, to avoid short circuits and damage to the gear. A minute passed.

Then two.

Three, and...

Finished.

She sprayed insulator over the cables and reached for the battery box, hit the old-fashioned on-switch. The power light went green.

"Should be flowing, Ike."

"*We've got power flow to the transmitter. Good job. Come on in.*"

Switching off her boot power, she used the SAFER to aim her back up toward the airlock. Feeling good.

I did it, by God.

"Lieutenant Burkett," Alexi Syrkin said. "I insist that Lieutenant Carney be arrested." His voice grated. He seemed to be talking through clenched teeth. "Right here on this ship. There's a utility compartment that'll double as a brig. You could put him there."

"That's not your call, Specialist Syrkin," Burkett said coldly. He sympathized with Syrkin but the guy was out of line. "He's no danger to anyone here. I'll talk to the Captain about a court-martial when the time comes."

"*Captain?*" Ike Faraday was talking to Mayweather over the all-personnel channel, and his voice came over Burkett's headset. "*We've got enough power to call base. Maybe you and the XO might want to…*"

"We're on the way," Mayweather said, drifting up beside Burkett. He led the way forward to the pilots. On the way, Mayweather flipped his headset mic out of the way. "Art, what's up with Alexi?"

Burkett pushed his mic aside, too. "He wants Lieutenant Carney arrested, Captain. Here and now. Locked up in a storage unit."

"Christ! Well, I get how he feels. Carney killed his brother in an unforgivable dumb-ass move—but that's just not his call."

"That's what I told him, sir. Lieutenant Carney made some kind of feeble apology to Alexi. Maybe he should try again."

They reached the flight deck and Mayweather grabbed the bulkhead over the hatch. He carefully ducked in feet-first, stopping between Linda and Ike.

"Sergeant Strickland, good job out there, but I understand you went on a little side trip."

"Yes sir, very much an unplanned one."

"Any worse for wear?"

"No sir. Topnotch."

Mayweather restored his headset's mic. "Call Sergeant Prosser, Ike, and patch my headset in."

"With pleasure, sir. Keep in mind, Captain, that this is just a big old battery powering us now, not our usual power source, so we might want to conserve it."

Too damned bad the ship had so little solar power, Burkett thought. Another "they won't need it" lack of foresight.

"Let's do this, Ike," Mayweather said.

Faraday tapped at the comms, looking for a satellite to route the call. They needed one equipped with quantum encryption, to make sure they weren't monitored by unfriendlies. He found a military communications satellite, confirmed the link, and transmitted.

"This is S-7, Lieutenant Faraday for Homegirl. You reading?"

There was a long pause as the call bounced around. Then a crackle and a young male voice.

"This is Corporal Feeney, on S-series comm watch. Sergeant Prosser's on her way in... Ah, here she is now, Lieutenant."

"It's Faraday?" Susan's voice was in the background. There was a scrabbling sound and then she came on the line. *"Ike! Lieutenant—what a relief to hear from you! What's the situation?"*

"I'll give you to the Captain, Sergeant."

Mayweather took a deep breath and began. "We were dogged by a missile, apparently fired from orbit. It exploded on our aft fuselage. Damage is mixed—no casualties, and we do have airtight integrity, but we lost comms and we were forced out of our course. Some maneuvering thrusters are gone. We haven't tried our main engine yet—sensors say it's functional, only we can't maneuver without more thrusters." He coughed. Some kind of dust in the air. "Fuel line to some of them has been interrupted," he continued. "Others knocked to pieces. We don't know who fired on us. We didn't get a clear image of the bogey. Had to jettison a cracked fuel tank and the other is low. Not enough to brake with if we come in, and we can only maneuver half-assed. We are in the Compass orbital belt."

"*Compass*," Prosser gasped. "*Medium orbit?*"

"Affirmative. We're holding geo-sync over Canada…" He gave the exact position and went on. "We have an injured civilian and a wounded prisoner, as the General is aware, and we have limited oxygen. Right now we're breathing, but if we don't get some kind of resupply or manage to land, we're in trouble. That's the short version."

"*At least you're all alive,*" Prosser replied, sounding breathless. She was usually more coolly professional. "*I just came from my office—got a call from Chance. There's chatter that Krozkov activated an orbital missile station, and fired it. We were afraid they nailed you.*"

"Orbital missile station." He snorted. "You mean the ones they claim are prototype space labs?"

She chuckled dryly. "*One of those, right. We can get a fix on you, now we know where you are. We'll do everything we can for you. Carney is ready to send up an S-series.*"

Burkett nodded to himself. An S-series orbital rendezvous would be the simplest way to resupply. There were always a couple of Drop-Heavy orbcrafts ready to launch at need. They could parallel the S-7 in a lower orbit, carry out phasing burns to bring them into a coelliptic orbit. Send EVA-ready personnel across with the supplies. Refueling would be tricky, but there was a maneuver for it.

Too bad the S-7s weren't equipped with orbit-ready robots, which could easily whisk supplies between vessels. Orbcrafts weren't supposed to be in space long enough to need them.

Prosser sighed. "*Only, there's already media noise about the raid in Moldova. The Moldovan government has complained to the UN. Moscow has issued a statement of support for Moldova and it was shocked, truly shocked, that the USA would attack Moldova this way."*

"I expected them to take that line."

"The White House isn't eager to accuse Moscow of the kidnap—no definitive proof in the pipeline. We need your prisoner for that. And—General Carney sounded out the President on a rescue, if you guys weren't… Anyway, the President isn't ready to send up another SubOrbital. He wants to deny the mission, keep it covert. Doesn't want to confirm it with a launch everyone's going to be looking for."

That kindled anger in Burkett. The President was juggling politics with the lives of everyone on S-7. *"Drop-Heavy is still unofficial,"* she went on. *"Our allies do a good job of pretending not to know. The President is… waffling."*

"What a surprise," Mayweather said. "Sergeant—our long-distance comms are powered by emergency batteries. We don't have a lot of calls left. We'll figure something out. Call if you have a resupply plan, or if the President realizes he's the fucking *Commander in Chief."*

"Roger that, Captain."

Mayweather cut the connection.

"It sounds as if we're going to have to get back on our own," Burkett said darkly. "We haven't got time for waffling."

The captain nodded. "You and Ike figure out what can be jury-rigged."

Rodriguez drifted up to the flight deck.

"Captain? Ildeva claims he's about to die."

TEN

"Is my heart, Lieutenant Burkett," Mikhail Ildeva said, adding something in his own language. "My heart, it is killing."

He does look pale, Burkett thought as he drifted up to them. Ildeva was slightly hunched in his seat, with Rodriguez floating beside him, looking into a med scanner that picked up his heart and blood pressure.

"What we got here, Rod?" Burkett asked.

"Lieutenant, he and Dupon need a real doctor in a real hospital—"

"Meaning you don't have a diagnosis?"

"Yes sir, that's what I mean. But I think it might be a kind of panic attack—bullet in the shoulder, his whole enterprise taken down, then he's dragged up into space. First time in freefall. Then the ship takes a hit. Who wouldn't freak out? I took him to the head a few minutes ago, he was okay, but on the way back he got kind of sick to his stomach... caught most of it with the air scooper."

"Have Private Dorman find *all* of it, Rod. We don't want any chunks in the air ducts."

"Yes sir. Anyway—I think if this man had a heart attack, it was a minor one."

"No, no, is my heart," Ildeva protested.

"His heartbeat's stable right now, Lieutenant," Rodriguez continued. "Blood pressure is average range. I'm going to give him something that'll chill him out, and keep a watch on him."

"Is another Bulgar, to talk…" Ildeva muttered, jerking his head toward the rear, where Syrkin was.

"You're asking to be moved over by Specialist Syrkin?" Burkett asked.

"Yes." He said something in Bulgarian and then, "Very please."

Burkett thought about it. On the one hand, he didn't want this gangster to feel like he was running the show. He was a prisoner, and he was going to cooperate whether he liked it or not. On the other hand, Burkett needed Ildeva alive. Wouldn't be good if the guy died of a heart attack.

Maybe Syrkin could calm him down—and it'd be good for Syrkin to be occupied.

"You know who the boss is here, Ildeva?"

"You the boss, Lieutenant."

"Not just me. *Every one of my team* is your boss. You're low man on the totem pole."

"Totem pole?"

"Never mind. Just remember, you're our prisoner. You do what we tell you. You know the word *cooperate*?"

Ildeva nodded earnestly. "Yes, yes, boss."

Is this guy playing me? Burkett wondered. *If he is, it's the last time.* He turned to the corporal. "Rod, did you have this man handcuffed and under control when you took him to the head?"

"For sure, Lieutenant. It was complicated doing it that way, but we got it done."

"Keep it that way, and make no mistake, he's a vicious, dishonest son of a bitch. Keep him under your thumb. And— hold on a minute." Burkett moved a few yards from the seat and called Mayweather on headset. He explained the situation. "But I'm not sure I trust him seated next to Syrkin."

"*Might work to our advantage. Let's do it, but talk to Syrkin first—see if he can get any intel from the guy.*"

"Yes sir."

Burkett drifted back to Ildeva and Rodriguez. "Rod, give him the meds and then get Tafir to help you, just to make sure, and you guys move him to Lem's seat. Move Lem up here. Be sure Ildeva's handcuffed to that seat."

"Copy that, sir. How's that noggin of yours, Lieutenant?"

"My head's clear. I'm good." His shoulder and side still hurt, but manageably. He tugged a ceiling ring, heading over to Syrkin, to tell him what was going down.

And to suggest that he draw Ildeva out on Moscow.

Sandy Chance was never comfortable meeting with Gen. Roger Carney, but events had come to a delicate, volatile pass, needing some fine-tuning. So here he was, standing in Carney's office at SubOrbital Base One, in the boonies of Colorado.

Carney was seated at his desk, speaking snappishly into a phone as if Chance weren't there.

Chance hadn't been offered a chair.

"You're giving me excuses!" Carney snarled into the phone.

Chance glanced around. Behind Carney was a tinted bulletproof window with a view of the Rocky Mountains, the humps of three hyper-hardened silo caps in the foreground. He'd bet that Carney had *asked* for a view of the anti-ballistic missile silos, even though they were mostly underground.

The walls of the office were crowded with photos of Carney chumming with presidents and secretaries of state. Two framed commendations flanked a photo of him sitting in a tank trying to look like Patton—probably taken in North Korea, but way behind the lines.

"Well, I don't give a goddamn," the General barked into the phone. "Just make sure the President understands!"

Oh hell, Chance thought. *How's he gumming up the works now?*

A uniformed staff sergeant glided in with a printout and laid it on the desk. The sergeant looked at Chance, as if trying to size him up. Chance read the man's ID badge: Sgt. James Rowell.

He didn't know Rowell. Crew cut, smooth faced, blue eyed, all his movements crisp and his expression pert. This base was so highly classified, the cooks in the cafeteria had to have top clearance. So why hadn't Chance been copied on this guy's paperwork? He was supposed to see all clearances.

Rowell must be new. Very *new.*

The sergeant frowned at the unlit cigarette in Chance's hand, and flitted out of the room. Carney ended the call and tossed the phone onto his desk.

"Chance, I hope you have something useful for me. I got the report from Sergeant Prosser. They're all alive, but otherwise it sounds bad."

"Mind if I sit down, General?" Chance asked.

"Hm? Yes, yes, go ahead."

The only available chair was an old wicker thing that creaked ominously as he sat down. Carney must've dragged it from office to office.

The general gets a check for office expenses, Chance mused. *What does he do with the money?*

"Your staff sergeant is new here, isn't he?"

Carney frowned. "Not so new, been here three months."

"It's funny, I usually get documentation on all employees. Didn't get his."

"Yeah you did. We follow protocol. You must've overlooked it."

Chance shook his head. "I didn't. Like to see it."

"So pick up a copy at Staffing while you're here."

"Who should've sent it to me?"

"Staff Sergeant Sheila Mendez."

"I know her. She's reliable. Odd that she overlooked it."

"Chance—why are we talking about this?"

"Surprised I didn't get the paperwork."

Carney snorted. "Every time I get saddled with CIA, I get sweated by their goddamn paranoia."

"General, if you knew what I knew, you'd be more paranoid than I am."

"That makes no sense," Carney replied. "Anyway, you're wasting my time. You know, there's a department that checks people's bona fides, background checks, all that. You don't need to do it. It's not usual for CIA to do all that personally."

"Drop-Heavy's not usual."

Carney tried to change the subject. "Put that cigarette away. Flipping it in your hands like a poker chip, making me nervous." He was flat-out glaring now. "What are you here for? Just give me the lowdown—the one you could've documented without coming here in person and wasting my time on this bullshit." The General leaned back in his chair, tented his fingers.

Chance wanted to tell him to go to hell, but he took out the Balkan Sobranies pack, and tucked the cigarette away.

"I didn't want a conference call, or anyone else in the room," he said. "I'll tell you straight up. I want to save the S-7, and you're one of the people who could order a launch to do that."

"I can't do it without the President signing off on it."

"You have the President signed off on the *mission*—and this is part of the same mission."

"I don't think he'd view it that way. Who the hell fired on us anyway?"

"We sent you the memo. You didn't get it?"

"Haven't got a memo from you for a good long while."

Chance wondered if someone had intercepted it. "We'll deal with that later," he said. "Good information, it was the Russians. Krozkov. He had command of those two stations, but they weren't supposed to be in use without the Russian president ordering it. If my sources are correct, Krozkov *didn't* get permission." He paused to let that sink in, then continued.

"So Krozkov is in trouble. He can probably make a good case, but when you fire an orbital weapon without checking with Anatoly Veronin, you're in hot water. Right now, of course, they're denying everything."

"I got a call from the White House Chief of Staff this morning," Carney said. "President thinks if we send a SubOrbital up now when everyone's looking for us to, it might look like an act of war." The General ran his long-fingered hand over his sparse white hair. "I think he's being too careful. CIA got an opinion about that? What's the director think?"

"The director thinks the Russians are engaging in viral media scare tactics. Hinting that the Russians are on the verge of declaring war. Just a lot of whispered disinformation to keep the President from assisting the orbcraft. The Russians would like to see everyone on S-7 die up there."

General Carney swallowed. Probably thinking about his son. "Any word on the Russians trying again? Another missile, or a laser hit?"

"It's possible, sure." Chance shrugged. "I haven't picked up any chatter on it yet, but the order would go out in a very need-to-know way."

Carney swallowed, muscles jumping in his face as he stared at the desk.

"My son's up there, Chance."

"Yes, he is."

General Carney looked up and made eye contact. "I'm not letting him die up there."

"You plan an end-run around the President?"

"Looking for one. I can't say 'it's all part of the same mission' when he tells me not to launch yet." He narrowed his eyes at Chance. "You got an idea?"

"Maybe our allies could do it. Trouble with anyone helping is, it'll take preparation. Time, and the S-7 hasn't got a lot of that…"

* * *

"How much time have we got, Art?" Mayweather asked.

Air pressure was steady in the rear storage room, so they were belted into the front seats of the Light-Up. Mayweather wanted to talk in a secure space. He didn't want to create unnecessary stress in the team or the scientists, and he didn't want the prisoner to hear.

"Well…" Burkett looked around at the interior of the vehicle. There were a few charred panels and he could smell the residual acrid reek of the explosives that had struck the LTV. "Near as Strickland and I can figure out, Captain, we have an average of about eighteen hours more oxygen."

"An average?"

"It'll vary some, depending on how active we are. Another thing is, toward the end we'll still be able to breathe for a while, but it'll get kind of thin—and stale. We need to watch for hypoxia symptoms…"

"Before just flat-out dying." Mayweather nodded dourly. "I see."

"We're sure to get some help before we run out."

Mayweather snorted. "We're *sure*, are we?"

Burkett *wished* he was sure. "Okay, we'll probably get help. Despite the political… complications." *Political bullshit*, he thought. "Meanwhile, we could do some orbital scavenging."

Mayweather grunted an assent. "Far as Ike can tell, the main engine's functional, and two maneuvering pods. We can travel in this orbit. If we change orbit, we'll need better maneuvering than we have—and more fuel.

"I figure someone can get fuel and oxy to us," Mayweather continued, staring glumly at the dashboard. "Maybe take some of the team and our guests back with them, whatever they have room for. It's your decision—but I don't think we should abandon the orbcraft unless we absolutely have to. We're going to have to spend some comm power with a general distress call if we don't get some kind of plan from Carney's people. Or the CIA. Or Space Command. Someone…"

Mayweather's shoulders were slightly hunched and his mouth was fixed in a scowl. The lives of the team and the passengers weighing on him.

"There's one space station in this orbit," Burkett offered. "Japanese. Most space stations are in lower orbit, but if we try to get to them, we'll use up our maneuvering fuel—might collide with the station we're trying to reach.

"Only, the one up here is abandoned," he added. "There might be some supplies there. We could accelerate, catch up with it."

"How? We'd still have impaired maneuvering. We could end up maneuvering ourselves into deep space."

"We're going to have to fix our RCS thrusters. The ones that can be fixed."

"Bring me a plan, Art. Get Strickland on it, too. She's the navigational genius. Good on a spacewalk. How rusty are your EVA skills?"

"I can manage, Captain, but she was an instructor. She'll keep me on the straight and narrow."

"As for oxygen, we can keep the squad and our guests from unnecessary exercise, when it comes to that. Burn less oxygen."

"Yes sir. Means I'll have to cancel that square dance I was planning, but…"

Mayweather gave a weak smile. "Joan likes square dancing. Line dancing, and all that." He looked wistful, probably wondering if he'd ever see his wife again. "Country music's not my thing but I took her to a square dance class for our anniversary."

"Now that's true love, sir."

"You bet your ass it is. Whole thing embarrassed the hell out of me. Dosey fucking doe." But he gave another slight smile.

"Do we tell everyone about the oxygen supply, Captain?"

"I guess we'd better." Mayweather rubbed his eyes and growled to himself. "But make it sound like it's all under control."

Then he looked narrowly at Burkett. "How's Ildeva doing next to Syrkin?"

"Seems to keep him settled to have another Bulgar to talk to. Rod's not sure if he really had a heart attack or not, but we're likely to be in rough straits for a while, and I don't want an asset like that to die on us. Syrkin can use the distraction—I asked him to see if he could draw Ildeva out on his contacts with Moscow. Get something intel could use."

"Good. But we need to keep an eye on them. I don't trust Ildeva."

"Roger that, sir."

"I tell you truly, Alexi," said Ildeva in their particular Slavic, "you and I, we must be related. Cousins! Because Olek was my second cousin."

"I guess we are," Syrkin said in the same language. He wasn't especially pleased to be related to Ildeva. "Or maybe not. Olek had a different mother." He was thirsty, and looked around for Rodriguez or Dorman so he could ask for water. The medic had asked him not to get up unless he had to use the head, but he and Lemuel seemed busy with Dupon. The Swiss scientist was floating on his back in a corner near the flight deck, Dorman holding Dupon's shoulders.

Dorman was standing on the deck thanks to electromagnet-fitted shoes. There were only two pairs aboard, apart from the boots that went with the biosuits—too slow to wear inside. Rodriguez was carefully putting a large black orthopedic boot on Dupon's injured leg. The scientist had his eyes squeezed shut, his mouth pressed into a line of pain.

Syrkin grunted. Rod must have given him a local anesthetic, but Dupon just had to milk it for drama. Alexi despised people like that.

Olek had died for that man.

"You knew Olek was going to be at St. Basil's, Alexi?" Ildeva asked.

"No. Not till we got there, and they told me. They wanted me to handle him, but I got this..." He touched the bandage on his head. "I was unconscious for a while. I wouldn't have let him wander off to search for some hand-screen. If he'd been with the team, right there with them, even an idiot like Carney wouldn't have fired at him." He saw Second Lieutenant Carney, a few seats ahead, sit up stiffly at the sound of his name, which must've stuck out in the Bulgar talk.

Let him wonder...

"The Americans got what they wanted from Olek." Ildeva sniffed. "What do they care if he is killed?" He gave a deep, dramatic sigh. "But Olek betrayed me. For CIA money, I'm sure. I saw him talking to your officer like such very good friends. You're lucky they didn't abandon you, too. They don't value us like their own kind, Alexi."

Syrkin frowned. "I grew up in the USA. I'm an American citizen."

"What has it gotten you? You tell me they court-martialed you—demoted you for doing your job. They killed your brother! How do you know they didn't intend to kill him all along?"

That cut deep. Syrkin was loyal to the Rangers—to the US Army—and Burkett had made it sound like shooting Olek was a deeply regrettable accident.

But maybe that was an officer covering his ass.

ELEVEN

"Strickland, you're with Burkett," Mayweather said. "You make those maneuvering jets happen for us or don't come back in."

"Yes sir," Strickland said. "The air in here is getting kind of, uh, pungent anyway, Captain."

"We'll ship washing machines and more soap next time, Sergeant."

She grinned. "Thank you very much, sir."

Burkett, Strickland, Dabiri, Lang, Andrews, and Carney were gathered around the Captain at the rear of the main cabin. They were floating in the air like a crowd of ghosts. Seven hours earlier, they'd been divided into watches and ordered to get rest when they could. Buckled loosely into a seat, some had managed to sleep.

Ken Carney looked sick, Burkett thought. The Second Lieutenant held on tightly to a ceiling ring and swallowed hard from time to time, probably to keep from barfing.

"Lang," Mayweather said, "you're in the copilot's seat. Interface with the EVA team and generally do anything you can to help Ike."

"Can do, Captain."

"Andrews, you take Dorman—looks like he's helping Rod

now. Get him when he's done with that, and you two conduct an inventory. Look for any oxygen bottles we don't have listed. Water supplies, medical supplies, every useful thing we have. List it all, even ammunition." This raised some eyebrows, but Mayweather chose not to elaborate. "Syrkin's on sick list but he might be well enough to help out later today—we'll see. Corporal Dabiri will check the biosuits."

He started to tuck his hand-screen away in his coat.

"And me, sir?" Carney asked.

Mayweather looked a little surprised, as if he'd forgotten about the Lieutenant.

"Um—Lieutenant Carney, you go with Corporal Dabiri and inventory the biosuits. Count them—I think there's enough for everyone, but do it anyway—and double-check to make sure they all look ship-shape. Don't rush through it. Look them over real close. There's a chance we'll need them at some point. Dabiri'll show you the suit locker."

"Captain," Strickland said, "the biosuits are pretty flexible but they're not exactly one-size-fits-all."

"Good point." Mayweather nodded. "I think the only ones that are fitted are yours and the ones for the officers. If we need 'em, we may have to kinda shoehorn some people in. Getting Dupon into one might be an issue, what with his broken leg. Things get hairy, we may have to wear them all the time, so keep the helmet handy, just in case."

Ken Carney made an *urp* sound.

Captain Mayweather glanced at him. "You're not going to throw up, I hope, Lieutenant? Use the snap-bag if you are."

"No sir. Nothing to throw up."

Mayweather nodded. "The first couple days here, it's a little hard to get the rations down," he said. "And listen— if any of our scientific guests need to go to the head, or anywhere else, you take them, Carney. They know how, but they really need someone with them when they're moving around, no matter what."

Carney winced at that. It was a job for a private or a non-com.

"All right, any questions?" Mayweather asked.

Des Andrews said, "Sir, it's kind of another subject, but kind of not…"

"Spit it out."

"We're already late. I don't know about you, but I gave an approximate time to my family I'd be returning… and anyway, our families know about how long these missions take. So— my folks have to be worried."

Burkett nodded. That same thought had been needling him. Ashley would be expecting him, or some word…

"And when I was sitting up front," Andrews went on, "I got the impression from what I heard from Sergeant Prosser that the Russians might be outing this mission. So—"

"We're all in the same fix," Mayweather said, nodding gravely. "I'm planning to get some kind of word to our families, soon as we can figure out what we're allowed to tell them. That'll have to do you for now."

Andrews nodded. "Yes sir."

"Good. Let's get to work. If there's anything you've got to run by me, I'll be in the computer compartment typing out a report—the XO is going to be going outside for a while."

Burkett and Strickland let go of their handholds and propelled themselves down the narrow passage with gentle tugs on pipes clamped to the wall, heading toward the rear storage deck.

There was a good possibility the S-7 wouldn't be able to land at Base Three or any other Army base. They might not have fuel to get that far, and even if they did, they wouldn't have enough maneuvering for a guaranteed safe landing. It could go wrong and they could take out the operations building. If they crash-landed, the big orbcraft itself could become a flaming hell.

Maybe they'd come down in the Arctic tundra. Or in the Sahara. Or in the middle of the Pacific Ocean.

Uncertainties just kept coming. Burkett thought of the domino lines people set up to make elaborate patterns. What was the pattern on this one? Where would it end up?

"Lieutenant," Linda said as they came to the closed steel hatch of the aft storage. "At some point we're going down to L, and there are Russian weapons stations down at that orbit, floating quietly along pretending to be something else. Suppose we end up in range? You think they'll fire on us again?"

"Can't be sure, but…" He looked through the thick window in the hatch. Everything he could see looked squared away. To the right of the door, the internal air-pressure indicator read STANDARD. "I'm going to guess there's too many people watching now to launch another attack. They'd get busted."

"Maybe they don't care."

Always a possibility—that someone doesn't give a damn, he thought. Burkett tapped the little keypad and drew slightly back. The hatch clicked and hummed open. Air smelling of motor oil and gunpowder wafted out to them.

Linda went through first, like a swimmer in the air, pushing off from the sides of the hatch. Burkett followed less gracefully, catching the toe of one boot on the raised bottom of the hatch frame. Straightening out, he let himself drift upward in the relatively high-ceilinged room—it was twice as high as the cabin—so he could look around.

Nothing floated loose. Weapons locker seemed secure. Linda was opening the gear lockers. The extra oxygen tanks had been returned to their racks. The LTVs were secured to the deck. Reaching up, he pushed off from the ceiling and sank down to where she was at the burn-gear locker, looking over the fueling units they'd need on the EVA.

"Bulky, these things, and we'll need five."

"We'll tether them like a chain behind us," Burkett said.

"They'll clunk on the hull—might damage them, Lieutenant."

"Okay, two shorter tethers, one for each of us, and we'll be crazy careful."

She drew a burn-feed unit carefully out. "Least it doesn't weigh much here."

"Any hint on the comms when we're going to hear about a rescue operation?" Burkett asked.

"Not last I knew, sir."

"Captain says we need to assume it's not coming."

She nodded. "I'll get the tethers…"

He took the complex of pipeage and wiring from her, an armful of machinery, and looked it over as she pushed off, once more seeming as if she could swim through the air.

Assume help's not coming, he thought as he looked over the burn-feed unit. *Because even if it does, by the time they get it together, it'll be too late.*

Eighteen hours of oxygen, the Captain had said…

And now it was down to sixteen.

Ashley Burkett dialed the number again, as she had every five minutes for the last forty-five. She was sitting at the redwood picnic table in the shade of the liquid amber tree. Nate was in school. What would she tell him when he came home?

Listening to the phone ring the requisite four times before the recording, once more she heard, "Lieutenant-Colonel Baxter is not currently available. Please call back, or call—"

She hung up. "I have a right to know, Baxter," she muttered. She'd tried the other number, and some brusque clerk had taken her message. No one called back.

The hell with that. She'd keep trying until someone answered.

Ashley waited the five minutes, nervously tapping the cell phone on the bench. In another minute she'd be up, pacing back and forth. She thought about having a Chardonnay. No, it was too early in the day. But maybe it wasn't.

A little under an hour earlier she'd seen something deeply disturbing on the WorldTalk channel.

"*...citing a leak from an unnamed intelligence department, sources affirm the rumor that a US Army Airborne spacecraft used for covert operations has been struck by a missile while in lower Earth orbit. The source says that the crew are unhurt, but the spacecraft was damaged and may have limited resources.*

"*A statement from China's Orbital Navy Command states that it tracked what may have been a missile before losing sight of it over the Atlantic. The Japanese Space Service reports that a SubOrbital craft fitting the description of known US infiltration prototypes has been spotted in an unusually high orbit...*

"*The Pentagon had no comment.*

"*WorldTalk military analyst former Gen. Lawrence Lopez has connected the alleged missile attack with Russia's complaint to the United Nations Security Council regarding an alleged covert operation carried out in Moldova, in which numerous men in a monastery were—according to the Russian Ambassador— 'summarily executed by American black ops commandos...*"

Ashley shook her head. Summarily executed? A lie, of course, but in the age of internet disinformation, lies could live on and on.

Nate shouldn't have to deal with that craziness, she thought. *But he's going to.*

Goddammit, Arthur Burkett. You dragged me and your son into this.

Of course, she'd had the discussion with her husband, more than once. "You knew the life of an Army wife when you married me." And, "You knew it was covert combat." With everything that kind of duty entailed. But there had been an understanding when they'd married. He was going to transfer out of combat-operations within five years.

The five years had come and gone.

Before this call, she'd been on the phone with Laney Placer, a family friend working at SubOrbital 3 as a supply sergeant. She knew what orbcraft had been deployed. Laney found a roundabout way of telling her that no other orbcraft had been launched besides the S-7. Which meant that the one referred to in the news report was Art's.

She ticked the phone app for WorldTalk news. Under a talking head there was a chyron:

DID AMERICAN COMMANDOS KILL 20 MONKS?

"Oh, for crying out loud," she muttered.

They'd killed twenty somebodies, anyhow, she thought, but not monks. Were there Ranger casualties?

Is Art all right?

She looked at the time, and dialed Baxter's office again.

"We'll give a press conference," Lieutenant Colonel Baxter said. "We'll tell them as much as we can. Which won't be much." He was just a window on Chance's computer screen, but he emanated determination. The guy was sure of himself.

"I agree," General Carney said. "They're slandering us. We need to clear the air, and we need to explain our movements when we launch rescue."

"I'm sure we should make any announcements yet," Darrell Winch said. The Secretary of Defense was a thick-bodied, thin-lipped man in a navy-blue suit, his round head shaven nearly bald. "Classified is classified."

"It can be declassified, Mr. Secretary," Chance pointed out.

In the little monitor window next to him, the Secretary of State shook her head. Laura McCallister was a big woman, tall and deep voiced, yet a slump in her shoulders hinted at her age. Her auburn-dyed hair was fashionably cut, but her broad face was seamed with age and stress. "It's tantamount to saying we committed an act of war, and a breach of international law—and we're throwing that in their faces."

"We rescued an American citizen," Carney said, "and two other hostages who were from allied nations. To me, the only question is, do we tell them everything about Moscow's involvement."

Baxter made a sound of exasperation. "The Russians are saying we killed a bunch of monks, Madame Secretary. We can't let that stand!"

"I've already denied that accusation," McCallister said. "We asserted that it was ridiculous."

Chance cleared his throat.

"One of those so-called 'monks' is now a prisoner on the S-7. We can show his video image from the spacecraft, if we have to. His face can be identified by UN security, and we have Moldovan officials admitting the place hasn't had a monk in it for more than a hundred years. No one believes the story anyway—Moscow hasn't even repeated the claim."

"Now they're hammering on a so-called invasion of Moldova," Baxter said.

Depends on your definition of invasion, Chance thought. He leaned back in his office chair. It was 7:00 P.M. and his secretary had gone home. She could have brought his nicotine gum, dammit. "Ma'am, as you know, Moldova is not a member of NATO. The latest statement from the Kremlin reminds us that Russia is their ally."

"Moldova's officially neutral," Carney said.

"You can be neutral and still have allies who agree to protect you," Chance said, running a hand over his unshaven jaw. "Russia can claim that it's bound to retaliate militarily against anyone invading that country. They can call our operation an invasion."

"It was *not* an invasion," McCallister said, "but it did break international law. There's going to be a condemnation from the Security Council."

"The hostages make it special circumstances," Baxter asserted, remembering to add, "Ma'am."

"Chance, what do you mean by retaliation?" Carney asked. "What they've already done? Or something more?"

"Using their logic," Chance said, "they can rationalize both the initial strike at the S-7 orbcraft and a follow-up. There could be another attack."

"That would be an act of war against the United States," the Secretary of State said, flapping a hand dismissively. "Not likely to happen."

"It already has," Chance said. "With the first missile. They hoped to get away with it. An orbcraft blows up and no one knows why. But they didn't pull that off. Now they want cover, in case they feel like they need to follow through."

"Suppositions," Winch snorted.

"If we don't speak out proactively," Chance said, "they may use our silence as their cue to take out the S-7." Something popped up in the urgent messages window on his hand-screen. "One quick moment, folks, I've got something coming in from the Russia team. It's urgent. Could be relevant."

When he saw what it was, he rocked back in his chair.

Well, this ought to make the point.

Chance took a deep breath, and said, "Ah, it seems like a TiL survivor managed to get some footage of our troops breaking into the monastery. There were recognizable faces, and recognizable uniforms."

"Was someone going to tell me this?" Winch growled.

"Just this moment learned about it, sir," Chance said. "It'll be all over the net in minutes. What's more, some trucker in the area got a shot of the S-7 taking off. You can't see it very well—but clear enough. They're going to flood worldwide media with this stuff."

"That's it," Baxter said. "We need to get ahead of them and make a statement. We need to spill our guts."

The Secretary of State closed her eyes, shook her head just once. Then she sighed.

"Yeah. I guess we do. I'll look into declassification."

* * *

We have to do this fast, Burkett told himself, *but we also have to do it right*. And no mistakes. A mistake out here could end their lives in a hot minute.

It'd be a cold minute now. Night had swept over this side of the Earth, its darkness spangled by city lights. Their biosuits were working hard to keep them warm in the extreme frigidity of space. The moon was a large gray ball scored by meteor hits, and the Earth was a cobalt sphere, so close he couldn't see the whole of this hemisphere.

Restoring the maneuvering jets was vital, even in a jury-rigged way. Without them, they wouldn't be able to maneuver in orbit, and he had no confidence in a rescue anytime soon. Even with the President's approval, it would take time to get it organized. This wasn't like sending a Coast Guard chopper to a sinking yacht.

We've got to help ourselves.

They were on their second burn-feed replacement, and it had been hard work getting it where it needed to be, because they'd had to walk most of the way. There was only one airlock, at the forward end of the vessel. Linda had been able to float along for the transmitter power job, but this time they had to move into areas of the hull with few or no handholds. And the two of them drifting along with the tethered equipment would probably have tangled.

So, they had to walk along the hull—sticking out sideways relative to the Earth—magnetizing their boots to do it. The strong, electrically generated magnetic field that held them to the S-7 used up suit energy a bit too fast for his liking.

Burkett held down the burn-feed unit while she welded it in place with the squeeze-metal tube. Both of them were squatting beside the unit. He could hear her hard breathing over his headset. The unit was an ugly mass of equipment that was going to stick up from the hull.

What would happen when they hit atmosphere, going home? Would these units sticking up from the hull affect their aerodynamics? Would the heat from the atmospheric friction boil the fuel passing through them? His early training in engineering suggested that they *might* make it intact, for one trip. No way to be sure.

"*Progress, Lieutenant Burkett?*" Sergeant Lang asked over the headset.

"One more after this."

"*How's oxy and power?*"

"We'll get it done, but it's got to be quick."

From time to time, the temperature in Burkett's biosuit would drop for a moment or two—not all the way to the cold of space, but enough that he could feel its chill probing for him. Then the warming mechanism would catch up again. He glanced at his indicators. The suit's power read 45%. Not quite half.

"We need to do the next one faster, Sergeant... if we can still do it right."

"*How come they didn't bring more of these units along?*" Strickland asked.

"They didn't count on missile strikes," he replied, then added, "Keep the talk to necessities." More talk meant more oxygen use. The biosuit could electrolytically split their exhaled carbon dioxide to make oxygen—but that only provided a small part of what they needed.

Strickland understood and gave a small salute with her gloved hand to acknowledge the order.

Outside the biosuit, it was 455 degrees below zero, Fahrenheit. Inside, it was getting steamy from his body heat and the suit's effort to stave off the external cold. When it was too hot inside, the suit stopped heating a little, and the chill would seep in once more and make itself briefly known.

Hello, astronaut. It's me again.

Just a reminder: I'll get you eventually.

The chemical weld set quickly.

"*Ready for splice pipe*," Strickland said. In response, Burkett tugged a bag closer, drew out the part, and handed it over. She wrestled it into place and welded its joins. Then she stood up, and he could see her nod inside the transparent helmet. Done.

He pointed toward the aft, blackened by missile blast, and they started off, clumping along the hull on their magnetic boots. Burkett towed a floating unit and Strickland towed tools. Their breathing was loud in the helmets. Burkett looked at his HUD display. The power level in his biosuit was at thirty percent.

"Sergeant, what's your power level?"

"*Thirty-three… no, thirty-one percent.*"

Jesus.

"Let's get this done and get back." Only, they couldn't do it hastily. If they did, every life on the S-7 could be lost. The squad needed these maneuvering jets. Desperately. But had to do it right.

What was the Delta Force saying?

Slow is smooth and smooth is faster.

They reached the blackened hull under the slightly bent stabilizer fin. There was the gnarled, curved panel where the oxy-methane feed had leaked off into space. The feed to aft had been shut down. Once the repairs were in place, it could be restarted and they could burn fuel for maneuvering jets, which was critical for navigation.

Twenty-one percent power, and they'd reached the end of their tethers. If he had more oxygen, he'd have made a joke about that.

"When we're done, go back via SAFER," Burkett said.

"*Sir,*" she replied in the affirmative.

Strickland knelt beside the gnarl and used her powered gloves to pull away a broken panel, carefully tossing it clear. It spun away into space. More debris.

Focus on now, Burkett, he told himself. A thought struck him. "Turn off boot magnetism. I'll keep mine and hold you down for your work." That'd save power in her suit.

She gave a thumbs-up. Opening her wrist panel, she flicked a switch and floated upward, off the hull. He grabbed her SAFER and pressed her back down, held her with one hand, passing her the floating burn unit so she could weld it down.

Coolly she went to work as if she were in some loft on Earth working on an art project, without a care in the world.

His power was down to twenty-three percent. Could that be right?

Strickland hurriedly welded down the unit, then reached out for the piping. He had it ready, handed it over. She had practice now and quickly set it into place, linking the unit with the pipes in the exposed under section of hull.

Eighteen percent power.

It seemed to be draining faster now. If they didn't get through with this quickly and back to the airlock in time, they would most definitely freeze to death out here. They'd die maybe ten seconds after the power ran out on their biosuits.

She put weld over the joins. *"Fuel can flow now… Wait."* Strickland straightened partly up, to look over the whole set-up. *"One more thing."* She had missed a spot. If she didn't weld it firmly, the unit would break loose on re-entry.

Hurry up, he thought. His own power reading was eighteen percent.

"Tube's empty, sir. Need more."

He turned, fumbled in the floating bag.

Seventeen percent power.

Was that the tube? No, that was an electric wrench floating away to join the space debris. *Shit.*

There—a tube floating up out of the bag. He grabbed at it— and caught it between the tips of two fingers. Tugged it down, let go, and caught the spinning tube with his other hand.

His breathing loud in the helmet, sweat in his eyes, he handed it back to her, then used the internal auto swab to remove sweat from his face. It wiped it off, but sent droplets to float up and stick on the inside of his helmet. It accumulated there, and dripped. *That's just fucking great.*

Linda was working quickly, applying the weld.

He had a sudden picture in his mind of Nate, looking at him from inside the front door of the house. Just before he drove away for this mission.

That look in Nate's eyes...

"*Done*," she said.

Eleven percent biosuit power. It shouldn't be dropping that fast!

"Let's go!"

He switched off his boot's magnetism, pulled the SAFER controller out in front of him, turned and activated the jets. He started back up the fuselage. Nine percent power. The damned things should have been made for longer space walks.

Feels like oxy's getting a bit thin, too.

"Push past me, if I'm in the way, Linda. Go full power," he said, distantly noting he'd called her by her first name. Almost laughing aloud that some part of his mind was concerned about ranking protocol at a moment like this.

She was up beside him now, glancing his way to make sure he was all right as the jets on their backpacks whisked them on their way. They couldn't go too fast or they might overshoot, and not be able to backtrack in time.

He eased off on the jet—then saw that the process of controlling the SAFER was using power as fast as the boots had.

Six percent remaining.

It was a strangely slow trip to the airlock, but not so strange, since the orbcraft was moving in the same direction. He was breathing hard. Oxygen definitely getting low. Where was the airlock? Sweat was in his eyes now. He blinked it away and squinted.

"*Sir?*" Linda caught his arm, guided him closer to the hull—he'd been angling away. "*Best slow down so we don't overshoot...*"

He tapped the braking jets.

Two percent, and the cold was seeping in.

I told you. You can't win against the infinite darkness. The cold. I'm here to claim you, Burkett.

One percent. At least Linda had more charge. She could make it.

He heard a strange sound in the helmet. Some pump in the biosuit seemed to be jittering, struggling. The cold...

Ashley.

Ice formed on the interior of his helmet. He couldn't see.

Nate.

His head ached. There was a sound like a bell ringing, a crack in his helmet... air seeping out... a hissing...

"Sir?"

His helmet was gone and he sucked in warm air. He was in the airlock and Linda—sans helmet, her hair floating around her head—looked down at him, her eyes wide with concern. He realized she must've pulled him into the airlock.

"I'm okay, Sergeant," he said, between gasps. "And thank you."

"I see why you have done this, Krozkov," the President of Russia said. "Why you fired on the Americans without my permission."

"Anatoly—my old friend—I did it because I had no choice."

Anatoly Veronin looked at Krozkov across the table, almost without blinking. He wore an immaculately tailored suit of wine-colored silk and earthy-brown velour. He had a cap of dyed blond hair which should've been iron gray, papery but smooth skin specially treated to make it seem young, and icy blue eyes. He was nearly eighty-three.

They were in a side-room of Veronin's vast Kremlin office, an elegantly appointed "private conference chamber" where sometimes he entertained foreign diplomats, or certain high functionaries in the armed forces, or specially trained young ladies.

The two sat in plush red-velvet chairs at an antique rosewood table with silver filigree, under a gorgeous Tiffany lamp shedding soft purple and red light. The very finest vodka waited, chilled but untouched, in front of them. The glasses still glimmered with dew. There was a humidor on the table, and the room smelled of cigars, but Anatoly did not offer him one.

"You think I'm indecisive." President Veronin leaned back in his chair, his head cocked to one side, wagging a delicate finger at his spymaster. "I have been accused of it, and you have hinted of it."

"Never!"

"I know, Krozkov. You make this decisive move—you take your chance to do it—because you think the Assembly wants someone new, someone like *you*. Someone hasty in his judgments."

Krozkov heaved a sigh. "My old friend, you hurt me."

Of course, Krozkov thought, everyone knew that Anatoly Veronin had become afflicted with the fear of decision so common in old men. He had not always been indecisive.

"There was no time for consultation," Krozkov continued, his voice softly apologetic. "If I had not acted, Anatoly, they would have taken those four to the United States. Three men who are key to the new Euro-American plans to dominate space—and that opportunist Ildeva, who will probably sing them any song they wish to hear."

"Is he a mere opportunist? Then why did you make him instrumental in the operation?"

"Ildeva has been useful. I believed he would keep things under control, but he became complacent. He failed to send out patrols, so he was surprised by the Americans. It was necessary to take out the S-7 to prevent Ildeva from getting to the CIA interrogators." He paused, then added carefully, "There was a window of opportunity—they would have been out of range in a matter of minutes. It was a chance to cripple their Drop-Heavy program, and, I thought, we will expose what they have done. So if it comes out that it was our missile, we must accept it, and declare that we were merely retaliating for an ally. At the ally's request!"

"Did Moldova request it?"

Krozkov shrugged. "President Shimlov has agreed to say it was at his request."

"How much did you pay him? You squander so much money, Krozkov."

"He was expensive. Anatoly, if ever there was a time to trust me, this is it! I have the full report for you…" Kroskov drew out a hand-screen. The President of Russia took his own smaller screen from a coat pocket, held it out. Krozkov touched his unit to Veronin's, and the information, preset to go, was instantly transferred.

Veronin showed no interest in looking at the report. He stuck his screen back in his pocket.

"It has been recommended by my aides that I fire you, at least," he said. "Some say arrest you. You attacked a foreign vessel without my permission, behind my back. Like a sneak thief."

"There simply was no time. I took a chance on my career—and yes, on my safety, Anatoly. But you and I have known each other far in advance of our current status. You were like a big brother to me, guiding me through SVR." He sat up straight and said proudly, "I reported to you the *instant* it was done, knowing you would understand."

"Does it sound like I understand?" The President growled deep in his throat and waved a hand dismissively. "What is it you recommend? Do you care to *share* it with me?"

Krozkov offered up a smile. "Amusing, my President. I recommend that we finish what we started. We have new systems in orbit, and that is what they're there for. The American craft seems to be in dire straits—we might be able to make the next strike look like some internal accident, or a debris strike. The Chinese lost a ship to debris just two months ago."

"And this recommendation—who else has heard of it?"

"Only my own people, in my department. I discussed possibilities with them."

"So—they will report it to their friends at the Assembly—"

"They never would do that, Anatoly! They know I would arrest them as traitors."

"They would and they *do* report… to certain people. I suspect you know that—and you allow it because sometimes leaks are to your benefit. The Assembly knows about the plan, and if I say I cannot agree to it, they will say I am indecisive. They will ignore the fact that 'no' is a decision! All of this is what you want.

"Well—I shall surprise you by acceding to your recommendation. Perhaps I am foolish, but I have no desire for Ildeva to spout to the world. But you must consult me every step of the way!"

"Of course, Anatoly. Always!"

"Always?" Veronin shook his head and gave a soft laugh. "Drink your vodka."

TWELVE

Burkett woke with a start. Someone had tapped his arm.
"What is it?"

"Susan's on comms, sir," Lang said. She handed him a bulb of coffee.

"Thanks." He put the bulb to his mouth, sucked coffee. With his left hand he unclipped his seat belt and let himself float upward. He noticed Ildeva in close colloquy with Syrkin, chattering away in Bulgarian. How long had they been talking? What was Ildeva saying? He had the look of a man trying to convince another of something.

Syrkin looked skeptical, but was listening closely. Burkett tugged on a ceiling ring and floated toward the open flight deck. Inside he found Mayweather hunkered in midair, listening to Susan Prosser on the comms. Her voice was, as ever, a perfect blend of cool professionalism and maternal comfort.

"*Captain, your mission is no longer classified. As usual, the Russians have been spouting disinformation, sir. They're saying you've killed a couple dozen monks.*"

"Monks!"

"*The Secretary of State has refuted that, of course. The Russian Orthodox patriarch spoke out, too—probably before Veronin could stop him—and said there were no monks in that*" monastery. *The President authorized Secretary McCallister to give a press conference. She told the press the mission was about rescuing an American and two allies from a crime syndicate with Moscow contacts, and added that you've taken a prisoner who has vital information.*"

"Were our squad members *named*?"

"*The internet named some of you. Lieutenant Burkett was seen on a video taken by one of the gangsters. And Sergeant Lang and Private Dorman. The Russians made those images public and, you know, web trolls with facial recognition software...*"

"Hellfire," Mayweather muttered.

The revelation sent a shock through Burkett.

"Guess S-7's busted," Faraday said, sounding amused.

"*Yes, sir, Lieutenant,*" Prosser said. "*But the first polls show most Americans regard the squad as heroes.*"

Burkett didn't want to intrude his private concerns in a military exchange, but this was vital. His family could be targeted by Russian agents, Thieves in Law, or just some lunatic individual.

"Susan, this is Burkett. Can you ask Colonel Baxter to get my family to Base Three—to my quarters? If you explain to Ashley, she'll be happy to go where she and Nate are safer."

"*I'll sure pass on the request to Colonel Baxter. Oh—Captain Mayweather, we've got a request from General Carney to talk to his son.*"

"We haven't got a lot of battery power for this thing left," Mayweather said. "Mainly because no one in charge of Drop-Heavy, including Carney, thought we'd need solar power. Tell the General his son is on duty, he's busy, he's fine."

Burkett winked at Faraday and Ike grinned back. It wasn't the first time Mayweather had blown off a general.

"How about a supply ship, Susan?" Mayweather asked.

"*We haven't got approval for the launch, Captain. There's a chance that you'll be fired on again. The Russians are stonewalling the UN. There are reports that Veronin is suffering 'intermittent cognitive decline.' If that's true, he's unpredictable. The President is afraid we'd lose two vessels instead of one. It's in discussion."*

"Discussion? We have twelve hours of oxygen left!"

"God. Um—I'll report that. Do you have a full written report you can scan to us, sir?"

"It's ready to go right now, I'll send it. Anything else vital?"

"Not yet, Captain."

"The report's coming—then comms are only for urgent advisements."

"Yes, sir. We're all praying and keeping you in our good thoughts, sir."

"Tell our families we're okay—and we're coming home. We'll get back one way or another."

"Yes, sir."

"Thanks for the update."

He waved at Prosser, who cut the connection.

"Well, that's a kick in the ass," he said. "Now the mission's public knowledge."

Burkett nodded, frowning. They had his picture from St. Basil's. He was still reeling from that—knowing it wouldn't be hard to find out where he lived, and who his family were.

Mayweather handed Strickland a flash drive. "Here's my written report. Send it." He turned to Burkett. "Lieutenant, tell everyone we're going to try to connect with that Japanese space station. I found the coordinates and all the data that's available. We'll see what we can scrounge there—there's only so much they could have taken with them."

"Yes sir."

Mayweather turned back to the copilot. "Sergeant—pull up an expert system to keep eyes on radar and lidar when you step away from the scanner. They need to be constantly monitored for bogeys. Seems we could be coming under fire again…"

* * *

"What is the expression?" Dupon said, scowling. "Out of the firepan into the flames?"

"Frying pan, actually," Dhariwal said. "Which does describe our circumstances."

Rodriguez had just given the three scientists a sketchy report on the situation. Dupon had pointed out to the medic that small wobbly globes of water were floating around, and Rodriguez muttered something about a cracked pipe caused by the missile strike.

He went off to find the leak.

"I wish they'd give us some work to do," Magonier said.

"I agree, Jacques," Dhariwal said. He looked up at a wobbly translucent globe floating past. "I wonder if that's potable. I'd like to suck it right down. I'm thirsty again."

"What's to lose? It could be that we are doomed," Dupon said, seeming to enjoy making the gloomy declaration. "Some political entanglement, some stupid policy aufschub, preventing rescue. Less than a day of oxygen. Water leaking from damaged pipes. The possibility of another attack."

"You had me at the short oxygen," Dhariwal said. "Don't like the sound of that. You two have any practical engineering these Rangers could use?"

"*Pah*, I'm a neurologist!" Dupon said.

"I have some, perhaps," Magonier said. "But—to apply here?"

"We could help some way," Dhariwal insisted. "Here comes Burkett." He gestured. "Lieutenant?"

"Yes, Professor?" Burkett arrested his motion by grabbing a ceiling ring nearby.

"Can we help with something? We're going stir crazy, and my mama didn't raise no slackers."

Burkett grinned. "Good for your mama. Lemuel taught you how to move around the cabin?"

"Moderately well. I have only one bruise."

"Only one is good." He waved Lemuel Dorman over. "Private, get these fellas some air cleaners. They can go after the vagrant water, and anything else they can find floating around that shouldn't be. After that, if they still want to help, you see what can be found for them."

"Yes sir."

"I will stay here," Dupon said, pouting. "My leg."

"These air cleaners," Dhariwal said, struck by a thought. "They use suction, yes?"

"Yep, just a small, specialized vacuum cleaner."

"Couldn't they kind of pull you around with the suction?"

"Just a little," Dorman said. "That'd use up too much power anyway."

"Ah well. I thought I might be jet propelled." Dhariwal unbuckled and floated upward. "Let's see what we can do."

Sgt. Megan Lang was worried about Alexi Syrkin. He was starting to move around the cabin, insisting he was well enough, but when he went to the head—the space toilet was a little booth not quite as big as the restroom on a passenger jet—she heard him talking to himself.

She was passing by on the way to the tiny exercise space in the biosuit compartment. Syrkin was alone, talking in Bulgarian, then English.

"I won't forget what you did, Olek," he muttered. "You were a hero. I won't let them forget."

Worried to hear Syrkin talking to a dead man, Lang went on to the biosuit locker. Most of the space in the locker was taken up by the rack of suits, but there was a small area at the end with grab bars set up on either side. She wedged herself into the space, took hold of the steel bars, pressed her back against the bulkhead and extended her legs to the opposite wall. She did leg pumps, hard, against the opposite bulkhead. There were a lot of exercises that could be carried out in the little booth, and it smelled strongly of sweat. Their training taught them that

exercise is vital to an astronaut, partly because of "fluid shift"—
without normal gravity, the body's fluids tended to concentrate
in the upper part of the torso. Not good for the legs. And sinus
congestion was a big problem after a couple of days. Soon they'd
be taking decongestants, for as long as they lasted.

Dabiri came into the locker, pulling himself along by the top
of the rack. "I thought we weren't supposed to exercise. Oxy
conservation."

"All I'm doing is some compression to balance blood flow.
Captain says it's allowed—for a minute."

"Me next, me next," he said. "My head's filling up with gunk."

"Your head is always filled up with gunk," she said, puffing,
reaching up to press on the overhead with her hands, her tiptoes
on the deck.

"And you always have something nice to say to me," Dabiri
said, looking over the biosuits. "I need to figure out if one of
these things will fit me."

"You still got that…" Lang paused to take a breath. "…that
Talos suit?"

"Aft storage, yeah, but it doesn't pressurize. Seems like we
should be wearing these things already. We get hit again…"

"They're easier than the old spacesuits, but not…" She took
a breath. "…not much fun to wear long-term." She paused to
wipe sweat from her forehead with one hand, the other keeping
her from floating up and knocking her head on the overhead.
"Biosuits are clumsy inside the vessel."

Tafir nodded. He cleared his throat. "We get down intact, you
want to catch some dinner with me at Juji's?"

"All the way to Phoenix?"

"Wherever you want."

"Fourth time you asked me out and I always say no."

"I figure it's because my physical beauty is intimidating,"
Tafir said, making his face comically sympathetic to her plight.
"But… you're the most badass woman in the Rangers, so I got
to keep asking."

She shook her head. "It's crazy to date another Ranger. Also, who asks their sergeant for a date?"

"You're the only sergeant I'd ask, I promise you," he protested. "Anyway, I'm about to get my stripes, Burkett tells me."

"Congrats." Dabiri was good looking and occasionally almost as funny as he imagined himself to be, but she wasn't going to date a Ranger, nor would she date a Muslim—not at this time in her life. She was only dating marriageable men, and for her, that meant someone of her own faith.

She had a long-term plan. Three more years of service in the Rangers, then transfer to non-combat or leave the military; find a Christian husband she could truly love, get married and have kids. She loved kids, and she wanted kids. Not terribly badass but it's what she'd wanted all her life.

Lang had grown up on a Seminole reservation in Florida near Lake Okeechobee, and her father had been a drunk—until he found Jesus. Everything had changed, then. He got sober and he went from being a problem to being her best friend and a good father. That was it for Megan—she and her mom and her sister took up Christianity in a big way. She knew a lot of prejudiced, cold-hearted people who called themselves Christians, but Megan knew real Christians, too.

Her best friend in college, Cindy, was a Buddhist, and Megan went to her same-sex wedding. Her close friend Ali was a Muslim, but Megan was determined to marry another Christian.

Nothing was going to knock Megan off course. That was the Rangers way. You choose a goal and you go for it till you get there. Why shouldn't it extend to everything you do?

It wasn't that she didn't trust Dabiri, either. She knew he was devoted to the band of brothers and sisters he fought alongside, whatever their religion. He was Muslim, but had no problem killing Jihadist terrorists—he regarded them as heretics. True, he wouldn't stand for people around him sneering at Islam. If they did, Dabiri walked right up to them and argued. It never came to blows.

"I know a great Mexican restaurant in Armstrong."

"Tell you what," she said. "I'm fine with Muslims—hell, you're like my brother, Tafir—but I only date Christians, because I don't date for fun. You convert to Christianity, and I'll go out with you."

"Whoa!" he laughed. "I'll have to get back to you on that."

She grinned. "Thought so. Hey, you'll make some Muslim girl a fine husband, big guy. Now get out of here, you're using up all the air in this little room."

He turned away, then turned back to say, "Hey, when I get married, I'll invite you to my Muslim wedding!"

"And I'll be there with bells on. Now out!"

He floated out of the locker, and she held onto the bars, but she didn't exercise. She prayed, quietly, to herself.

"Our Father who art in Heaven…" She said the Lord's Prayer and took a small towel from her pocket, wiped the sweat away, and left the locker. She had security watch.

In the main cabin she found Alexi Syrkin drifting near the ceiling, upside down, pulling himself along. It looked like something from a horror movie.

"You training?" she asked.

"Yeah, Sergeant, I am. I got to get back into moving in freefall. I used to be good at it." He did a tuck and roll, coming out in a standing position a foot off the deck.

"Might not be the best time now. We're running low on oxygen, and you've been injured," Megan said. "You got a pretty good knock in the head. Takes some time to—"

"I'm fine!" he snapped. His face was knotted with anger.

Lang was startled. "Not so sure you're fine," she said. "You look like a snapping turtle 'bout to take off somebody's foot. You need to get back to your seat, Specialist."

"No, it's not necessary."

"Wasn't asking, I was telling." She glanced at her watch. "See, we're getting set up to do a burn. The ship is going to jolt, so we're gonna feel some gees. We'll be doing significant linear acceleration. Meaning you need to be seated."

"When the Captain orders it—"

"*I'm* ordering it. Into your seat *now*, Syrkin."

He turned to glare at her, his face white with anger.

Okay, that's not good, Megan thought.

Then he let out a long breath, and seemed to relax a little, looking away.

"Fine… *Sergeant*. I'll be good. I'll be strapped down."

Megan frowned. *What did he mean by that?* She watched him make his way to his seat next to Ildeva. The gang boss called to her.

"Missus Sergeant!" he said, giving her a "come here" with jerks of his head. *A charmer.* Lang tugged a ceiling ring, then pushed down close to Ildeva.

"What do you want?"

"Please, I go at toilet."

She winced and looked around for Rodriguez. This was one of his chores, but he was busy with Dupon, giving him some kind of injection in the lower right leg. Local anesthetic, probably. She let out a long breath.

"You know how to use the thing now, Ildeva?"

"The thing? Toilet? Yes."

"I'll take you over there."

"I can go, only me."

Buckling in, Syrkin chuckled. "Yeah, where's he going to escape to?"

"You're to be escorted anywhere you go on this vessel, Ildeva," Lang said. She unlocked his cuffs from the chair, then used one set to cuff his hands together, in front. "Let's go."

Thank God there's a door on that toilet, flimsy though it is.

Ildeva drifted up, almost hitting Syrkin in the head with his boot. Lang reached out, guided the gangster by the shoulder.

"I'll take you. Just relax and cooperate. If it looks like you're going to bump into anything, use your hands very gently to stop yourself. Easy with everything, in space." She grabbed a ceiling ring with one hand, with the other took his collar and pushed him gently toward the head. Slightly crooked in the air, his arms extended in front of him, he drifted that way and she moved ahead of him, braced herself on the wall by the head, and caught him by the shoulders.

"Look you," he said. "You don't belong in uniform, so pretty woman."

"Shut up and get in the booth. Grab the door handle and pull gently."

He did, the door came open and, using the back of his shoulders, Megan eased him inside. Every movement about the cabin had to be easy, not too much force, or you'd fly into something and rebound off something else.

Closing the door on Ildeva, she waited. A few minutes later there was a vacuum-cleaner sound. The thin folding door rattled as he tried to turn around to open it. Megan opened it for him and he came out too quickly, colliding with her, his forehead smacking her lower lip. She grabbed at a ceiling ring, arrested her momentum, and realized he was clutching at her with his hand.

"I can give better life, for real woman," he said squeezing her right breast with his manacled hands.

"What the *fuck*—" she snarled, giving him a gut punch that sent him wheezing back into the toilet. He bounced from the inner wall but she reached out with a foot and pushed him gently back in. "Grab the walls and hold on."

Rodriguez drifted up. "Sarge—you're punching my patient?"

"He grabbed my boob. And knocked me in the mouth with his head, and said stuff to me—" In fact, Megan wished she'd just slapped his hand away and told him off—but it had been a reflex.

"I saw it, Rod," Burkett said, coming up beside them. "I don't blame her. He grabbed her... her breast. He deserved that slug in the gut."

"Yes sir," Rod said, "I'm sure he did." The gangster was still wheezing. Rodriguez felt the pulse in Ildeva's neck. "But this man's got a bullet hole in him."

"She didn't hit him there. Anyhow, check him over. I'll talk to Sergeant Lang."

"Okay, Lieutenant. Hey Megan—Sergeant—I do understand."

She nodded and Rodriguez drew Ildeva away, dragging him through the air back to his seat. Ildeva was saying something in a hoarse voice, about Americans torturing prisoners. Lang turned to Burkett and was only a little surprised to see him grin at her.

"You should've hit him in the nuts."

"Good thought for next time, sir."

"What did he think he could accomplish by grabbing your…?"

"You can say *boob*, sir. He was just trying to demean me. It was a message. 'You're just one of my whores.' He feels weak and defeated now, so—he looks for a woman to take it out on."

"Sounds about right. Anyway, try not to rough him up if you can avoid it, but I'll tell you what, he's lucky we had orders to take him prisoner."

Megan nodded. Her breast actually hurt from Ildeva's grip, and she was sure he'd been violently abusing women all his adult life. She wished she'd been allowed to put a bullet in Ildeva's head herself, that dark morning at St. Basil's.

"Lieutenant—I'm kind of worried about Syrkin," she said. "He seems out of it. Talking to himself, and forgetting I outrank him, you know?"

"I'll clear him up on that. Right now, make sure everything and everyone's squared away and then buckle yourself in. We're gonna do a burn for that Japanese station in about five minutes."

THIRTEEN

Harley Spencer lived in the hills overlooking Alexandria, Virginia. Cherrywood was all exclusive estates surrounded by high stone walls. The streetlights on the walled, winding road were so many and so bright it hardly looked like nighttime when Chance drove through. But it would soon be 11:00 P.M.

As he pulled his barely street-legal 1975 Mustang GT up to the wrought-iron gates of Spencer's mansion, a security drone swooped low to check him out. Its cameras swiveled, taking in his face. It would already have his license plate. Harley Spencer, PhD, would have informed the house's security system that Chance was expected and, having confirmed his ID, the drone soared away and the gates rolled back.

Chance pulled around the circular brick driveway and parked in front of the neo-colonial entrance. It wasn't as well-lit as the street. He climbed out of the car—and was a little startled when a glowing face appeared in the shadows to one side. It floated toward him. He made out the rest of it after a moment: a CGI face atop a man-shaped robot.

Man-shaped from the waist up. Below that it was a V-shaped chassis of chromium on wheels. The face of a friendly and efficient middle-aged man smiled brightly at him, blue eyes crinkling, lips moving in perfect concert with the plummy voice coming out of its metal neck.

"Good evening, Mr. Chance!" it said, in an urbane masculine voice. "My name is Burgess. Mr. Spencer sent me to welcome you in."

"Good evening, Burgess," Chance said, feeling foolish, as he always did, talking to house robots.

"Come right this way, sir," the robot said. "You are expected."

Considering how difficult it was to get this meeting, Chance thought, *I sure as hell ought to be expected.*

Harley Spencer rarely left his house. He was agoraphobic and a night owl, given to insisting that he suffered from several chronic illnesses—which CIA evaluators deemed sheer hypochondria, part of a suite of "eccentricities."

Computer genius? Yes. Billionaire tech innovator with a love for the *idea* of space travel? Yes. Had he provided key technology, along with Griskin, for the S-series orbcrafts? Yes.

Could he help Chance save the S-7?

Maybe.

Chance followed the robot through the self-opening doors, down a marble hallway—the floor white marble, the walls red—to an elevator beside a staircase.

"You will need the elevator, sir. Mr. Spencer is underground."

"Naturally."

"If you say so, sir."

Chance stepped into the elevator, a box of glass and green steel, and rode two levels down.

The elevator opened onto a mahogany-lined hallway where a tall, gangly, stooped man in an ankle-length, sunset-colored dashiki paced up and down. Thirty-nine years old, Harley Spencer was round-cheeked despite his overall thinness. His short hair was bleached white, his nose a point in the midst of his face. He turned with a sudden jerk, seeming startled, his blue eyes wide, pallid face showing a sudden blush. He wasn't used to company.

"Chance?" he asked, licking his thick lips. He had a rather high voice, but Chance suspected that if Spencer were to relax, maybe take a tranq, his voice would lower an octave.

"I'm guessing you recognize me from the videophone, Harley. We've spoken on it a number of times. Is there somewhere secure we can sit down and talk?"

"Every inch of this property is as secure as I know how to make it." Spencer led the way down the hall to a double door of paneled wood, which slid aside as he approached.

"That was the realest semblance 'bot I've ever seen, Harley," Chance said. "From the waist up."

"Burgess is the latest, from my own developers. His model isn't yet released to the public."

Inside, Chance found himself blinking around at a big lozenge-shaped room, much of the wall space taken up by exquisitely high-resolution screens showing images of space. The biggest screen showed Earth from orbit, switching every few seconds to a different view from another satellite: Africa, Northern Asia, North America, the Pacific, India.

Another monitor provided nearly-real-time footage of a lander descending into the sublunar moon base. It switched to views of the four major space stations. Another featured views from James Webb II: planets, galaxies, nebulae. Yet other screens offered charts, and feeds from unmanned exploratory vehicles in the outer planets.

This room was Harley Spencer's voyeuristic space travel. Space by proxy. Spencer sat in a smart chair in front of a control panel and began waving his hands over the haptic controls.

"I'll pull up the latest on the orbcraft. Position, trajectory. Some imaging."

"You're tracking the S-7?" Chance asked, sinking into a swivel chair beside him.

"Oh yes. Everyone is now. Here you go…" A distant image of the S-7, shot from a satellite, appeared on one of the screens.

It looked motionless, but Chance knew it was whipping briskly along in orbit.

Harley shook his head. "It's amazing no one has the will to help them. I don't understand it."

"The Chinese and the Indians and the Japanese were ready to help till the Russians suggested that sending aid would be taking sides in a conflict. Now everyone is stalling, and the President is afraid of starting a war."

"History will despise them all if the Rangers die up there."

"I agree," Chance said. "You helped design that vessel, Harley. Ike Faraday and Linda Strickland, and to some extent Randall Mayweather, are experts on the orbcraft—but there are aspects that only a designer and hands-on engineer might know. You could help them yourself."

Harley frowned at an image of Saturn for a long moment, then nodded. "I have something in mind—something that could affect the geopolitical picture. Which might build support for a rescue. Suppose that we could confirm the launch-point of the missile that struck the S-7?"

"In a way that we could share with people? They'd be able to see for themselves?"

"That's the idea. See, the S-7 was outfitted with image-sensitive embeds on its hull. They're used to track space debris, mostly, but they could pick up a distant energy source like a missile. They wouldn't get it at the point of origin, but the record can be filtered through a computer model. We can project the probable point of origin."

"Some sort of algorithm?"

"Several, but yeah."

"I'm not sure that'd be considered evidence—it's extrapolating. Still, it'll help make the case. Any thoughts on extending their survival window?"

"Scavenging in orbit. There are space stations that aren't in use."

"They're already on that. How about the oxygen supply?"

Harley shook his head grimly. "Would be getting low, and the S-7 isn't equipped with water electrolysis to make oxygen. It just wasn't in the mission plan for a Drop-Heavy orbcraft to be in space for much more than the time it took it to get to and from Zero Point. We included extra oxygen in case of emergency, but not *enough* extra."

"It's too bad your team didn't design-in some kind of escape craft."

Harley shrugged. "We *had* a plan for that—me and Griskin. Drop pods. But it would've taken a long time to work them into the overall design, and Carney didn't want to wait. Nor did the CIA."

Chance grunted. When he had to, he kept his conscience buffered away, folded into some mental drawer. More than once he'd developed foreign assets who'd died in the field. Olek Syrkin was one more. Dead. Chance and his Slavic asset specialist Betsy Torrato had run Olek Syrkin, and they both knew it would be high risk. Every death of an asset bothered Chance. It was something he lived with.

The S-7, though, an orbcraft full of people, had been badly knocked about by a missile and now everyone aboard was at risk of an ugly death. That was harder to shoulder. Most of them were especially good people. Hell, they were heroes, and now Chance was hitting every beat trying to find some way to pull the S-7 out of the fire.

Chance's conscience wormed its way from the drawer and chewed at him. He'd been the guy who insisted the S-7 take the scientists and Ildeva all the way to Base Three. They might have assigned a couple of Rangers to take them in an LTV, through Ukraine, for pick-up in Odessa. But he'd nixed that plan.

If they hadn't had the prisoner and the three hostages along on the S-7, it was likely Krozkov wouldn't have fired on it.

I should have known.

Should've known Krozkov might try to shoot the craft down in orbit. He'd seen briefing papers on their new orbital battle stations. *Putative* battle stations, but it seemed likely that's what they were. He should have warned Mayweather. And now that the Russians seemed willing to start a world war in orbit, anything was possible.

"You going to talk to Griskin?" Harley asked. With a flick of a finger he ordered coffee.

"That's my next stop. Not looking forward to it." Harley Spencer was neurotic, but Chance liked him. Griskin, however— Darryl Griskin, CEO of InterplanetaryEx and the biggest contractor for the SubOrbital series, was a major pain in the ass. Compared to Griskin, General Carney was a creampuff.

"So, you are requesting an emergency resupply for the S-7, ma'am?" The reporter was a young, dark-haired man in a polo shirt and tan pants. He looked like a Native-American mix.

"I'm not requesting this," Ashley said firmly. "I'm demanding it." Ashley felt uneasy—not just at having her first press conference, but also because of what Colonel Baxter might think. This was likely to be picked up for national news. Baxter was a good man, and Ashley hated to go behind his back, but she couldn't bear it anymore.

She and Nate were standing outside in the dusk, facing down a phalanx of television cameras. They were posed in front of her house, Nate clutching her hand. She was wearing a dark blue business suit, which she hadn't worn in a long time. It was to look serious and a little official.

Nate was in shorts and a green *US Army Rangers* T-shirt that Colonel Baxter had given him. He gaped in awe at the television cameras. She wanted to tell him to close his mouth but decided against it. A drone camera shifted for a better angle overhead and Nate gawked up, blinking.

"My husband, and more than a dozen other brave Army Rangers, are being abandoned by the country they have risked their lives for over and over again," Ashley went on, her voice trembling only a little. "They're short on oxygen, they're in a damaged vessel, and they haven't got the fuel they need to land. Now, we have lots of spacecraft who could get it to them and only politics is delaying it. I'm asking that the President show just a little of the courage of any one of these men and women serving on the S-7."

"Ma'am, isn't there a risk of a rescue craft being shot down?" a middle-aged blond reporter asked. She wore a tight brown-leather skirt suit. "Isn't that what's causing the delay?"

Ashley spread her hands. "The Air Force has a spaceplane ready to go—and the crew is eager to take the risk. The Russians aren't likely to take a shot at them, too. They don't want a war. Let the Air Force do its job and rescue these American heroes! I've put up a petition online and last I looked it already had two hundred thousand signatures."

"Ma'am…"

On and on it went, for ten minutes more, before she put up her hands.

"That's all for now, thank you for coming."

She couldn't wait to get back in the house.

It was called N-22, in English parlance. N for Nihon, which is what the Japanese tended to call Japan.

Space station N-22 was shaped like a cross, three of the arms being cylinders, the fourth a boxy rectangle. Looking over Faraday's shoulder, Burkett noticed that one of the cylinders looked oddly dimpled, wrinkled in places. Mayweather had provided a report on the Japanese station that said the multilayered shielding outside the inflatable sections had failed when orbital debris—a large spear-like meter-length shard of titanium—slammed module four at a speed of 28,000 kilometers an hour.

The module deflated, killing two Japanese astronauts. Burkett felt a little sick, contemplating their death by decompression.

Though three modules were still perfectly intact, the station had been evacuated as the Japanese space bureau awaited approval for repair—or maybe for ditching it in the Pacific Ocean.

And thank God, Burkett thought. The Japanese hesitation meant that N-22 was available to loot. Too bad it didn't have fuel they could use.

Did Drop-Heavy have permission from the Japanese?

Right now, Burkett didn't care.

"First approach for semi-dock begins in thirty seconds," Faraday said.

"Better get into your tuxedo, Art," Mayweather said, coming to the hatch. Burkett turned away from the flight deck and made his way past Rodriguez, who was in close conversation with the three scientists.

"Rodriguez, take a seat. Everybody—strap in."

"Yes sir."

Burkett slung himself across the cabin to the biosuit locker, where Dabiri had already suited up.

"You ever wear the old pressure suits, Corporal?" Burkett asked as he worked his legs into a suit.

"No sir." Dabiri used a tool to seal the seams of the suit over Burkett's legs.

"It was like the thing was using you, instead of you using it," Burkett said. "Felt like you were in a medieval suit of armor compared to these."

"You wore medieval armor? You're even older than I thought, sir."

"You keep it up, I'm going to punch little holes in your biosuit," he said. Then he added, "How you holding up?"

"Good, Lieutenant. The usual weirdness in my sinuses, but the nausea is mostly gone. Glad to be going on this one with you."

"Linda's had more than her share of external radiation exposure, so you get to enjoy your share now, Tafir."

"I just like going outside, sir."

"Won't be outside long."

"Well, hell, then maybe I'll stay in here. Sir."

Burkett smiled. Tafir got away with jokes like that by using a very precise tone of facetiousness that sounded more self-deprecating than mocking.

"*Lieutenant?*" Mayweather called on the headset. "*Strickland checked the news for us up here—your wife just made an appearance on television, broadcast around the world. She had a press conference, and she has a big online petition going.*"

"What? I mean—" He felt blindsided. "A *press* conference?"

"*She called out the delays in sending the fuel we need. So, she demanded, by God, that the President grow a pair!*" Mayweather didn't sound as if he disagreed.

"Tell me she didn't say that, sir!"

"*Not in those words, but that was the impression. I'll bet Colonel Baxter's head is spinning.*"

"Holy crap," Dabiri said, listening in. "'Grow a pair!' That's great!"

Burkett had a carousel of conflicting reactions. Proud of her courage, happy she was trying to save his life, embarrassment, hope—and fear that it might make her someone's target. He took a deep breath.

"Let's get back on track, Tafir." There was an indescribable shift in the vessel around them as Faraday made fine adjustments, segueing into docking position. "Feels like we're almost ready. Get into your suit."

"Roger that, sir."

Still imagining Ashley standing in front of news cameras, snarling at the government, Burkett helped seal Tafir into the suit and fastened his helmet on for him. Dabiri reciprocated; they could put on their own helmets but this was faster.

Then they tugged their way to the airlock.

FOURTEEN

"Has Ildeva told you anything interesting, Syrkin?" Mayweather asked softly.

They'd happened to meet at the recycle chute, Syrkin and Mayweather tossing out their empty food packages after a skimpy meal.

"Only hinted, sir," Syrkin replied.

"I'm not sure you should be talking to him at all. I don't trust the bastard."

"Seems to keep him quiet, sir. Anyway—he said he'd tell me something surprising, soon. Lot of hints like that. I'd better keep at him."

"For now." Mayweather nodded. "Sounds like they're about ready to go EVA…" He drifted forward to the flight deck.

Relieved, Syrkin made his way to his seat and pulled down into it beside Ildeva, thinking that to satisfy the officers, he had better pretend Ildeva had made some tantalizing claim. Buckling in, he realized he was planning to lie to his CO. Which was surprising. Then again, it wasn't. Since Olek had been killed, he felt they were all strangers.

"Look at that bastard Carney, all chummy, gabbing with the Captain," Ildeva said.

Syrkin grunted. Second Lieutenant Carney was up at the flight deck, talking to Mayweather while Burkett and Dabiri went EVA. Smiling, nodding. Cozying up to the Captain. Maybe thinking ahead to the debriefing back on base. He had to explain shooting a CIA asset and he needed Mayweather on his side.

"I tell you, Alexi," Ildeva said in Bulgarian, "your brother was my close friend. And my second cousin. He was *family*."

"That's what you said, yeah." Syrkin squirmed a bit in his seat.

"Alexi—you know my childhood? My father—a drunk. My mother—always running off with some man. Can I blame my father for dropping her from a helicopter into the Black Sea? No. I learned from Papa, drunk or not. Because he was old-time Thieves. Started during Soviet Union, and he taught me: find men you can stand with, work with them as a team, to get what you *all* need from the rest of the world. You see? It's us against the rest of the world, Alexi. That is the hard truth."

Perhaps, Alexi thought. Perhaps it was indeed the truth. He wished they'd have let him go on EVA. Anything to get out of here. Have a change. But the others didn't seem to trust him. He'd gotten a knock on the head, so what? They'd all had concussions before. He was fine now. Mostly.

Alexi glanced at Ildeva. "I never heard anyone in my family mention you were a relative."

"Maybe your family doesn't like that connection," Ildeva replied. "They were too self-righteous, living in the land of the banking gangsters, to have anything to do with a real gangster, eh? But I tell you—the CIA bastards blackmailed Olek to betray me. It must have been that. Maybe they threatened your family. 'Do as we say, Olek, or we can make your family disappear.' You remember, back when they were running death squads in Central America?"

"That was under Reagan. Decades ago."

"You think they've changed? They were caught torturing people in the Iraq War! The CIA changes faces, but not methods, Alexi. They probably blackmailed him."

"They paid him."

"And so? Was that enough alone? No! Alexi—I saw him die in that cowardly attack. It was no accident. His blood is on their hands. They will never do more than slap this general's son on the wrist for his death."

"That much I can believe."

"And me—what will they do to *me*? His friend—his relative! They will torture me in a black site prison. Or leave me to choke for air on this rocket ship while they escape. They *are* going to run out of air, you know. So—maybe they will push me out an airlock."

Syrkin frowned. Was it possible? If it was a question of Ildeva's life and one of the others... maybe so.

His gaze fixed on Ken Carney, speaking so earnestly to Captain Mayweather...

The orbcraft maneuvered to within docking reach of the space station—but the S-7 wasn't designed for docking.

Drifting over the upper hull of the S-7, Tafir went ahead to the boxy module where the airlock was, using his SAFER to move toward the hatchway where normally a supply ship would dock. Burkett had a surge of dread as he floated over the hull. It was being in EVA, again. Adapting to psychological stress was part of being a Ranger, but almost freezing to death in space had affected him—another few seconds and he'd have been done for.

You think you're hard as nails and then, all of a sudden, that's right—you're human.

"*Lieutenant,*" Dabiri called over the headset. "*We brought those tools for nothing. The damn thing's unlocked!*"

Moving up behind Tafir, Burkett aimed his flashlight into the cup of the dock. The Corporal was turning a wheel—and the hatch swung gently, slowly open.

"*Okay to go in, Lieutenant?*"

"Yeah, but take it slow."

Dabiri pulled on the edges of the hatch and ascended into the airlock. When he was clear, Burkett followed, finding himself in a dark rectangular compartment of metal. A hatch was sealed in front of them. Instructions in Japanese ideograms clustered on plastic insets beside the interior hatch.

"*Not sure what button to push, Lieutenant, afraid I might hit 'eject' or something.*"

"Hold on," Burkett said, taking out an instrument shaped like an old-style smart phone. He held it up to the vertical row of Japanese instructions and tapped. Its small screen translated. "That one!" He hit the tab that translated as "Pressurize."

A yellow light flashed, and kept flashing. The hatch they'd come through closed, and twenty seconds later his HUD showed rising air pressure around his biosuit. He relaxed a bit. The pressure reached Earth normal and the yellow light was replaced by a steady green light.

Another tab, translated, said, "Entry on Green." Burkett pressed the tab and the interior hatch swung open—gently, slowly.

"Keep the helmets on, sir?" Dabiri asked.

"Better, yeah. We don't know if the air filled with fuel or something when the station was damaged. Could be toxic."

Dabiri pulled through the hatchway and Burkett followed. They were in Module Two now, which automatically lit up as they entered. It was a cylindrical room about twelve meters long, nine in diameter, with quilt-padded walls of white synthetic, neatly set off by lockers of equipment, food distribution drawers, emergency supply units, exterior view screens in place of windows, and tilt-out worktables, each marked with ideograms. The Japanese penchant for carefully designed living space was apparent.

Burkett's headset crackled. "*Lieutenant Burkett*," Strickland said, "*we received a communication from the Japanese government. They say given this emergency we can take possession of the station, and use whatever we want. Warned us to be careful of stability.*"

Faraday chimed in, "*I think they were trying to tell us, 'Don't accidentally knock the thing down into some dangerous orbit, you clumsy American bastards.'*"

"Least someone's being neighborly," Burkett said. "Good deal."

He noticed Dabiri looting a long chain of linked freeze-dried dinner packets from a locker.

"Twenty here," Tafir said. "Japanese freeze-dried yakisoba is gonna make a nice change from our so-called vegetable beef stew." He accordioned the chain up and tucked it into the satchel on the side of his suit.

"Corporal, if you're done raiding the fridge, we'll try module three."

"Yes sir."

Burkett led the way to module three, a room where padded walls curved down to a steel deck. There were eight microgravity bunks—basically Velcro-closed sleeping bags attached to the soft bulkhead—and a couple of media centers. At either end was a space toilet and sponge-off booth, set beside stretchable exercise cords. Several blank screens had probably shown scenes of Earth. All was carefully arranged. He saw no oxygen storage compartments, but the deck seemed to have lockers built into it. Turning on his magnetic boots, he let them pull him to the deck, then tugged at the deck inset rings.

There they were: tanks of oxygen mix.

"Guess we can't go into module four, sir," Dabiri said.

"It was ruptured, decompressed. So—nope. Too bad, it's their laboratory, might be useful stuff in there."

"This station has to have positional jets for restoring position, Lieutenant. Can we cadge some of their fuel?"

"Specs for the N-22 says its OP jets are hydrogen-oxygen. We can't use that stuff for S-7. Not our engine design. But we might have some other use for it…" Burkett had some ideas coming together in the back of his mind. Seeing what looked like a life support indicator panel, he walked over to it, having to tug a little too much to use his magnetic boots. He turned the magnetism down a bit.

"Let's see if the air is breathable in here, Tafir."

Burkett translated the input keys and selected "Cabin Air Quality."

Ideograms appeared on the small screen, translating to "Air Quality Optimal."

"Says it's breathable."

"Let me do this, sir."

"Corporal—" But Tafir had already unfastened his helmet. He lifted it off and took a deep breath.

"Smells like soy sauce. Makes me hungry."

They moved the oxygen-nitrogen mix cannisters to the S-7 by grouping chains of them on tethers. It would help—but they still had sixteen human beings sucking oxygen on board. There was enough in the extra tanks, Burkett figured, to give them an additional thirty-six hours, but they might well need more.

The next stage—he'd had to get it approved by Mayweather—was more complex, and arduous. Researching the specs for the N-22, Burkett found that it wasn't terribly difficult to detach the modules from the space station—it had been constructed in orbit, after all—but it required a team of four, working inside and outside.

"Which will be good," Mayweather said. "I have a feeling our people need more EVA time to be ready for anything."

Puzzling over the module detachment system, Burkett tried not to obsess on the possibility that Ashley might be targeted in some way. Would she be safer at Base Three? Suppose the base itself was targeted?

How far would the Russians go?

Focus on problems you can do something about.

Burkett and Corporal Dabiri worked inside the N-22, while Sgt. Des Andrews and Private Dorman worked outside. Activation of release clamps inside the N-22 had to be initiated at the same time as external levers and wheels were thrown. The modules could be disconnected, Burkett figured, without losing pressure, as long as the proper seals were activated.

Andrews and Dorman secured the module by tethers attached to upper hull hand-rings on the S-7. Modules two and three were detached and tethered to the rear of the orbcraft. Module one had a fuel tank attached to the bottom. They were able to release it and attach it to module two.

"Sir," Dabiri said as they worked, "if we can't use it as fuel, why do we want the oxy-hydrogen?"

"That's above your paygrade right now, Corporal," Burkett said, pretending to be snippy about it.

"Sir, I think you enjoy saying that stuff is above my paygrade."

"Roger that, Corporal Dabiri."

The project took three hours to organize and carry out, but when they were done they had not only the air in the modules, which could be compressed into tanks or breathed directly inside—they also had the volatile fuel mix.

"When we get back to base," Mayweather said, "I'm going to send the Japanese embassy a basket of flowers and a case of Kentucky's best bourbon."

Sitting at his desk, Chance puzzled over Staff Sergeant Rowell's clearance reports. Everything seemed fine. General Carney's staff sergeant had been a Green Beret, an expert commando, and had even instructed. Had won awards in Army hand-to-hand combat competitions, fought in Libya, received a silver star for bravery. Killed several terrorists barehanded in a night insertion to rescue prisoners.

Rowell's final combat mission was in Estonia. He'd gotten a bad wound, bum leg, physical rehab, desk job.

But Chance had been forced to ask twice to see the clearance checks. Why had they been held back? Maybe just an office snafu, after all. Or maybe there was something in the files he hadn't spotted. Something he wasn't *supposed* to see, tucked away in all the seemingly irrelevant data.

Estonia.

Chance reread the file on Rowell's combat time there. Winter, six years ago. Baltic Alliance base near the Baltic Sea. Eastern Estonians of Russian antecedents tried to break off, form a Russo-centric state, with arms and financial support from the Russian GRU. The Baltic Alliance had been unprepared, asked for American troops from their base in Finland just a hundred miles north.

An Army battalion was sent to Estonia, established a temporary base—which was overrun by separatists in a surprise attack. Rowell was wounded, taken prisoner. Three months later he was exchanged for two Russian "advisors."

The takeaway was that Rowell had been a prisoner of separatists run by Russian Intelligence. For three months. What had happened in those three months? Was he tortured? Recruited?

Could be there was nothing there. But…

Chance accessed Defense Intelligence Agency inter-agency files, and looked up Rowell's psychological assessment. Ayn Rand fan, it said. Very reserved, mistrustful of interviewer. Possible sociopathy but no clear diagnosis. "Could be simple battle fatigue." Subject's father had lost the family fortune, and Rowell resented it in a big way. He said his ambition, after he got out of the military, was to make another fortune. How? *"I'll find a way."*

Chance told his phone to get him General Carney's switchboard. A human-sounding but inhuman voice asked Chance for his name, clearance number, and who he wanted.

"Staff Sergeant Sheila Mendez."

A click, another, and a woman answered the phone. It was still daylight back in Colorado.

"*Sergeant Mendez.*"

"Sergeant, this is Sandy Chance at the Central Intelligence Agency. I have the clearance file you sent over on Staff Sergeant Rowell. Seems comprehensive. But listen—and don't take this personally, I am most definitely not blaming you, Sergeant— but General Carney told me you were sending me all this stuff previously. Months ago."

"I did. I put it in the pipeline. I sent the files."

"Never got to me. Thanks for resending them. But… what happened the first time?"

There was hesitation on the line. "Tempting to say it was a screw-up on your end, Mr. Chance, but we're having some… some glitches around here. Some computer issues. We had some kind of break-in on our SubOrbital files—had to plug that leak."

"I remember," Chance said. "Carney says it was just one of those 'we found a hole in our firewall before anyone else did' things. He claimed nothing got out."

"Didn't, as far as I know."

"You don't sound certain."

She chuckled dryly. "General Carney's my boss. I'm as certain as he wants me to be."

"I take it you think this was an internal issue—maybe someone's faulty IT work?"

"Could be. Maybe."

"Rowell involved in any of the security IT?"

Another hesitation. "Yes. We also had Pentagon security come in."

It would have been easy for Rowell to stop his files from going out to the CIA, then, Chance figured.

"You don't think anything could've gotten out through that hole—anything regarding the Drop-Heavy missions, Sergeant?"

"We don't know, Mr. Chance, but we did manage to keep everything buttoned up about the mission in... am I supposed to say? Everyone knows now. The mission in Moldova."

Or maybe, he thought, *it was kept need-to-know until someone got onto it just as the mission was ending.*

Right before a missile was launched.

"Sergeant—what's your impression of Staff Sergeant Rowell?"

"Efficient. Very loyal to the General. Loves opera. Got a medal or two in the field. Not much else I can tell you. Keeps to himself."

"You have my contact information. If there's anything else you think could be of interest to the agency, please send it on. Discreetly. I won't reveal my source."

"I'll... keep that in mind, Mr. Chance."

"Call me Sandy, if you want to. Thank you for your help."

Chance broke the connection. He drummed his fingers on his desk, looking out at the night. The circle of lights around the helipad.

"Get me Director Blackwell."

Blackwell answered. "Chance—what?" There was a yawn in her voice.

"Long day, I know. One thing more, ma'am."

"Well?" He heard ice clinking in a glass. Chance guessed she was in the back seat of the self-driving limo, relaxing on the way home.

"We have a seven-level risk at SubOrbital One. I want authorization to have someone followed, and monitored."

"You're saying there's a mole there?"

"I'm saying it's possible."

She made a *tsk* sound into the phone. "Come on, Chance. You've 'spotted moles' before and it turned out to be a mirage. General Carney won't like this if you're wrong."

"Yes ma'am, but we can't take the risk just to soothe the General. Especially now. We have sixteen lives—four of high intelligence value—targeted up there in orbit. We have the very real danger of…" He didn't want to sound melodramatic. But he almost said, *a world war.* "…of serious escalation, Madame Director."

Blackwell exhaled a long, annoyed outbreath that made the headset she'd be wearing hiss.

"All right. I'll authorize it. Tell your people to be as discreet as a nun dating a priest. You hear me?"

"Yes ma'am. I hear you."

Blackwell hung up and Chance made two quick, urgent phone calls.

FIFTEEN

It was no use at all.

Alexi Syrkin could not sleep. 2nd Lt. Kenneth Carney was snoring in his seat just two rows forward from Syrkin. Everyone but the watch was trying to sleep and the serrated sounds coming out of the murderer of his brother tormented Syrkin. Carney would be quiet for a moment, then a raw sawing noise would come right at Syrkin, right into his brain. He could feel the sound, in there. A cutting, icy feeling.

He sleeps well, Syrkin thought. *He feels no guilt, no remorse. Why should he worry? A general's son has nothing to fear.*

Close beside Syrkin, Ildeva slept, too, floating loosely in his bonds, his head tilted to one side, his mouth wide open. Snoring an octave lower. Ildeva's snoring didn't bother Alexi.

Syrkin could hear the reaction control system thrusters burning—a slight rumble transmitted through the hull from beneath the thruster. For this orbital shift, the RCS was under control of the ship's navigational computer. He unfastened his seat belt, the netting moved out of the way to let him float to where he could see through the open hatch to the flight deck.

Earth was crowding up, filling the windshield as if waiting to engulf them. The S-7 was moving into position to drop to Zero Point over Base One, where they were going to try a landing—

assuming the USAF spaceplane brought them a sufficiency of frozen methane-oxy fuel for braking. The emergency fuel transfer might work, if the spaceplane got here in time.

Lieutenant Carney would go cheerfully back to Earth, skate through the inquiry, and off to some cushy job set up by his father.

Ildeva was right. The Army would never convict Carney of anything. They'd go through the motions, give him a slap on the wrist, and send him back to shoring up his career.

There would be no justice for Olek Syrkin.

Perhaps it *was* the plan to kill Olek all along. The CIA didn't want to have to pay him off. Probably thought he'd outlived his usefulness. Syrkin wasn't sure—but it was possible, and what had he, Alexi Syrkin, done about any of this?

What had he done, in fact, to protect his brother? Olek—who'd stood up for Alexi more than once.

Nothing.

I should have thought about protecting Olek. I was trying to be in the forefront of the action for the sake of my own career. Prove that I deserve to be promoted once more. Which had gotten him clipped by a bullet, and while he was unconscious, Carney had murdered Olek.

I have to make up my mind, Syrkin thought. *What must I do, to make it right?*

Another cutting snore and Carney mumbling—laughing in his sleep.

Laughing! Something funny in your dream, Carney? Are you enjoying your little joke?

Suddenly he knew what he must do. He could not live with what had happened, not without justice—and the only justice for Olek would come from Alexi Syrkin.

It must be done quickly, before they were back on the ground. Before Carney could be protected.

Syrkin reached up, pulled at a ceiling ring, torqued his wrist, turning himself toward the aft and then tugged to head that way, floating over Megan Lang's head. She was deeply asleep. He could even see her rapid eye movement. But there was Lance Corporal Cha, on security watch, drifting over to him.

"Where you off to, Alexi? We're supposed to be seated and secured right now."

"There's no appreciable inertia from these little burns," Syrkin said, waving a hand dismissively. "I'm just going to the head."

"Make it quick."

"Who'd want to linger?"

"You got me there."

Cha turned away, pushed off the back of a chair to drift toward the flight deck. Syrkin waited to see if he'd turn around. He didn't.

Syrkin turned away, tugged toward the aft again. He saw everything so clearly. He could see a bit of food that had escaped from someone's careless mouth, floating like a miniature asteroid next to him. He could see pits and grain on it.

He could see every seam, every mark on the deck below. He could easily count the metal rings on a cable running along the ceiling of the passage to the rear as he headed to the big storage compartment. He smelled the stale air thick with the odors of sweat, rubber, piss, old food. With sixteen people aboard for so long, the air filter was overwhelmed.

Syrkin reached the hatch to aft storage, glanced over his shoulder. Corporal Cha wasn't in sight. Probably had taken his seat. So Syrkin opened the hatch, floated through, closed it, and pushed over to the weapons locker. Because they had an "enemy combatant" aboard, the metal cabinets were locked up. But Syrkin had a key.

He opened several lockers, then picked out a semi-automatic pistol, and a KRISS Vector submachine gun. Its recoil suppression would help in weightlessness. Strapping the SMG over one shoulder, he holstered the pistol, thinking that he had to formulate a clearer plan. Should he kill them all and then himself?

His head throbbed as he tried to think it out. Should he...

Should he kill Ken Carney and Mayweather—then use the weapons to hijack the S-7? Maybe they could still take fuel and he could force the pilots to fly the orbcraft to his own choice of destination.

Where?

There was a Russian base in the Crimea.

Why not? Why shouldn't he change sides? Hadn't his own side abandoned him and his brother? He was Slavic, and the Russians were Slavic. Ancient ties.

He was no longer a Ranger. That had ended when the Army had murdered Olek. Now, he was just a soldier without an allegiance—except to the dead. A soldier with a mission of his own.

General Carney glanced up from his paperwork. "What is it?"

Rowell smiled—just enough. "Sir, we're getting some inquiries from the CIA. Seems Agent Chance has some... personal issues?"

"Chance? I'm not surprised. Pain in the ass."

Rowell gently placed a folder on General Carney's desk, looking out the window behind Carney at the view of the mountains as he did so, as if the folder was of no real importance.

"Beautiful view today, sir."

"Is it?"

Rowell cleared his throat and tapped the folder. "This file, General, contains some personnel issues regarding Chance... some idea that he might be unstable. Prone to... imagining things?"

"Really?" General Carney blinked. "Of course, in a way it's his job to be paranoid."

"Is it, sir? At any rate... Director Blackwell seems to be wondering if you'd come across anything like this with him. You know—they do a general field inquiry about agents, every so often. If they're unstable, are they still loyal? That kind of thing."

"She told you all that?"

"Oh—her aide spoke to me. Thought it needed explaining, sir. Seems Chance drinks a bit too much when off duty. Can be fanatic when there's no cause... that kind of thing. I'm sure it's nothing to worry about."

"Yes, ah—as well to know about it. Thanks, Rowell. Maybe I should call the Director, ask about this..."

"Oh, she's incommunicado. Some kind of conference in Prague. So her secretary says."

"Okay, remind me later."

"Yes sir. I'll do that."

Rowell bustled out of the room, and Carney reached for the folder, looked the file over.

"Normal shenanigans. Not sure why they... not really procedure... fine." The General shrugged, tossed the folder aside, and went back to calculating his new property tax increase.

"Just promise me, no more press conferences, Ashley," Baxter pleaded.

"Talley, are we friends or not?" Ashley was sitting with her chair pulled up to Baxter's desk, her hands on the desktop. She'd dragged the chair up this close to make sure she had his attention.

Lieutenant Colonel Baxter winced, then forced a smile.

"Ashley, I'm your friend, my wife's your friend, my kids are your friends—mi casa, tu casa, the whole thing. Hell, I'd give you a big cash loan interest-free if you asked me for one. I'd cut your lawn while Art's off in space, I'd wash your car, and I'd protect you and Nate with my life. But—" He spread his hands in a shrug. "—I can't give you classified information."

"You can tell me just how much danger my husband is in."

"I can't tell you what we don't really know, but we're optimistic he's coming back." Ashley slapped both hands down on his desk and leaned even farther forward.

"Is there any real, ongoing effort to rescue the S-7?"

"Of course there is! I can't tell anybody what it is, but I *will* tell you that your husband and Captain Mayweather were able to get additional oxygen, thanks to the Japanese. The Rangers had to do it themselves—very resourceful, too. So that's encouraging."

"Is the President going to keep sitting on his hands?"

"I—well, I wouldn't describe it that way. He's my Commander-in-Chief. But, um—like I said, there is a plan. I've been given strict instructions not to discuss it with anyone. It's classified."

"You think I'd blab to the media?"

"No, *hell* no! But—we're under orders to maintain what the CIA calls 'strict informational hygiene' when something's classified at this level. Listen, Brenda's annoyed with me because I won't tell her anything else, either." He smiled ruefully. "If I did, she'd be on the phone telling you lickety-split. But if I can't tell my own wife, how am I going to—"

"Talley—there *has* to be more you can tell me! And don't blow smoke up my ass."

Lieutenant Colonel Baxter leaned back in his chair and frowned.

"Um—he's still in some danger, Ashley. They all are, and do *not* pass that on. We don't know if the Russians are gonna have another run at the S-7, but... we're not ruling it out."

Now it was Ashley's turn to lean back. She swallowed hard. There was a good chance Art was going to die up there. At her last meeting with him she'd been cold, angry. That would be his final memory of her.

"Any word on a resupply vessel?"

"I... you know what, I think you had an impact. Rumor has it, something's planned. Something Air Force—but do *not* quote me."

"Oh, thank God."

"I can't confirm or deny right now but... you seem to

have kicked the President's butt." She imagined kicking the President in the ass, and smiled.

"Can I… Can Susan arrange for them to talk to us?"

"Ah. I've been trying to get permission for that. If it's possible, we'll do 'er. They did get another five-megawatt battery from the Japanese station, to run their transmitter." He paused, then continued. "Let me ask you a question now. Is the base making you comfortable? How are you and Nate doing in Art's quarters?"

"We're fine. I didn't like being dragged over here, but we're comfortable."

"We didn't force you to come."

"You scared me into it. Same thing."

"Well. Anything I can do to make it better, make you more comfortable, say the word. My kids are planning to come over and play board games with Nate if he's up to it, tonight."

"Oh, he's counting on it. He's playing checkers with Sergeant Crossley right now." She suddenly felt drained. "Just… when you can tell me anything more?"

"When I can, I will, Ashley. I promise you."

She got up, nodded to him. She had a little glowing ball of hope in her now, after what he'd said about the Air Force, but there was still a good chance Art wouldn't ever come home.

Ashley went out the door, feeling sickeningly helpless.

Never mind, she told herself. Bearing feelings like that was part of being married to a Ranger.

Syrkin slung the submachine gun over his head and neck so it dangled behind him. The pistol was tucked in his waistband at the small of his back. He hid two clips for each weapon inside his shirt. A combat knife was strapped to his ankle. He thought about a Kevlar vest, but it would bulge under his shirt. He didn't want anyone to wonder about him till he was ready.

Syrkin quietly closed the aft storage compartment behind

him and pushed forward, down the hall toward the crew cabin. His heart was thudding; his mouth was dry; his head throbbed, but he felt strangely euphoric, too.

The orbcraft burned a couple of attitude control thrusters, adjusting course, and he felt the rumbling when he put his hands on the bulkhead as he stopped at the entrance to the crew cabin. With something approaching delight, Syrkin saw that the watch had been changed while he was gone.

Corporal Cha was back in his seat. And Lt. Ken Carney was floating in a corner, watching over the cabin, a pistol on his hip. His back was to Syrkin.

It's fated, Syrkin thought.

He pushed from the corner bulkhead toward the biosuit locker. He got through the door into the locker and heard no word from Carney. The man hadn't seen him. Syrkin chose a suit he thought would fit him—noticing that one of them was gone. They'd already put Dupon in one for his transfer to the spaceplane.

"Lieutenant Carney, sir!" Syrkin called out. "Could you look at this in the biosuit locker and tell me if it's…"

He let it hang there. Carney hesitated, probably because it was Alexi he was talking to. He hadn't tried to square things with Syrkin—Mayweather had told him to wait on that—and he wasn't sure how they stood.

After a moment, Carney drifted over to the door and looked in.

"Yes, Specialist Syrkin, what's the—?"

Carney's eyes went wide when he saw a pistol butt coming down.

Syrkin cracked him hard on the head, but precisely, as he'd been taught in SAMBO training. The blow pushed the limp, weightless lieutenant down toward the deck, but Syrkin caught him and tugged him back into the locker. He took Carney's sidearm and pushed it into the tool satchel on the belt of a biosuit. Then he shoved Carney into the deepest corner of the locker.

Carney still had handcuffs on his belt, issued when the prisoner was brought aboard. Syrkin used them to cuff the unconscious officer's hands behind his back, running the cuffs' chain around an exercise bar.

"I wish Olek could see this," Syrkin murmured.

He searched Carney's pockets, finally coming up with a handcuff key. Which should fit Ildeva's shackles.

Hiding the SMG behind a biosuit and tucking his pistol into his belt, under his shirt, Syrkin affected a look of boredom and slipped into the cabin.

The orbcraft braked, slowing in lower Earth orbit. Burkett, Mayweather, and Sergeant Lang got up, crowded around the flight deck as a USAF spaceplane approached with their additional fuel. Everyone in the cabin was eyeing the flight deck, trying to subdue their excitement at this key stage in their rescue.

Let them get the fuel, Syrkin thought as he floated over to his seat beside Ildeva. *I'll need it. Then I decide how to take over, and who to kill first.*

SIXTEEN

Sandy Chance found himself stuck watching Darryl Griskin get his full-body massage.

He was in Colorado at the combination residence and offices of the CEO of InterplanetaryEx, at 8:00 A.M. Chance was feeling his jet lag and craving a smoke as Griskin's hefty blond Swedish masseuse rubbed the tech tycoon's naked back and buttocks.

A very thin media center screen was tilted under the massage table so that Griskin could watch WorldTalk while he was getting his rubdown. The room smelled of cedar paneling and rubbing oils. It was a little too hot in here, and Chance was sitting on a wooden bench nearby. Griskin was swimmer's-body muscular—he had a very good trainer. He was uniformly tanned, and his hair — it wasn't really hair, but Chance had to look very, very closely to see that.

Each individual black synthetic hair had been implanted within each follicle, giving Griskin a cut that was immaculately shaped into a classic widow's peak. It didn't grow, it never needed to be cut, and it was one style, forever and ever. Chance stared at it in fascination.

Griskin was a fortyish good-looking man—or he would've been if not for the put-upon sulky look on his face that seemed as permanent as his hair.

"Sorry about the heat," Griskin muttered. "Part of the regimen. Look at that bastard, Chance. Senator Grosvenor. What a prick."

Chance leaned over a little to see the lowered screen. Grosvenor was gesturing wildly at the interviewer and monologuing in his North Carolina accent.

"*What we have here is a United States space vessel and its crew, and several important scientists—one of them an American* citizen—*being used as a foil, one of those robot ducks the hunters like to shoot at. Just being used as a damn political football!*"

"I don't disagree with him," Chance said.

"Not that part—that's just bombast," Griskin insisted. "He's going to repeat the litany any second now."

"*And why are they in this fix?*" Grosvenor demanded, scowling. "*Because people like Darryl Griskin didn't care! He contracted to build these SubOrbital craft and he tossed them off without thinking they might have some kind of emergency situation. No escape pods, not enough emergency oxygen—just a bad design all together. And how many billions of dollars did we pay him? It's obscene!*"

"There it is—you see?" Griskin said. "It's all my fault! They're blaming me! I did what the contract asked for. If you want to know why there weren't more safeguards, ask Carney. He didn't have the patience for it. Christ—blaming *me*? What grade-A bullshit. What's happening out there is the Russians' doing!"

Chance wiped sweat from his forehead. "Darryl, I came out here, in person as you insisted, flying all night, because you said you had a plan to help the S-7. There is a plan happening now, but if you—"

"Hilda!" Griskin barked, pushing up from the table. Startled, the big blond woman backed away.

"Yes, Mr. Griskin?"

Griskin sat up and ran a hand over his stiff synthetic hair.

"That's all, I'm good, I'm… leave us please."

"Yes, Mr. Griskin." She turned and hastened out as Griskin grabbed a towel to cover his privates.

"Chance, you've got to get them to call off this Air Force spaceplane resupply. They can't get enough fuel up to the S-7. I've got the biggest damn payload-carrier in the world. UltraLift is almost ready to go. I'm going to send along a camera crew when I rescue the S-7, make it a big media event. It'll take a little while to get the fuel payload aboard the rocket, do all the checks, find the right crew, but…"

"Darryl, here's the thing. We have a narrow window of time to do this. The Air Force spaceplane's already loaded and ready to go. It's just waiting for the President's green light, and for the S-7 to come around to optimum position to transfer the fuel. They even have a plan to take the injured scientist off. They've got room for one extra passenger."

"This is absurd! That vehicle does not dock. They're going to put an untrained man in a spacesuit and EVA him over?"

"It'll be almost no journey at all. A few meters."

"That's crazy."

"It's faster, and we need fast. They've replenished oxygen some, but… not enough. There are other reasons I'm not at liberty to mention."

"What, the Russians again?"

"Not at liberty, Darryl."

"You know what's going on here? I have enemies at SubOrbital command. Carney for one. He's trying to make me look bad with all this!"

"Did you have anything else to tell me, Darryl? I've got a stop at Base One before I go back…"

Fuming, Griskin ignored the question. "I'll tell you something else—the President is trying to bring me down. That's why he's not taking my calls, the son of a bitch! Investigate that, why don't you? Who's he working for, really?"

"I'll get on that, Darryl."

Chance got up and moved toward the door.

"Where the hell do you think you're going?"

"Too hot in here for me, so I'm getting out of the kitchen. I'll keep you in the loop as much as I can." Chance hurried out, figuring he'd go to his hotel and crash for a while before his meeting at SubOrbital One.

Or he'd try. He doubted he'd be able to sleep till the USAF spaceplane had reached the S-7.

"What the hell is that floating behind your spacecraft there, S-7?" the pilot of the spaceplane asked. *"Looks like you've got toilet paper stuck on your shoe."*

Burkett was listening to the radio comm on headset, as Faraday replied, "You're hilarious, Cranford. We got air in those things. Japanese inflatable modules. We were short on oxy mix. We can compress that stuff and breathe it in here or shift over there in an emergency."

"Sounds crazy to me but you're in a crazy fix. Prepare for semi-dock."

"We're ready when you are."

There was intricate tech talk as the two vessels jockeyed for semi-dock, with the spaceplane's lower-hull airlock aligned over the airlock on the rear upper hull of the S-7, but not hooked to it.

Syrkin's voice crackled over the headset.

"Lieutenant Burkett, sir, are we going to EVA to help transfer supplies?"

"Nope, too delicate," Burkett said. "Specialist robots bring them into the airlock. We already have Dupon in a biosuit. He's going out. Why you ask?"

"Thought I could be useful out there, sir."

Burkett didn't respond. There was something in Syrkin's voice that worried him. He wasn't sure what it was.

The indicators showed the air was sucked out of the airlock and stored away. A security camera showed the external hatch opening. The hull camera revealed a robot emerging from the spaceplane with a red methane-oxy fuel cannister in its pincers. It floated its payload silently and precisely into the airlock. Seven canisters would fit there, and a crate of compressed oxy-nitrogen mix. Probably enough air, certainly enough compressed methane to get them back to base.

The robot finished the transferal in less than five minutes, and then departed. A clank transmitted through the skin of the S-7 as the outer hatch closed and the indicator showed repressurization.

Des Andrews, Megan Lang, and Lemuel Dorman went to the airlock and began very carefully shepherding the fuel cannisters into storage—all but one. That one was moved to the internal fuel siphon assembly. The three Rangers hooked it up and the assembly slowly melted the methane and drew the vapor into the main fuel tank. Then the next cannister would be moved into place.

Faraday was already working with Strickland to plot their course to Base One. Burkett felt an uneasiness he couldn't trace. Something wasn't right. Then he watched as Strickland led Dupon to the airlock. The scientist wasn't as rational as scientists were supposed to be—he was too scared. His voice came over the headset.

"Are you sure the helmet will be airtight?"

"Absolutely sure, Mister Dupon. I double-checked."

"And I won't go floating off when... ah..."

"Soon as the hatch opens the robot will pick you up, gently as a baby, and carry you into the other ship. I just wish they had room for our other guests." She guided Dupon through the little maintenance hatch. Complaining in French, he went up the ladder—no effort in weightlessness—and she followed to make sure he was squared away. Two minutes later she was back on the cabin deck.

"*Ready as he'll ever be, Lieutenant.*"

Burkett turned to Faraday. "Airlock depressurized? Air Force robot ready?"

"Cranford says it's *go*."

"Open the hatch. Let's get this done."

The noise of the servos whined softly through the craft.

"*Mon Dieu—what is that thing!*" Dupon said in the headset.

"You were told about the robot," Burkett replied gently. "Just close your eyes and let it pick you up. I've had the experience, they're gentler than people are."

Dupon moaned.

Faraday said, "It's got him… heading back to spaceplane… right into the airlock. Airlock closing."

Still uneasy, Burkett turned and glanced around the cabin. There were empty seats. Carney was gone—was he in the head? And two other seats were empty.

Syrkin and Ildeva.

"Cha! Who's on security?"

Cha looked up from his seat. "Lieutenant Carney took the watch after me, sir."

Burkett spoke into his headset. "Syrkin! Where are you? Where's Ildeva?"

"*He's in the head, sir,*" Syrkin responded. "*I was checking on the biosuits. Lieutenant Carney had a question about them. I, ah…*"

"Carney, get back out here with Ildeva!"

"*He took off his headset to try on a helmet, sir.*"

"Bunch of goddamn kids," Burkett growled. "Send him out here, and if the gangster is in the head, tell him to save some for later and get back to his seat!"

"*Yes sir!*"

Burkett glared toward the door to the biosuit locker.

No one came out.

"Cha—go see what the hell the hold-up is! Check the head!"

"Yes sir!" Cha unbuckled and, in his hurry, pushed up a little too hard, clunking his head on the steel ceiling. Swearing softly, he tugged a ring to go toward the head, next door to the biosuit locker. Burkett turned back to the flight deck to confirm that Dupon was safely stowed on the spaceplane.

"That payload secured over there, Ike?"

"Yes sir. He's in his seat."

"Fuel in the line?"

"It is, sir. Correct pressure. Doesn't seem to be leaking."

"Good, back off the spaceplane, say hasta la vista, and set a course for Zero Point over Base One."

"Already got the course, sir. Hasta la vista it is."

SEVENTEEN

Harley Spencer was in his basement room, with big swathes of nearby space on screens around him. Tonight, however, he ignored the solar system—except for the part immediately around the planet Earth.

He was absorbed with the task he'd been working on since Chance had asked him for help. Harley was carefully collating the courses of Russian orbital assets—provided by the National Geospatial-Intelligence Agency—with his parallel logarithmic and spatial-geometry calculations for missile-launch origination.

On the stainless steel table next to him were three empty food trays, neatly stacked, and seven empty cans of energy drink arranged into a shape roughly like a rocket. His hands were shaking a little as he clicked "render code." The computer purred, and he studied the results—the orbital tracery on the sky chart, a readout specifying origination of the tracked object, and the end of its trajectory.

Harley sat back in his chair and stared at the screen.

This couldn't be right. If the CIA knew about this, Chance would have told him. He trusted Agent Chance. There would be no reason for him to have held back, and the CIA agent would be in the loop with the Defense Intelligence Agency and the US Space Command.

If they knew, he'd know.

Spencer shook his head in amazement. "They missed it," he muttered. "And I found it."

He ran the figures again. Same result.

Not only had the Russians fired a missile at the S-7—he had been able to trace the missile path back to their middle-orbit so-called "observation station"—but their supposedly geosynchronous station had moved out of its fixed position over Russia. It had moved to an orbit above Base One. Meaning the Russians knew about Base One—knew its relationship to the S-7.

They must have been planning to fire on the S-7 again when it reached Zero Point. Otherwise, why move to that position?

Harley had done some online research and found the shifted satellite—actually a disguised battle station—listed as a Sat-12008-N, named "Gogol-1." There were no indications it was armed, but it was as big as any space station. Room for armaments—and personnel.

All right then. He had to report this to Carney first, then Chance, then the press. The world needed to know. It needed to start watching this satellite.

"Get me General Carney's office on the line," he told his interface. Not just anyone could even get through to Base One, but Harley Spencer had helped design the facility. He maintained a great deal of clearance, and had been in many video meetings with the General.

Carney's office line rang twice.

"*General Carney's office.*" The voice was officious.

"This is Harley Spencer. Clearance four for Base One." Meaning he'd been the fourth person cleared, back before the base was built. That should impress this staff underling. He waited while a computer verified his voice print.

"*Yes sir. He's not in right now. Can I give him a message?*"

"This is urgent. Can you get him on the line? Put out a call for him or something?"

"*No sir, I'm under orders not to disturb him just now.*"

"Who are you, please?"

"*Staff Sergeant Rowell, sir.*" If he was Carney's staff sergeant, he must have proper clearance. Just tell him, then.

"Well, Staff Sergeant Rowell, please inform the General that I have evidence that a Russian orbital battle station has moved itself directly over Base One. This battle station is the source of the missile that struck S-7. Not only is it almost certainly planning to hit the orbcraft again, it might well attack Base One itself."

"*Are you quite sure of this?*"

"I am. There are other Russian satellites making anomalous orbital shifts," Harley continued. "They're planning something. They're lining up as if they're about to make some highly coordinated moves. They might be EMP pulse attacks, or... I'm not sure, but it's bad, Rowell."

There was a pause. Harley could hear his own tinnitus.

"*Are you at home, sir?*"

"What's the relevance of that?" Harley replied. "Yes, I'm at home, but he can call me anywhere."

"*I see, sir. I'll get in touch with him. I'm sure he'll get back to you as soon as possible.*"

"Make it quick." He cut the connection, then told the computer to get Sandy Chance on the line.

"*This is Agent Chance's office. Please leave a message.*"

Shit, voicemail. "Chance, this is Harley Spencer, and uh..." Wait, was he cleared with the CIA? It wasn't the same as the Drop-Heavy program clearance. He had some national intel clearance, but not all the way up. How would the CIA react if he started babbling secrets over the phone? "Anyway, uh—call me back. Quick. I have something urgent. Very, very urgent."

He cut the line and began to chew on the knuckle of an index finger, an old habit he thought he had broken.

Chewing on the knuckle wasn't enough. Harley stood up and paced back and forth in the small space beside his desk. Should he call the press now? No, that would be horrible protocol.

He had to tell the authorities—and the right authorities were Carney and Chance. Didn't he have a name at the Defense Intelligence Agency? What file would it be on? He wasn't sure.

"Screw this." He decided to call Chance and just leave it on his machine. Let the CIA charge him if they wanted. He told the computer to give him Sandy Chance's office again. It rang once, twice—and then stopped.

The computer went dark.

Then the room went dark.

He heard the door open—it did it automatically, with battery power, when there was a power failure.

"What the hell! Burgess!"

The house robot rolled silently in. A small lamp on his chest lit up so that he provided the only light in the room. "There appears to be a power outage, Mr. Spencer."

"No kidding! Fix it!"

"I have tried to do so, Mr. Spencer. The power reset is not responding."

"We have backup power. We have huge batteries! We have generators!"

"Yes sir, but all activated by separate… control… units… which—" Burgess broke off. His holographic forehead furrowed in puzzlement. "Apologies. Seems to be… sort of cyber-intrusion… which bores into systems… Deep Bore. It's… attacked me by wi-fi. All of our systems going down one by one… Cell phone communications down…

"It's destroyed your car's… systems… I think I can… protect the… car, but… They're attacking your… recognition…"

"*Who?* Who's doing this, Burgess?"

"Unknown, Mis… ter…"

That's all Burgess managed. He fell silent, and the light went out on his chest. Feeling his way, Harley found his desk chair and slumped in it.

Breathing hard, Harley Spencer sat in the darkness for what seemed like a long time. Clearly, this was something he couldn't fix himself. Not here. Deep Bore cyberattacks damaged all RAM, all data, all backup, and they did it so seriously, systems couldn't be restored. They could only be replaced.

But he had to tell the CIA what he'd learned, and it seemed he had to do it in person. That would mean leaving the building. On his own. Without his phone or his car's computer.

He had to warn Carney, and Chance. There were people's lives on the line. The Russians were planning a major move in space. They might be planning to take full control of orbital space.

All of it. Entirely.

But how did he tell anyone about this?

Wait. His hand-screen. Harley took it from his pocket, opened it...

...and quickly confirmed that it was dead. The Deep Bore cyberattack had penetrated that far. Harley felt under his desktop for the lower desk drawer, passed his hand over its sensor to open it.

Of course, it didn't respond. He felt for the latch and pulled it open manually. Reaching inside, he found the emergency kit. Using his fingers in the dark, he opened it and felt inside. There. The little flashlight. He switched it on.

The light was reassuring.

There was an emergency phone in the kit. He tried it. Was unsurprised when it didn't work.

That was it, then. He had to go... outside.

It'd been a long time. And in these conditions. No purchase-phone, no car. It was impossible! Panic swept over him. Better to wait inside for someone to look for him, yes?

No.

Fighting the panic, Harley Spencer got to his feet, and forced himself to go to the door.

* * *

"What will you do now?" Ildeva asked breathlessly. He was crammed behind Syrkin, next to the unconscious Carney. Syrkin had given Carney's pistol to Ildeva. "Why do you have those boots on, Alexi?"

"Because it'll be easier to fight with my feet on the deck—at least some of the time. Now shut up."

Syrkin was waiting. He was wearing biosuit boots, detached from the suit, and he was nicely fixed to the deck when Cha came in, looking around.

"Where's Carney? And that Ildeva guy?" Then he gaped, seeing Ildeva crammed in behind Syrkin. "What's he doing back—"

Syrkin stepped forward, raising the gun for another smackdown, but Cha was trained in martial arts and weightless-conditions combat. He blocked the blow with his right hand, while pressing his feet to the floor, grabbing the door's edge with his left. He shifted his center of gravity to the right, so most of the force of Syrkin's attack with the gun butt was deflected. Cha kicked out with his left foot.

The kick caught Syrkin's right side, but he'd used his Systema-based response to dodge the attack and it didn't land squarely. He stepped back, grunting, as Cha shouted into his headset.

"Lieutenant, I'm under attack!"

Cha pushed off from the deck, flying forward, trying to tackle Syrkin—who slithered aside using a Systema move. He brought the pistol down hard on the back of Corporal Cha's head. The comm specialist made an inarticulate sound of pain—and then went limp.

Ken Carney groaned. He was waking up.

Syrkin took hold of Cha, swung the weightless body around so it faced outward, a human shield. He held Cha by his collar, held the gun up to the back of the Corporal's skull.

Burkett was suddenly there in the doorway.

"Put that fucking gun down before you get us all killed, Alexi," Burkett growled. "You hit an oxygen line and you'll blow a hole in the hull. You really don't want to die that way."

Burkett was looking right into Syrkin's eyes, looking hard, and Syrkin was startled for a moment. The habit of obedience to rank was strong in the Rangers, and he had a lot of respect for Burkett. For one second, Alexi Syrkin wavered inwardly. But…

It's too late. I'm committed.

"Back off or I blow his brains all over you, Burkett."

"You a Ranger, Alexi? Or are you not?"

Syrkin swallowed. He felt like he was falling into a black hole.

"I'm not. That ended when you and the CIA railroaded my brother. When your pawn murdered him."

"Olek wasn't murdered, Alexi." Burkett's voice was softer now, but his eyes were just as hard. "Accidents happen on a battlefield. I lost a good buddy from friendly fire. You took a crack in the head and you need medical attention. Now put the weapon down so we can get you some help."

"Uh-uh, soft-soaping isn't going to work, Burkett. I need you to bring Captain Mayweather here."

"You want to negotiate with him?"

"I'll exchange Cha for him. Then I give you further orders."

"Lieutenant!" Carney wailed. "Help me!"

"Carney is like fly in web!" Ildeva crowed.

"Let Cha go, and we'll talk," Burkett said.

Syrkin shook his head. "Ildeva, step out here, carefully," he said. "Point your pistol at Burkett. We want to make sure he doesn't make a move we'll all regret."

The mob boss sidled up close beside Syrkin, pointing Carney's pistol at Burkett.

"Now listen up!" Syrkin shouted through the doorway. "I want everyone to stay in their seats unless I ask for them. I've got a KRISS Vector here too, and if you fuck with me, I'll spray it all over the cabin and we'll *all* take the consequences!"

"You hearing this, Captain?" Burkett said into his headset.

"*I hear treason and cowardice*," Mayweather said, his voice hoarse. "*I'll exchange myself for Cha.*"

Meeting Mayweather on the flight deck, Burkett pointed at the Captain's headset and gave the hand signal for silence. Burkett already had his own headset silenced. Mayweather nodded and whispered to Faraday and Strickland, both sitting nervously in their pilot seats. They cut theirs, too.

Burkett glanced over his shoulder, saw that Rodriguez was at the entrance to the biosuit locker trying to get Syrkin to let him examine the hostages. Typical of the medic. He'd done that on his own initiative.

Burkett turned back to Mayweather. "Sir—I only have a few seconds," he whispered. He'd talked Syrkin into giving him that much time to arrange the exchange carefully with Captain Mayweather. "Respectfully, it's not yet time to exchange. I'm not sure he'd even give us Cha or Carney for you, whatever he says."

"Back the fuck off or you're dead in three seconds," Syrkin shouted at Rodriguez. "One, two..." Burkett turned, saw Rod, white-faced with anger and frustration, retreating from the locker.

"Maybe if I'm in there I can talk to him," Mayweather said softly. "Or overpower him."

Burkett shook his head. "Ildeva has Carney's gun—he'll be watching—and Syrkin's got the KRISS Vector as well as that pistol."

"You have a better plan, Art? Rush him?"

"I have a Plan B, Captain." He turned and gestured to Dabiri. The corporal was sitting in the front row, now, reassuring the scientists. The looks on their faces told Burkett they were afraid their nightmare was going to begin all over again.

Seeing Burkett's signal, Tafir slipped quietly out of his seat. Burkett signed for him to turn off his headset and Dabiri complied. He moved swiftly, silently to the flight deck—just out of Syrkin's line of sight.

"I'm going to distract him—try to block his view," Burkett whispered. "There's something I need you to do, and fast…"

EIGHTEEN

Reaching the end of the Cherrywood private road, wearing blue jeans, running shoes, a blue T-shirt, and a light blue jacket, Harley Spencer found himself in darkness. He was out of reach of the nearest streetlight.

Harley wasn't scared of the dark. He was scared of the *world*, and his next few steps would take him out into it: vast, open, unfettered world, crawling with unknowns, and ten million malevolencies.

Bad enough just walking out of the house. He'd broken into a cold sweat, moaning softly to himself. Fear encircled him with clamps of ice, but he made himself take several steps before looking around. There—his car, but it didn't respond to his voice code. It just sat there, dark and silent, and refused to open for him.

Most of the houses on Cherrywood were dark, no lights showing in their windows. Even so, Harley had considered rushing to a neighbor and asking for help. Only, he didn't know his neighbors. He'd never met a single one of them, and they all had locked gates in front of their elegant, manicured homes. If he shouted from the street, they might call the police—but would the local cops help him?

His ID was in his electronics—in his phone, and his hand-screen. He didn't have a printed ID card. He'd just have to hope that one of them recognized him. Even if they did—what about that time he'd had a meltdown at the mall, and the cops had taken him into custody? He'd broken a store window. They'd kept him in a holding cell for two hours before his lawyer got him out.

"No favoritism for Mr. Big Shot," one of them had said.

Would they keep him in some cell tonight, ignoring him while the Russians did their dirty work? They were supposed to give each prisoner one call, weren't they? But who would he call, at this hour of the night? Would Chance answer this time?

Should I call Rowell back? No way. He'd sensed something *off* about the guy, and it was after talking to him that the Deep Bore carried out the viral attack on all things Harley Spencer.

A call to the press from the police station wouldn't yield quick results. It'd be, *"Crazy guy claiming to be Harley Spencer calling from the police station."* His lawyer wouldn't be taking calls at that hour, either. No. The cops wouldn't be his first go-to.

Harley's mind was whirling. His stomach too. He felt sick and disoriented, cut off from everything he knew: the digital world, the internet world, the world's armature of technology. How many times had he argued with people who claimed America was too dependent on electronics?

"Hard to argue with 'em now," he muttered aloud, just to hear a friendly voice. If he could get over to Langley, to CIA headquarters. Talk to the duty agent. It wasn't all that far. A few miles. He could flag down a cab. But no—they were all self-driving now and the cab's computer always asked for a valid cash-card or phone transfer before driving anywhere.

Just head for Langley, he told himself. *Think of something on the way. Maybe you'll find someone who can help...*

But Harley felt rooted to the spot. To either side were big square-edged concrete posts, topped with steel spheres, each post with a sign:

CHERRYWOOD ESTATES
PRIVATE ROAD

Once he stepped out past those posts he was really on his own.

There were some scary-looking people camped out along the main road. Some of them were likely to be predatory. There were the cops—Harley was as afraid of them as of the street people. There were rumors of wild-dog packs. But his most powerful fear was undefined. Just the vast empty uncertainty of it all.

Harley glanced up at the sky. A few stars were visible. He was fully aware of the irony: he had a fixation on outer space, felt its allure, and yet he was afraid of wide-open spaces. Turning his gaze to outer space was an escape from the chaos of the human world.

Chaos. He had to face it sometime.

Harley stretched, took a couple of swipes at the world with his outstretched arms, then growled to himself, psyching up for the next step. Looking at the sky again, he thought of the damaged S-7 up there. Men and women of courage, US Army Rangers, struggling to survive against the odds.

Well then, he told himself. *There's more than one kind of courage.*

"Fuck it," he said.

Heart pounding, Harley Spencer stepped across the invisible barrier, and out into the street.

"Dean? Sandy Chance. You got a minute?"

Chance heard the usual slurping sound from the other end of the line. Rogers was probably sucking some thick coffee concoction through a straw.

"A minute is really all I got, Sandy," the DIA agent said. "Video conference in two minutes. Something from the Chinese specialists. What's up?"

"Thanks for sending the files over… I hope to have one for you pretty soon. I was wondering—"

"One for me about *what*?" Rogers interrupted.

"Not cleared to release that yet—just conjecture anyhow." He wasn't at all sure about Rowell. Didn't want to give it to Rogers, who might go off half-cocked. "Was wondering if the guy you had, the one who wanted asylum—"

"Pfensky?"

"Yeah. I thought maybe, by now, he coughed up a name for that mole in SubOrbital."

"Well—no."

"So, you guys cut him loose? No deal with him?"

"Uhhh…"

Chance suspected there was something Rogers was loath to admit. A screwup.

"Yeah?"

"We had him in custody of the French police—he came to our people in Paris, see—and, uh, the French cops blew it. Pfensky went missing from his cell. His body turned up three days later in the Bois de Vincennes. Burn marks all over it. Bullet in the head. Never had the chance to give us a name. You got anything on the mole?"

"Not sure there is one, but there's a certain—"

"Whoa, someone's making crazy hand signals at me, I gotta get off the line. Conference. China. You get it."

Rogers hung up.

"I'm done talking, Burkett," Syrkin said, his voice grating between clenched teeth. He had one hand on Cha's collar, holding him down. Cha had regained consciousness, but his hands were tied behind him with one of the heavy plastic straps used to secure the biosuits. Blood droplets floated up from Cha's scalp wound, and Burkett could hear his raspy breathing.

"Alexi…" Moving in close, very slowly, Burkett put his hands, palm facing palm, out in front of him. "Cuff me. I'll take Carney's place. You'll still have Cha. Come on, Alexi. I'm a bigger fish than Carney."

"*No, Lieutenant*," Carney shouted, surprising Burkett. "Don't do it. I'm okay!"

Syrkin turned to glance back at Carney. "Well, the little murderer has some balls!"

That moment of distraction gave Burkett the chance he needed. He couldn't jump Syrkin—Ildeva had that pistol pointed at Burkett's head. Instead, he lowered his hands and put them behind his back.

Which was the signal Dabiri would be waiting for. He'd been floating near the deck between Strickland and Faraday, his arms braced on the edges of the open hatch. He pulled forward, hard and fast—Burkett caught the motion from the corner of his eyes—flashing just over the deck between the two rows of seats, toward the back of the cabin.

Dabiri whisked into the narrow passage leading behind the cabin to the aft storage compartment. For a split second he might've been in Syrkin's line of sight, despite Burkett deliberately posting himself in the way, but Syrkin was focused on Burkett. He pushed the pistol's muzzle against Burkett's forehead, hard enough so he floated back.

"You can die right now, or you can get out of the fucking way and get Mayweather in here," Syrkin said. "Do you understand me or not?"

"You'll exchange Cha for Mayweather?"

"No promises!" Syrkin barked. "Send Mayweather, or people die."

"He'll come, but how do I know you won't kill him on sight?"

"I won't kill him unless I have to. He's going to order you to change course. We're landing in a whole different part of the world."

"I see."

"You *will* see, my friend. You're going to be a guest of Russia."

"You've been a Russian agent all along." He didn't think so— but he was stalling to give Dabiri more time.

"You don't believe that bullshit. I'm going to make a deal with them. Now fuck off!"

"I'm not a murderer..." Carney said. "It was an accident."

"And did you say to Alexi that you are sorry?" Ildeva asked, kicking Carney in the head. It took all of Burkett's willpower to hold himself back when he saw that. He forced himself to turn away, to push off, drifting slowly back toward Mayweather. Looking for every chance to give Dabiri a few more seconds.

"Lieutenant," Dorman murmured, as he passed. "Maybe I could—"

Burkett shook his head. Other faces looked at him imploringly—every one of them wanting to *do* something.

"No," he said. "There's two guns and a submachine gun, and ours are in the weapons locker. Just hold hard."

"So you're not a murderer, Carney!" Syrkin yelled behind him, laughing bitterly as Burkett reached the flight deck. He glanced back toward the aft passage.

No sign of Tafir yet.

"Don't whine to me with that idiotic term 'friendly fire'!" Syrkin continued. "The CIA told you to kill him! They probably paid you! *Murderer!*"

"I was tensed up and I..."

"Shut up!"

Burkett caught a flash of motion at the far end of the passage. The hatch opening. Dabiri had gotten it done in record time.

"Okay, Captain," Burkett murmured, as he came face to face with Mayweather. "We go *slowly* to the—" Then he heard a scream from the biosuit locker, and a gurgling shriek. A metallic thump.

Carney's voice, extra high pitched.

"Syrkin! Don't!"

Burkett hesitated for two seconds. Maybe he should rush them. But if he did...

Then Carney's body, leaving a wake of blood in the air, came floating out of the biosuit locker. He was facedown but his eyes were staring at the ceiling, because his head was twisted around backward, blood from broken bone ends gushing from his torn neck. The handcuffs trailed from one wrist.

"Oh God," Mayweather muttered.

"You see what happens!" Syrkin bellowed. "Cha is next— then I open up with the KV! We'll see what nine-millimeter submachine-gun bullets will do in that cabin. I want Mayweather—now!"

"Tafir's on the way, sir," Burkett whispered.

Mayweather gave a slight nod, licked his lips. "Syrkin—hold on," he said loudly. "I'm coming now!"

Captain Mayweather took a deep breath and his eyes got cold. He pushed out from the flight deck, drifting toward the biosuit locker. Blood was a red gelatinous floating amoebic form outside the locker, a cloud of viscous dark red that would spread out and touch everyone.

Burkett started after Mayweather. "I'm going to get Lieutenant Carney's body out of there," he called. Morbidly thinking that Carney was turning out to be useful after all.

Syrkin didn't object—the blood was spreading out, getting in his way.

"Do it fast! Get your ass in here, Mayweather!"

Burkett caught a ceiling ring, changed direction, and reached into the cloud of blood, its smell filling his nostrils. He grabbed the dead man's limp arm and tugged him toward the aft storage, as if he were going to put the body there—but in fact he was blocking Syrkin's view.

Dabiri was in the combat suit, edging up to the biosuit locker.

Now, Burkett thought, *how do we get Cha out alive—Tafir will have to be fast.* Glancing back at the entrance to the locker he saw Cha's face, looking up under the rising cloud of blood—his face red with his own blood. Cha gathered himself and pushed off, hard, with his legs, against something behind him. He rocketed out of the locker door, tearing loose from Syrkin's grip, bound hands behind him, his head down.

He struck a chair with his shoulder a meter from the locker and grunted, spun with the impact, and Syrkin fired the handgun.

The bullet missed Cha, ricocheted madly in the cabin. There came a reverberating clang like a big high-pitched bell being rung five times in a single second, almost too fast to follow. Burkett listened for a scream of pain or the sound of an oxygen pipe bursting.

It didn't come, but there was another sound, coming from the locker. Was that Syrkin putting a fresh clip into a gun?

Stupid, Ashley thought. Waking up at 4:30 in the morning. Drinking a whole bottle of wine by herself.

I never do that. And—I did that.

She hadn't drunk that much in fifteen years, because she knew that a lot of alcohol late at night screwed with her sleep. The few times she'd done it, back in the day, she'd woken in the wee hours, halfway to dawn, with a horrible, buzzing, utterly undesirable lucidity. This time she'd been drinking while watching some old movies, trying to get her mind off Art.

Oh yeah, another glass of Cabernet will help.

Only it didn't.

She sat up, fully awake, remembering. Seeing him in her mind's eye, her husband gasping as the oxygen ran out in the damaged ship...

Ashley's head throbbed and her stomach was turning flip-flops, and she wanted so badly to be asleep. To not think about what Art might be going through right now. To not wonder if he was even alive.

She hadn't awakened beside him for months. The separation had seemed the only way to really make her point. To show him how serious she was. It had left her lonely and frustrated and unsure what to do next. For the umpteenth time, she remembered their parting that morning. She shouldn't have talked to him that way, right before he was going out to put his life on the line.

Don't torture yourself, she thought. *Nothing wrong with wanting my husband home, after all his years of service. After all those bullet scars. Nate needs him. We both need him here.*

Now she might well never see him again.

I should be ready for that, she thought. *But I'm not.*

It had come close to happening more than once in the last ten years. And the medals—she should be proud of his medals, but she'd come to hate the sight of them. Every medal meant he'd carried out some outrageous act of bravery; he'd put himself in harm's way yet again.

"Art…" she murmured. "Arthur Burkett…"

Ashley let out a long, resigned breath. No way was she getting back to sleep, so she got up, put on her bathrobe, and went into the kitchen to make coffee.

Nate padded in as she was filling the pot with water. He was hugging himself against the early chill.

"Mommy?"

"Hey, Private Nate. What you up for?"

"I heard you. I can't sleep very good."

"Me neither. You want to have some cereal? We could watch Moonman cartoons."

His smile was like turning on another light in the room.

NINETEEN

Clanking, muttering sounds from the biosuit locker. Burkett heard Syrkin talking to himself in Bulgarian, and English. Something about justice.

Dammit, Dabiri...

He looked across the cabin to Cha—Rod was treating him in a sheltered corner.

Then Syrkin shouted, "I'm giving you ninety seconds, Burkett, in case the shooting damaged the atmosphere feed, but just ninety seconds! I want Mayweather—*here*."

There was a roiling motion in the cloud of blood.

Then a bellow of rage from Syrkin as Dabiri in the Telos combat suit plunged through the red haze and into the locker. Syrkin fired the sidearm, and Burkett intensely hoped the combat suit's armor could take a round at point-blank range. That was the risk Dabiri was willing to take.

"*Lieutenant!*" Des Andrews called out. "Can we—"

"Hold on!" Burkett responded, tugging a ring to come to the bulkhead by the locker door. He heard sounds of a struggle, and several thumps—and then the racket of a submachine gun, a short burst: thunder and then a hailstorm...

A scream. A gurgling cry of despair.

"Tafir—" Burkett called, on his headset.

"*I'm here, sir. I think they're both dead. Ricochets, and it's a real mess. We've lost some biosuits for sure and I can't see for the blood in the air.*"

"You sure Syrkin's dead? You disarm him?"

"*I have the weapon, sir. Most of his head's missing. So…*"

Burkett waved away some of the cloud of blood and looked into the locker. He could see the two bodies, Ildeva and Syrkin, floating, arms akimbo.

"*He was trying to hit me with the SMG—I think I broke his jaw while he was doing it. He squeezed off a long burst. Ricochets were contained in here and it was like…*"

His voice trailed off and Burkett nodded, even though Dabiri couldn't see him. The two men were cut to pieces. The CIA wouldn't be pleased about losing Ildeva.

"You okay, Corporal?"

"*Yes sir.*" Tafir's voice over the headset. "*Armor held up. Bruised is all. Maybe a cracked rib.*" Burkett caught sight of him as he wiped blood off his visor with a gloved hand. "*Can't see much in here but… I don't think there's a hull breach, anything like that.*"

"You have anything against being a sergeant, Corporal Dabiri?"

"Me sir?"

"You're going to be one as soon as we get back, if I have anything to say about it."

"Can you make it a general?"

"Shut up and go see Rodriguez." Wiping blood from his eyes, Burkett turned to the other Rangers. "All Army personnel unbuckle for emergency clean-up!" He paused to cough up some of Carney's blood. "Ike, turn on the air filters, full bore! Dorman, hustle out the industrial vac. Megan, Andrews, help me with these bodies."

All the time he could scarcely breathe, thanks to the spreading cloud of blood. Mayweather drifted up beside him. Burkett had never seen him look so grim. Almost deathly.

"Lieutenant, I want you to write a report to go with mine. You say exactly what happened. This is my responsibility. I'm the damned fool who said to go ahead and put that gangster with Syrkin. I just…" He shook his head. "I mean—Syrkin was a *Ranger*."

"I understand," Burkett said. "I didn't believe Syrkin would turn, either. When he was getting kind of squirrely, Rod was wondering about traumatic brain injury. From the head wound when he was grazed. Hard to diagnose. Maybe that's what happened. Add in an officer killing his brother, and the Ildeva influence… I don't see it as something you could have anticipated. You had so much on your plate…"

"Thanks for the thought, Art, but I don't need any excuses. Let's get cleaned up." Mayweather turned away, his face a picture of mourning—not just for Ken Carney, but for the honor of the squadron.

* * *

"So, this isn't *your* self-driver?" Harley asked.

"Actually, the title is all fuzzy now," Bowman said. His words were mushy, thanks to his having lost half his teeth. He sat in the front seat, the passenger side of the Toyota pickup. Harley sat in back, behind the empty driver's seat, watching the eerie motions of the untouched steering wheel. "The police just sort of laugh at it. I convinced them that I'm *getting* the title, and I've gotten to know a lot of the patrolmen, so…"

It was just after dawn and there were few cars on the access road leading to the CIA headquarters at Langley. Harley and Bowman—a bearded, glint-eyed, gap-toothed homeless man in a stained jogging suit he'd met on the avenue—were trundling along in a rattletrap crash-damaged self-driving electric pickup truck. Some human driver had T-boned it at some point, making it almost V-shaped, and it had to be driven in slants within its lane, angling this way and that, to get down the road. It was averaging twenty-five miles an hour.

"Explain to me how you managed to get control of the car—without real, um, clear ownership?" Harley asked.

"I hacked it. I used bounce-fi, and an exploit that's sort of my personal property, my own, to get control."

"You know a lot about IT?"

"Used to. Had my own start-up. People like you crushed me."

"Then you believe I'm Harley Spencer? I wasn't sure."

"I know your face from all over the internet."

"Bowman, I haven't knowingly crushed anyone, but listen—are you one of those people who are so used to living on the street they can't really think about leaving?"

"Hell no, but it costs a lot of money to get even a rental, and the waiting list to get help... The company that runs all that assistance, since the privatization, it ignores most of us..."

"You have all this capability, so you must have a phone."

"Sure, I have a goddamn phone," Bowman snapped.

"If you'll give me the number, I'll give you a job. You obviously have talent, and we have a place we can put you up. It's a suite we use for visiting business contacts. You can live there as long as you like, long as you behave in a civilized way. If you need rehab, we'll set that up, too."

"You'll never really do it."

"Try me," Harley replied, surprising himself. "You gave me this ride—and this is no ordinary trip I'm making tonight. I owe you, Bowman."

They turned into the access road for the CIA headquarters. About a hundred yards down was a checkpoint with a closed gate of black metal. There were large, hooded, quite visible cameras—visible as a kind of warning—atop white-painted poles to either side of the checkpoint. Nevertheless, a sign bade them:

WELCOME TO THE
CENTRAL INTELLIGENCE AGENCY

"Welcome!" Bowman snorted. "As if!"

He stopped the vehicle partway down.

"Bowman—you don't think this'll look suspicious, stopping here?"

The fellow shrugged. "They'll probably think we're lost, but when they check out this truck, they might think it's wired with bombs or some goddamn thing. I'm not going any closer."

"Fine. Give me your phone number."

Bowman squinted at him, then shrugged again, dug in his grimy pocket for a pen, found a scrap of paper on the floor of his truck, wrote down the number and handed it over.

"Don't give that number to the CIA."

"I won't. Now—I need to use your phone."

"Um… okay."

He handed over the old-school cell phone, and Harley realized he didn't actually know Chance's phone number. His computer knew it. His hand-screen knew it. But Harley had forgotten it long ago, never having had to dial it himself. He sighed and called information.

"Central Intelligence Agency Headquarters in Langley, Virginia."

Eventually he got a lengthy voice menu. After navigating the voice menu, Harley was at last connected to an operator with a female voice that might've been human and might've been an AI. He couldn't tell.

"This is Harley Spencer," he said. "I'm a consultant to the CIA and I worked on a… special program. With General Carney and Sandy Chance, among other people. I have urgent information regarding national security for Agent Chance. I know he often spends the night here but… I don't seem to have his number with me… Anyway, I'm right outside. At the gate."

"*You're at the gate* now?" It sounded like a real woman.

"I know, it's a weird hour, but…"

"*We're closed now, except to authorized personnel.*"

"Please—just put him on the line. I've had to borrow this phone."

"*Sir, if you don't have his number, then how are working with him?*"

"I know, I know—my phone is dead and it's all on there." *Don't tell them about the cyberattack*, he told himself. *You'll sound like someone with a paranoid delusion. They must get calls from those people all the time.* "We're having a nasty blackout at my place. My network's down."

"*I recommend you return home, charge your phone, and try him then, sir.*"

"This is too urgent. Just tell him it's Harley Spenser. Tell him it's about the S-7."

"*We're getting a lot of calls about the S-7. It's all over the news.*"

"Okay, let me talk to the duty agent."

"*Sir, I suggest you reach the person you are trying to call in a different way. I… hold on.*" There was a pause filled with soft static. Then she said, "*Is that you in that… vehicle, sir?*"

"Yes, that's…"

"Okay, that's it," Bowman hissed. He snatched back the phone and broke the connection. "If you're really Harley Spenser, don't hold this against me—but get out of the truck, bro. I heard what she said. They're coming out here."

"Oh, well—"

"I don't want to be detained in some weird CIA holding cell. *Out!*"

Harley sighed. He couldn't blame Bowman. "Okay. Thanks for the lift. I'll be in touch."

Bowman rolled his eyes. "I just bet you will."

Harley climbed out and walked toward the checkpoint in the gray morning light. The beat-up truck turned awkwardly around, running up onto the grass verge and leaving tire marks, then zigzagging back toward the main road.

He regarded the CIA headquarters in the rising sun. It looked like a college campus, with broad lawns all about it. Many of the buildings exhibited the 1960s idea of modernism. The drone that buzzed overhead to scope him out gave another impression.

It hovered, inspecting him. Harley ignored it and, feeling tired and footsore and hungry, walked up to the checkpoint hut manned by SPS—three security protective service officers. Two men and a woman wearing what looked like ordinary police uniforms—but they were the CIA headquarters' own police force. They were all fairly young and looked unnervingly serious as they peered at him from the checkpoint booth. They were all armed.

One of the officers opened a sliding window.

"Can we help you, sir?" He was a young man with short black hair and narrow eyes. He might be Filipino, and no older than thirty-five.

Harley cleared his throat. "I spoke to the switchboard operator—I need to see Sandy Chance. He's an agent specializing in aerospace, ah, security. He and I work together. I had some problems with my car and phone—it's a long story—but I left him a message. I need to talk to him personally. I have urgent information for him." He licked his lips. How much should he tell them? They were lower-level employees. Everything he had to say was classified. Harley had no desire to do any amount of jail time, and if anything was to be kept sub-rosa, it was the information he had for the Agency. "I have a power blackout at my place, can't call him directly—and I really can't say any more. People's lives are at stake!"

"At this hour he's probably asleep, sir. Can I have your name?"

"I'm Harley Spencer. I'm a consultant, among other things, for a certain CIA project."

"And your ID, please?"

"Ah, yeah. It was on my phone—which is fried. I've never

had a printed ID card. Um—you ever hear of Deep Bore malware?"

"No sir. You have no ID? I'm going to have to ask you to step back from the booth. You'll be scanned by the drone, then we'll take you into custody. Just till this is all sorted out."

"Custody! There really isn't time for all that."

"Step back from the booth, sir."

Harley wanted to shout with exasperation. He wanted to be inside a building, where he didn't feel maddeningly vulnerable, not shoved in a van and taken who-knew-where. He wanted a cup of coffee and maybe a little something to eat and he wanted to talk to Chance face to face.

But he stepped back from the booth.

"One more step, sir."

He stepped back again, aware that a car was driving up behind. An unusually rumbly car. Its headlights outlined his silhouette against the street.

The car drove past him, and up to the level crossing barrier. The driver flashed his ID at the SPS officers. The car was an old Mustang.

"Sandy!" Harley shouted. The barrier raised, and Chance drove obliviously through. He hadn't recognized Harley from behind, especially in this setting. Harley bolted after the car, waving his arms, shouting, "Sandy! It's Harley Spencer!"

He passed through the barrier just before it came down. He thought he saw Chance looking at him in the rearview. Then the taser hit him in the back. The electricity jolted through him and he fell, quivering, to his knees.

Harley was paralyzed, and the taser hurt, and the car was screeching to a stop and the SPS officers were shouting at him to put his hands on his head.

But he couldn't move to do as they asked.

Well then, he thought, *I guess they'll just have to shoot me.*

TWENTY

"You're saying we can't maneuver?" Burkett asked.

"The guidance system for AC thrusters took a direct hit from that ricochet, sir," Faraday said. They were both hunkered near the floor, holding onto the underside of the indicator panels, looking at the dangling wires and jangled electronics. "It's a simple device, but both the computer controls and manual run through it. There's no backup. Meaning we have to find a way to tell the jets when to go on and off. Linda—uh, Sergeant Strickland—thinks maybe we can wire something up."

"And this'll take how long?"

"Hard to say, Lieutenant."

"Where's the Captain?"

"Working on his report, I think."

Burkett nodded wearily. The cabin was as clean as they'd been able to get it, but it still stank of blood. There were several misshapen bullets floating around that they hadn't captured yet. Three men were in body bags in storage: Alexi Syrkin, Mikhail Ildeva, and Olek Syrkin. Burkett felt like he'd get out and push this orbcraft to get back to base if he had to.

General Carney had sent his son on a dangerous mission, but he'd be looking for someone else to blame.

Maybe me. Burkett wouldn't blame the General for that.

He should have found a way to neutralize Syrkin without Ken Carney having to die. And die ugly, too. At least Cha looked like he was only mildly concussed.

Captain Mayweather floated up to the flight deck. "How's the guidance system look?"

"Trashed, Captain," Faraday said apologetically, as if it were his fault. "We're thinking of a jury-rigged electronic firing system."

"What's the ETA on something that works?"

"Ah—as fast as we can do it, sir."

They were silent for a long moment, pondering the variables and not liking the odds.

"The General's going to flip out about Ildeva," Burkett muttered. "And the CIA—I feel like I lost our asset."

"I don't think he knew all that much," Mayweather said, smiling crookedly. "But we *did* get something from Ildeva. You ever hear of the 'administrative oversight patch,' Art?"

"You mean—that's real? I thought it was just some made-up bullshit to scare the non-coms."

Mayweather chuckled. "*Not* bullshit. On mission, there's a computer record of everything that's said—not only on our headsets, but *near* them. Even when they're on a private channel to another headset, or simply switched off."

"Uh oh," Faraday murmured.

"Only, we don't listen to all of it. Your typical CO will erase 'em after the mission. Anyway, I do."

"That's good."

"You been telling dirty jokes on a private channel, Lieutenant Faraday?" Mayweather asked.

"No sir, Tafir and I were… it was just a little… well, some were kind of…"

"Definitely dirty jokes, sir," Strickland said blithely. "Right here in the control center, in front of a very sensitive woman."

"Really? I didn't notice one here," Faraday said. "And you are betraying the trust of pilots everywhere."

Burkett rolled his eyes. "Enough! Captain, you got some intel from Syrkin?"

"I went back and isolated the conversations between Syrkin and Ildeva. Ran them through the computer translator." Their translation programs, for hundreds of languages, could be transmitted to headsets wherever needed.

"Ildeva was pushing Syrkin to mutiny," Mayweather continued, "so he gave Syrkin some tidbits. Seems Ildeva got drunk with one of Krozkov's bodyguards, who heard talk of a mole in the SubOrbital project at Base One! He said all this to show that he had the inside dirt—so that Syrkin would trust him when he said, 'We know the CIA. They will roll up an agent who's no use to them.'

"Only that part was a lie. No one planned to kill Olek."

"So Ildeva was useful to us after all," Strickland said, looking up a wiring plan.

"Anything about the missile attack?" Burkett asked.

"Only to confirm that the Russians have their clandestine orbital military program. Like we figured, the attack on us came from orbit—so that confirms the source."

Burkett nodded. "Captain, if we need a guidance system for firing attitude control, maybe we can borrow one from the Light-Up. You've got some circuitry in there for firing missiles."

"That might work," Strickland said. "Take some time though…"

Mayweather grunted. "Then let's get on it. Without ACT, we don't land this multibillion-dollar vessel."

Burkett pushed off toward the rear of the cabin, Mayweather following. Dorman and Andrews were still working on scrubbing blood from the bulkheads over at the entrance to the biosuit locker. The job was seriously depressing. Burkett was feeling the comedown, the emotional crash after all that had happened with Syrkin.

It was like mentally driving on an obstacle course, veering around obstructions to stay on the road, when part of him wanted to stop and ask, *Was Syrkin possibly brain damaged? Wasn't he traumatized by the death of his brother? Shouldn't I have saved him?*

And then, *Will Ashley leave me after all this because it's the final straw, just too much for her to take? And Nate—how much is all this getting through to him? Does he think I'm dead already?*

The adrenaline gone, the thoughts all came crashing into his head. With the discipline of long service, Burkett swerved around the mental obstacles, and pulled himself back on course.

He got to the Light-Up in aft storage, climbed in, and set to work.

"You awake now, Harley?"

Spencer opened his eyes and blinked away the blurriness till the face came into focus. Sandy Chance, looking down at him with almost human concern.

"Yeah. I guess so. They gave me something... but I'm... yeah." He looked around at the hospital room. There were a couple of electrodes on his chest, and an IV in his arm. "I think they kind of overdid it. I'd have been okay. Can I have some water?"

"Sure thing." Chance handed him a glass and lifted him by his shoulders so he could drink.

"Thanks. Weird how good water can taste. Hey—how long was I out?"

"Couple hours. They gave you some Valium to relax your back muscles. The taser did a number on you."

"No kidding. Back hurts like a bitch."

"Sorry about that—one of them recognized you, but before he could speak up, I came driving through and you lit out after me and—" He shrugged. "It got a bit ugly and the others kind of overreacted, but that's their job, really. They said you had some kind of technological breakdown? I thought you were like a god of tech or something, man."

"Seems I'm overrated," Spencer said. "I couldn't reach you, so I called Base One. Some asshole name of Rowell gave me the runaround. I told him some of what I had found out—and next thing I knew there was a major cyberattack on my entire house. And more than my house. Even fried my house-bot and my car. My digital ID was gone, everything. Deep Bore program."

"Oh, Christ. That one," Chance said. "Russian-made. Yeah, they send out a drone to your house and it latches on and floods your systems with malware. Signal override just burns through firewalls. The agency has insulation against it, and so do I." He lowered Harley onto the mattress and sat back in the chair by the bed.

"Chance—it's weird." He was still dazed, a little dreamy. "I... everything led to my leaving the house without any phones, without any connection to... you know... and... I was so scared to just go outside, but lives were at stake, and there was nothing for me at home and I... just walked out and looked for you. It was—what's the expression?—*transformative*. I just broke through some kind of wall in myself."

Chance nodded, his forehead creased. "Rowell, you said? You talked to him and then all this happened? I wonder if that's enough to get him taken into custody. I mean—proving he initiated it."

"I suspect he did—but I don't know."

"We're onto him, only my boss says I need more proof."

"Oh Jesus!" The last of the mist cleared from Harley's mind and he sat up, wincing with pain at the motion. "I'm fucking babbling here! Listen—I've got some critical intel for you."

They were on the flight deck when Sergeant Strickland told Burkett that the S-7 was headed downhill fast.

"Lieutenant, we have a problem. We're in lower Earth orbit, we've got a temporary, half-assed guidance system. The ricochet hit the old system—which shorted out attitude control three and five. We can't activate altitude AC thrusters up there. It's not something you can reach from inside."

Burkett sniffled—his sinuses were congested like everyone else's. A little too long in weightlessness.

"Meaning we've got too much downward momentum?"

"Yes sir," she said, "and we can't get a navigational glide-in unless we get all the navigational jets running, Lieutenant."

"I see." Burkett felt a cold hand clutching at his throat. But he maintained his outward cool.

"Sir—if we don't get this operating fast, we're going to burn up in the atmosphere."

"Got that. Show me on the diagram where this fried piece of wire is. I'll EVA and fix it."

"Sir, I'd like to volunteer. I—"

"You have electrical repair training? What you did before was mostly just switching out units."

"Sir, I can work it."

"My old man was an engineer," he said. "Provided wiring for mine operations. I was his apprentice for almost a year. Long story short, I'm the guy for the job."

"We haven't got much time."

"Then work up the circuit patterns and placement while I'm suiting up, Sergeant, and upload it to HUD database. I'll download it when I get the helmet on."

Reluctantly, Linda turned away to the ship's computer interface as he pushed off, headed toward the biosuit locker.

Dabiri was still there, inspecting to see if all the blood was off the suits.

"Find me one I can wear, right now, Tafir," Burkett said. "Fast. No bullet holes. I'm going EVA."

"Roger that, Lieutenant. No bullet holes. Can't promise about moths."

* * *

Thirteen minutes later, Dabiri zipped him into the suit and handed him the helmet. "You ready for this, sir? We're up to our ankles in the exosphere already."

Burkett pulled on the helmet and locked it down. "You just ask Captain Mayweather how you can be useful in here."

Another five minutes, hurrying through every step, and Burkett was in the airlock as the air was pumped out of it, into the S-7's main oxy storage tank. The door swung open on raw vacuum. He pushed out through the airlock, grabbing the ring outside the hatch and activating his SAFER, using its jets to propel him toward the vessel's nose. He could see that the S-7 was skating on the exosphere, the highest and thinnest layer of Earth's atmosphere

"*This better be fast, Lieutenant,*" Mayweather said over the headset.

"Yes sir, that's my plan," he said as the hull rolled by under him.

"*If you burn up out there, how'm I going to explain it to Ashley?*"

"Captain, burning up out here is *not* my plan."

But he knew it was a good possibility. They were angling down into the thermosphere, and it didn't help that they were on the sun side of the Earth. It was starting to really bake out here.

If the orbcraft was dragged down by gravity before he could complete the job, the S-7 would gather momentum and he'd be snapped off both tether and boot-lock. Then he'd watch the orbcraft burn up as it fell into the atmosphere. All his fellow Rangers, his friends, his brothers and sisters, incinerating right in front of him.

Burkett would be falling, by then. He'd burn in the atmosphere too. He'd cook alive, regardless of his biosuit. How long would a death like that take? The sun was a white glare in the corner of his visor. The Earth seemed to be shining with heat, its atmosphere fulminating. Waiting to burn the S-7 and Nate's old man to a cinder.

Burkett's helmet HUD showed the target panel, up ahead. He took the power tool from his belt, hoping the drill's battery would hold up for the whole operation. He noticed the temperature rising in his HUD. A degree. Another…

Almost froze the first time I was out for repairs. Going to burn up this time. Somehow figures.

He pushed the thoughts away.

Concentrate!

Burkett turned off his maneuvering jet, reached the service panel, turned on his boot magnetism, then touched down so the boots gripped the hull. He squatted and began to remove the big screws on the panel. Two of them came up. The trick was to remove them partway, just enough so they let go of the hull. If he unscrewed them to the last thread, they'd float off into space and he wouldn't be able to seal the panel.

He started the third—and it stuck. Did not want to let go. He went to the fourth—and it stuck, too. Maybe the heat affecting them.

"God d—" Burkett started to cuss, and broke it off. He didn't want to panic anybody listening on the S-7. He glanced at the Earth. Twisty threads of upper atmospheric gases were coalescing, twining like ghostly ballroom dancers. Enjoining, thickening.

"*Lieutenant?*" Faraday said, in his headset.

"Hold tight, Ike."

He changed the bit on the drill—losing the original, which became part of the endless collection of orbital debris—and used the new one to drill out the old screws. Then he used the bit to pry at the edges of the panel. It had hinges on it, and it responded, lifting up.

Space, all around him, was changing. It was going white, and there was a sense of momentum tugging at him, of the orbcraft picking up speed. Downward speed.

"Listen," he said, taking out the other tools he needed, and the replacement wire. "The instant the power's on, burn fuel for higher orbit. Don't wait for me. That's an order, Ike."

"I... *sir, I'll have to check with the Captain.*"

"Do as I tell you!"

He located the blackened wire, bubbled with molten copper, and he clipped it out of place, then spliced, spliced like a son of a bitch, spliced faster than anyone had ever spliced.

The temperature was going up in his helmet readout.

Ashley. Nate.

"*Current's positive, Art!*" Mayweather yelled, so loud in the headset it hurt Burkett's ears. "*Get back in here!*"

"Accelerate up and out, sir!" He closed the panel and did without the screws. As he clomped toward the airlock the hull shivered under him, reverberating from the attitude control burn. The orbcraft tilted, nosing into the thermosphere.

Switching off his magnetic boots, Burkett turned on his SAFER jet, and flew toward the airlock.

He could really feel the heat now.

There—the airlock. But the orbcraft was shifting, tilting up under him as Faraday fired the attitude control rockets. The S-7 was going to hit him—to knock him into space. He switched off the SAFER and switched on the magnetic boots in the same second. The hull rose to slap him—and the boots took hold. He was whipsawed in his suit, afraid it would burst.

Then the motion steadied, and he clomped toward the airlock, climbing in. The hatch closed after him.

"We've rigged a functional guidance system," Burkett said on his first call to Base One since the bloodletting. "Kind of crude

ATC control, but we can navigate to Base Zero Point. We're going to jettison the air modules and a hydrogen fuel module and we'll be ready to burn."

"*Your timing is scary, Lieutenant,*" Susan Prosser said, her voice taut even over the comms. "*S-7, do not coordinate Base Zero Point.*"

"Repeat that?" Burkett asked.

"*Don't go anywhere near Base Zero Point,*" Prosser said. "*The Russians have a bead on it. They have moved a battle station to ME orbit, geosynchronous with Base One.*"

"Holy shit," Faraday muttered.

"Ike, can it," Burkett said. He was floating just behind Faraday, who was in the pilot's seat on the flight deck. "Don't move forward. Burn nose jets and move back, then head for a higher orbit and wait for orders. This comes from General Carney."

"We can't go home?" Faraday snorted in disbelief. "Are they *insane?*"

"Do it, Ike, and make it snappy," Burkett said, bracing. "Captain, did you copy all that?"

"*Affirmative, coming forward, Lieutenant,*" Mayweather replied. Burkett thought he heard Mayweather mutter a curse under his breath.

The engine rumbled as Faraday triggered the burn—a sound inaudible outside the ship, but inside it vibrated through the deck—and the S-7 shifted about them. Burkett could feel the inertia tug him a little forward as the orbcraft moved backward, and then back as the vessel tipped spaceward.

"Linda, we got full scan going?"

"Yes sir, both the computer and my eyes are on top of it. So far only some debris about a quarter-klick off, no bigger than a breadbox and no internal heat sig."

"Don't even blink till we're out of the firing line, Sergeant."

"Inserting toothpicks, sir," Strickland said as she rechecked radar and lidar scans. They were within a hundred kilometers of Zero Point. Would the Russians already be tracking them? Could a missile be on the way?

"*Burkett?*" Another voice came on the comms. "*Sandy Chance. She's patching me in from Langley so there might be a lag but uh… is the CO there?*"

"Right here," Mayweather said, pulling himself into the hatchway.

"*Gentlemen, we gave Harley Spencer the data he requested, he worked it out with his system which confirms that the missile was fired from orbit—and it came from the Russian 'Observation Satellite' Gogol-1. He's located the current position of Gogol-1— right over Zero Point. This so-called OS is big as a space station because it's that too. There are sure to be crew aboard, and our observations show three shuttered ports that could be ordnance launch tubes.*"

"Thank God for Spencer," Mayweather said. "We'll have to find another landing site."

"*Yeah, about that—we think we have an active mole in Drop-Heavy. I have a good idea who he is. Seems like he didn't get hold of the preliminary mission plans, but he's got his hands on everything since the drop. Chatter we're getting is, the Russians are making a major move to control orbital space, and they don't care about the political fallout. They came here to take you down—and my guess is that Base One may also be a target.*

"*The thing is,*" Chance continued, "*the President grounded the rest of Drop-Heavy because Congress wants to investigate this whole thing and they're insisting and everyone thought you were coming down anyway until now. Then we find out Gogol-1 has moved. We don't have anything armed up there from US Space Command, and they seem to be moving other assets into place and… uh…*"

"You telling us we have to stay up here?" Mayweather said. "Deal with this ourselves?"

"*I hate to be the bearer of bad news, but—yes. Those are your orders. I've got 'em right here. They figure since you're already deployed, you're in a unique position. No one's specifically gotten around to forbidding the S-7 to take action."*

"Chance, we have the rescued scientists up here," Mayweather pointed out.

"They'll just have to suck it up. Look—this is like a house of cards ready to tumble down on us. If we don't push back, they control space—and that means everything below their battle stations is in the crosshairs."

"You think there's a risk they'll attack Base One?" Burkett asked. "That'd be an act of war."

"Definitely, they'd risk it," Chance said, his voice heavy with concern. *"Base One is the heart and brain of Drop-Heavy. Take that out and it'd throw the whole program into chaos. They'll say it's self-defense. They're betting we won't launch nukes just 'cause they take out one base—and they're right. No one wants a nuclear holocaust."*

"The base should be evacuated, Chance."

"That's being... talked about."

"Talked about!"

"Take it easy, Art," Mayweather said. "They'll evacuate it."

"Down to most essential personnel anyway," Chance said.

"I'm not leaving my post while you're up there," Prosser said. "Anything I can do to help you—"

"There's something else," Burkett said.

"My responsibility to report this, Lieutenant," Mayweather said. "We have bad news for you too, I'm afraid. Sandy, I'm sorry to report that the General's son is dead. Lieutenant Carney was killed—in action. He was trying to stop Alexi Syrkin."

Killed in action? Burkett thought. *Why not?*

"Alexi Syrkin? Olek's brother?"

"Syrkin didn't take Olek's death well. Carney was responsible for it. Ildeva talked him into the idea that the CIA did it on purpose, and by that point Syrkin was already a powder keg. Am I right to assume that Ildeva was full of crap?"

"*Yes, he was. We wanted Olek intact. He could have been usefully debriefed.*"

"Plus Specialist Syrkin got a head wound, maybe that was a factor. He melted down and tried to mutiny. He's dead, Carney's dead—and I've got more bad news, Sandy. Ildeva's dead, too."

"*Son of a bitch! He might've been a wealth of intel!*"

"Chance," Burkett said, "how many of these battle stations are there?"

"*There are six others—but they don't seem to be fully activated yet. I think the idea is to cripple SubOrbital, then the Russians push their other battle stations into place.*"

"They do that, they could hit the other bases."

"*Why would they stop there? Hell, Moscow seems to be spinning out of control. They could hit Washington DC, Burkett!*"

TWENTY-ONE

Blood on the biosuits.

Dabiri and Dorman were in the locker, inspecting each spacesuit for damage and bloodstains. Four bullet-impacted suits had already been removed, locked in a cabinet as too damaged to use.

"Not finding any obvious damage on these," Dabiri said. He was feeling claustrophobic in the locker, finding it hard to concentrate. Remembering Carney's battered body. The broken neck, the staring eyes. Right where he was now, in the little room that reeked of blood.

"I'm finding hella blood," Dorman growled, using a scrubbing pad and a hand vacuum to clean the suits. "And bits of, like... entrails. Hell, I was already nauseated before I got in here."

"You need a vomit bag?"

"I keep one with me at all times, bro."

"Sick shit, what went on in here," Dabiri said. "When he fired off that SMG. All those ricochets turned this little space into a meat grinder."

"Not even an exaggeration," Dorman agreed. "Syrkin's body was barely holding together."

"Right up until his brother got killed, Syrkin seemed like a stand-up Ranger."

"Fuck," Dorman said. "There's a bullet hole in this suit. Thought we'd found them all."

"One more suit we can't use. Running short of them."

"Man, we already ran short. They're talking about new orders, and they're saying we're not going back down."

"You scared?"

"Corporal, I'm feeling sick, and this isn't what I trained for," Dorman said. "We had some space time, but nothing like this. This vessel has no missiles, it's got no laser cannon. It can't open fire. It's a transport. What're we gonna do, ram them?"

Dabiri snorted. "Burkett and the Captain, man, they have ideas. What're you going to do, Private? Raise your hand and say, 'Please sir, may I go home?' You're a Ranger, Lem. Shit, all the combat you've been in, you're lucky you're not dead already. You saved my life in Libya. You could've been a sergeant if you wanted to. Now you're crapping out?"

"Just—don't feel competent to deal. Because you know what command has in mind, don't you?"

Dabiri was silent, looking over another biosuit. "I think I *do* know what they're thinking," he said, "and it's crazy shit, but—you already knew the Rangers was crazy shit, Lemuel."

A pause. Then Dorman cackled.

"You're right. I did."

"Do you remember 3D Chess?" Mayweather asked.

"Barely," Burkett admitted.

They were crowded into the flight deck with Faraday and Strickland a few hours after the call with Chance, looking at the three-dimensional image projected by a dashboard holo unit. It showed a hundred square kilometers of space. In the center of the image was a red triangle designating Gogol-1.

"That's what we have here," Mayweather said. "They know where we are, in all three dimensions of cubic space, and we know where they are." He wiped sweat from his forehead. The hatch was closed, their headsets switched off, to keep this planning session secure for now, but the closed hatch meant it was hot and stuffy despite the air circulation vent. "We didn't fall into the trap, so they're probably waiting for orders from the GRU."

"There's one of Griskin's 'junk yards.'" Faraday pointed out a tight cluster of fine yellow points. The captain nodded. Those points, numbering in the thousands, were concentrated within a square kilometer, and were known to every space traveler or remote navigator.

A Griskin-designed mobile satellite from InterplanetaryEx detected space debris and used a plasma field generated by an ion engine to move them to the orbital junkyard. There, collected orbital debris was contained till it could be safely directed earthward to burn up over remote oceanic zones.

Some of the debris was large, like broken pieces of satellites or spacecraft or jettisoned material. It included an abandoned space station, and obsolete satellites about the size of refrigerators. Some of it was miniscule. All of it was potentially dangerous.

Once, two missions ago, they'd spotted debris near the S-7 that was the size and shape of a bowling ball. Turned out it *was* in fact a bowling ball, released with a hundred others by a bowling lanes company, with flashing lights on it spelling out "Cimarron Lanes." It was barely visible from Earth, but they'd obtained shots of it floating in orbit.

The company got in trouble for that.

"We need to move into position for an assault," Mayweather said. "First, we make an offer to our guests. We put them in biosuits, move them into one of the air modules. Then we set that adrift, somewhere it can be picked up within an hour or two by a sympathetic neutral nation. India has a maintenance ship working on its big India Destiny satellite. We could set the module moving slowly that way, ask them to pick our scientists up. Make it look like we're just jettisoning the modules. Russians will be watching the S-7, they won't realize the scientists are in the module…"

"A lot could go wrong, sir," Burkett said.

"If they remain with us, they're going to be at far greater risk."

Burkett nodded. "I'll talk to them about it. And speaking of talking to people—Captain, the squad's going to be a little shaken up by this change of orders."

"They're Rangers," Mayweather said. He appeared to assume nothing more needed to be said.

"Yes sir, and they'll do their duty, and more, like they always do." He pushed the thought of Syrkin from his mind. "But respectfully, sir, if there was ever a situation where a soldier's not going to feel 'grounded,' it's this one. They're used to a short trip in orbit, but none of them have ever engaged in combat here. You might consider giving them a talk. We're all going to need maximum focus."

Mayweather scowled, but then he nodded. "I'll do it after they're briefed. Sergeant Strickland—any hint of incoming so far?"

"No sir," Linda said, keeping her eyes glued to the radar.

"We're above them in orbit, now," Faraday said. "Their weapons are pointed Earthwards. They can turn their station toward us, but that'll take some time to work out. They're probably arguing about it right now."

"Shame we don't have missiles of our own," Strickland said. "We're going to have to be creative about this."

"I have some ideas," Burkett said.

Half an hour later, when the plan was blocked out and two maneuvers were carried out, Faraday piloted the S-7 to a position more removed from the enemy, but not too far away to engage.

Word came from below that Base One had mostly been evacuated, but there were volunteers staffing parts of it. Families on SubOrbital bases would be moved to "secure locations." Burkett wondered what that would be like for Ashley and Nate.

Taking a final look at the operational holograph, Mayweather took a deep breath.

"Smells like my gym locker in here. Come on, let's talk to the troops." He turned on his headset. "Squad, this is your commanding officer. Assemble outside the flight deck. We need to talk."

Floating beside Captain Mayweather, Burkett looked at the squad assembled in a half circle around them—all but Strickland, who was on watch for incoming missiles. Even Ike Faraday was there for the briefing. The two remaining scientists, Magonier and Dhariwal, were in their seats nearby, listening. The squad members floated like spirits over the deck around the CO and the XO.

"Comme une conference de fantomes," Magonier murmured. Burkett had enough college French to translate.

Like a conference of ghosts.

"We're not ghosts yet, Doctor Magonier," he said, but maybe there were a couple here, he thought. Ken Carney. Ildeva. Syrkin. Their bodies were in bags, in lockers near Olek's.

Sgt. Des Andrews, Sgt. Megan Lang, Cpl. Tafir Dabiri, Lance Cpl. Kyu Cha, PFC Lem Dorman, Lt. Ike Faraday, and Cpl. Rod Rodriguez waited for Mayweather to start. They looked serious, respectful, some better at concealing the underlying worry. But it was visible in their narrowed eyes, however. Their compressed lips.

"Squad," Mayweather began, "you probably heard we have new orders. I know what you're feeling. Hell, we've been through a lot, and we're short on supplies. We've increased our oxygen stores but it won't last forever. We haven't got endless water, either. We're all feeling some of the side effects of weightlessness. We're trained for space but this is, frankly, way more than we prepped.

"We risked our asses on the ground mission, as we've all done many times, and it got ugly. We lost a Ranger up here on the orbcraft, and he died hard. We dealt with blood in a way we've never had to before. We all have families we're worried about. We all want to go home. But—we can't, not quite yet.

"We've been ordered to remain in orbit. Some of you probably figure this end of the mission isn't what you signed up for. Ranger training was all about airborne and ground combat, but we knew what we were getting into when we signed on for SubOrbital. We had to know it might come to this."

He paused, pinched the bridge of his nose and sniffed.

"This sinus thing is no goddamn fun. Though it blocks the smell in here."

They all gave out a sympathetic chuckle at that.

"What we've learned is that we're on the frontline here. The Russians are making another move, and this one is big! They're planning to establish widespread military control of orbital space."

The squad members glanced nervously at one another.

"They're using an orbital battle station they call Gogol-1 to threaten Base One. It's positioned in High Zero Point right above SB-1. They have other battle stations coming online, maybe in a few days. Intel suggests they want to destroy the S-7 and Base One before they fully initiate the other stations. Pentagon could deploy more orbcraft, or ground-to-orbit missiles, but the President feels that might spark a world war.

"You can see how important this is. We're going to need that Ranger willingness to push the envelope. To go beyond."

Mayweather cleared his throat and went on. "Now—the Commander-in-Chief and the Pentagon want us to approach Gogol-1 to get a clear sign of aggression from them, draw them out so when we make our move, it'll be self-defense. We don't want to look like the aggressors and give the Russians an excuse for all-out war."

"Just tell us what to do, sir," Strickland said.

Mayweather nodded. "We have no conventional ship-to-ship armaments—but we do have a plan. I won't lie to you—it might well be riskier than anything you've ever been through." He looked around at them, making eye contact with each man and woman.

"We're going to do something kind of old-fashioned right now. You haven't had to do this since you were in Ranger training, but we're going to recite the Ranger Creed."

They'd all learned it by heart, long ago. Burkett knew that reciting the Creed might seem corny to someone outside the Rangers, but they all had memories that made the Creed profoundly true for them.

"Recognizing that I volunteered as a Ranger," Mayweather intoned, "fully knowing the hazards of my chosen profession, I will always endeavor to uphold the prestige, honor, and high esprit de corps of the Rangers…"

Burkett recited with the others and found himself remembering a gray day in the mountains of Northern Georgia. Leaping into an icy river in full battle dress with a hundred-pound pack, up to his neck in foul, startlingly cold water, using a rifle butt to clear the razor-thin ice, slogging toward the other bank alongside dozens of other trainees.

The water got deeper. Halfway across he felt like he wasn't going to make it, teeth chattering, gasping for breath as his lungs seemed to seize up with the cold. His clothing felt like it weighed five hundred pounds. Bianchi, next to him, was barely keeping his nose out of the water.

And then Bianchi was outright sinking.

Burkett grabbed him by the collar, lifted him, and tugged him along. Somehow that helped Burkett, too. Other trainees reached out to assist. They all made it to the far shore.

"Acknowledging the fact that a Ranger is a more elite soldier who arrives at the cutting edge of battle by land, sea, or air, I accept the fact that, as a Ranger, my country expects me to move further, faster, and fight harder than any other soldier…"

Central Africa. The helicopter's Air Force pilot said the LZ was too hot for insertion. Captain Becksworth told him to move to a small clearing nearby. Pilot said no-can-do, too many trees crowding the clearing, closest he could get might be seven meters above the ground. Becksworth shouted at him to let the Rangers worry about the altitude.

Under fire, the heli choppered over to the clearing, descended as far as it could—and Becksworth jumped for the ground, Burkett and the other nine Rangers after him. Seven meters down.

On impact, Becksworth cracked an ankle. As the chopper heaved off into the sky, he used his rifle as a cane, stood up, drew his pistol, and led them through the trees and into combat, firing his pistol with good effect.

"Never shall I fail my comrades. I will always keep myself mentally alert, physically strong, and morally straight, and I will shoulder more than my share of the task, whatever it may be, 100% and then some.

"Gallantly will I show the world that I am a specially selected and well-trained soldier…"

Libya. Rangers fighting side by side with Libyan soldiers to liberate Tripoli from the "African Islamic State" terrorists. Burkett and his squadron were running down a narrow street in the gray dawn light, leaping over bodies of dead civilians who'd been executed by AIS. Then the trap closed around them. The yellow stone buildings seemed to erupt with gunfire. Someone shouted through a bullhorn, demanding surrender.

The Rangers jeered at that—and charged…

"Energetically will I meet the enemies of my country. I shall defeat them on the field of battle for I am better trained and will fight with all my might. Surrender is not a Ranger word.

I will never leave a comrade to fall into the hands of the enemy and under no circumstances will I ever embarrass my country…"

Venezuela. Burkett ran to a shell crater, head lowered against the driving rain. Three terrorists stood over a Marine prisoner who'd been made to kneel, all four in a growing puddle of muddy water. They were about to execute the Marine.

Burkett shouted to get their attention, jumped in, opened fire.

Three Tango down. The Marine was back with his platoon twenty minutes later.

"Readily will I display the intestinal fortitude required to fight on to the Ranger objective and complete the mission though I be the lone survivor. Rangers lead the way!"

"Rangers lead the way!" Burkett said, with the others. His eyes were misty. Feeling a little foolish but also proud of his squadron—proud of being a Ranger.

I needed that at least as much as they did.

TWENTY-TWO

Forty minutes after talking to the S-7, Sandy Chance was buckled into a window seat of the Air Force's fastest troop transport, usually used for top level officers. He was the only "trooper" aboard. Chance held this special privilege because the President had announced DEFCON 3: Roundhouse. A state the US Government had not been in since the Yom Kippur War in 1973.

The possibility existed that the Russians could have a nuclear warhead on Gogol-1. No evidence for it, but... it might be there. So right now, everything about the Drop-Heavy program was an intelligence priority.

As he studied the files on his hand-screen, Chance felt the drop in his belly that meant the transport was making a steep descent. They'd flown to SubOrbital Base One in Colorado in under an hour and a half.

No putting it off—he had to talk to Carney, right now. He called the General's private phone. General Carney answered.

"Who the hell is this? I don't recognize this number."

"It's Sandy Chance, sir." He added the "sir," though he wasn't required to, not being military. He knew Carney must be hurting, knowing what happened to his son.

"Did you get my memo, General?"

"Yeah, handed off to me in person at my goddamn house by some spooky wonk from the DIA. I'm trying to deal with my son being murdered, and you—why didn't you just send it to my email, for Chrissakes?"

"Did you read it, sir? We think your base is insecure. Any plans, any orders, have to stay need-to-know only. That includes your staff sergeant."

"Goddammit, that man is a war hero! And you're making wild accusations—"

"Sir—we're taking precautions. I've got a team on it right now, and if there's no evidence to support the suspicion, we'll all be relieved. Meanwhile, not one of your orders to the S-7 is to go to anyone but Captain Mayweather. It must go to him *directly*—no one else sees it."

"Who the hell are you to order me around, Chance?"

"I have the authority of the President of the United States in this. It's all in the memo. Sir." Who could blame Carney for not being able to process everything? His son had been beaten to death on a US vessel. "I understand how you must be feeling. Just follow the protocol, that's all we ask. And I'm deeply sorry for your—"

"Don't tell me you're sorry for my loss, you little weasel." His voice was low and menacing. "You're cronies with that S-7 bunch!"

"General, that squadron is the best we have in Drop-Heavy."

"The best? They let some lunatic murder my son! They're all going down for this, Chance!"

"I understand how you feel, General Carney—"

"No, you fucking do not."

He broke the connection.

Chance grimaced. Would Carney follow protocol? If a Presidential order didn't convince him, what would?

* * *

Fifteen minutes later, Chance was driving a black electric sedan, signed out from the base. He took the access road to the highway and went out into the scrubland. It was a blustery midmorning with dark clouds racing overhead. The foothills of the Rockies rose brown and red in the distance; beyond the hills, the mountains jutted blue and snowcapped.

The plateau around him was blossoming; sand scrub and sage and high-desert flowers rolled away to either side of the narrow highway.

Ten minutes took him into the small town of Kirke. A strip of supply shops, gas stations, bars, and fast-food franchises lined the highway. Side streets leading to the neighborhoods. A little less than a thousand people here, according to the city limits sign. Chance found the Rough Rider Motel on the east end of town, its early 1960s sign showing a rodeo rider on a bull waving a hat. It had lost its neon and the cowboy no longer waved.

Shrubs grew through cracks in the parking lot. The row of rooms was faux adobe. There was only one car, parked in front of room nine, which was Agent Cary Frelling's room number.

"Come on into my honeymoon suite, chief," he said, opening the door and ushering Chance in with a flourish of his freckled hand. Frelling was a stocky man of middle age, wearing khaki trousers and shirt and a tweed blazer. He had receding red hair, a spray of brown freckles on a brickish, weathered face that typically held a rueful expression.

Chance looked around at the room, took in the noisy air conditioner drooling from the only window. Colorless carpet, a flat screen on the wall over a dresser, a bad seascape beside the bathroom door, a bed that looked lumpy even from twenty feet away. An old dining room chair seemed forgotten in a corner.

"Have a seat, chief. Take your pick."

"You check for bedbugs?"

"Scared to."

Chance snorted and chose to remain standing. "This the only motel in town?"

"There was a bed and breakfast, but NRD thought I'd be too noticeable there. For no reason at all." Technically, Frelling and Agent Chris Fisher both were National Resources Division, but it was actually just a secretive domestic operations subset of the CIA.

"Where's Fisher?"

"Today is Rowell's day off, so Fisher's watching the staff sergeant's house. Not even as interesting as paint drying. I'd be with him but—" He spread his hands, pooched out his mouth. "—I had to be here to meet you." Frelling had a perpetual tone of subtle mockery about him.

"Just give me your report."

"Nothing more beyond what I sent you yesterday. Rowell has rented a house in town. We were told max discretion, so we didn't try to break in. Might've seen that the lock was jiggered or something, but I'll do it if you want me to."

"Fisher following if Rowell goes out?"

"We release a drone to do that, mostly. Fisher has the drone, but it kind of depends on where Rowell goes. Small drone, not much range. Kind of overcast, so we're getting shitty satellite observation."

"You put a tracker on Rowell's car," Chance said. "You checking that?"

"If the car moves, the tracker calls my screen. Then me and Fisher yak about whether to follow him. During the day there's not that much traffic around here. Rowell would notice us. But—where's he going to go? It's not like he's going to meet a Moscow agent here."

"Moscow's likely got him using a detached uplink," Chance said. Undercover GRU agents didn't communicate with Moscow directly from overseas cover, rarely from screens or cell phones. They had a relatively small satellite-link device set up somewhere—like a rooftop a ways from where they were staying, or some old outbuilding in the country.

"He'd go there," the CIA agent added, "somewhere out in the woods, probably. Be good to find it, but so far, we got nothing from orbit. Moscow uses quantum encrypted microwave bursts. Hard to trace." He looked around. "You got any coffee? I need coffee and a cigarette."

"There's one of those cappuccino booths on the highway."

"Let's go in your rental. We'll swing by Fisher's stakeout. Call ahead—let him know we're coming by. I just want to look at the place."

Frelling unfolded his hand-screen, making a tick-tock sound with his tongue, something Chance found annoying since he did it *every single time* he was performing a minor task.

"Fisher," Frelling told the screen. It called the other field agent. There was a flickering light on it showing the call was going through.

No response.

"What the hell?" Frelling made a face as if he were personally offended. "Is his screen not charged, or what?"

"Let's get the coffee. We'll try again in a minute."

They went to the fancy coffee kiosk and found it staffed by a bored college-aged girl in a red bikini. Chance looked at her in momentary confusion.

"Yep, bikini girl baristas, chief," Frelling said after they'd ordered. "It's a thing out west. Since I was a kid." Chance rolled down the window of the rented Hydro and lit a cigarette, took his coffee from Frelling.

"Drive to Rowell's, try to come at it from behind, if there's a way to do it."

Frelling drove to the street behind Rowell's place and slowed to a crawl, stopping at the house behind Rowell's backyard. Most of the homes in the neighborhood were little one-story cracker-boxes, shaded by poplars and oaks. Few people were about. A couple of houses down, an elderly couple sat on their front porch in lawn chairs, talking to a tubby neighbor who was leaning on a rake.

"How's Fisher doing out here?" Chance asked. "The one time I had him in the field it seemed like he watches too many spy movies."

"VR games, more like—he's barely thirty. Always trying to prove himself. Said we should break into Rowell's, just disregard the advisement. I was concerned he might go off half-cocked. Could be he did just that."

"Shit. Where's his car?"

"We move the cars around—he's probably parked a few houses down on the other side." He opened his hand-screen and tried calling again. Shook his head. "Not answering."

"What's his car look like?"

"Old blue Chevy Hybrid rental, two-door." Frelling drove down half a block, turned, pulled up at the corner so they could see Rowell's street. "I'm not seeing his car. That spot's where he'd mostly likely be."

The empty parking space by the mossy curb was a half block down from Rowell's place, chosen so the trees fronting the suspect's house would cover the car. Fisher would have been able to see from a discreet distance when Rowell came and went.

"You think he'd have followed Rowell on his own?"

"He was making noises like I should let him do that, because our drone is too short-range, but... that'd be crazy."

"You didn't tell him flat-out *not* to do that?"

"I think my words were, uh, 'I don't think that'll be necessary.'"

"Christ. That's not a *no*." Chance growled softly to himself. "If he's following, he'd have the drone up too, right?"

"I think his idea was let the drone follow, then follow from way back. Follow the drone as it followed Rowell."

"What's Rowell's car?"

"Rented white SUV. It's not here. The driveway's filled with the landlord's rusted old RV, so Rowell parks on the street. He's out and about."

"Check the tracker on Rowell's car."

"Sure thing." The tick-tock sound with his mouth as Frelling took out his hand-screen, unfolded it, tapped it a couple of times. "Fuck."

"What?"

"No signal. Rowell found the tracker."

"Which tells you he knew what to look for. How is he *not* an operative? You got that screen linked to drone view?"

"Yeah." Frelling tapped the screen again. The image on it went dark. "It's not active. Probably in Fisher's trunk."

"How about latest flight video?"

"Getting it, and... there."

Chance leaned over and they both watched the footage of the drone following a big white SUV from on high. The SUV drove in a leisurely way down a highway. Telemetry placed the drone about two miles southeast of Kirke at the time. The footage had been recorded about seventy-five minutes earlier. The SUV turned right, leaving the highway for a side road. It trundled past a cattle-loading pen. The drone followed.

Followed... followed... more than a mile and around a curve. Then the drone slowed, and hovered. The SUV moved out of camera view, turning left into a bushy cut-out. Twenty seconds later a blue compact car swung into the shot. The camera descended. The blue car stopped, growing in camera frame as it pulled up to wait for the approaching drone. Fisher would retrieve the drone before it ran out of power.

The drone landed behind the car and the last shot was a glimpse of the agent's hands as he put it in the trunk. The footage ended.

"You see that? The shitty drone they gave us?"

Chance ignored him. "Where he stopped—not far from

that cut-out. Maybe fifty yards. Hasn't occurred to him Rowell might have turned off the road."

"Oh Christ, the damned fool," Frelling muttered.

"More testosterone than brain cells," Chance said. "You armed?"

"Couple guns in the trunk."

"We'll head out there. Stop when we're out of town and get the guns out." Frelling nodded and they drove to the highway, and followed it southeast. Chance spotted the steer loading pen off in a field.

"Turn here and stop."

Frelling turned, stopped the car, and popped the trunk. They got out, and Frelling opened the big metal case.

"I'll take the carbine," Chance said.

Frelling took a double-load niner handgun.

They got back into the car in grim silence and drove on. A mile… a little more. Chance saw the cut-out, up ahead. Barely visible.

"Stop the car."

Frelling pulled up and Chance got out, crossed the road, looked through a break in some junipers. The SUV had gone. He returned to Frelling's rental and they drove on. The road's curve straightened out and they saw they saw the blue compact skewed half into a ditch in the shade of some poplars.

"Oh shit," Frelling muttered. He pulled up about thirty meters back and they both looked at the underbrush on the right, a field to the left. Beyond the field was a line of trees. "Let me get out first, chief."

"Fuck that, I've got the carbine. More range."

"You think Rowell's out in those woods?"

"I don't see his SUV. I think he drove on, took another route back to town. Or to the base. But keep watch."

Chance got out and looked over the top of the car, peering at the field. No car tracks on it. Blackbirds were pecking around near the trees. Probably no human being hiding in there, or the birds wouldn't hang around.

"I don't think he's over there," Chance said.

Frelling got out, came quickly around to Chance's side of the car; both of them hunkered, half expecting a gunshot. Nothing but the sound of crows cawing from a nearby treetop.

His mouth dry, pulse thudding, Chance stepped over the grassy ditch to the underbrush to the right—there was a rusted, half-fallen barbed-wire fence running through the shrubs.

"Frelling, take cover behind the car, keep down, watch those trees and Fisher's vehicle. Shout if you see anything."

"Chief—seriously, let me do this."

Chance ignored him. He was the one who'd chosen Fisher for this job. He'd liked Fisher, despite his way of acting like a dog straining at the leash. Should have known better. Some idiotic avuncular impulse.

That's what happens when you get middle-aged and you've got no children, he told himself bitterly. *Should have pushed to have Rowell taken in before now.* He'd been hoping to catch some accomplice, where there probably wasn't one in the area.

Stepping over half-fallen wire, Chance pushed through the underbrush, using it as cover, and worked his way up toward the car. Breathing hard. Brush bugs rose up buzzing about him; blackberry vines bit through his trousers. He could smell sage and some other acrid plant, and cow patties somewhere. There was a rustle in the brush, and he froze.

A grouse flapped out, and away.

Watching, listening, he moved on. A hawk screeched from far overhead. A couple minutes more and he came up opposite Fisher's car, about five yards away. Between two scrub oaks, Chance went down on one knee and peered through the open passenger-side window.

Fisher was behind the wheel, slumped over. His head shattered. Exit wound in his right temple. Angle suggested the shooter had fired from a higher vehicle—like an SUV. There was a bullet hole on the right side of the dashboard, splashed with blood and brains.

Chance could picture how it had played out. Fisher had been clumsy about surveillance and Rowell spotted him, lured the young agent into the country. Found a place to wait for him—some little turn-out where the SUV was hidden from the road by trees. Fisher passed him, oblivious, thinking Rowell was up ahead.

Rowell drove up alongside and shot him through the window.

A sick feeling rising in him, Chance stood up and pushed through the brush. He climbed awkwardly over the fence, avoided a patch of blood-splashed sagebrush, jumped over the ditch, and waved to Frelling.

Rowell probably didn't know there was a second agent on his tail, close by, or he wouldn't have risked killing Fisher. He would have seen Fisher put the drone in his trunk, so he knew about that. Rowell would be planning on ducking out of Base One, pronto.

Make an agent disappear, whether FBI or CIA, and when the agent failed to report, someone would notice. Rowell knew that. He was probably at his uplink, somewhere off in the countryside, arranging for Moscow to extract him with all possible speed. Maybe *today* at some point. Maybe he was driving to an extraction point right now.

Chance leaned the carbine against the fender of the blue compact, got on his hand-screen and called a friend at the Denver FBI. Agent Gabe Steiner.

"Gabe? Chance. The Agency has a present for the FBI. We're going to turn over a Russian agent to you, once I've had him arrested by the MPs. He's killed one of our agents. We'll interrogate him after you've booked him." Chance gave him the lowdown on Rowell and Fisher, asked him to call the sheriff's department, have them cordon off the area around Fisher's car till the FBI arrived.

"Listen, Gabe, I'd take it as a big favor if you'd deal with the kill scene personally, if your chief allows it. You guys can transport the body to DC once forensics is done."

"*Okay,*" Gabe said. "*It'll take time to get agents out there. What are you gonna be doing?*"

"I'm going to SB-1, make sure the MPs follow through. General Carney over there's a little sketchy on security. One way or another, I'm going to take Rowell down."

TWENTY-THREE

"You two gents ready to make your appearance before the whole world?" Burkett asked. "Because sure as hell the Pentagon will release it to the media."

Dhariwal glanced at Magonier inquiringly. Magonier nodded. "We're ready, Lieutenant."

Ike Faraday was the only pilot there. Sergeant Strickland was EVA with Sergeant Andrews, working in one of the modules. Mayweather and Burkett were crowded into the flight deck with the two scientists. Faraday was focused on watching for incoming from Gogol-1.

The S-7 had come to a geosynchronous position over a point in Colorado, 120 klicks east of Base One. Burkett worried Gogol-1 would fire on Base One. There were anti-ballistic missiles at the base, but there were no guarantees. The Russians had evasion-capable hypersonic missiles.

They needed to act soon, at least to keep the bastards busy.

"All right, gents," Mayweather said. "Step... okay, float... right into the center of the flight deck, and we'll activate the camera. You'll see a green light on the control panel. Look toward that."

The two scientists pressed gently against the sides of the hatch and floated in, using the back of Ike's seat to brake.

"Code Hitchcock," Mayweather said. "Authorizing camera and sound in flight deck S-7. Go."

"*Recording*," a computer voice said from the control panel. Dhariwal cleared his throat and spoke to the world.

"I am Dr. Lucius Dhariwal, based at the Massachusetts Institute of Technology. With me is my colleague, Dr. Jacques Magonier of Sorbonne University. We were abducted, along with Frederic Dupon, who is now back on Earth thanks to a small spacecraft which did not have enough room for all three of us.

"The United States Army Rangers arrived in this vessel, designated S-7," he continued, his voice steady, "and stormed an abandoned monastery where we were held prisoner. The Rangers rescued us. We are now in orbit, in the S-7. We have been given the opportunity to enter a module from the N-22 station, to await rescue, while the S-7 undertakes a military mission in space.

"The captain has made it clear that the module will be safer than staying with this vessel, but we have both freely chosen to stay here. We feel we can be of help. We were moved by the bravery of these Rangers, we have been touched by their care for us, and we wish to be part of this effort. We feel we can be useful. I am making this statement of my own accord, quite freely, to make it clear that this is something we choose to do.

"Our situation is not the fault of the personnel of the S-7. I wish to say that I feel a deep love for my parents, and my sister Dani, and I hope to see them very soon." He took a deep breath. "And now—Doctor Magonier..."

Magonier made much the same statement in French, adding sentimental effusion about his wife and children.

"Recording ended," Mayweather said. The green light went red.

"When will people see that?" Dhariwal asked.

"Not until after we've engaged Gogol-1. We'll send it as soon as they know we're taking them on."

"Captain," Faraday said. "Apparently the President of Russia is talking trash about us now."

"What do you mean their orders have been changed?" Ashley demanded, stalking up and down the living room with phone in hand. Nate was sitting on the couch, watching her with wide eyes. "They're supposed to be back by now! First you guys bum-rush us to this godforsaken hotel in Denver, and then you tell me he's not coming home? That's bullshit! They've more than done their duty, Talley."

"*Ashley, I'm sorry, but it wasn't my decision. Rangers have to be ready for anything.*" Baxter was working hard to keep his temper. She could hear it in his voice. "*I'm sure they'll finish up and, uh…*"

"What is it they're doing? Are they going into a fight up there?"

"*I can't tell you that. I… Hold on.*" She heard him talking, his voice muffled, to someone in the office. "*Ashley—the Russian President is making some sort of statement. You might want to check it out. I'll get back to you soon as I—*" Ashley hung up and, heart sinking, turned to the big flat-screen hanging on the wall.

"Television, WorldTalk channel," she told it.

The screen flickered on, and there was the President of Russia, a seam-faced old man with swept-back dyed-blond hair and a nicely tailored charcoal-blue suit, looking stern and oddly paternal as he stood at the UN podium.

Ashley sat beside Nate and put her arm around his thin shoulders, felt him nestle closer. Through a translator, Veronin spoke from the television.

"*…and so, the United States has committed an act of war by invading our allies in Moldova, through this covert spacecraft* *operation. This was followed by the American attack on one of our observation stations in orbit.*"

"Why you damned liar," Ashley muttered. "They did nothing of the sort."

"They didn't?" Nate asked. "Somebody at school said—"

"Never mind what some idiot at school said. Talley Baxter might not tell me everything, but he doesn't lie to me. They didn't commit any acts of war, and they didn't attack anything in orbit. Hush, now."

"*The observation station, Gogol-1, is equipped for self-defense. It fired a warning missile, which did minimal damage to the American vessel.*"

"Another lie," she gritted. "It wasn't minimal."

"*The Gogol-1 was then approached in a threatening manner by US Air Force spaceplanes, coming dangerously close to the observation station.*"

That might be true, she supposed. They'd be confirming it wasn't for observation—it was a camouflaged weapon.

"*This aggression forced Gogol-1 to relocate,*" Veronin continued. "*It has been moved into a position which can be strategic, if necessary. I must warn you all that if we have to take further steps, we will. We are not going to be pushed out of space by the illegal aggression of the United States.*"

"We've got incoming!" Strickland called, her voice taut.

"Where away?" Burkett asked, rushing to the flight deck so fast he almost collided with the bulkhead.

"Gogol-1's fired a missile," Faraday said, staring into the holographic scanner. "But it's not targeting us. Its trajectory is straight down for Base One!"

"Get them on comms!"

"They already know," Mayweather said, floating up beside Burkett. "They're watching close, and there's no cloud cover down there. There's nothing we can do!"

"Called it in," Strickland said.

"*S-7, this is Sgt. Prosser.*" Her voice came over the comms. "*We're aware of incoming and ABM interception there is locking on.*"

"Let's hope it's not a nuke," Mayweather said.

A nuke, Burkett thought. *Would they go that far?*

The base's anti-ballistic missiles were AI-guided and very effective. The latest, top of the line, but if a nuclear warhead was set to detonate on its way in, there'd be a radioactive cloud settling over the whole area. Maybe even as far away as wherever the Army had moved Ashley and Nate.

They waited, and watched.

Burkett found himself noticing all the things he tried to ignore. They'd been in space longer than usual, and with the blood and extra sweat and dust, the air filters were clogged. The air was muggy, almost foggy from impurities. While they used hand-wipes and very small amounts of water, one at a time in the space toilet, they had hardly bathed. It was beginning to tell.

Burkett's clothes seemed to cling, to scratch at him. Somehow the waiting, the uncertainty, along with the scant sleep they were getting, made all the effluvia, the reek in the air, more pungent.

There was something else in the air.

A possibility…

"Captain," Burkett said, "Gogol-1 is focused on Base One right now. Suppose we use that distraction? This might be the time to get the drop on them."

Mayweather nodded. "The modules set up?"

"I think so, sir. It should work. Gogol-1 is medium low orbit. We could go to medium high."

"They're probably keeping eyes on that region."

"We could be saving Base One by making them turn their attention fully toward us, sir."

Mayweather nodded to himself.

"Ike, let's go to high medium, as close to geosynchronous with our present position as we can manage, then we'll figure the optimum approach to Gogol-1 from there. And—" He turned to tell Burkett to take a seat, and they both realized that everyone who'd been seated was up, a floating crowd behind the flight deck.

"Captain—did they fire on the base?" Lang asked.

"Yes, they—"

"Explosions in the upper troposphere Zero Point over Base One!" Strickland announced, breathless and rapid-fire. "ABM effective. And… no nuclear signature!"

Burkett blew out a long breath of relief.

Mayweather smiled. "They knocked down the incoming!"

"You think Gogol will fire again, sir?" Strickland asked.

"Almost certainly. Maybe they're working on a way around the interceptors. We'd better move!" Mayweather and Burkett pushed toward their own seats as Mayweather bellowed, "Soldiers and scientists get your butts in seats! You've got thirty seconds! Ike—a thirty count and then burn out of here."

Agents Chance and Frelling drove rapidly toward the checkpoint outside Base One. Frelling was at the wheel; Chase stared up through the windshield.

He caught white flashes high up in the thin overcast, then two slowly dispersing clouds of red and brown. Missile impacting missile. Less than twenty seconds later a chunk of steaming metal fell in front of Frelling's car, and he had to swerve hard to avoid the smoking crater from missile debris.

They were relieved to reach the checkpoint without being hit by anything. There they found three Army MPs gawking at the sky. Chance was annoyed.

"What the hell, Petersley?!" he called, leaning close to Frelling to yell out the driver's side window. Petersley was the one MP here Chance knew, a gray-haired man, mouth open, squinting at the sky. "You can't do anything about what's *up there*—stick with what might be around here!"

"That you, Chance?" Petersley said, squinting at him now.

"Thought I heard gunfire," a younger MP said. He looked like a football linebacker stuffed into the wrong uniform. "Then—" He laughed. "—I realized it was stuff falling out of the damned sky." He pointed to the big blacktopped space behind them. Three plumes of gray smoke rose in the fifty yards between their location and Building A.

"We called in to have a man arrested," Frelling said, his voice dripping irony. "You hear anything about *that*?"

"Yes, we did," Petersley said, pressing a button to lift the barrier. "Go on in, you should find him in cuffs in the brig. First time we used that brig. Carney—General Carney—is probably reading the guy the riot act now."

"Carney's here?" Chance asked.

The older MP nodded just once. "Refused evacuation."

Frelling gave them a small salute and drove on, weaving around craters. Off to the left they saw a building with a smoking hole in its roof, but no flames. Chance had a quick cigarette as Frelling parked alongside the short line of cars outside the front of the administrative center.

"So you think Rowell's here?" Frelling asked. "Why didn't he just bolt after killing Fisher?"

"Maybe orders. Maybe something he has yet to do here. Come on."

"Not many cars," Frelling said, as they got out.

"Skeleton crew only," Chance said, tossing the half-smoked cigarette away as they got out of the car and hurried toward the front. "Rowell may have taken advantage of that. His background is commando training, and he's known to have killed enemy troops hand-to-hand. He doesn't look like it in person, acting like a secretary, but that's who he is."

"There are MPs inside, right?"

"Yeah." They pushed through the front door. There was a small lobby, with a US flag on one side of the tile-floored room, a US Army flag on the other. Normally there'd be an armed military cop seated at the check-in window, but it was conspicuously vacant.

"Huh," Frelling said.

"Yeah, huh," Chance said. "Go out to the car, get our guns, bring 'em in here lickety-split."

"Should we get some MP backup from the checkpoint?"

"Not yet. Maybe the guy's just taking a pee break and they're short-handed—but bring the guns. You take the carbine, I'll take the automatic."

Frelling hurried out. Chance went to the open window in the wall and looked through into the next room. He didn't see anyone at all. There was a desk phone with a blinking red light on it, out of his reach. It was a corded phone, which often was better for security. A swivel chair was pushed away from the counter. There was an outdated desktop PC and the door buzzer.

Beyond was a small room and an open door to a hallway. He started to call out, then thought better of it. If he had to, he could get through.

Frelling came in with guns and ammo. Chance took the niner. "Go to that side door there, I'll see if I can buzz you in."

Frelling went to the door; Chance reached in, pressed the buzzer. No buzz. He pulled the little button console closer—and saw that a wire had been pulled out of the back. "Christ. I hate climbing through windows. Come on, Frelling."

He pushed the PC out of the way, put the gun on the counter inside, and clambered clumsily through the window, barking a shin in the process. "Shit." He had to crawl onto the counter and swing his feet to the floor. "Hold on."

Chance went to the door into the lobby. It was locked, and the unlocking mechanism had been yanked out. "Can't open it. You'll have to use the window."

Gun in hand, he waited for Frelling, who grunted and knocked the broken buzzer onto the floor as he climbed in.

"Sorry, chief."

Chance picked up the phone, pressed a button marked "Front CP."

Petersley answered. "Yo."

"There's nobody at the front desk, and someone's pulled the buzzer wire. I don't know where the MPs are. I need a couple of your guys in here."

"General Carney gave me strict orders, no one leaves their post. I can't take orders from you, Chance."

"This is no time to get all grandma about chain of command!"

"You don't know General Carney like I do."

"I know him *better* than you do. *Get in here!*"

"No can do. Maybe you can find someone else. Supposed to be guys patrolling the fence perimeter, but I haven't seen them."

"Well, get 'em on the horn and... fuck, never mind." He hung up and pressed a button that said "GM Office." The phone rang. No answer. Then he heard Rowell's voice. A recording.

"*General Roger Carney is not currently available. Please leave a message with your name and...*"

The bastard sounded so calm and professional.

Chance hung up. "Come on."

He led the way down the hall behind the greeting counter, heading toward the administrative offices. The overhead lights fluttered. There was a smell in the air. A mixture of two rank scents. He remembered it from Beirut.

They got to a cross-hallway. To the right were the administration offices, including Carney's. Chance signaled Frelling to hang back, and edged up to peek around the corner. The hall was empty.

No—no it wasn't. There was something in a shadowy place,

down at the end of the hall. A man sprawled on the floor. Chance turned to Frelling and spoke softly.

"I think we've got a man down. Which could mean Rowell is free—and armed."

Frelling's eyes widened. "All righty then." He took a deep breath. "You going to let me go first this time, chief?"

"Naw, just… watch my back. This hall runs both ways. Come on." Chance looked around the corner again toward the figure sprawled on the floor, then started off, the gun heavy and cold in his hand. The smell he'd caught earlier grew stronger. Blood and gun smoke.

Chance listened closely as he went, and heard muted voices, two angry men in a room farther down. No words emerged, just the tone, the short, sharp shape of the phrases.

He and Frelling came upon the splayed body of an MP lying on his back, arms flung out: young, blond, with a startled look on his face, his eyes wide as if amazed at so early a death. His jaw was swollen, misshapen. There were three bloody holes in his chest and his sidearm was missing from its holster.

Looked like Rowell had smashed the guy's jaw—then disarmed him, shot him with his own gun.

"Oh jeez," Frelling muttered.

"*Quiet,*" Chance whispered. They stepped carefully around the body and a congealing pool of blood, came to a partly open door. Chance raised his gun and pulled the door toward him. Another Army cop, dark skinned and black haired, lay face down, head at an awkward angle, his helmet lying beside him. No blood. Someone had broken his neck.

No one was visible in the hallway beyond the dead man.

Chance took a deep breath, his mouth paper-dry, and they stepped around this body, too. They were beside Carney's office now. The door was open. No one inside. Papers littered the floor, and a couple of the framed pictures had been knocked from the wall. They looked around, and then went on. Chance came to a closed door that was clearly marked:

INTEL CYBER A
AUTHORIZED PERSONNEL ONLY

He'd been one of the authorized personnel, last time he was here, talking to Sergeant Susan Prosser and looking at photography of Russian satellites, including Gogol-1. They'd moved Susan to a mobile command post.

Chance listened—and heard someone talking, more quietly now—and maybe the tone was bitter. The door to Intel Cyber A wasn't completely closed. Chance carefully edged it a few inches open so he could hear what they were saying.

"They're going to rain hell on us." Rowell's voice. "And you're going to die, Carney, unless you open the safe. Then we can both get out of here."

"I'm going to die anyway," General Carney said, and he laughed acidly. "You'll kill me. Maybe I deserve it. My son… I should have known better. I've lost a tubful of blood already, and I just don't care." He laughed again. "You haven't got time to torture me, either. Just kill me and leave, you damned fool."

"I won't kill you, Carney. You'll make a great hostage."

"I won't cooperate with being a hostage. And I don't have the combination."

"If anyone has it, you do."

"You didn't have to kill Lucy. She wasn't going to get in your way."

"She ran. She'd have brought help. Now there's no help coming. I'd have had all I need from here and been gone if you hadn't changed the codes. It's down to you, Carney."

"What happened to you, Rowell?" the General asked. "Brainwashed when you were captured, or what?"

"No one brainwashed me!" Rowell seemed angry at the suggestion. "I'm going to be a millionaire many times over. I need those codes, Carney!"

"Can't help you. Not even my fault the codes are sequestered.

The CIA was getting nervous, so they locked up the interceptor codes—and I do *not* have access."

"You're lying, and I'm not tolerating any more stalling!"

Chance pulled open the door and stepped softly into the hall beyond. Ahead was Intel Cyber A-2; to his right, frosted-glass double-doors to A-1 stood open. A big room humming with computer stations and screens. About eight meters inside the room, Rowell stood almost within reach of Carney, pointing a Glock pistol at him. The General was on his knees, his face swollen, blood dripping from his torn mouth.

"Just fucking shoot me, asshole," Carney barked, his head drooping.

Chance extended his right arm and got a bead on Rowell, but even if he caught Rowell in the head, the man might get off a shot and kill the General.

With his left hand, Chance reached back, gesturing *hold there* to warn Frelling not to make any quick moves.

But Frelling was already stepping out, aiming his gun.

"Rowell!" he shouted. Probably hoping to get Rowell to turn the gun away from Carney.

It worked. Rowell swung the gun around but instantly fired, and Frelling grunted and fell back. Chance fired in return, and one of Rowell's ears vanished in a small puff of blood.

Rowell fired again and Chance felt a big steel baseball bat hit him in the left shoulder. The impact of the bullet in the bones of his shoulder spun him and he fell on his face.

"No!" Carney yelled.

There was a scuffling sound. In a strange state of detachment and numbness from the shock of the bullet, Chance rolled over and sat up, raising his gun. His right arm felt droopy, unnaturally heavy, but he willed it to raise the 9mm. Carney had tackled Rowell, knocked him over, but Rowell was aiming the gun. Another gunshot. Carney's body jerked and went limp.

Rowell got to his feet in time to turn to Chance, raise his gun—and get two quick rounds from Chance's. The bullets caught Rowell in the throat and he staggered backward, trying to keep on his feet. His gun fired once, shattering one of the glass doors. Then he fell on his arching back, and his feet shook as he bled to death.

Hellfire, Chance thought. *We needed that prick for interrogation. Dammit, I need a cigarette.*

Frelling...

Then the shock and pain rippled through him, and everything went velvety black.

TWENTY-FOUR

"Anatoly," Krozkov said, "now is not the time for indecisiveness. You must give the order."

They were in the Russian President's private conference chamber, as he styled it. In fact, it was merely an old-fashioned den, an elegant library where the books were probably never consulted. A very expensive antique, gold-inlaid mahogany table was placed in the center of the Persian carpet. Here the two men sat opposite one another, each with a crystal flute of vodka.

"Krozkov, you are underestimating American pride," Veronin said. He picked up the small glass of chilled vodka, held it under his nose, sniffed at it, and put it back down. "They will not stand for it. Our missiles are no longer faster than theirs."

"The Americans will cringe in fear if we use a nuclear warhead on their Base One, Anatoly. We can use the Putin II. Not a hydrogen warhead but it will make its point. They will accept that we have them under our guns from space, and they will surrender. At *long last* they will surrender to us!"

"Or they won't surrender."

"Historically, they have backed off. Except for the Cuban business, but that was so long ago—and in this game, with our orbital battle stations, we will have them checkmated."

Veronin rubbed his eyes wearily. "Krozkov, all our intelligence data suggest the Central Intelligence Agency knows full well that Gogol-1 is the only *armed* battle station we have in orbit, and they have so advised their President. The others have no personnel as yet. We do not have crews ready. We do not have nuclear warheads in our battle stations. We could not move a nuclear warhead to the battle station without it being detected.

"We could bluff," he continued, "but—they would not believe us because they have very good intelligence on the matter. You got us in too deeply, too soon, when you fired on the S-7. And now this attack on Base One! They shot down our missile quite handily."

"We were only trying to get an estimate of their anti-ballistic capability," Krozkov countered. "We had heard these new ones installed at Base One were not reliable, but that data was outdated. So now we know, Anatoly. We make adjustments, and we will fire two missiles at their anti-ballistic system—"

"They launch from within a hardened bunker, Krozkov," the President said, sighing. "There are launch tubes inside the bunker."

Krozkov was a little surprised that the elderly President was so up-to-date on military intelligence. Krozkov cleared his throat and took a sip of vodka.

"Very good vodka. Your own brand?"

"From one of my distilleries." Veronin sipped a little and then said, "I am still considering my options with regard to Gogol-1, Vladimir. It may be that we have gone too far to stop this. Their Congress is already calling for sanctions against us, and the sanctions will come. They have moved their new stealth battleships—the Zumwalt destroyers—into the Bering Sea and the Arctic Circle."

"It was I who sent you that memo. They imagine that we're unaware of the stealth ships, but they can be seen if you know what to look for. It's only saber-rattling."

Veronin snorted. "They have moved to Defcon Two! The United Nations is more unified than usual in this matter—they, too, will mount sanctions against us. Already we are excluded from the security council." He scowled and shook his head. "It may be that we are indeed left no viable choice but a decisive military option.

"Perhaps if Gogol-1 can destroy the command base," he said, "the American SubOrbitals will be thrown into confusion and we will have time to man the other battle stations and supply them with nuclear warheads—as covertly as we can. After the base is destroyed, we could stall them by calling for a ceasefire—the Americans rarely turn them down. Then, we decide if we're to break the ceasefire."

"With sanctions already underway, and the Americans moving toward war, there is no point to holding back—you are saying it yourself," the spymaster crowed.

"The point? The point, Krozkov, is that they have at least as many nuclear weapons as we do, and most of their S-series spacecraft are at other bases. They could easily arm them. There are rumors of the US Air Force working on retrofitting the SubOrbitals with nuclear weapons. So, you see... I don't know. Not yet."

Perhaps, Krozkov thought, it was time to make his move. He had planned to wait till next year. He had the sequence worked out with certain of his agents, and certain high functionaries. They would drug Veronin's bodyguards, then remove Veronin himself in a "medical emergency."

They would say he'd had a stroke—and he would be under guard, cut off from communication, unable to deny it. Then Krozkov would be made "president pro tem"—a supposedly temporary takeover that would become permanent. After a respectable time, Veronin would "die peacefully in his sleep."

If he acted forcefully against the American space command, he would seem to all Russia like the right man at the right time. Strong, and proactive.

A moment later, as Krozkov pondered this, Veronin played into his hands.

"I tell you, Krozkov, that the next step is *your responsibility*. You will give the order, as you did when you fired on the S-7, but if you order Gogol-1 to destroy the American base, then it had better be successful. *If* it is—then I will consider arming the other battle stations."

Chance woke up in a military hospital, lying on his back. Machines connected to electrodes on his bare chest hummed and softly beeped. There was an IV in his right arm. He looked at his left shoulder and arm and, with relief, saw that nothing was amputated. It was heavily bandaged around a puckered suture where they'd cut into him. He wondered if they'd had to put some pins in to keep his shoulder bones working.

Kinda funny, he though. Not long ago he'd visited Harley Spencer in a hotel room, and the guy was hooked up the same way. Now they'd traded places. Spencer was back in his comfortable hiding hole, with his services restored.

Chance's mouth tasted like burnt rubber, and his eyesight was fogged. He couldn't feel much pain—they'd put a pump on his shoulder, which picked up incipient pain signals and responded with exactly measured doses of the anesthetic.

I've got farmer's tan, Chance thought. His arm was brown up to where his shirtsleeves started, where it became pinkish white. He tried moving his fingers and they responded. That was good, too.

Looking around, he saw that he was in a pale-blue cubicle, sealed off from another bed by a white partition. What, he didn't merit his own room?

"The pricks," he muttered.

"That you in there, chief?" Frelling called from the other side of the partition.

"Frelling? You hurt bad?"

"I lost about six inches of intestine, but they say I'll heal up. Feel like shit, though. How about you?"

"Better than I deserve." He winced. Funny how self-condemnation could become self-pity. Maybe it was defensive, anticipating what was coming. He figured he was going to be raked over the coals for his failure to stop Rowell before he killed Fisher, two MPs, and General Carney.

"Hell, you deserve a medal, chief. You found Rowell and stopped him. With that guy in place, you think Base One would be safe? Much less the S-7."

"Any news about that?"

"No one's come by to say anything, but I only woke up an hour or so ago. I checked WorldTalk. News is being really mysterious about the S-7. Most likely the Pentagon's keeping everyone in the dark. Far as I can tell, Base One hasn't been attacked again, but I'd be kinda surprised if they just backed off."

Chance nodded. "Krozkov's behind this, and he doesn't like to give up. They're gonna be looking for a way around the interceptors."

I'm talking too much, he thought. *The drugs.*

"Anyone else in here with us?"

"Nope. Just you and me."

"Christ. My roommate." Damn, but he craved a glass of beer and a cigarette. He noticed a nicotine patch on his left arm. That wasn't gonna make it.

There was a familiar ringtone from the stainless-steel table to his right. His hand-screen there.

Reaching out, he winced with a flash of pain from the motion, and retrieved the screen, unfolded it with one hand.

"Chance."

"Sandy?" It was Sylvia Blackwell. CIA director. Likely calling to tell him he was under investigation for the fuck-up that left four men dead, including a three-star general. "You're answering the phone?" she said. "You can't be too bad off."

"No ma'am, not bad. They seem to have sewed me together.

I only woke up a few minutes ago."

"Your nurse tells me you have some broken shoulder bones, but they got the bullet out and the surgeon thinks the shoulder will be functional, more or less, in a few months."

Why not just out-and-out ask her? "Did you call to ask for my resignation, ma'am? I was sort of mentally composing it."

"Resignation? Don't be ridiculous. You stopped Rowell. I'm the one told you to hold off—I wasn't sure you were onto anything, and I thought if he was a Russian asset, he might have a partner we could pull in, too." There was a brief silence, then she said, "No, it's on me. I waffled. We should have just picked him up. Carney was in denial about the whole thing, though. I think Rowell was whispering to him that we were responsible for his son's death."

"The General's dead, isn't he?"

"Yes, he is."

Chance paused, thinking that his opinion of Carney had gone way up, at the last moment of the General's life.

"I heard him tell Rowell he wasn't going to give him any interceptor codes, and the bastard had a gun to his head. I'd be dead if he hadn't tackled the guy at the last moment. Rowell killed him for that. The General had sand."

"He'll be remembered for it."

"I don't feel like I... well, maybe I *should* resign."

"Don't do it for me. No one's blaming you. I want you in the loop, for now, even if it's from your hospital bed."

"Any news on SubOrbital 7?"

"They're working on carrying out their new orders. That's all I can tell you on this line. But... those Rangers had better act fast."

"We're in position for the first maneuver, Captain," Faraday said.

"Good," Mayweather responded as Burkett came into the flight deck and hooked his harness—adapted from EVA equipment—into the hastily-rigged stability netting. As the officer with the most space-navigation experience, he'd be staying there. Mayweather's specialty was ground combat.

Burkett peered through the windshield. The sun was behind the Earth at the moment, so he could see a few stars—and there was the Russian battle station, glinting in moonlight. Gogol-1 was still too distant to see its details with the naked eye, but he'd studied it via digital telescopy. The S-7 was moving slowly closer to the battle station.

"Computer is picking up radar from Gogol-1," Strickland said.

"Figures they'd be tracking us," Burkett said. "Radiometrics sharp? They're not jamming us?"

"Nope," Faraday said. "Computer and my own eyes tell me the radiometrics are sharp. We're on the right declination, right attitude, thirty-out."

Burkett nodded. It was a concern: radiometric navigation, a sort of three-dimensional GPS in orbit, was the key to moving around in space. The Russians had signed a treaty disallowing radiometrics jamming, and apparently whoever had designed Gogol-1 hadn't gotten permission to ignore the treaty.

"Everything's set up," Mayweather said. "I better take my seat. Lieutenant Burkett's in command of the operation, but you'll hear from me on headset."

"Roger that, sir," Faraday said.

"Copy, sir," Strickland said.

Mayweather moved out to his seat and strapped in as Burkett braced himself against the inner cornering bulkheads of the flight deck.

"Why'd they cheap out on putting a third seat in here?" he asked, watching the seconds to burn tick off on the navigation console. Thirty-three seconds… thirty-one…

"Something about payload mass, keeping everything small as they could," Faraday replied. "Real reason—maybe keeping unnecessary people out of the flight deck... sir."

Burkett smiled at the small dig. "We'll see who's necessary. Burn one when ready."

"Burning one in three," Ike said. "Two..."

He thumbed the burn tab and the attitudinal rockets on the upper part of the S-7's nose fired for exactly 1.4 seconds, while rockets on the forward underside fired for 0.5 seconds. The combined burns tilted the orbcraft to aim directly at Gogol-1.

"Burn two," Burkett said, firming up his hold, and he felt the jolt as Faraday started the burn.

Burn two was the big one. The main engine, big thrusters going briefly full bore, would rocket them toward Gogol-1. As Burkett held on against the inertia, he could see the battle station expanding in the windshield. It was shaped like a fairly conventional octagonal-cylinder, without the usual fanned-out solar panels. Gogol-1 was about the size of a nuclear submarine, Burkett thought, and the comparison was disturbing. Its launch tubes were tilted down at Earth now, below Burkett's line of sight.

As they approached, Gogol-1 changed its orbital attitude, shifting to bring the launch tubes up toward the S-7.

"They're trying to get a bead on us, Lieutenant," Faraday said, switching off the main engine. "Maybe we should perform our maneuver, uh, sir?"

"Not quite yet," Burkett said, but it was going to be tricky. He hoped that Dhariwal and Magonier had calculated this as precisely as they claimed.

As the S-7 rushed closer, the octagonal appearance of Gogol-1 became more complex, some sections bigger than others, until it looked almost like a camshaft floating in space. There were the openings of the launch tubes, four of them; blade-like metal shields slipping aside, the missile tubes irising open as he watched. Like eyes opening to look right into the flight deck of the orbcraft.

"Lieutenant..." Strickland cleared her throat. "Sir, they'll think we're going to ram them," she said breathlessly. "They'll open fire!"

The orbcraft was within two kilometers now. Burkett had it worked out in his head. They had only a handful of seconds left.

"*Sir?*"

And it was... now.

"Burn three, and release the towage!"

"Burning!" Faraday called out, and the upper AC thrusters rumbled. The S-7 tilted and fired a braking thruster. They slowed—Burkett was afraid his stability rig would snap with the force—and the two modules they towed behind them were carried with forward momentum over the top of the S-7.

"Release!" Burkett called. Faraday hit the transmitter that remotely unbuckled the second towage cable.

"Released!" The second module rushed forward over the S-7, heading at Gogol-1.

"Incoming!" Strickland said, almost a shout, as Gogol-1 launched missiles.

"*Burn four!*" Burkett shouted.

The main engines roared. Already tilted downward, the S-7—still pulling one of the modules—rocketed under Gogol-1. The released module from N-22 continued on the orbcraft's original course, essentially slingshotted toward the enemy. A split second later two Russian missiles rocketed past the S-7, but Burkett knew the AI-guided projectiles would change course and pursue their target.

He watched the view from cameras they'd attached to the exterior of the big module—cameras that were little more than the astronautics version of GoPro—showing the Russian battle station beginning to fill the frame.

Closer. Closer...

"Twelve seconds to impact!" Faraday said. "They'll try a burn to dodge it—"

"Detonate in three!"

"One, two—"

The pilot pressed the transmitter button. The plastic explosive, standard Ranger issue, detonated inside the module, igniting the tanks of liquid oxygen-hydrogen fuel. With the oxygen that inflated the modules feeding the explosions, the blasts filled the camera frame with red fire for a split second before the cameras became shrapnel—along with the metal parts of the inflated modules, the Japanese tools Burkett had deliberately left floating inside, and the spare nuts and bolts they had taped to the explosives.

The screen went black.

"End burn four!"

Burkett worried that they might get hit by stray debris from the blast, but they were already several klicks out. In fact, the S-7 was heading with unnerving rapidity toward deep space.

"Enemy incoming has changed course, accelerating to pursue us."

"End burn four. Fire retros," Burkett said.

It was a nervy move. They were slowing to let the missiles catch up to them.

"They're two klicks out," Strickland called. "One!" A half-second pause. "Nearing impact!"

"Release, burn, and detonate!" Burkett said.

The towage was released directly in the missiles' path. Faraday waited two seconds, accelerated with the main engine, then waited one more—and transmitted the detonate signal. The plastic explosives in the final module detonated, setting off the third oxy-hydrogen tank, and the missiles were consumed in a ball of fire laced with spare parts and shattered module bands. They exploded, visible in the aft camera view as twin balls of white fire that instantly blinked out in the vacuum of space.

The S-7 was still accelerating—going unnervingly fast, considering they were headed out away from Earth—and yet shrapnel overtook them, clattering on the rear engine cowl.

"*We hit just now?*" Mayweather asked over headset.

"Shrapnel, sir," Burkett said. "Lang, Andrews, Dorman, Dabiri—check for damage." They acknowledged on the headset, but Burkett barely took notice. He was already issuing orders.

"Ike, burn retros, set a course for their zenith, fifteen klicks out. Then brake into synchronous orbit and we'll see what damage we did to the Russian station, if any."

How many missiles do they have on that thing?

TWENTY-FIVE

"How many missiles are left, Lieutenant Batkin?" Andrei Arsov asked as he vacuumed his own vomit out of the air.

"Can't you count?" Second Lieutenant Batkin asked, the question coming with a snort of contempt as he rose up from his gunner's seat. "Four remain!" Batkin, a squat man whose wide face seemed incapable of anything but a scowl, liked to lord it over Andrei, who was a junior lieutenant, even though the second lieutenant's rank was only higher by a very slim margin.

Arsov was bleeding from a wound in his forehead. He'd gotten a smack from a bulkhead when they'd been knocked about by the Americans. The first and middle fingers on his left hand were broken, and he was using his right to vacuum vomit.

When the blast and shrapnel hit the Gogol-1, the battle station had gone into a spin—hence the nausea, the broken fingers, and battered head. Only the commander's considerable skill had managed to stabilize the battle station once more.

Batkin was unhurt, Andrei noticed. He had been strapped into a gunner's seat at the time. They had no actual guns, only missiles, which were Batkin's responsibility. There were some small arms, and a broken laser cannon that had fried itself when they'd tested it on orbital debris.

"My head feels like it's still being banged on the bulkhead, Lieutenant," Arsov said. "So I can't count very well, right now. Also, this vacuum is getting clogged."

"Then give it up and get back to your battle position," Batkin said brusquely.

Arsov snapped the little vacuum onto its wall hook, turned away from the aerial sludge of the last of his breakfast, and pushed toward the radar station. His "battle position" was pointless, really. There were two radar stations at opposite ends of the station, and his was broken. Its transmitting cone had been shattered in the attack.

He lowered himself into the seat, which was partly sunken into the deck like the other operations seats, and buckled himself in. Pointless though it was, it was a relief to just sit here, held by straps.

What was going to happen to them? He himself had stopped a breach in the hull—Andrei just happened to be near the spray sealant, and was able to use it even as the strong current of air tugged him toward the void. If he *hadn't* been there, they might all be dead now. He had also used an extinguisher to stop an electrical fire. Despite his battered head and broken fingers, he had done these things.

No one had taken note, but he was too tired to care.

How had he gotten himself into this? Philosophically, he was a man of peace. Andrei never wanted to come to a battle station. He wanted to work in commercial astronautics. Moving payloads in space, or perhaps debris cleanup or EVA work on satellite maintenance. That was his dream, but he hadn't enough training to be hired by commercial space companies.

The only way he could afford to get the training was to join the Russian Orbital Army. He'd succeeded in being transferred into the ROA because he knew a good deal about the theory of orbital work, and they were short on skilled men.

But this? Somehow, he had ended up here, trying to kill people down below, in a place called Colorado. He worried every day—

if day was the word—that they might cause a nuclear war. He might be up here, looking down on the nuclear explosion that took out Vladivostok. Knowing that his mother and his sisters were burning.

Even if that didn't happen, when were they going to get relieved? When would they be back on Earth? There was no talk of resupply, no plan to abandon the station and return home.

There were four of the small but powerful missiles left, and two quite theoretical, untested orbital mines. They had food for perhaps another week, and how much breathable air? It was already quite stale—and now it was polluted by smoke. The Commander wouldn't say how much oxygen remained.

There were seven men still alive. Sergeant Filipov was dead. The shrapnel that had penetrated the hull had bounced around inside and ended in his skull. Lieutenant Grosha was dead—the sudden spinning of the battle station had flung him against the corner of a heat regulator, and it had snapped his neck. Lukin had a broken arm, Malinov a shattered knee. They had been given morphine.

Andrei had received none.

I am feeling sorry for myself, he thought. *I must accept my fate and do my duty.* He remembered the line from the station's namesake, the novelist Gogol, often quoted by Commander Volsky when things seemed rough: *"There is still gunpowder in our flasks!"* But how could things get any worse, short of the hull suffering a major breach?

Such a breach could happen. The Americans might well be back.

"Well, Arsov," Volsky said as the commander's shadow fell over him. His voice was guttural. "Have you nothing to do but stare at your knees that way?" There was not much reproach in his words, however. Despite his gruff voice and weathered face, his outthrust lower lip and fierce black eyes, the commander was actually a man capable of empathy.

Volsky floated down, holding onto a panel of the radar tuner, so that he came into a sort of weightless squat beside Andrei. The right sleeves of his uniform jacket and shirt were cut away, and there was a bloodied bandage on his upper right arm.

"Sir, I was ordered to my station by Lieutenant Batkin. I have confirmed that it is not functional. This transmitter is destroyed."

"Yes, I know. Did you see to your injuries?"

"Some aspirin and topical medicine."

"You forgot to bandage this." Volsky took a sticky bandage from his shirt pocket and pressed it to the wound on Andrei's head. "It is bleeding, though not much."

"Thank you, sir. I am waiting for Udinsky to splint my broken fingers but he has enough to do, dealing with Sorrin."

"Ah. Udinsky thought Sorrin had a small wound in his abdomen, but in fact he had considerable internal damage from a fragment of bulkhead. He has just died."

Six left now, Andrei realized. *Two badly injured.*

"What can I do to help, sir?"

"Udinsky says he saw you seal the breach in the bulkhead. Yes?"

"Well—yes sir." Arsov felt an inward glow at this acknowledgment. "It was small."

"Still, very quick thinking. We will need that, but you look quite pale. I will have Udinsky attend to your hand, give you a vitalizer shot, and a little numbing agent—not too much, we need you alert. To carry out your part of the plan."

"The plan, Commander?"

"Yes," Volsky rumbled. "A very simple one. First, we make some additional repairs. The sealant is only temporary. We have twenty magnetic sealing cups that will better secure the breaches. I'll put you in charge of applying them to any areas that need them. Then—we destroy the American craft. I feel sure they will return to attack us again, so we must act offensively. Once that is done, we use our thrusters to reach a lower orbit, and travel in that orbit eastward. We will contact the Siberian base—they are best equipped to send help for us—and I will inform General Prositov that we have carried out our orders, and the Gogol-1 is unfit for habitation.

"We will return home. How do you like my plan?" He raised his bushy eyebrows inquiringly.

"Superb, sir, if I may say so."

Volsky chuckled. "You see! There is indeed still gunpowder in our flasks! Wait here. I will send Udinsky over, and then you will take over Sorrin's position at secondary radar. We will locate the enemy, and destroy them."

"I still don't see why we're in this alone, sir," Des Andrews said, frowning, as he looked for a biosuit that would more or less fit him. Andrews and Burkett already had their electromagnetic boots on so they could stand on the deck to suit up easily. "Why shouldn't other S-series help us out, Lieutenant? Or maybe surface-to-orbit missiles. They do exist."

Looking critically at his own suit, Burkett replied, "We're not set up for this geo-orbital situation, Sergeant, because we abide by our treaties. Like the one that says we won't *deploy* surface-to-orbit missiles. There are some in storage, but the only prepped surface-to-orbit missiles are protecting DC, which the treaty allows. Orbitally fired missiles like the ones that hit Base One are supposed to be against the treaty rules, too."

He brushed a fleck of old dried blood off his biosuit. "Seems like Veronin and Krozkov make their own international laws, but we're going to bust them for it." Blood or no, Burkett was stuck with this suit. There'd been one that had fit like a glove, but it had been wrecked by Syrkin.

"It'd take too much time to scramble the other S-series," he continued. "We're here right now, so we've got to stop them before they're in a position to kick off the rest of their missiles at SB-1. Anyway, it's not like our orbcrafts have cannon or missiles, either. They're no more designed for orbital combat than the S-7."

Andrews nodded. "I get it. I don't mean to sound like I'm dodging a fight, Lieutenant, but reinforcement isn't exactly an unknown concept."

Burkett nodded. "Des—we're not alone in this. We get intel from Sergeant Prosser and the CIA, and we got a fuel resupply from home. Griskin provided a control code for the combine, but I'm not going to blow smoke. We're walking a tightrope out here. It could get ugly. I heard a few minutes ago that the Russians are saying we committed an act of war by striking their battle station."

Andrews turned to him, staring. "They fired on an American base!"

"Russian foreign minister is saying that was self-defense— that someone had locked onto Gogol-1 from below. That, of course, is a damned lie, but some people will choose to believe him."

"I'm surprised the battle station is still operational, sir."

"Seems damaged, but—they're maneuvering back to a position over Base One. We think they plan to destroy SB-1 to get rid of its communications and digital infrastructure, weaken the command system for Drop-Heavy so they can make their next move. We can't let them do that." The two men began to pull on the suits, helping each other with sealing. The lower part of the suit was designed to pull easily over the boots, but it still required tugging and grunting before it could be sealed.

"We're going to make sure they use up—damn, this thing's stuck—the last of their missiles," Burkett continued. "CIA figures the station has three, or at most four, missiles left. We're either going to take that vessel out, or we'll provoke them into using up what they've got—and hopefully we'll *evade* those missiles. In the end, if our next move doesn't work, we might have to attack the station EVA."

There's a good chance the wrong people might die in a fight like that, he thought. Andrews was silent, and Burkett glanced at him. Saw a mild look of surprise on the Sergeant's face, and a slight smile. Burkett figured he was surprised that the XO had shared so much with him. But Mayweather was going to tell everyone the same thing. They had to be ready for what was coming.

Sealing the torso of the biosuit, Burkett glanced through the hatch, saw Dhariwal talking to Magonier. The scientists looked gloomy. He suspected that they regretted, at least a little, their decision to stay with the orbcraft. But if they hadn't, the S-7 would have had only one module to work with. The orbcraft might not have survived the attack on the Russian station.

Still, Burkett felt bad for the two men. They hadn't asked to be kidnapped, and they were going above and beyond. They weren't professionally ready to die for their country, like the Rangers.

He found himself thinking about Ashley, and Nate, wondering what they were doing right this second. There had been a plan for the Rangers to have a video transmission talk with their families, but Mayweather had nixed it. They didn't have enough stored power for *everyone* to call home. Why should only the officers get to talk to their wives, their loved ones? Morale was critically important right now.

Resentment, though unspoken, wouldn't help.

"Helmets and SAFER on, Sergeant. Let's get out there."

Twenty-eight minutes later, Burkett and Andrews were EVA in a debris cluster.

"Hold on here for a moment, Sergeant," Burkett said. They braked with their trajectory joysticks and took stock—as well as they could, seeing by moonlight and suit lights.

Most orbital clusters were fairly diffused, with debris separated by kilometers, so it was difficult to see two pieces together. Griskin's junkyard, however, had been gathered together by his robotic plasma thrusters, organizing the materials into twenty cubic kilometers for mass disposal. So individual objects were fairly close, sometimes as little as ten meters apart.

Griskin's clean-up plan included a remote-controlled "debris combine." The device gathered up space junk in specially designed nets, towing it to a low Earth orbit over a safe disposal area, for eventual release into the atmosphere. Later he hoped to shoot the other, bigger debris into deep space, setting it on a course for the sun.

Burkett looked around, trying to get oriented. The sun was still hidden from them, but that wouldn't last long. Meanwhile, his HUD reported that his biosuit was working hard to keep him warm. Dhariwal, Magonier, and Linda Strickland had managed to ramp up the power storage in the suits, so maybe there'd be no heating crisis this time.

To his right was the enormity of the darkened Earth—dark but haloed in light—seemingly a perfect globe from here. The seas on the dark side seemed cobalt, partly streaked by gray-black clouds. He saw a grid of lights he thought might be Denver. To his left floated Sergeant Andrews, turned to gaze down on the Earth. The S-7 was behind them, but a quarter-klick away to keep a reasonable maneuvering distance from the space junk.

Burkett checked his HUD's directional display, found the radar bounce from the combine, touched the magnification tab on his helmet, and zoomed in a bit closer to a distant hourglass-shaped object of metal panels alternating with solar-power panels.

"Tracking Griskin's combine," he said over the headset.

"*Roger that,*" Des said. "*Hold on. I see it too.*"

"We make for that. About forty meters from it there's a net

full of space junk, thanks to the high-tech garbage truck. We'll see if it'll be useful."

Andrews used his trajectory joystick, triggering tiny gas jets on his SAFER, and turned his suit so he could look back at the S-7.

"Orbcraft's a long way off. Looks crazy small from here. You ever been this far from a spacecraft out here, sir?"

"Hell no. It's spooky, all right, but if we use the SAFERs like we were taught—minimal thrust—we'll get where we're going and back."

"You lead, I'll follow, Lieutenant."

"More people should think like you," Burkett suggested. "Come on."

They used the jets to propel them toward the center of the cluster of debris, where the combine waited. The objects in the three-dimensional field had been drawing slowly together, since they were herded nearby. Even small objects exerted gravitational force.

It made Burkett nervous, as he and Des entered this inner cluster. Too many random factors with broken metal edges, drifting along too closely. At least—unlike most space junk—this debris was moving relatively slowly, having been held in place by the plasma thrusters and their own weak gravitation.

"This is... weird," Des said, taking in the slowly whirling scraps of metal and plastic and frozen liquid around them. The liquid was urine in clumps of yellow crystals, refracting the moonlight and the flashing from their helmet lamps.

"Yeah, it is." Burkett saw a circular steel console with trailing wires—it looked like a robotic jellyfish. He was reminded of footage of the undersides of the big drifting islands of garbage in the oceans. Random shapes, familiar and yet unfamiliar, slowly floating past one another.

"There's one of those goddamn bowling balls, glowing at us."

"Move slowly toward the combine, Sergeant, keep one finger on the braking button. We need to conserve maneuvering jets."

"*Roger that.*"

Burkett led the way. They weren't in immediate danger of colliding with anything, most of it was some meters away, but they had to stay alert. He watched a unit that looked like a broken cylindrical vacuum cleaner strike one of the bowling balls. The impact sent the ball spinning toward them, for a moment looking like a rogue planet. Burkett had to use his joystick to dodge right a couple of meters to get out of its trajectory, and it passed between him and Andrews.

"*This orbit's a billiard table,*" Des muttered.

Burkett corrected his course. A roll of plastic wheeled by, turning end over end. The big spindle of the combine became more and more detailed as they got closer. The sun began to edge over the Earth to their right, like the stone on a wedding ring, and it lit up one side of the hourglass shape, revealing a thin cable extending from it.

In this light the cable looked like a strand of spider silk, stretching out toward an object about five hundred meters away—the object resembled a bug wrapped in a spider's web, from here, but it was a netting full of space junk. On Earth, Burkett had read, it would weigh about twenty tons. In the microgravity of orbit, the junk collection weighed very little, which meant it could be moved relatively easily.

Lucky, Burkett thought, that Griskin hadn't gotten around to moving the net over its disposal target on Earth.

He accelerated a little toward the combine, and then a shadow whipped over him, and he caught a glimpse of something like a giant razor blade coming at his head: a meter-square slab of ragged-edged metal. In an unconscious overreaction he pressed the joystick too hard. He was pushed rapidly down, relative to his former position, by the SAFER's small nitrogen-gas jets.

"Son of a mother…"

Burkett hit the brake-motion, and several jets fired to stabilize him, but when he looked around, he couldn't see Des Andrews anywhere. Not in any direction.

"Des? You okay?" It occurred to him with a chill that Des might've been hit by the sheet metal debris. "I don't have eyes on you! Go to the combine! Do you copy?"

"*Sir, I'm okay, but...*" There was a crackle. "*Not...*" What was wrong with comms? "*...can't...*"

And then endless static.

TWENTY-SIX

"Andrei! How goes the jamming?" the Commander asked, kneeling by Andrei's position, the radar and comms post recessed into the deck. He held onto a stanchion to keep from floating away in the station's weightlessness. "Did you get it to work?"

"Repairs were successful, sir. I caught some of their transmissions. They are not able to say much. Almost nothing."

"Very good! That will give us an edge. I knew that device would come in handy."

Arsov nodded. "Yes sir." He glanced past Commander Volsky at the dead men floating nearby. They were tied together in a bundle of corpses near the ceiling of the battle station's main cabin, with another line holding them to a ring on the overhead. The storage they would have put them in was too badly damaged. Thus, they floated nearby as if quietly listening to everything that was said.

"And the radar, Andrei?"

"On radar, the S-7's last known position was about fifty kilometers away at…" He read the elaborate three-dimensional position out, hoping he'd got it perfectly right. "They were about a quarter-kilometer from the outer bounds of the Griskin debris dump, sir. They detached two objects, possibly men on extravehicular activity, and they moved to another position, putting the debris dump between us and them. This was just two minutes ago—I was about to call you, but I was double checking."

"They sent men out, and then moved? That's an odd thing to do."

"Perhaps it wasn't men. Perhaps… weapons of some kind?" Volsky seemed to be scarcely listening. He was frowning at the radar screen.

"They are keeping the dump between us. Interesting. Well, of course, that will obscure our readings of them."

"Yes sir."

"I am awaiting orders from the General, and he is awaiting orders from Vladimir Krozkov. But… perhaps we can briefly change our position to make an attack on the American orbital craft a little more feasible. I am concerned that if we fire all the missiles at the base, we may be all but defenseless against the Americans. We must at least roust out the mines…"

Burkett realized he had not only gone relatively "down" from his last position—using the SAFER nitrogen jets to stop his errant motion had pushed him a half-kilometer farther out from Earth. He looked around.

One twitch of the hand, and I'm headed for the moon.

It really did feel like being on the edge of death. Looking out into space from here, with the stars blotted by the glare of the emerging sun, he saw only deep, infinite blackness. And wasn't that what death was supposed to be like?

Burkett turned to look at the Earth. It was so immense. He could see green tones in the Rockies. Underbrush, trees—life. Somewhere, not far from there, were Ashley and Nate. The knowledge reassured him.

Taking a long slow breath, he let it out gradually, to slow his pulse. Then called the orbcraft.

"I am not sure you're reading this, S-7, this is Burkett; error with my joystick, lost the correct position, do not see Sergeant Andrews. Do you read?"

Static.

He waited. A crackle… perhaps a slight fillip of a voice. A foreign phrase. One word came through clearly.

It sounded like, "Vrag." The accent was Russian.

Every biosuit helmet had a translation database. "Translation, Russian word: vrag," Burkett told it.

A female-sounding AI voice said, "'Enemy.'"

"Great," Burkett muttered. Then he turned his attention to the available readings. The helmet's heads-up display wasn't entirely working. He couldn't find the combine's position from where he was, but he was able to scroll back, in a sense, to order the HUD to disgorge past readings, and find the last fix he'd had traveling to this position.

There. The usual positioning wasn't working, but he knew a trick.

"Triangulate position eleven with this position and Base One." The result came, and he did a little trigonometry. "Give me radial direction to that figure within cubic area C."

He had a direction now, and aimed the joysticks, following a radius line through the established geometric sphere to its center—his position before getting lost. He moved "up" and forward. Glancing at his SAFER bar, Burkett saw that his maneuvering nitrogen was 75% depleted.

Never quite enough of what this biosuit required, he thought. *Thanks, SubOrbital Supply.* If he lived through this, he'd clamor for some serious redesigns.

Breathing slowly and carefully to avoid using too much oxygen, Burkett maneuvered on toward what he hoped was the debris combine. Godsend that Sergeant Andrews had heard his order about meeting there.

How close were the Russians? Would they come after him, somehow? The CIA might be wrong about their available weapons. He looked around but couldn't see the battle station.

Just concentrate on getting back on track, he told himself.

He pushed a little harder on the joystick, picking up speed, then released the button, coasting rapidly. In under a minute he began to see debris whirling slowly past, mostly just ragged pieces of metal of every conceivable size. Exquisitely careful with the joystick now, Burkett used very little maneuvering gas when he had to swing wide of the space junk. Then he got back on the radial line.

Another three minutes and he saw the metal-and-plastic hourglass shape of the combine, up ahead. Still no sign of Andrews.

"Des, do you read me?" he called.

Still only static.

He got closer, within fifty meters of the object, and Des Andrews emerged from the other side of the combine. His headset crackled.

"Y'...'kay, Lieuten...?"

Burkett waved in answer, and Andrews waved back.

In under a minute, he and Des were floating side by side in the shadow of the combine, their suit lights illuminating the dark side of the device. It was about thirty meters in length, and the widest parts at both conical ends were twice as wide as the "waist" where the cones met. Hardened charcoal-colored plastic panels alternated with thin steel around the cones. Two of the panels near the object's waist had circular switches.

The radio being unreliable, Burkett gestured for Des to carefully lean forward, to touch their helmet facings. They did so with a soft *clack*. Des was only inches away, but his voice transmitted through the glass sounded as if it were coming from a distance.

"You heard my orders on the radio?"

"No sir. We were headed for the combine, I figured I'd better go to it. Either that or go after you, but I couldn't see you, Lieutenant."

"You did right. Let's switch on Griskin's toy."

"Sir—couldn't this thing be switched on remotely?"

"It won't switch on remotely. InterplanetaryEx was afraid someone would hack the code remotely and misuse the combine."

"Misuse it like we're going to, Lieutenant?" Burkett smiled. A little light irony out here felt good—like they were back on Earth.

"Look to your right—see those two switches? They open the panels—you'll see a green button. I'll give a signal, and we each press a button simultaneously, and then a keypad will light up. Then we each put in a set of numbers. Mine is 550, and yours is 798. That'll light it up. Then it'll take our orders, if we can get the damned radio working. One thing at a time."

He pulled away, reached out for the nearest panel switch, and turned it. The panel slid aside. Des moved to the other panel— too far away for one man to accomplish both operations—and opened it.

When Des gave a thumbs-up, indicating that he had located the green button, Burkett gave a hand signal. They pressed the buttons... and inside the panel a keypad lit up. The codes were entered...

...and nothing happened.

Burkett waited, one gloved hand on the panel frame. Then he felt a vibration pass through the metal, into his hand, and a moment later the two ends of the hourglass shape lit up, the light glowing an eerie green from small circular openings around the object's dual bases.

That's it, he thought. *Back to the S-7.*

Burkett turned and used his helmet's zoom, trying to get a fix on the orbcraft. No sign of it. He checked to see if he was looking at the S-7's position. He was—but he wasn't. Because the orbcraft had moved.

It was gone.

* * *

"What the hell do you mean you lost contact with them?" Chance demanded, sitting up. The motion sent a lance of pain through his left shoulder and he gritted his teeth as Lieutenant Colonel Baxter replied, the regret in his voice coming through even on the hand-screen.

"*The Russians are jamming them. We shouldn't be talking about this—*"

"The fuck you say. If they've been shot down, I need to know it!"

"*We have no evidence that's the case. The Agency's being informed. You're on sick leave. I just took your call because we're…*" He seemed reluctant to say "friends." "*…because we've worked together a long time. That's all I know.*"

"Just tell me—Base One. Fully evacuated?"

"*All except the launch crew in the interceptor bunker.*"

"Bodies taken out?"

"Yes. All of them. Volunteer team of Rangers went in, documented it as fast as they could, and took out the body bags. Everything you said checks out."

"That last bit I already knew—I was there! This is bullshit. If no one's at Base One, where's ground control for the S-7?"

"*Mobile unit a mile from SB-2. Only essential personnel.*"

"Yeah, well, *I'm* essential, whether they know it or not, and I'm going over there."

"*You taking too many painkillers, Chance? You're not talking rationally. You've got a busted shoulder. Lie there and wait for information.*"

"I don't take orders from you, Baxter."

"*If you don't chill out, I'm going to call Director Blackwell,*" the Colonel said. "*I've got to go; we're still trying to establish communication. I'll let you know if we succeed.*" Before Chance could reply, Baxter broke the connection.

Grimacing, Chance started to get out of bed, just as Rosella, the plump Filipino military nurse, came in.

"You don't get up, Mr. Chance," she said. "You need the head I'll bring you a bowl or whatever."

"I'm checking out of here. I've got business."

"You are going nowhere till you're properly discharged." Her voice was calm, and yet chilled with authority. "You're still healing. You could get an embolism if you go bumbling around. Lie back down or I'll call an MP."

On the other side of the partition, Frelling hooted with laughter.

"She's got you by the nuts, chief!"

"Frelling, *shaddup*," Chance snarled. He stared at Rosella. "What do you think you're doing?" She was injecting a clear fluid into his IV.

"You're going to take a nap, Agent Chance. Nurse's orders."

"The hell I am! I... it's... oh Jeezus. I think I... have to... to lie down."

TWENTY-SEVEN

"What are we going to do when Burkett gets back and finds us gone, Captain?" Megan Lang asked, floating up to grip the flight deck hatch frame. "We're about fifty klicks from our former position."

"I'm fully aware of that, Sergeant," Captain Mayweather said irritably. Was she doubting his strategy? His orders?

Because he sure was doubting them.

As he hung onto a strap, watching Sergeant Strickland and Dr. Magonier working to add a new fixture on the radio, to do an end-run around the jamming, Mayweather was seriously doubting his own judgment. Partly it was because he'd had very little sleep in the last seventy-two hours—which wasn't ideal for making good decisions—and partly because… Syrkin.

He was haunted by all that had happened with Alexi Syrkin.

"It's a… complex situation, Sergeant Lang," he said. He'd almost said *a bloody mess*. "Just before the radio went down, we were radar scanned by the pricks in the battle station. There's a good chance they might be planning to spend one of their remaining missiles on us. Radar and lidar has them set up near their original position over Base One, but closer to us.

"We've moved to an area that's more difficult for them to

target, just temporarily. But I still want them to know we're here. It seems to have restrained them from firing the missiles so far, so I'm staying within their radar range. Burkett and Andrews have a job to do, and we'll pick them up en route to our staging position."

But if we don't time it right, he and Andrews are going to die out there. Only we can't confer with them because of the radio jamming...

Megan nodded. Something in his tone seemed to have struck home.

"Yes sir. I understand."

"Any progress on that thing, Sergeant Strickland?" he asked. Magonier had a plan to piggyback their radio comms on their radar transmissions. It'd be an intermittent pulse of communication, but it might work. Magonier had had been part of a team that had developed the method for EuroIntel.

"Oui, yes, j'espere—yes," Magonier said, screwing a wire down onto a modulation device. Both he and Strickland wore magnetic boots so they could work without floating away. "Radio will now go through this unit. It is on a quite different frequency than any the Russians would think to jam."

"Okay, we can try it now, sir," Strickland said, standing up and moving, her boots clanking to her seat. She activated the radio, and Mayweather spoke.

"Lieutenant Burkett, we have a new system in place. There may be some lag. Do you read me?"

"*I read you. Only you moved the ship, so...is this goodbye?*"

"Don't tempt me, Burkett. Russians were getting a fix on us, we had to dodge it. What's your status?"

"*Mission complete, we're heading back to—to where you were before anyhow.*"

"Yeah!" Lang said, happily slapping the bulkhead.

"*Actually, Andrews is towing me back. I ran out of maneuvering nitrogen. Told him I could get him a job with Triple-A, but he's not interested.*"

Even Mayweather smiled. "A relief to hear your voice, Art. We'll meet you there."

It was getting hot in the orbcraft. The coolant system was overburdened, partly because the air filters were choked up. Holding onto the strap at the hatch, looking past Faraday and Strickland at the flight deck's readout, Burkett had his eyes on a green blip in the holographic chart: Griskin's combine.

"Is the combine out of the junkyard?" he asked.

"Yes sir," Strickland said. "Moving slow, exactly the way we told it to move."

With luck, he thought, *if the Russians notice it, they'll take it for just more space debris*. They were focused on the S-7 and Base One.

Burkett coughed. Over the last hour he'd noticed he wasn't breathing easily. He thought the air was becoming a little blurred, like a slightly steamy window. Certainly, it smelled heavily of everything human, along with solder smoke and old food. There was something else in the air, too—a sense of imminence.

This is it. One way or another, it'd all be over soon. He'd seen the Rangers typing into hand-screens. The solemn looks on their faces told him it was letters to family. Goodbye letters. Hoping they had a chance to transmit them before it was over.

The S-7 sent an updated status report to Lieutenant Colonel Baxter and Sergeant Prosser. Then they carried out a short main-engine burn, along with maneuvering thrusters, and now the orbcraft was on its way to the zenith position a quarter-klick "above" the battle station. Soon the assault team would have to get into biosuits.

There was no way to get into the battle station—not alive. The Russians would be in close control of the airlock, but there might be another way to capture Gogol-1.

"Where's the Captain?" Burkett asked, glancing over his shoulder.

"Doing something in aft storage," Faraday muttered. "I think he was looking for a spare air filter. God knows we could use one."

"How far from attack position?"

"Forty-two kilometers and ninety meters," the pilot said.

"Oh shit!" Strickland burst out, gaping at one of her monitors.

"Any chance of a more professional announcement, Sergeant?" Burkett said.

"Gogol-1 has launched three missiles, sir! They're headed for SB-One!"

"They're really booking, full speed and direct," Faraday muttered, looking at the screen.

"There's no one there," Strickland said. "What're they hoping to accomplish? Do they really want a world war?" As they watched the blips on the holo monitor, several Rangers crowded into the hatch behind him.

"In upper atmosphere now," Faraday murmured. "Slowing, feathering for heat resistance. And… ah! The interceptors have launched!"

Another two breathless minutes—Strickland checking for anything coming in their direction, too, and not finding any—and then—

"Direct hit on two missiles! They're down! But one got through!"

"Is there another interceptor?"

"Yes," she said, almost inaudibly. "Um—yes sir. It… seems to have missed. Russian missile has directly impacted Building A."

"Three billion dollars in Drop-Heavy command infrastructure," Burkett said, unable to keep bitterness from his voice. "I… we…" He didn't finish it out loud. *We were supposed to stop that from happening.*

Suppose it triggered a world war.

"The base was deserted, though," Faraday said. "Nothing but drones there. That's something."

Burkett nodded. "Yeah."

"*What's gone down?*" Mayweather said on the headset. "*I couldn't get it clear.*"

"Russians launched missiles at SubOrbital Base One, Captain," Burkett said. "Two shot down, one got through. Building A is destroyed. No one was there to be killed, but—"

"*Agency thought they might have four of those things left. They may have saved one for us, Lieutenant.*"

"Seems likely."

"*Everyone feel as physically shitty as I do?*"

"I believe that would be a big yes, there, Captain."

"*Break out the energy bars. The powerful ones with the cognitive enhancement. Everybody gets one. Team Alpha into biosuits, right now—and everyone else gets their butts back in seats. We're due to be in combat range in about eleven minutes, if the computer's right.*"

"Yes sir."

Team Alpha for this operation was Lance Corporal Cha, Cpl. Tafir Dabiri, Sgt. Megan Lang, and Burkett. As Burkett finished issuing orders, Sergeant Prosser called from SB-2 with a news report.

"*President is finally growing a spine,*" she said. "*He's warning that if Gogol-1 gets any reinforcements or even resupplies, he'll consider it an act of war. Any further rocket launches by Russia into space, at this point, will be also regarded as an act of war. He's demanding that the battle station surrender before anyone else is hurt. The Russian foreign minister claims Gogol-1 was only defending itself and says that there are no plans to order a surrender.*"

"*CIA reports to Drop-Heavy that Krozkov is reportedly taking over the Kremlin—anyway, he's in charge of all this, and Veronin is a no-show.*"

"Not long ago Veronin was banging his shoe or something at the UN," Burkett said.

"*He's gone to ground somewhere,*" Prosser said. "*Leaving Krozkov in charge of the ROA.*"

"Great," Burkett replied. "Krozkov in charge. He's hawkish on everything."

"If the President is growing a spine," Faraday said, "how are we not getting reinforcements?"

"*Because the Russians say that will be an act of war against* them. *Things are hair-trigger, Lieutenant Faraday. Best thing is to end this quickly. We can't just starve them out of that thing, because they fired on a US base. We need to take Gogol-1 down for that. Maybe that's the President's political calculation—for the next election.*"

"Sounds like Alpha had better suit up fast," Burkett said.

They were in their biosuits, apart from the helmets, when Faraday called.

"*Lieutenant Burkett, to flight deck!*"

Burkett pushed off, drifting rapidly forward—by this time expertly, using chair backs to correct direction. He was there in seconds.

"Lieutenant," Strickland said, "there are two objects right in our path—I thought they were just space junk, and maybe they're supposed to look like it, but they are *identical.* Stellated dodecahedrons, computer says, each about three meters in radius. They look like goddamn Christmas tree ornaments."

"Identical? Those are orbital mines! How close?"

"One thousand meters and closing!"

"Evasive, Ike," Burkett said as he gripped the strap and checked the holo monitor.

"Already on it, sir," Ike said as his fingers danced over the controls. "Hold on!"

"*On my way forward*," Mayweather said in the headset.

The monitor showed the two objects, one directly above the other, relative to the trajectory of the S-7. The orbcraft fired braking retros, then forward attitudinal thrusters so the vessel tilted to slide down below the oncoming mines. Burkett held on against inertia as they burned to undercut the mines, and glanced back to find Mayweather holding onto the back of Rod's seat, his face strained.

"Where are the mines now?" Burkett said, trying not to shout the words.

"One's close behind us—"

"Jesus God, I left the aft compartment hatch open," Captain Mayweather burst out, turning and pushing madly toward the rear.

"Captain, send Dorman, he's in the back of the cabin!" Burkett shouted. But racing to the aft, Mayweather ignored him. He rushed to the aft hatch.

"My fault, I gotta close the…"

Strickland scanned the data. "Maneuvering thrusters knocked one of the mines off toward Griskin's junkyard, but the other one—"

There was the perfect merging of a *thud* and a *clang* as the ship wrenched in space. Only the computer's thrust stabilizer kept them from spinning off into infinite night. The impact of the exploding mine, coming from the rear of the vessel, threw them forward and then backward. Burkett was wrenched from his hold, flung toward the aft, tumbling over the cabin seats. His head spun as his body did the same, but he glimpsed a ceiling ring and grabbed it, arresting his motion, grunting from the jerking in the joints of his right arm and shoulder.

No time for anything to be dislocated, he thought.

The vessel stabilized and Burkett caught his breath. "*Depressurization in the aft compartment*," Faraday said in his headset. "*All other areas of the ship have airtight integrity.*"

Rodriguez's voice was next. "*Lieutenant Burkett, you'd better come back here...*" There was something especially grave about his tone.

"Coming. Ike, get back on track for now. Stay alert."

"*Roger that, Lieutenant.*"

Dazed, stomach still flip-flopping, Burkett used his left hand to tug another ring and flew quickly to the entrance to the passage. Inside, he saw that Rodriguez was bandaging Captain Mayweather. There was blood floating in a small cloud nearby. One of Mayweather's shoulders was crooked. The Captain was floating on his back, held stable by Dorman as Rod worked over him.

"He needs to get into his seat, sir," Rodriguez said. "He's got to move around as little as possible."

Mayweather groaned with pain, coughed.

"Art...I've got an order for you." His voice was hoarse.

Burkett swallowed hard. "Yes sir?"

"Pursue the mission." His face pasty, Mayweather grimaced as Rod tightened the bandage. "Whatever it takes."

"I'm pretty sure he's got a concussion," Rod said. "Bones broken. He got bounced around in there after he got the hatch closed, banging from wall to wall." He shook his head. "He needs more than I have to give, Lieutenant."

"Captain, we need to get you to help," Burkett said. "Maybe the Air Force can get a surgeon up here." Descending into strong gravitation might kill Mayweather.

"Sure." Another cough. "Soon as the mission's done. We're almost there. Can't stop now. Look at me, Lieutenant. You think I'm delusional because I got a knock on the head?"

Burkett looked into his eyes. "No sir."

"Then you know this is a real order. Carry it out. Those are my orders. These men are witnesses."

Burkett took a deep, shuddery breath. "Yes sir. Rod, get him strapped down and ease his pain best you can."

Rod nodded. "Good call, Lieutenant." Burkett turned

away—then turned back to Mayweather and met his eyes. He saluted him.

Mayweather used his functional hand to manage a weak response. "Good luck, Art."

Heart sinking, Burkett took a deep breath and pushed toward the aft hatch. He looked through the hatch window—and saw stars. The mine had exploded under the engine's tail thruster, on the underside of the orbcraft below aft storage for the Light-Up and other ordnance. There was a big gash in the deck where the mine had blown. Stars sparkled through the gash.

Everything had been secured except a big repair kit used for the Light-Up. The box and its power tools clanked around the hole in the deck—the gash in the hull wasn't terribly wide. The air had been sucked out by the vacuum of space, but some of the tools were large enough to be stuck.

"Ike, is main engine operational?" Burkett called.

"*Yes, it is, Lieutenant,*" Faraday replied. "*At least, that's what systems tells me. We haven't tried a burn yet. I'm pretty much braked out here. No seeing any more bogeys from the battle station—not yet.*"

"They're waiting for an optimum shot. Story is they have only one missile left."

"*Yes sir.*"

Strickland's voice came through fuzzily. "*Computer reports the mine detonated under the engine, probably by remote control—most of the impact on the underside. Seems to have busted through the lower deck.*"

"It has, but with luck... Actually, this gives me an idea. Dabiri, you copy all this?"

"*Yes, Lieutenant,*" came the Corporal's voice.

"Get your helmet, meet me at the airlock in two minutes."

TWENTY-EIGHT

"Is he really coming back, Mom?" Nate asked.

Ashley hesitated. They were sitting on the back porch, holding hands on the glider in midmorning, listening to cicadas and the sound of a plane rumbling overhead. The air was sweet with the exhalation of a recent rain.

This morning they'd been in a nice hotel, placed there by the Defense Intelligence Agency. Ashley decided they were going home. This was where Nate wanted to be—so they could wait here for Art.

Ashley didn't think it likely they were in danger here. She hoped she was right.

"Mom? I asked a question."

She answered evasively. "Hasn't your dad always come back?"

"Yes."

"We need to have faith that he'll come back this time too. One thing I'm sure of, he's doing everything he possibly can to get home." Ashley felt a little ashamed, managing her son's expectations this way. Not wanting to guarantee anything, but not wanting to outright lie to him.

There had been new orders. A new mission, and she could guess what it was. The White House said that the Russians had broken the treaty. A world war was simmering, and she was almost as afraid for Nate's life as for Art's.

Wouldn't it be odd if she and Nate died here, in nuclear fire—while Art was still alive in orbit?

"Mom you're hurting my hand."

"Oh—did I squeeze it too hard?" Ashley lifted his hand up and kissed the palm. "I'm sorry, sweetie."

"When will he come back?"

"I think we'll know very, very soon, Private Nathan Burkett." He smiled wanly. "I'm not a real 'private.'"

"You're my hero, is what you are."

"If it was nighttime, could we see Dad's spaceship, up there?"

"Maybe if we had a big telescope and knew just where to look, but about the time we get that, he'll be…" She swallowed. "…he'll be walking up behind us to look through it too."

Nate laughed.

She hugged him close, looked up at the blank blue sky, and wished it was night out. It'd be nice to look up at the stars—and just *believe.*

First Lieutenant Burkett fastened his helmet in place. Dabiri helped him secure it, and Burkett did the same for him. They were about to head for the airlock when Burkett got the call.

"*Lieutenant?*"

Burkett knew, from Rodriguez's voice on his headset. He took off his biosuit helmet and pushed into the cabin, to Mayweather's seat. Randall Mayweather's head was lolled forward over his chest.

"He died about a minute ago, Lieutenant," Rod said, a thickness in his voice. Burkett noticed that Mayweather had something clutched in his right hand. It was his Ranger's Airborne pin.

Rod noticed Burkett staring at it. "He pulled that off his hat, just before he died, Lieutenant. Seemed to need it in his hand. He gave me a message for his wife... And he said to tell you you're in command. That was about it."

Rodriguez closed his eyes, his lips buckling. Burkett swallowed hard, as the other Rangers gathered silently around.

"Have a good trip, Captain," he said. "We'll see you there, sooner or later." Then he saluted Mayweather. The others saluted, too, snapping theirs in place almost simultaneously. Burkett finished the salute then frowned at Ike.

"What're you doing away from your position, Faraday?"

"Sorry sir." The pilot put a trembling hand to his face. He went back to the flight deck. Strickland followed him.

"Should I get a body bag, sir?"

Burkett shook his head. "No. Not yet. He's in his seat on his command. We'll leave him there for now. In case we..." He shrugged. "Just in case."

He didn't want to say, *In case we get shot out of the sky.*

"Corporal Dabiri, let's go. We're going to carry out the Captain's orders."

Burkett and Dabiri came in through the back door.

Faraday had lowered the "rump ramp," as Tafir called it, at the aft of the orbcraft, so that some of the loose tools had floated out into space. Burkett and Tafir used their SAFERs to maneuver into the storage compartment, then activated their electromagnetic boots.

"*Creepy in here,*" Dabiri murmured.

Burkett had to agree. The aft storage deck, lit only with a red emergency light, looked like some other place entirely. He glanced back through the ramp entrance, saw a slice of the Earth glowing blue and white.

He led the way to the armory and selected the smallest

charge of plastic explosives he could find. Ranger-grade plastic explosives were not thermobaric—they didn't need a surrounding atmosphere to detonate. There was enough reactive iron-oxide blended in to do the job.

Putting the explosive and its radio detonator in a pouch, he then selected a much larger brick of plastics. He opened the side of the scarred old Light-Up vehicle, then attached the larger explosive and its radio detonator to the floor over the gas tank. Burkett climbed out and clumped over the deck to the back of the LTV, where he opened the back door of the vehicle.

"*Let's load 'er up.*"

They put all the tools they could find, along with a spare oxygen tank and twenty mortar rounds, into the vehicle.

"*Mortar rounds going to blow up in space?*" Dabiri asked.

"*They can—if launched and properly impacted, they'll detonate. Not sure if that's what we're doing here. Just taking the shot.*"

"*We're going to be making a mess, Lieutenant.*"

"*More fun for Griskin.*" He paused and studied their handiwork. "*I think we've got enough in here. I don't want it too packed in.*" Burkett climbed out and placed the smaller plastic explosive and detonator on the back bumper of the Light-Up. "*Corporal, you unhook that side, I'll get this side.*"

"*Roger that,*" Dabiri said. They each had a lockdown key and quickly used it to unclamp the wheels of the LTV. It floated up just a hand's breadth over the deck. "*But won't it slide out when we accelerate, sir?*"

"*We're going to close the ramp for now, once we're outside. Let's get the rest of the plastics we're gonna need and get back to the airlock.*"

They retrieved four more blocks of explosives, shut off their boot magnetism, then used the SAFERS to travel outside the ramp entrance. Returning power to their magnetic boots, they walked up the bulkhead to either side of the ramp hatch.

"*Like flies on a wall,*" Tafir said.

"*Close the ramp hatch, Ike,*" Burkett ordered.

"*Closing aft hatch, sir.*"

"*Let's move, Corporal.*"

Burkett and Tafir hurried over the hull, back to the airlock, climbed in and got it pressurized, opened the door to the ladderway—and Burkett got another call.

"*I think the Russians have locked onto us,*" Strickland said.

"*Tell Ike to do whatever he needs to.*"

Burkett and Tafir took off their helmets and hurried forward down the ladderway to push off toward the flight deck.

"Incoming?" Burkett asked. His heart was banging away. He told it to chill out. It ignored him.

"Not yet, sir."

"Give it a twenty count, Lieutenant, then accelerate directly at the battle station, fast but not full speed." He gripped the straps he'd rigged. "Let's get their attention riveted on us. Dabiri, get to your seat and transmit the detonator markers to Ike."

"Yes, sir."

"Sergeant Strickland, you clear on what to do with the combine?"

"I… yes, sir."

"Some hesitancy there?"

"I just—oh, incoming, sir!"

"Where away?"

She read off its position, fifty klicks out. "A missile, direct from Gogol-1."

"Ike, when it's about to close, accelerate out of its way. Linda—" There wasn't time for the extra syllables in "Sergeant Strickland." "—accelerate the combine, release when you're at the programmed point, don't wait for me."

"Yes, sir."

"Here it comes," Faraday said. "Hold on." He changed course and increased acceleration. Burkett held on against the inertia. The missile zipped past them but changed course to pursue.

"Reduce speed by one quarter, Ike… Let it get closer…"

"It's gaining, sir."

"Open the ramp and give us some TV!"

"Ramp opened."

Burkett watched it open on the security monitor.

"Detonate charge one."

"Detonating!"

The small charge blew, just enough force to propel the Light-Up out the back of the vessel—right into the missile's path.

"Fifteen seconds till the missile closes with us, sir!" Linda said.

"Accelerate, wait five, and detonate!"

"Sir!"

The orbcraft accelerated powerfully—and then Faraday detonated the big charge inside the floating LTV. Mayweather's beloved vehicle...

It exploded, dispersing shrapnel, tools, and explosives directly into the oncoming missile.

"And the missile... is *gone* sir!" Strickland said, grinning.

"Close the ramp, Lieutenant Faraday."

"Closed, sir."

"Releasing the net!" Strickland called. At her preprogrammed direction, Griskin's combine raced toward Gogol-1 from an angle on the far side of the battle station, towing a net full of space junk.

Suddenly the combine changed directions, getting out of the netting's way.

The loose mass of junk continued in the towing trajectory—and fast. The net, a ball of hard metal objects of all kinds, flew like a comet toward Gogol-1—its extra netting the comet's tail. It opened up just as Griskin designed it to, the fine threads breaking so that the debris would disperse just enough...

* * *

Arsov stared at the radar screen in disbelief. Something must have gone wrong with the scan. The missile had vanished.

Batkin and Volsky were hunched behind him, looking over his shoulder. Andrei cleared his throat.

"Sir—it's just gone, and the enemy craft is still there."

Volsky grunted. "The Americans have destroyed the missile. Our last missile. We'll have to get out of here. I'll set the course myself."

"Sir!" Arsov gulped down the lump in his throat. "We have an incoming object... it's not the American spacecraft. It's closing—"

A *crack*, a flash of heat and blinding light—

The spacejunk cluster striking the battle station was moving at a little more than orbital speed. Orbital speed, seven kilometers a second, was itself so fast that a small object the size of a baseball could smash through a hull and bulkhead with such force that the impacted metal would liquify. The pieces that struck Gogol-1 did so with various degrees of efficiency, some glancing off the armor, some breaking through but stopping at the bulkhead. One piece of steel followed a previous impact. The inner wall was breached, molten metal striking the two wounded men strapped down in the sick bay, burning through them. They added their screams to the screaming of the air as it was sucked into the void.

Andrei pushed up from his post and kicked off his radar monitor, grabbing the breach stopper from its emergency post by the hatch to the next compartment. He pushed fast toward the breach, drawn now by the current of air—pushing the magnetic plug ahead so when he arrived it slapped over the sizzling gap.

He was going so fast he barely had time to cushion his head with his arm as he struck the bulkhead. Dazed with pain, he heard Batkin shout that the commander had been struck by something...

TWENTY-NINE

Gogol-1 was all but blind.

Strickland and Faraday agreed on that after a close observation of the battle station. The debris assault had knocked out the station's radar and lidar antennas, and its exterior cameras. All that remained, apart from one radio antenna, were a few ports—small windows. Since the station had a completely blind side, facing away from the Earth, the S-7 was able to come within an eighth-kilometer.

Alpha Team, suited up, standing by in the aft storage compartment.

"*In position, sir,*" Faraday said over the radio.

"Open the back door, Ike."

"*Sir.*"

The ramp unsealed and lowered. Burkett could see Gogol-1 through it, in the distance, superimposed darkly against the shining globe of the Earth. Bits of debris glinted close to the battle station.

Switching off his boot magnetism, he used his SAFER's maneuvering thrusters to take him out of the orbcraft. The others followed, everyone moving as rapidly as they safely could.

Blinded or not, Gogol-1 could still hurt them, Burkett knew. It could fire its maneuvering thrusters while they were approaching. But Strickland had picked up a radio exchange between Gogol-1 and its ground control. The computer's clumsy but generally correct translation suggested that there was some disagreement going on between the commander of Gogol-1 and his superiors.

He was asking for permission to relocate, but so far they'd put him off. Burkett didn't know how much time he had before the Gogol-1 started its maneuvering thrusters. Alpha team had to get this done *fast*. If the station became aware of an enemy on its hull, the Russians could fire the thrusters to try to catch the squad in the heat-blast, or to shake them off like fleas.

Burkett's plan required stealth.

Behind Alpha team, the S-7 did a very short burn from its main engine, just enough to get it gliding along till it could swing around and approach Gogol-1 from the Earth side. That would focus attention on the orbcraft, away from what was happening on the station's blind side. Faraday knew what to do once he was out there.

From a half-kilometer out, quite visible through the Earth-side ports, he would be calling the Russian station, introducing himself as the S-7's new commander—which he was till Burkett got back—and asking to talk to someone who spoke English. If they didn't have an English speaker, he'd use the computer translator.

Faraday would demand an unconditional surrender. He would assure them that once they surrendered, he could have another SubOrbital craft up here fairly quickly, equipped with surgeons and medical supplies and with room to take them back to Earth. They would be treated well.

"At least get them talking, if you can, Ike..." Burkett had told him. "If they don't answer, just keep radioing anyway."

His EVA team knew what to do. Maintaining radio silence, each Ranger maneuvered to a preselected cluster of thrusters, big orange metal cones in groups of three, each a little less than a meter deep, nozzles aimed like trumpets outward from the station. Two of four groups of maneuvering thrusters on the other side had been destroyed by the debris from Griskin's net, their nozzles twisted into tangles of metal.

Without the thrusters on the battle station's dark side, Gogol-1 would be unable to maneuver in any direction but out toward deep space.

Burkett ceased accelerating with the SAFER, floating on sheer momentum to his target. He stuck out his gloved hands to catch the rim of one of the big orange-metal cones, arresting his motion, careful not to bang into anything. He glanced at the others—Lang and Dabiri were performing the same maneuver. Corporal Cha had been the last in line, and was just coming in, moving rapidly toward the cones. Burkett realized Cha was moving too fast, coming at them at an awkward angle.

He might hit a battle station thruster with a corner of his SAFER...

He did. The *clang* of impact was transmitted through Cha's SAFER, through the suit, to his helmet, and to the headset. The sound made Burkett cringe inwardly. The impact knocked Cha back and he grabbed at the nearest cone, caught it, but the reaction from the grab whipped him too close to the hull and he banged a boot into it.

Cha quickly righted himself, gripping the circular top of the cone with his hands like he was driving a bus. Burkett could hear his rough breathing over the headset as Cha found his sealant gun and set to work.

Suppose the Russians had heard the noise?

Suppose they fired the thrusters?

Telling himself they'd mistake the sound for a minor impact of the debris still floating nearby, Burkett pulled his EVA sealant gun from the tool pouch on his hip and extended it as far as he could into the orange-steel cone—tensely aware that at any moment the Russians could fire the thruster, burning his arm off, blasting him into space.

He sprayed the self-hardening metal-based cement into the small tube at the base of the cone, blocking up the thruster. Within seconds it would be harder than granite.

One down.

Burkett went to the next cone in the cluster, and then the third, carrying out the same operation. When he completed the job, he let out a long shaky breath of relief, and was able to back away from the cone.

He glanced at the others, saw that Lang was done with the maneuvering cluster, and was moving around to the main engine nozzle. It was the last nozzle—and a much bigger one. She'd have to enter the cone—helmet, biosuit, and all—to get it done. She was the smallest among them, so she had the job.

Almost done. Almost ready to move back to the extract point. The S-7 would come back around for them.

Kyu Cha and Dabiri were finishing their operations. Tafir had completed sealing, and was attaching a large block of plastic explosives to the hull. The explosive was intended to force a surrender—or take out the station if surrender was refused. Burkett hoped he'd never have to detonate it. The Defense Intelligence Agency badly wanted to capture the station, and take some prisoners back alive.

One way or another, the President wanted this resolved, *today.*

Dabiri finished. Cha was on the last maneuvering thruster. Seemed to be taking his time now.

Lang showed up at the edge of the battle station, returning from the main engine thruster. This station wasn't going anywhere unless someone towed it.

Burkett signaled for Lang and Dabiri to head back out for extraction, then he'd follow with Cha. Soon as they were all at a safe distance, he'd tell Faraday to let the Russians know about the stymied thrusters, and the bomb on their hull.

There was a motion at the upper horizon of the battle station.

A space-suited shape was silhouetted up there against the glare from Earth.

Most likely the Russians had been space-suited since the debris assault. Cha's noise had brought a soldier outside to check. There was something in one of the man's gloved hands—a very large combat knife.

The Russian used his suit's own version of a SAFER, its jets sending him straight down the slant of the hull at the nearest American intruder: Corporal Cha, who was turned away, about to head out from the station.

"*Cha!*" Burkett shouted on headset. "*Tango! Accelerate, head out fast!*" Burkett carefully aimed his own nitrogen jet and rushed to intercept the Russian.

Though his yellow and red spacesuit was a little bulkier than a biosuit, the Russian was just as fast, and he was closer to Cha.

The knife flashed in his helmet light as he impacted with Cha's SAFER, one arm going around Cha's helmeted head. The two men spun off together, whirling out past the shadow of the battle station, catching oblique rays of light from the sun.

Burkett kept accelerating, but he knew he couldn't get there in time.

The Russian's knife hand methodically slashed at Cha, who writhed in the soldier's grip. A spout of red was forming a cloud of blood around them both.

Then the frantic movement slowed, and Cha was drifting off alone, twisting, arms and legs like a ragdoll. The Russian was an outline in the red cloud, slowing its spin with maneuvering stabilizers. Turning toward Burkett.

He was only ten meters from the Russian. Without a knife.

Glowing hellishly with sunlight, the cloud of dark red roiled. Burkett slowed, unwilling to plunge blindly into it. The Russian emerged, wiping blood from his helmet visor with one hand, the other one gripping the wet, red knife.

Trailing blood as he came, the Russian dove right at him. Burkett knew this would be over before Lang or Dabiri could reach him.

Fishing in his tool pouch with one hand, Burkett changed direction, then turned, flanking the Russian. The Russian turned his way.

Burkett grappled the Russian's knife hand...

In his right hand, Burkett gripped a large, fully charged power drill. He jammed the spinning drill bit into the flexible spacesuit material between the Russian's helmet and his collar bone. The Russian tried to torque away, but Burkett caught him by hooking his right leg around the Russian's left, pulling him closer so he could press the drill deep into the spacesuit mesh. Struggling to keep control of the Russian's knife hand, Burkett pressed down with all his strength.

The two men whirled as they grappled.

The titanium bit sputtered and then began to dig in. Metal shavings spiraled up, and though Burkett couldn't hear the scream, he could blurrily see the enemy's face through his blood-smeared visor.

The Russian tried to free his knife hand, but Burkett knew that he had two choices: hold onto that wrist or die. He held on. The Russian writhed as the bit went through his Adam's apple, through his throat, and through his spine.

He spasmed, limbs jerking... and then went limp.

Burkett waited.

The two men spun together in space. One alive. One dead.

Then the living man pushed the dead one away.

Panting, his eyesight obscured by points of light, Burkett stabilized out of the spin. He turned to see the orbcraft arriving about five hundred meters away...

THIRTY

"**Y**ou are the commander?" the Russian asked, his very youthful voice coming through the comms. He had a strong accent but seemed to be reasonably assured in English.

"Yes," said Burkett. "I am. The other was temporarily in command."

Burkett was buckled into his seat, feeling deeply weary, his head throbbing as he spoke to the Russian on his headset. They had just found Cha's body—no minor task—and Dorman had gone out to bring it in the back door.

How many dead men did they have aboard now?

"*Sir*," the Russian said. "*I am Lieutenant Andrei Arsov of the Russian Orbital Army. Now that you have killed Lieutenant Batkin—*"

"That was his name? The guy with the knife? Batkin?" Burkett wasn't sure why, but he wanted to know the guy's name.

"*Yes, Batkin. Now that he is dead, only remain three, here. Medic Udinsky, myself, and Commander Volsky. The commander was injured. His throat is weakened—he can only whisper so I speak for him. One of his eyes is now blind and he has a swollen knee, but Udinsky says the knee, it is not broken.*" He hesitated a long moment and then asked, "*You have a bomb on our hull?*"

"Yes, we do. As you were told already. We are observing you.

Don't try to leave your station until we tell you to, or we'll detonate the bomb. Anything but complete surrender, and we will detonate the bomb. You could not move the station, even if there were no bomb. We have seen to that."

"*Yes. Ah—we wish to...*" There was a pause. "*To unconditionally surrender.*"

"Good plan," Burkett said.

"*How can we then get help for the Commander?*"

"We have a request out for approval to take you three aboard. You have spacesuits?"

"*We do. We three are in suits. Very painful for the Commander.*"

"The US Space Command has an orbital medical laboratory—USSC-ML. It's mostly for research but it's also a functioning clinic. There are two doctors there. We'll take you to them. There also are military personnel at ML-1 who will take custody of you. You'll be their prisoners. I give you my word, you won't be mistreated. They'll get you down to Earth quick as it can be safely done."

Arsov said something to himself in Russian. Burkett didn't understand the words, but it sounded like an expression of relief.

"We'll be in touch shortly," Burkett said. The communication ended, he leaned back in his seat and closed his eyes. With any luck he'd be seeing Ashley and Nate soon. Maybe after all this she'd make up her mind—for good and all—to leave him. The worry must have been excruciating.

The thought was painful. And he seemed to see Cha's body, in its ruptured biosuit, tumbling away in space like a bloody child's toy...

"*Sir?*" It was Ike, on the headset.

"Yes, Lieutenant Faraday?"

"Sir—can we really trust these people to come aboard? What if they have bombs in their spacesuits? What if it's a suicide mission?"

"I don't believe that's the case, but since you're worried about it, I think I'll send you to their battle station to check them over, with Dorman. You call the guy and arrange it. Now, I'm going to take a nap. Wake me when we take the prisoners aboard."

THE KREMLIN
MOSCOW, RUSSIA

"You wished to see me, Anatoly?" Krozkov asked.

Standing on a Persian rug before Veronin's desk in the President's elegantly furnished administrative office, he was unsettled at having been literally called upon the carpet. It was a place where Veronin rarely made an appearance. Nor had Krozkov been in this particular room for some years.

Anatoly Veronin was sitting behind the desk, his elbows on its leather covering. He was smiling gently, and toying with a very expensive nineteenth-century gold fountain pen. Veronin collected fountain pens. There was nothing else on the leather-topped desk, except a buzzer, itself a rather old-fashioned object. No electronics.

"Perhaps you have decided to order the rest of our orbital battle stations to be manned and armed," Krozkov suggested.

The old man chuckled. "Certainly not. The station you armed has been captured. Many of the crew members are dead, and *I* did not order the attack on SubOrbital Base One—"

"Anatoly!"

"No, I did not. I said you will make the decision—as you made the decision to fire on the American spacecraft: without my permission. All on your own! I expect you thought it would make you look strong, so that when you carried out the pretense that I had fallen sick, you would seem the right man to take my place."

"The pretense of…?"

"Don't playact, Krozkov. I have a splendid, high-definition video of you discussing the plan. It was provided to me quite recently by the man who will take your place. Your former aide, Feodor Ivanovic Smyrnoi. He has come to me, recently... perhaps he realized I was beginning to piece your plans together. Very wise of him."

Krozkov stared. "Feodor? That—that spineless..."

"Yes. He will be quite amenable to my wishes. Unlike yourself. You got Russia into a beartrap, Krozkov. Now..."

He pressed a buzzer.

The door behind Krozkov opened and he heard heavy footsteps. He did not turn to look. He knew who it would be. Chersky and Vaminoi. The quite enormous, heavily armed thugs that Veronin kept handy.

Krozkov snorted and waved a dismissive hand. "This is all nonsense—I have my own people, Anatoly! I have many powerful friends..."

"And you will be seeing them soon. Since they've all been arrested—it happened during the early hours, soon after midnight. I decided to save you till I could say goodbye to you in person this morning."

Krozkov gaped at him. "I don't believe it."

Veronin's smile widened. "You shall see proof in person. Your associates were taken to Lefortovo prison, where you, too, will soon be. All of them. Even down to your mistress— we like to be thorough. I wonder... how is your health? You know, if you don't take care of yourself, Krozkov, you could have a stroke.

"Chersky, Vaminoi—take him away!"

The President of the United States was on the comms, declaiming in his deep, silken voice. He was, in fact, speaking directly to everyone aboard the S-7. Burkett figured it was mostly so the President could tell the nation that he'd personally spoken to the national heroes.

"*I was in a tight spot*," the President said, with his usual focus on himself. "*I owe you people! I was under a lot of pressure to retaliate after the Russians hit the base in Colorado. 'Take out one of their bases!'—as if we could do that without a risk of escalating retaliation. I said we'll retaliate in space. And by God you did it! I owe you—the whole country owes the SubOrbital 7 its thanks. Bigtime!*"

"Mr. President, I'd like to say," Burkett put in, "that a lot of key electronics work and engineering help came from our guests, Professor Dhariwal and Doctor Magonier."

"*And we're going to thank them too. You can tell Doctor Magonier that he's going to be the toast of France when he gets back!*"

"Mais bien sur," Magonier said, shrugging. Dhariwal laughed and clapped him on the shoulder.

"*And by the way, I know your squadron has lost people. They will be remembered, I promise you.*"

Yeah, Burkett thought. *The Rangers will remember them.*

"*Now*," the President said, "*Veronin is about to make a statement to the world, through his UN Ambassador.*" There was altogether too much satisfaction in that voice. "*I got an advance look at the text.*" He chuckled. "*Veronin explains that it was all mostly a misunderstanding—a result of some treachery in the Kremlin. He says Krozkov deceived him. It was the spy chief who pushed us to the brink of war, he says, and he claims he has indisputable evidence that Krozkov was in fact planning a coup!*

"*Personally, I think Veronin was playing the 'long game' with Krozkov all along. Now, Russia is suing for peace and has even offered to pay for the damage at Base One. He denies that this fellow Rowell was his agent, of course, but he says perhaps Rowell worked for Krozkov—a sort of rogue agent working for a rogue intelligence chief.*

"*You still there?*"

"Yes, Mr. President," Burkett said.

"*We've generously offered to return two of the three prisoners from Gogol-1 to the Russians, in exchange for a favor or two, but the youngest one, Andrei something, has asked for asylum and I think I will give it to him. We have to show the Russians who has the upper hand now. I'm sending a USAF spaceplane to tow the Russian battle station to our DIA observation station. We'll have our best techs up there look it over.*" He paused, and Burkett thought he heard a slurping sound, as the President took a drink. "*Now, I understand that your S-7 won't be able to land?*"

"No sir, it won't. The damage from the mine has completely ruined its aerodynamics, and in the atmosphere a lot of heat would boil up—might cause an explosion. We're going to need a ride, sir. Can you send a limo?"

He was astonished to hear himself blithely joking with the President—but he was feeling a bit off his game. Exhausted. Worried. Maybe battle fatigued.

Cha, floating away...

Luckily, the President laughed. "*We're sending you a brand spanking new SubOrbital—it's fueling up right now—to pick you up and bring you home. And then, we have plans for you, Lieutenant. For the whole squadron...*"

THIRTY-ONE

It took him almost a week to recover. Burkett was in bed most of the time, at Base Three. Sometimes his son came to spend the night. There was a bunk for Nate, but he slept beside Burkett, his arm draped protectively over his father because sometimes Dad had nightmares.

The nightmares were pretty bad for a few days. Ken Carney. Randall Mayweather. Corporal Cha. The blood-covered spacesuit flying out of the red cloud toward him...

Ashley came and did some nursing. He didn't need much. He was mostly just exhausted, had a low fever, and he was done in by the clampdown of full gravitation. Like all the others from the orbcraft. The ones who survived.

Burkett woke up on a Sunday morning, feeling stronger. His fever had passed. Which was good, because he had several funerals to go to this week. Including Captain Mayweather's.

Getting out of bed, he felt only a slight vertigo. When he stretched his joints hurt, but not badly. The main thing was, Nate was sitting nearby, on the floor, watching Saturday morning cartoons.

"Is that the *Daughters of Ninja Turtles*?" Burkett asked.

"Yep!"

"I like *Pirates of Snout Island* better. About the pirate dogs."

"Not as good."

"Says you. Seen your mother today?"

"Mom came in and she was real, real quiet. She didn't want to wake you up. The President was talking about you again."

Burkett groaned. "He's really making political hay from this."

"What's political hay?"

"Tell you later. I have to have coffee first."

"Mom says they want you and the squad at the President's… at the White House, some garden?"

"The Rose Garden? Crap. I'll probably have to do it."

"Can I go?"

"I won't go without you."

"And Mom?"

"Unless she doesn't want to. You want to go to the officers' mess, get some breakfast, Private Burkett? Pancakes and eggs?"

"Yep… um, yes sir. But—waffles."

"Waffles it is."

Burkett showered and shaved, which left him feeling even better. He put on some civvies, jeans and sneakers and a Hawaiian shirt, and took Nate's hand for the walk over to the officers' mess hall. On the way he admired the blue of the sky. What a pure blue it was, today.

"I'm starting to like the sky way better from this side of the atmosphere," he said.

Nate laughed. They ate, and then Lieutenant Colonel Baxter came in, waved to Nate, grinned at Burkett, and sat down.

"Got some news for you, Art. You're no longer a lieutenant, as of tomorrow."

"Busting me to private like my man Nate?"

"You're gonna be a captain. The President's arranged for every damn Ranger on that ship to be promoted. Even Lemuel Dorman."

"He'll hate that."

"He kicked up a fuss. The man just does *not* want to be

promoted, but—it was the Commander-in-Chief's idea. It's his orders, so Dorman has to suck it up. Dabiri will be a sergeant. Sergeants are getting 'battlefield commissions' to become lieutenants. Ike will be a captain."

"I'll be damned. That's good, anyway. He deserves it. They all deserve it." Sergeant to lieutenant was something that didn't often happen—non-com to commissioned—but the Commander-in-Chief could make it happen.

"You're all getting festooned with medals. Congratulations."

"They should give Ike his own SubOrbital."

"I'll support that if he wants it. You going to give that interview to WorldTalk?"

"Not for the foreseeable future. I'm going to pretend I'm too ill, hope they lose interest. You think about what we talked about, sir, on the phone?"

"Art, it's not like I would dare deny you anything. You want to transfer out of SubOrbital combat duty, you can do it. What I'm hoping is, you'll take the offer to be an instructor."

"If you mean a *ground* instructor. After I finish being a lobbyist, then—yes sir."

"You're going to be a lobbyist?"

"I'm going to push for retrofitting the S-series. Funding to get escape pods, more oxygen, more and better supplies, a couple of exterior laser cannons—at least. Whatever those soldiers need. Those vessels need to be more than fancy buses. They need to be ready for extended periods in orbit, and capable of defending themselves. And every new piece of combat gear needs to be fully tested."

"Damned right it does," Nate said.

They both looked with astonishment at the boy.

He shrugged. "That's what Mom would say."

Baxter laughed. As if on cue, Ashley walked up to the table. "Talley! Good to see you," she said.

"Now it's 'good to see you'? She gave me such hell, Art!"

Burkett smiled at her. "Did she? That's interesting." He

admired the tight-fitting white dress she was wearing. Showing some legs and cleavage.

Baxter stood up. "Art, I'll testify at those hearings, whatever you want. I'm behind you a hundred percent. Ashley—" He kissed her on the cheek. "—I still love you no matter what."

She laughed. Baxter gave a small salute to Nate and walked off.

"I'm transferring out of combat duty, Ashley," Burkett said, as if it were just a casual remark. He took a sip of his coffee.

"I know you are. I know everything that goes on in Baxter's office now. I have my spies."

"Sit down and have some waffles, Mama," Nate said. "They have raspberry syrup."

"I'm not sitting down, I've had my breakfast," Ashley said. "You guys are coming with me."

Nate got up and took her hand. "Where we going?"

"We're all going home. To our house in town."

"Daddy, too?"

"Why shouldn't your dad come home to his own house, Nate? He lives there." Ashley looked at Burkett. "Well? You coming or not, soldier?"

Burkett stood up and gave her a brisk salute. "Let's go home, ma'am."

ACKNOWLEDGEMENTS

Thanks to Jeff Conner for godlike patience, Steve Saffel, Daniel Carpenter, and Dan Coxon for editorial sweat, Brock Hinzmann for futurism input, and Carl Rogers, Andrew Kosove, and Broderick Johnson from Alcon Publishing.

ABOUT THE AUTHOR

JOHN SHIRLEY is the author of numerous novels, including *Demons, Wetbones, Cellars, City Come A-Walkin', A Splendid Chaos, Bioshock: Rapture, The Other End,* and the Eclipse cyberpunk trilogy. His newest novel is *Stormland*. His story collection *Black Butterflies* won the Bram Stoker Award. His new story collection is *The Feverish Stars*. He is co-screenwriter of *The Crow* and has written teleplays and animation.

VERTICAL

Cody Goodfellow

Michael Foster, Cam Buckley and Maddie Acosta – all former activists in the infamous urbex crew Les Furies. Together they scaled buildings, broke into the spaces no-one else could, and chased a rush that still haunts them.

Now though, Michael is stuck recovering from an injury, coding in a dead-end start-up. But Les Furies cannot hide forever. A journalist has uncovered Michael's identity, and he is being sent anonymous videos of his time in the crew.

When he discovers that Cam and Maddie are planning on reuniting the crew one last time, to scale the Korova Tower in Moscow, he is sceptical. But the tower has never been scaled before. Breaking into the world's tallest building on Russia Day is too good an opportunity to pass him by.

But Michael is about to discover that the vertical city has another purpose, one far more sinister than he could have imagined, and this one final ride for Les Furies might well be the last thing any of them ever do.

SEPTEMBER 2023

TOO MANY BULLETS

Max Allan Collins

A HELL OF A FINALE TO A
DECADE OF ASSASSINATION

It began with John F. Kennedy in 1963. Then Malcolm X in 1965. Martin Luther King in April 1968. And then, in June of the same year, President Kennedy's brother Robert fell before an assassin's bullets at the Ambassador Hotel in Los Angeles.

But how many shooters were there, really? And who sent them? In this astonishing, meticulously researched novel, bestselling author Max Allan Collins – Mystery Writers of America Grand Master – takes Nathan Heller, "Private Eye to the Stars," from the scene of the crime to Hollywood's seediest haunts, from striptease joints to Washington D.C.'s corridors of power to a deadly desert showdown outside Las Vegas, all in pursuit of the truth about a conspiracy that may have put the wrong man in jail, let the real killers go free, and snuffed out the life of a man poised to become the next president of the United States.

OCTOBER 2023

THE LOST FLEET: DAUNTLESS

Jack Campbell

After a hundred years of brutal war against the Syndics, the Alliance fleet is marooned deep in enemy territory, weakened and demoralised and desperate to make it home.

Their fate rests in the hands of Captain "Black Jack" Geary, a man who had been presumed dead but then emerged from a century of survival hibernation to find his name had become legend. Forced by a cruel twist of fate into taking command of the fleet, Geary must find a way to inspire the battle-hardened and exhausted men and women of the fleet, or face certain annihilation by their enemies.

EDEN

Tim Lebbon

"Tim Lebbon gives us a near-future as terrifying as
it is exhilarating, and—most frightening of all
—irresistibly beautiful. Surrender to Eden."
Alma Katsu, author of *The Deep* and *The Hunger*

"*Eden* is a smart, thrilling, relentless, eco-nightmare that will
worm its tendrils deep into you. Let your own ghost orchid grow."
**Paul Tremblay, author of *A Head Full of Ghosts* and
*The Cabin at the End of the World***

Earth's rising oceans contain enormous islands of refuse, the
Amazon rainforest is all-but destroyed, and countless species
edge towards extinction. Humanity's last hope to save the
planet lies with The Virgin Zones, thirteen vast areas of land
off-limits to people and given back to nature.

Dylan leads a clandestine team of adventure racers, including
his daughter Jenn, into Eden, the oldest of the Zones. Jenn
carries a secret—Kat, Dylan's wife who abandoned them both
years ago, has entered Eden ahead of them. Jenn is determined
to find her mother, but neither she nor the rest of their tight-
knit team are prepared for what confronts them. Nature has
returned to Eden in an elemental, primeval way. And here,
nature is no longer humanity's friend.

For more fantastic fiction, author events,
exclusive excerpts, competitions, limited editions and more

VISIT OUR WEBSITE
titanbooks.com

LIKE US ON FACEBOOK
facebook.com/titanbooks

FOLLOW US ON TWITTER AND INSTAGRAM
@TitanBooks

EMAIL US
readerfeedback@titanemail.com